"THIS IS NOT A SOCIAL VISIT."

Admiral Courtney's tone was frosty. Garvin reflected that he had pulled strings to get the Admiral out of the Psych Rehab Facility—the funny farm, to be blunt—and on the expedition roster, to say nothing of marrying him to Garvin's own girl . . . but past favors didn't seem to be on the Admiral's mind now. He wasn't armed, but his two henchmen were.

"Captain Roderick David Garvin, I relieve you of command of the *Saturnienne* and place you under arrest," the Admiral said.

"Before I call this a mutiny," Garvin said softly, readying himself for the move he must make, "I'd like you to clarify your grounds."

"The unjustified killing of two of the ship's crew and—"

Garvin had been shifting his stance, getting the improved pattern among the three men that he wanted. "Cut the talk and arrest me!" he shouted—then scooped up the wine cups and dashed them in the faces of the trio.

The thunder of an 11.2-millimeter sidearm shook the room . . .

OPERATION MISFIT

E. Hoffmann Price

A Del Rey Book

BALLANTINE BOOKS ● **NEW YORK**

To my son, Dan—
". . . From the hills of Montezuma
   To the shores of Pohang-do . . ."

A Del Rey Book
Published by Ballantine Books

Library of Congress Catalog Card Number: 80-66164

ISBN 0-345-30946-4

Manufactured in the United States of America

First Edition: August 1980
Second Printing: January 1983

Cover art by Darrell K. Sweet

Chapter 1

The minds controlling the Psychological Rehabilitation Facility were smarter by a country kilometer than Rod Garvin had suspected them of being. On the other hand, having devoted his life, something like twenty-nine years and a couple of months, to bucking the system, establishment, Hierarchy, Garvin was not going to be rehabilitated and socially reconditioned as readily as the supervisors of the Pyscho Factory had anticipated. On the other hand, there had been phases during which he admitted to himself that if he emerged from the course and remained the original, the immutable Roderick David Garvin, he'd buy drinks for the house.

By "the house" he meant fellow inmates of the Facility, although he had not thus far figured out how he could include the most valuable, the most respected and admired of his associates. This was because they were in maximum security, for intensive care. An outstanding example was Space Admiral Josiah Courtney, who still persisted in asserting that he had designed a cruiser which, taking off from Martian Mining & Ecological Project, could make it to the orbit of whatever planets circled the nearest fixed star.

Garvin, always conservative, had not been put into intensive care, with its corresponding restrictions. He had merely asserted that he had modified current spaceship designs and power plants which would permit him or for that matter, anyone capable of operating a garbage collection unit, to loop Saturn and transmit image-impulses to prove that he'd made it, that he'd cruised within spitting distance of the concentric rings and the flock of moons.

Garvin had comrades interested in matters other than spatial: Jim Ward, for instance, believed that the universal computer system which was the heart of Democracy's political, social, economic, and ideological control could be bugged so that it would render any judgment which a programmer wished to implant in the composite psyche of the Plastic Populace. He further declared that fact and falsehood could be mixed beyond unscrambling. What prodded Ward into crusading was that for more than eight years, he had been submitting evidence to show that he'd paid a Kredit Kard charge of two hundred thirty-eight and seventy-nine hundredths *pazors* for four bottles of champagne, four pipes of opium, and one night in bed with a duly licensed Pleasure, Vice & Recreation Girl. That the girl, Marcelle Livaudais, had submitted affidavits declaring she'd got her payoff, plus ten *pazors* extra, as a gift.

Meanwhile, Marcelle, retired from the PVR Corps, was married and the mother of two beautiful children: but the computer still spewed threats of lawsuits against Jim Ward. Since Citizen Credits had accumulated to his account, year after year, he could pay off and emerge, free and clear, provided, that he recanted his antisocial views.

Whether Ward balked as a matter of principle, or whether he'd fallen in love with Amelia, the receptionist, was not yet clear to Garvin. At first glance, he had decided that Amelia was equipped with built-in refrigeration, and that Ward was a pervert with a passion for the metal-and-plastic female which Science was perfecting.

There were other inmates, not one of whom was commonplace as the standard Plastic Citizens who believed as they had been directed to believe. All in all, however, Admiral Courtney and Jim Ward contributed most to Garvin's plan for outpointing the Hierarchy, and if need be, the Consortium which considered the elected Hierarchs to be self-moving chessmen in a never-ending game.

Nor was it a bad life: Garvin, being a Serf, because he elected to put in forty or more hours a week as superintendent of Spaceways Shops, enjoyed and made the most of his opportunity to experiment and improve his plans, the details of the supercruiser. He did not envy the Plastic Citizen the five-hour week. Garvin spent his spare time at the Psycho Factory, being rehabilitated, except of course for weekends at home with Flora.

At the moment, he wore a gray uniform, soft-soled shoes, and a white skullcap with a lavender, a green, and a blue button—color coding which indicated, respectively, *eccentric, harmless* and *extended liberty.* He was pushing an ionized broom which picked up dust, cigarette butts and miscellany. These he released into the plastic bag of the push cart by triggering the polarity changer, so that every particle darted from the bristles.

A taped voice spoke from the chassis of the pushcart: *"It is not the humble task alone which rehabilitates you. More important is the spirit in which you perform your occupation therapy. The zeal with which . . ."*

"Chinga tu madre!" he exclaimed, but silently. Garvin had not forgotten the time he'd vocalized his retort. The two-way squawkbox, tied to the computer system, had reported him to headquarters, fifty kilometers distant. When his task was completed, Amelia, the refrigerated beauty out front informed him that it was not his obcenity, *per se,* but his antisocial attitude which had got him three days, two hours, fifteen minutes thirty-nine seconds additional therapy.

Since polo and other equestrian sports were included in the gracious life of the Magnificent Democracy, it was natural enough for Garvin, hearing the bell tinkle, to turn toward the waiting psychiatric technician and say, "Now that I'm through turd-bustling, what's the next assignment, Dr. Kearney?"

Garvin knew that Kearney wasn't a doctor of anything, but tact had its value in an institution. The dumb-looking, pleasant technician gestured, led the way to a processing alcove, and said, "Sit in the swivel chair.

This session will be devoted to unsupervised reverie and introspection."

However he might plant himself in what looked like a barber's or dentist's chair, there were screens which faced him, and wall areas with abstract patterns; speakers and modulators hemmed him in; the entire battery of stimulators responded to the control buttons on each arm of the chair. Controls gave him whatever height and angle he fancied.

"Well, thanks, Doctor. Any suggestions?"

The blond young man smiled, shook his curly head, and called over his shoulder as he cleared the doorway, "It's all yours, Rod. Have a nice day."

As he seated himself in the comfortably upholstered chair with axial swiveling and universal back rest adjustment, an ever more frequently recurring thought plopped up out of the depths of consciousness: *These sons of bitches must be reading my mind. How do they do it? They don't look bright enough to tell shit from wild honey.*"

That the question recurred was what had begun to worry Garvin. Something was undermining his self-assurance. He remembered ancient classics, banned from the curricula the past century, and obtainable only in libraries. Although at least thirty percentum of the standard population could read, virtually ninety percentum of such talented ones were too indolent to do so. The Plastic Populace had become a massive psychic sponge from absorbing eight to ten hours per diem of tridimensional televideo coupled with stereo-audio propaganda, much explicit, and as much by implication. Thus, no point in censorship, and meaningless to burn books. Any such gestures would arouse a temporary interest in reading. More and more, Garvin was reminding himself that he had much in common with *"Odysseus, the Man never at loss."*

"If I'm so sure of myself, how come this yakking about never being at loss? . . . Maybe I don't realize how much I am at loss . . . And then a surge of resolution: *"I'll bugger them through their oilskins, if it takes till judgment day!"* He grimaced, and added realistically, *"It'll take something like a farrier's rasp."*

Before pressing the first button, he began to "count" his breathings, a Taoist trick he'd learned from an old Chinaman while freighting well-drilling equipment into Turkistan for reclamation of desert around the Turfan Depression. The unspoken query which was to filter to the surface would relate to new notions, thoughts, beliefs—but, *were* they new, or were they old stuff, from before this rehabilitation business? If new, then reject them. Whether true or false, they were someone else's, hence deadly. From the beginning this had been his attitude. However, his defense must have its loopholes, else he'd not have developed such an obsessive, almost paranoid defense.

He pressed another button. Screen and audio came to life. A belly dancer pulled a luminous black opal from her hair, slapped it to her navel, where she held it in place by localized control. He'd never seen, not even behind the lines during the African Liberation War, such accomplished teat-and-rump wobbling, nor ever heard such alluring fiddle and flute wailings, nor stirring thump of drums.

The dance of the *Ouled Nayl*—most of his comrades had pronounced it *Oiled Nail*—was good!

There was chanting. He flicked the starter of a miniature recorder, an instrument he'd smuggled in while enjoying *extended liberty*, as provided by *Title xiv, Vol. V, Rehabilitation Code.*

He dug from his shirt pocket a kit of filters used in technical photography. One would absorb red; others, blue, green, violet; a fifth was a polarizing screen. He shifted his glance from the orbit of the big black opal, blinked, and realized that it, rather than the girl's natal endowments had had an hypnotic effect. He tried each color filter on the arabesque abstracts, recently installed in wall panels behind "Fatima," a colorful background against which she wobbled kallipygous treasures and mammary luxuries.

Until he'd tried each color filter, his testing was negative; but when he held the polarizing filter to his eye and slowly rotated it, he saw through the color maze and as it merged into gray, he read against the now neutral background, ". . . *freedom from fear; freedom from thinking. Let the Hierarchy save you the trouble, the Hierarchy knows. Relax with the Supreme Hierarch . . .*" Presently the text changed to "*Controlled thought is true thought . . . Nine Freedoms and Seven Securities . . . Correct Thought is the essence of Universal Harmony and Happiness . . .*"

Garvin wagged his head contentedly, now that he'd got a further look into tricks which the psychologists had figured for impressing doctrine on the unconscious, simply through bypassing the normal perceptions. He wondered what tricks of sound his recorder would reveal.

When the technician came to tell Garvin that the session had ended, Garvin requested and got permission to take two hours of extended liberty. On his way out, he paused at Jim Ward's cell. He said to the tall, square-faced and stubborn man with the deep-set, fierce eyes, "I'll bring you a bottle. What would you like?"

"Anything in the dispensary, I'll drink it."

Garvin whispered, "How about the sketches and specs?"

Ward fished from the pocket of his gray robe a wad of pencilled sheets. "Take these to Hamlin Daly." He lowered his whisper until it became a test of lip reading. "Did you get the address? Check it back to me."

More marginal whispering, and then Garvin raised his voice: "Don't get drunk on what I'm bringing. How much extended sentence did you get for feeling up Amelia, the time she brought your delinquency report to sign?"

"She didn't report me." Lechery gleamed in his eyes. "Soon as I'm on the loose, I'm taking her out for the weekend."

"Soon as you get loose?" After staring for a long moment, Garvin got the point. "So she's going to connive, get you released and you'll have to be grateful and lay her?"

Ward ignored the question. "The thing for you is not, repeat, not to get off the privilege list. Don't get restricted."

Chapter 2

As he stood on the conveyor belt which took him from the Rehab Facility, Garvin pondered the results of his experiment with the polarizing filter. The mosaic patterns which adorned the façades of the towering buildings flanking the traffic way now had a new meaning: in each abstract design there lurked commands, suggestions. Although his ordinary awareness, his everyday consciousness did not perceive the thought-control slogans, each was digging into and taking root in his subconscious. All this was to shape mass thinking, and, like it or not, he was one of that mass, one of the Plastic Populace.

Garvin's response to his discovery was mixed: he had an urge, bordering on desperation, to escape into remote and uncontrolled territory; and there was likewise the determination to outwit the system. He stood at the guard-rail, weight shifted, shoulder edged forward, as if to strike or stab. He straightened, shook his head. The cocked eyebrow, the incipient twist of the mouth were accompanied by a glint of whimsy. He'd never decided whether to accept the life style of 2080 AD and amount to something, or, to relish the absurdity of the way which most of the denizens regarded as the mangificent life.

Sun-squint contributed to his paradoxical expression. It was difficult to decide from the look of him whether

7

the keynote was lurking ferocity, or bawdy laughter. He'd been tanned by sun bouncing from North African sand dunes, sun blazing from the peaks which swooped skyward over the deserts of Eastern Turkistan.

From freighting in remote regions, Garvin advanced to the Lunar Shuttle and lost no time in winning promotion to the major space enterprise, the Government's Martian Mining & Development Project. This was good while it lasted. It would have lasted longer, but for Flora, who talked her influential kinfolk into getting him a less hazardous job, one that wouldn't keep him away from home so much of the time.

Marrying on impulse, neither knew enough about the other. Garvin, for instance, had not even suspected that Flora was a remote cousin of Alexander Heflin, one of the inconspicuous group which controlled the visible Government: not until he was transferred from space and into a so-called promotion as superintendent of the Martian Spaceways & Engineering Department.

There were times when Garvin wondered whether he loved his wife.

The piped commerical which regaled conveyor passengers offered hope: ". . . *vacation homes, retirement homes, luxury settlements, and year around homes in the Andes. Look from heights above Cuzco and Tihuanaco at sunset in the vast Pacific . . . serenity for your sunset years, and let your sunset begin before noon . . . skiing in Khatmandu . . .*

Suggesting mass resettlement was another approach to the problem of too many people. Free abortion plus cash bonus and a two-week, all-expense trip to Honolulu hadn't been the answer. Neither had free narcotics, slot machine distributed. The ostensible reason for taking the lid off dope had been that crime motivated by the high cost of illegal drugs would be eliminated; the actual reason was that overindulgence should kill a significant number of addicts, and keep most of the others in an anaphrodisiac stupor. It hadn't worked that way. Once there was no prohibition, the demand for narcotics tapered off to insignificance. Again, sociologists and psychologists fell on their faces, and thought control failed in the one area where it would have paid off.

Garvin laughed. People stared. To give them their stare's worth, he rode one exit past the Beverage Dispensary and walked back. Nearing the groggery, he heard the familiar sound of flute, fiddle, and drum, the chanting in Arabic. The salesperson in charge ignored Garvin. He was half hypnotized by the dance of the Ouled Nayl and her navel with the black opal setting. Garvin's bitter glance scanned the array of bottles.

The Secretary of State had decided that the North American passion for Scotch and Bourbon had stirred up international resentment, evoking charges of discrimination, chauvinism, and attempted culturicide by ignoring the beverages of other countries. Accordingly, Bourbon and Scotch were marked up to ten times the cost of stuff from underdeveloped countries.

"*Que se chinguen, los cabrones!*" Garvin muttered, and poked his kredit kard into the auditor slot to get his current balance. He had to get accustomed to thinking in terms of the *pazor,* the new currency unit: *P* for *Peso*; *A* for *agorot*; *Z* for *zaira*; *O* for *ore*; *R* for *rupee*. *Pazor* kept other countries from being humiliated by dollar supremacy when the dollar was high, and from despising it when the rate was low.

Garvin finally addressed the salesperson: "Get your eyes off that fanny wobbler, just one God-damn little moment, *please!*"

The dancer's image blurred out. In her place came *Skiing in Kashmir*, and Indian music.

"Wyja screw it up?" the clerk demanded.

"How'd I screw it up?"

"Your first sergeant voice flipped it to a difference beam. Why can't they make automation work right! What's the problem?"

"I don't have enough *pazors* for Bourbon or Scotch," he falsied, since this Plastic Citizen wouldn't understand the actual reason. "And the kind I can afford, what are they like? I'm buying for a buddy."

"Sorry, I can't tell you."

"How'd you pass your job examination? You ought to know. What's that Rajput Punch? Anything like Pimm's Mug?"

"New regulation. I am not allowed to tell you."

Garvin drew a deep breath. "I'm being psychologically reconditioned, but I'm not crazy enough to believe that."

"You're way behind the times. Or you'd know that yesterday we got voice-controlled automation."

"What the hell *for?*"

"To keep salespeople from getting hoarse, talking to customers. Union finally got it. Better working conditions."

"Then how do I tell the difference between Batavia arrak and slivovitz? Do I have to buy a bottle of each and sample it?"

"You ask the machine."

Garvin addressed the programmed dispenser: "What the hell's Rajput Punch? Is it fit to drink?"

"*Demerara rum is distilled in the upper reaches of the Demerara River Valley, in Guyana. It is dark, earthy, pungent, a drink for men of iron. For further information, apply to Pleasure, Vice & Recreation Bureau for Bulletin Number—*"

"Not that crap, I asked you about—"

"This delicious liquor is offered in 151 degrees proof. It is a favorite additive for tea or coffee while skiing in Khatmandu or—"

"Shut it off and give me two bottles of Demerara rum!"

"Sorry, but I can't. This shop is one hundred percent automation, but I'll feed your kard into the slot and punch the buttons."

"What are you here for?"

"I keep the computer from feeling rejected."

He flipped Garvin's card into the machine, jabbed the code numbers, and out came two bottles. Garvin was surprised to note that each was Demerara rum. The sales-person turned to the three-D screen and grumbled, "You really bitched it up with your concrete mixer voice—nothing but condominiums in Cuzco and the Karakoram."

"Don't you ever get your fill of teat-and-rump gymnastics?"

The man regarded him curiously. "No. Do you?"

Garvin pounced for the mall.

A feminine voice, right in his ear, outwheedled the publicity broadcast from an information booth. "Show you a good time, dearie—"

"Kiss my ass!" Garvin snarled.

"That'll be two *pazors* extra."

Belatedly, her perfume suggested that he'd been hasty and rude. The girl was long legged, elegant, and regarding him good-humoredly, as though his retort had amused her. A choice number. Her apricot-colored gown trailed nearly to the paving. It parted unpredictably, revealing flashes from ankle to collarbone, flicker-glimpses, tantalizing vistas. Intellectual, witty, and all in all, a sweet package, going with his snotty quip.

Garvin grinned amiably. "If I'd not been in such a fighting mood, I would have bid five *pazors* to kiss yours. Tough thing about it all, I have a date—" He tapped his forehead. "At the Rehab Facility. A couple of jugs for a full-time inmate. And once I do my part-time hitch, I have domestic problems."

Garvin's second survey made her even better. Red blonde hair. Something Syrian about the eyes, which were large, dark, shaped like those of Nefertiti, whose imitation alabaster head and shoulder tourist bait they sold all over Cairo. Legs, North China style.

She nodded, smiled understandingly. "I know! I've just closed shop for the day, and for a change, nothing to do this evening."

"Hook shop?"

She shook her head. "A nice little restaurant. My real business is sort of a hobby."

"Hobby?"

Her smile was dazzling. "I'm a nymphomaniac. Well, as I told you, I have a lovely little place to eat."

"I bet it is."

"I was referring to the restaurant. Drop in when you have time and we'll discuss domestic problems."

"So you're a psychological counsellor?"

"Best therapy in the world! You'd love it."

"I better get going before I'm tempted to go AWOL."

She dipped into the gossamer tangle of garment and

found a card. Garvin glanced at the inscription. Her name was Lani.

"It's a bit confusing—now, if you had pictures, I'd know whether your line is gourmet, or new positions."

"You can't lose," Lani assured him. "Not even if you're on a diet and loaded with allergies."

As the high-speed conveyor whisked Garvin across town and toward the technical complex, his encounter with Lani reminded him again that overpopulation was the magnificent society's prime problem. The Pleasure, Vice & Recreation Girls, licensed professionals, were a sociological experiment in polyandry. The PVR Corps was hailed as the answer to excess population—it worked in Tibet—why not in progressive North America.

Each PVR Girl with half a dozen steady lovers and an indeterminate flock of once-in-awhile patrons. She'd prevent a substantial number of impulse marriages; she'd whittle down the number of unwed mothers—and if she did, through sheer mishap, become pregnant, she'd be no more so than the wife with only one captive customer.

This, however, did not work according to plan. In Tibet there was a shortage of women. In the Magnificent Society, such was not the case. Garvin's optimism and resolution bounced up to par: like nature, he, too, would outwit the planners.

He found Hamlin Daly in his one-man shop. Daly specialized in diverse crafts, many of which were entirely lawful. The latter included electronics and computers. When the space program bogged down, Daly had bailed out, instead of waiting to be phased out as a surplus pilot.

The work bench in the corner was barricaded by solenoids, helices, wired and photo circuits, transistors, capacitors, electrical motors in all stages of disassembly. Bottles and other unclassifiable odds and ends compounded the clutter.

The beads of his abacus rattled like distant machine gun fire. Finally, Daly recorded a result, looked up, and cocked a sardonic glance at his visitor. He was pop eyed and wore an expression which promised to become a good-humored grin.

Garvin handed him Ward's notes. "Jim said this would interest you. Jim Ward, at the Psycho Factory. I've got to dash now. Next free time, I'll be back."

"So you're one of the customers?"

Garvin nodded. "How'd you keep out?"

Daly chuckled. "By not thinking out loud." Then, after a shrewd eyeing, he resumed, "Sit down—I'm not so busy. What's on your mind? I mean, aside from Jim's deal."

Garvin told him of the slogans which the polarizing filter had isolated from the arabesques of the wall. Daly wagged his head, grinned in anticipation of the pay off, so that Garvin concluded, "Old stuff to you?"

Daly nodded. "It's like the old-fashioned color-blindness test chart, except it's foxier. You don't know you're reading the stuff, but it registers even though you don't realize it. And, every once in a while, those psychologists turn out to be right. God-damn right it works. And so you're hooked!"

Garvin handed Daly the miniature recorder. "See if you can make more out of this than audio words and music. Take your time. I won't be back for a couple of days."

"Mmmm . . . could have some high-frequency stuff on a separate track—not ultrasonic, but so high you don't notice it, not with standard ears." He chuckled sourly. "Now that you're catching on, what'll you do with your answers?"

At the door, Garvin turned back. He handed Daly a bottle of rum. "Forgot this."

Rapid transit got Garvin back to the Rehab Facility five minutes ahead of deadline, which left him time for a word with Ward. "Daly looks congenial, but he's a weirdo, using an abacus. Why doesn't he count on fingers and toes?"

Jim snorted. "He was probably figuring out something like Y equals X to the minus e-squared power. With my gimmick and his experience, some of us are going to be computerized out of here."

An orderly came racing in. "Rod," he sounded off, "Frozen Plumbing has a message for you."

"How many demerits am I in for now?" he asked the vacancy of the hallway as he made for the front. Then, at the desk, "Yes, m'am, Amelia, what'd I do or fail to do?"

"The Board orders you remanded to the custody of your wife, immediately. There's a printout at your home."

Amelia considered for a moment. A flash of kindness, female compassion, true humanity, made her quite attractive. "Relax, Rod. You can't always be wrong."

"What's it all about? I bet you'll miss me!"

"I don't know, really, I don't." She extended her hand. "Good luck, and I will miss you."

Chapter 3

Like most of the conservative minority, and particularly the Serfs who were overtaxed to support the Magnificent Democracy, Garvin wore the slacks and jacket standardized half a century ago. The only significant changes over the years had been variation of color and of textile patterning. There were pastel shades, a full range of spectrum primaries and secondaries, with many a shrieking plaid. A considerable segment of the Plastic Citizenry expressed individualism by wearing exotica of design, such as Chinese tunics of the Tang Dynasty, variants of European Renaissance, Mogul kaftans, turbans, and baggy trousers.

When Garvin emerged from the seventy-second floor, Flora met him in the hallway. "Darling, I've been so busy listening for the buzzer and getting dressed, and—"

Before she had both arms fairly looped about him, he was glad to be home well ahead of schedule; he forgot that he'd been remanded to Flora's custody. Instead, he wondered how she'd ever stayed on the loose long enough for the likes of him, exfreighter and exspaceman, to get at her.

When Flora broke away, Garvin backed off for a good look at an ever-exciting package. The scarlet *sari* draped over her straight-back dark hair accentuated splendid dark eyes. The next garment was of gilt bro-

15

cade, too short to be a jacket, and a bit too long to qualify as a bra.

"What—no black opal?"

"Oh, you saw that one, too?"

"Maybe I'll meet someone who didn't! But you make a better production of it."

Bare midriff, a multicolored Kashmiri skirt, accordion pleated, and swirling at the least hip-sway—he backed off to survey the entirety. "You're a conversation piece!" He eyed her from gilded sandals to artfully thickened Indian eyebrows. "Or do you want a drink first?"

Flora didn't have the masquerade look of the many wenches who didn't know better than to risk exotic outfits.

"Madame, it's lecherous—it's fascinating—"

He didn't know whether to fanny-fondle, dip into the sort-of-bra, or try a combination play. And then it was too late.

"Oh, I forgot—" Flora darted for the computer column and yanked off the paper supported only by perforations. "You read it while I mix us a drink. It's wonderful, sugar, it's worked out so marvellously-beautifully!"

Skirt aswirl, she wafted toward the alcove, Kashmiri *nautch* girl turned barmaid. Garvin, however, didn't hear the tinkle of ice or the jingle of bracelets. His face became longer, the sun-lines, deeper. He looked older and older as he read the details of the Recantation Ceremony. His release from the booby hatch had been to give him time for home study of the routine in which he would be the star, at ten, the following morning: a production which would draw more of a crowd than had the end of any Liberation War. The nearest resettlement area became a must!

Garvin didn't hear Flora's happy chatter as she turned from the bar with a tray of snacks, stemmed glasses, and a cocktail mixing glass with strainer. He did however hear the silence which took charge when she saw him, noted his posture, hunched, head thrust forward, hands clenching the printout as if digging into an enemy's throat to make the eyes bug just a little further.

He looked up. This prolonged the silence. After soundless groping, she asked, shakily, "What—uh—happened? Are you—"

"I had a feeling that leaving the funny farm was loaded." He regarded Flora for a moment. "I was right. Did you read it?"

She nodded. She licked her lips.

"And so you put on a fun and games dress." He drew a deep breath. "The great improvement, water baptism to wash away all error—that had offended Christian voters, so now, fire to incinerate error."

"But—but—it's not that sort of fire."

"Of course it isn't! That would offend the Parsis. Beautiful symbolism—thanks to Nikola Tesla in the early days—his inventions have been taken for granted the past two centuries—"

"Darling—" Her voice rose, quavered. "It's harmless."

"Haul your arse out of sight, I've had it."

She'd already got the message, and was turning. Abruptly, she snatched the tray, straight armed it, smashing glassware against the back bar, scattering ice all over the tiles.

"Those slimy bastards," he said, slowly, to be sure that her choked sobs would not blot out a word. "Cousin Alexander must have put them up to it. Recanting isn't enough. Got to have a public production—" He turned, and as if addressing someone who faced him, he found the Tagalog words he'd nearly forgotten: "*Puta 'ng na mo!*"

That spoken, he sat down to study. After an hour or more, he took Lani's card from his wallet, and fingered the keyboard of the visiphone. No answer. Busy with a customer or out on a call? All the better. His mood was no compliment to an attractive girl. He retrieved the crumpled printout, smoothed it, and tried to memorize his lines. "I'll read the crap," he grumbled after moments of futile wander-wittedness. "Read it, and bitch up the act!"

Whether Flora's enthusiastic burbling had been cooperation or treason became ever less clear, as he pondered the New Recantation. And then another possibility engaged him. The Consortium which told the elected officials what to think and when to think it rarely wasted a move. Apparent silliness was the shrewd figuring of minds seeking dominion over the Plastic Masses.

Showmanship? Of course, but, much more than that.

"A trick Tesla never thought of."

He picked his way among broken glassware, then backed off from the bar. This was no more a time for liquor than for honeymooning. He fingered the keyboard again, and got Hamlin Daly—as he'd expected, still at the shop.

"High-frequency messages," Daly said, "can be slowed down in the play-back, so you can hear them. But those you can't hear seem to do the job. You're plenty right."

He hung up. Garvin was now certain that woven into the music and song of the *Ouled Nayl* was propaganda to be imprinted on the auditor's subconscious.

"Those bastards probably hypnotized Flora . . ." No time for apologies, not now. Instead, he sat down to review the words he was to recite, and he groped for hidden messages, and for ways to block the commands which undoubtedly would be loading tomorrow's ceremony. Blocking was better than trying to erase.

Chapter 4

That the traditional ceremony of recantation had been simplified by eliminating medieval pageantry gratified Garvin and at the same time alerted him. Instead of walking barefooted, wearing dunce cap and penitential robe, he rode from home in a Government car with his official escort. Slowly, the open vehicle rolled along, its propulsion jets barely whispering. Slowly, so that the heretic could be viewed deliberately by the thousands bellied up against cables stretched along the Avenue of International Good Will, and toward the tremendous pyramid which rose, terrace on terrace from the park.

For the first time, Garvin truly saw the overfed and underworked who fattened on taxes gouged from the ten percent of the population which put in a forty-hour week. It was not their variety of dress which caught his eye. To that, he'd been accustomed all his life. Looking at the Plastic Faces, male and female, he found no friend nor had he expected any. He and fellow eccentrics, the voluntary, the self-made Serfs, were a submerged class. They could not rightly be called "forgotten" since their existence was not noticed, except officially, as at tax time.

Those were bland faces, devoid even of curiosity: this pageant was a proper diversion from boating, polo, tennis, a change from cultural pursuits, a relief from the employment drudgery which Thought Control had imposed as a necessary psychotherapy to make each citi-

19

zen feel wanted and necessary. This show was another of the many acknowledgments of the right to be entertained.

These contented people were diverse in stature, complexion, facial structure, cranial contour. However they varied in physical aspect and in the *let's pretend* costuming they fancied, there was nonetheless uniformity Garvin had never before perceived. This was not because of deficiency in his power of observation. It derived rather from never having seen so many of the Magnificent Democracy packed in solid array. Each face was akin to every other face: these were the thought-controlled, the evolved product, generation after generation, the result of a process before the Magnificent Democracy won its name. Theirs an emotional rather than bodily or mental homogeneity.

Emotional automation. Emotional uniformity.

They had become as they were after more than a century of the security which their ancestors had at first tolerated, then accepted, and finally had begun to crave. There was not a purposeful face among the kilometer of spectators. The open-faced expression of bland acceptance, childlike confidence, this was standard; the incipient gaping mouth had not yet reached the fly-trap stage.

Going to be something nice . . . something from the old days, when Nikola Tesla showed Thomas Edison and the world at large how to handle alternating-current electricity. Tesla the Yugoslav was indebted to Mr. Edison for a job, back in 1884 AD. Mr. Edison was indebted to Tesla for knowledge which made electricity more than a force to drive street cars and fire up murky yellow carbon-filament bulbs. From Tesla's genius, the Space Age had blossomed. No one, least of all that genius himself, ever foresaw such a possibility.

And now forgotten Tesla was going to convert a congenital heretic into a believer.

The hedge of uniform faces aroused in Garvin a ferocious antagonism, the will to resist ritual designed to make him one of them. Flora was one of them, though she didn't look like them. Their afterbreakfast parting had been amiable . . . affectionate. Flora had her points, and she knew that the mere prospect of recantation built up intolerable pressure. They'd sat down to synthetic sausages, ersatz grapefruit juice, mock kippered herring. She'd been so grateful that he was going to become a plastic citizen as all right-minded persons were from childhood . . .

Deploring Flora was more than Garvin could manage. She was a sweet package of woman, and good hearted, too. He wondered whether some of those who bellied up against the cable were good hearted. A lot of them must be.

But this was dangerous thinking.

"They're shit-heels and dummies. Flabby parasites!"

The procession was nearing the great pyramid of synthetic adobe bricks, a colossal magnification of the Pyramid of the Sun at Teotihuacán in the Valley of Mexico, an imitation designed to promote Latin American friendship. Garvin got his mind away from Flora and dangerous thinkings. He recalled the substance of papers he'd taken, as a brat in school, a confidential report which someone had dropped while degutting a briefcase packed with sociological reports. He'd never forgotten that analysis of civilization, an estimate which a sociologist had prepared more than a century previous. The thought was that ". . . *but for one ten-thousandth of one percent of the world's population, civilization as we know it not only could not advance, but could not even maintain itself . . . if it were possible to select, at birth, each potential sustainer of science, art, and culture, and strangle each such infant, one out of every million births, the world as we know it would relapse to savagery . . .*"

Flora's cousin, Alexander Heflin, and that handful of others who constituted the Consortium which ruled the land, was perhaps one of those exceptionally able few. They were the system, and bucking the system seemed ever more and more a nonprofit enterprise.

What made the outlook dismaying was Garvin's awareness that if there had been a strangling of special infants, he would have been ignored, and for good reason. He couldn't prepare himself to resist the forthcoming psychic attack. He would have to improvise against what they had designed after long pondering.

And since he was an in-law of Alexander Heflin, it was vitally important that he be converted to Right Thought. At times it seemed to Garvin that they were using a pile driver to sink a carpet tack.

The towering pyramid was in the center of a vast park, an ultramagnificent glorification of the formal gardens which the English-oriented natives of Vancouver, B.C., had devised. The gardeners who groomed the floral slogan, *"Freedom from Want . . . Freedom from Fear . . . Freedom from Thought . . ."* got off their knees, hitched up their jeans, and regarded one another. After a glance at the penitential car, one muttered, *"Hühne dreck!"* and the other, *"Merde, alors!"* And with this appraisal, they returned to grooming the inspirational slogans.

After thrice circling the park, the vehicle swung into the space at the foot of the stepped pyramid. Garvin's escort solicitously herded him to the uppermost terrace, which was canopied, and draped in national colors. Deputies of the Board and the audiovideo teams awaited him. A brass band with archaic instruments sounded the national anthem. And then, the business.

Well away from the board, the press bench, and the communications teams was a pair of metal columns to each of which was clamped half a dozen glittering spheres, the lowest at ankle height, the uppermost at shoulder level. He had no more than a good look when the chairman asked, amiably, "Mr. Garvin, you've digested the briefing sheet?"

"Yes, indeed, sir." He waggled the paper. "Brought it with me, in case I get stage fright."

The chairman smiled, nodded. "One of us will act as prompter. The high frequency display won't be noisy, and there'll not be enough ozone to bother you. If it makes you sneeze—" He fished in the pocket of his white vest and brought out a roll of throat disks.

"Thanks, " Garvin said, "ozone never bothers me.

It would have been tactless to add that the cough drops might contain an hypnotic as well as a throat-soother.

"The display is somewhat on the principle of the aurora borealis, a corona discharge. It is to symbolize your renouncing unscientific attitudes. A good many of our fellow citizens would not be convinced by words alone, whereas seeing you pass through the fire would leave them free of doubt as to your sincerity." He paused, gravely, introspectively, impressively. Then, "We need your cooperation. Uncontrolled originality of thought is destructive of Democracy, however well motivated it might be."

"I understand," Garvin agreed.

Unobtrusively, a mike had been moved toward him from a distance, and to a spot apparently calculated and marked.

The spokesman continued, "You may turn your back to us, to face the witnesses. Please relax. The power goes on gradually."

And so it did.

In the shadow of the vast canopy Garvin saw the lavender corona's glow, wavering about each of the burnished globes. There was not yet any sound. As the corona deepened to purple, a vibrant misty luminescence spread until it seemed as if a transparent curtain had been drawn between the columns. The acrid tang of ozone, sharper than he'd ever noted it, even in the highest of mountain ranges, became ever more stinging.

A dazzling flash of blue reached from the uppermost ball at Garvin's right and across the gateway to the middle ball on his left: a miniature lightning flash, crackling like a whiplash. Amplifiers built it up. The sound was a thunder-whack-tearing-ripping—

Garvin couldn't remember how many millions of volts it took to bridge the gap. He'd frogotten the extent to which ionization of the air reduced the resistance of the gap. The *beep-beep* from behind was his cue. He stepped to the marker on the pavement between the electrode columns and into the field of the high-tension, high-frequency discharge—several million volts and he knew not how many hundreds of thousands of oscillations per second as the precisely balanced capacitors and inductances sustained the shimmering discharge.

There was no sensation. The extremely high frequency of the current kept it flowing on the surface of his skin, with no penetration of his flesh. A good show: the tricks known to every radio ham, nearly two centuries ago, had been forgotten by the masses, buried by modern science.

He gestured, right and left, as the briefing sheet directed. Bluish streams of electrical energy reached from finger tips to the chrome-planted globes of the columns. The streamers shifted, up and down, from globe to globe.

From the pyramid's height, Garvin could not see the face of any individual as other than a small blob, but the mass movement was plain, the swaying of spectators against the cable, making the barrier belly out as though to uproot the stanchions through which the cables were threaded.

A good show.

Beep—beep—beep—tiny ticks of sound—

And then Garvin began reciting. He didn't glance at his briefing sheet. He wasn't even sure that he was actually speaking, although the sounds were precisely in synch with throat muscles which were getting a workout as new to them as to him. The voice he heard was stately, oratorical, formal, with well-timed pauses.

"Belatedly, I realize the absurdity of proposing to cruise beyond Jupiter, to make a circuit about Saturn. After deep thought it has become clear that my convictions were unrealistic, that my expressing them was harmful to the community. I am grateful to the Board which helped me to recognize my error, and for giving me this opportunity to address you, my fellow citizens, to let you know that I have rejected my cherished delusions."

Then, although he ceased vocalizing, there was a soundless echoing, a silent resonance, as if he were repeating his declaration. As he stood there, desperately struggling to block the reiteration, fear gripped him: he was silently rejecting every statement he had only pretended to reject. In the end, he would believe every word of the falsehoods he had spoken to the Board and to the crowd.

The shimmering corona changed color. The terraces and stairways of the pyramid quivered, wavered, became darker, ever darker. The more he fought the echoing of his oratory, the less substantial he became. He was diving headlong through darkness until, in the instant before total anesthesia, he shaped, inwardly, a total denial of his recantation. And then he realized that orderlies steadied him as he swayed and his knees were about to buckle. One offered a whiff of an aromatic restorative. Solicitously, Board men gathered about him. There was no longer any corona; the power had been cut.

"Feeling better?" one queried, and another, "Can you carry on?" A third cut in, "That was splendid."

Garvin nodded.

The electronic vocalizer sounded off. This was synthetic speech, the work of master technicians who had reduced the recorded voice of an ancient speaker into sound components, and had then rearranged the spare parts. They had reconstituted intonation and timbre and inflection until it seemed that the founder of the system were speaking, and that this was the golden voice of one never since his day equalled in a persuasiveness, whereby the uttermost absurdity became convincing.

The Voice was evoked to sanctify the ceremony.

"Roderick David Garvin, be pleased to recite the fundamental acceptances of Science."

When the applause finally subsided, Garvin declaimed, "I believe in the existence of e, in the Method of Least Squares, and in the Theorem of Mean Values. I believe that the Mean Value is that value which is as likely as not to be exceeded. I believe in the interchangeability of energy and matter, and that the two are expressions of a single identity. I believe in the Theory of Limits, in the Infinite Series, in Euler's Criterion of Integrability and in the Thought Control Board, World without end, Amen!"

Intoning the affirmation and at the same time denying inwardly all that he said was beyond Garvin's endurance. He did not feel the hands which checked his collapse. His next perception was when stretcher bearers carried him from the elevator and into his own apartment.

Garvin wondered whether, despite inner resistance

carried to the cracking point, he had become a potential believer. Only critical self-observation could tell who had prevailed. If indeed he had won this bout, it had been such a near thing that he would not risk a second baptism of high voltage. Meanwhile, he'd sell Flora the idea that resettlement, no matter where, was the next move.

When the attendants closed the door behind them, Garvin said to Flora, "Remember that drink you were going to fix? Let's pick things up, from just before the glassware exploded."

Chapter 5

Flora had a talent for dress design. The previous night's Hindustani outfit had suggested that she inclined toward the ripe and luxurious. Now, to celebrate Garvin's release from the Psycho Factory, she wore a Tang Dynasty tunic, dove gray, with headgear of kingfisher breast plumage, pearl embroidery, and jade pendants which reached from ear lobes almost to her shoulders. Instead of suggesting opulence, her lines were sleek, a sensuous understatement.

She was pouring hot *shao hsing* into tiny cups Garvin had brought out of Khotan, in Eastern Turkistan. Greenish-bluish eye shadow came into play as, bending to pour, she glanced slantwise through long lashes.

Garvin snatched the four-stringed lute he'd liberated while on Asiatic excursion. Plucking the strings, he sounded off a few phrases of a Turki ballad.

> *Ay wah de gooveh*
> *Maal i dindeh,*
> *Fustan ala youmi . . .*
> *Yok, baba jeem, YOK!*

Except for the refrain, he always botched the words. No time for singing, he announced, set the lute aside, and tossed off another thimble of rice wine.

"Oh, go ahead and play—I'll dance."

"Wait till I know how the Fat Boys took the way I loused up a smooth ceremony."

"Darling, it was marvelous, blacking out—I watched it on the screen. It showed you were heart and soul in it all—you should have seen the faces, the Board, I mean. And then a pan shot of the crowd—you had them nailed, every last one!"

"So you think I've got it made? Then I'll tell you the next move. Got it figured out."

Her brows rose. They leveled off during his groping for the right words. Then, "You don't need any suspense build up! Tell me!"

"How about a long honeymoon?"

"Oh, how marvelous! Where?"

"Well . . . here and there. For a good look at new country. We'll take our time picking a spot to settle down."

Flora blinked and went wide eyed. "But you were speaking of a *honeymoon*!"

"I still am. We had one before we settled down in this hell hole, only we didn't look at enough places first. This time, see the country around Cuzco, then there's Khatmandu, which has become a lot more modern than you'd imagine."

"You and your everlasting wanderlust!" she chided, trying to conceal a total letdown.

"This isn't wanderlust!"

"Then what *is* it?"

"I'm choking on this poisoned air."

"Rod, you silly! We have the purest air, better than Nature ever had, even before the industrial age began."

Garvin drew a deep breath. He was in for it now. Every time he tried to explain himself, he fouled things up. In a few more words, well chosen, he'd be fighting for another lost cause.

"In the way you mean, we do have the best. Even in my lifetime, I've noticed a lot of improvement." Seven–eight years older than Flora, he felt venerable every time he looked at her. "Sure, you're right. And the recycled sewerage we drink tastes a lot better than the chlorinated muck we used to get out of lakes and so-called deep wells. What I mean is something you never hear mentioned."

Flora frowned. "What's the cryptic unmentionable?"

"The crowding. A million people breathing down your neck."

"Oh, but we're adjusting to that, we don't hate the nearness of others as we used to. Remember the broadcast about Feilchenberg's experiments? How the rats became cannibals even when they had a balanced diet? The cause was crowding. Then they they were conditioned not to be resentful, and they quit cannibalism."

"God damn it, darling, yes! With enough adjusting to crowding, they went back to eating kibbled rat food instead of fellow rats. You make a career of being adjusted to everything. What's wrong with this Magnificent Madhouse is that there aren't enough people dying, there isn't enough infant mortality, not enough of these decrepit old fossils dying.

"For billions of years the world had a grand ecological system. Little animals ate plants. Medium animals ate plants and little animals. Big animals ate plants, medium and small animals, and sea food and stuff.

"All the eaters breathe out carbon-dioxide waste. The plants breathe out the oxygen from the carbon dioxide they've taken out of the atomosphere. Their oxygen-excrement keeps us alive. Animal dung feeds them."

"That," she suggested, "is not news!"

"I'm getting to my point—hear me out! All solid, visible, tangible, smellable or tastable waste goes through the cycle and comes back to us like roses, nectar, or good buckwheat cakes. But the air is reeking with psychic excrement that's never recycled.

"That's what's driving us nuts and fruit. So I'm going where we'll not be chin-deep in mental manure, spiritual offal. We'll get into the Andes, or the Himalayas, where the foothills are fifteen–sixteen thousand feet high, and then you see the big ones go zooming up."

"You mean—we're to resettle—and live with— savages?"

"I got yanked from a space run where the only pollution was the twenty-mile trail of exhaust dust. None of it was human thought defecation, human emotion-manure—"

"You really mean . . . leave our beautiful things and life-style . . . Rod, I *couldn't*! Not into horrible places where you can't poke your nose out of your own kitchen window without having one of the aborigines take a shot at you."

"Oh, for hell's sweet sake! I used to tell you yarns of those countries till I was hoarse and tried to shut up, but you wouldn't let me. I made a career, telling you bedtime stories, thrillers."

Her voice rose, crescendo. "But *Rod*! Hearing it was fascinating. *Living* it—that would be *awful*. I couldn't! I won't!"

He pounced to his feet. She started as if he'd menaced her with a weapon. She couldn't speak until he was nearly at the door.

"Where—ah—are you going?"

"Back to the funny-farm where I belong."

It wasn't until he was down to street level that he realized that the Rehab Facility would be closed to him, except as a visitor. Pausing at a dispensary to get a couple of bottles, he turned to make for the shop of Hamlin Daly Enterprises. Before he'd fairly changed direction, he had a second thought.

The day was young. Flora's reaction to the recantation was undeniably more valid than his appraisal of his playing the role of penitent. It would be a good idea to have a talk with Flora's cousin, Alexander Heflin. Garvin's preliminary preparation was to step into a haberdashery, where he had himself outfitted with head cloth and gold threaded brow-band; an ankle length *jellaba* of fine cashmere; red leather slippers and a broad bladed *jambia* in a silver scabbard. This weapon he thrust into the embroidered sash which, with a Moslem rosary, completed the outfit.

Garvin's costume was to indicate that he had actually become a believer, not in Allah nor His Prophet, but in the Administration. The Administration was ass-kissing the Imam of el Yemen, who in retaliation for a real or fancied slight had raised the price of San'ani Mocha,

Coffea Arabica, the parent of all coffee which rated the name *coffee*.

Not everyone was admitted or admissible to the presence of Alexander Heflin. Perhaps as many as one-tenth of one percent of the Plastic Populace suspected that he existed, much less that it was he who told the duly elected Supreme Hierarch what to think, what to do, and when to do it. Garvin's card got him undelayed passage through office after inner office, until he faced his wife's fifth cousin.

Alexander Heflin brushed aside the solitaire layout which covered a good bit of the acre of teak desk top. He got up, thrust out a hearty hand; his tanned aquiline face blossomed into a happy glow. "Glad to see you, Rod! You cooperated marvelously!" Pressing a button set the hospitality department in motion. A panel of tropical hardwood slid aside, and a self-propelled cart rolled out, stopping just a centimeter from the desk. "Austerity's the keynote! All I can offer is the bottles you see."

"What! No Mocha San'ani with orange flower water?"

Alexander chuckled, eyed the Yemeni robe. "That's getting into the spirit of things. What's on your mind, Rod?"

"Now that I'm on the loose again, I ought to have a fresh start all around."

"There's been no awkwardness at the shops—you've been carried full time, and your time out has been charged to . . . mmm . . . general and technical education."

"Well, thanks, Alex, but that isn't what I was thinking of. Call this an appeal to Caesar."

Alexander's gesture which started brushing back his sleek black hair was completed as a two-handed pantomime. "Now that my laurel wreath is on straight—you're selling me an idea! Why not a classical touch, wreath and toga?"

They filled glasses, and they drank. And then. "Something's on your mind, Rod. Without being Caesar, maybe I can help?"

Garvin snapped back to his feet, thrust the chair

aside. "Meet me half way. Now that I admitted I was out of order, talking about circling Saturn, how about getting me back on the Mars route? Fifty-fifty—I play your game, you play mine."

Slowly, the master of the show shook his head. "I'm sorry, awfully sorry, but that's out. Call it a matter of policy."

Fighting on foot was not paying off. Garvin seated himself, and asked, earnestly, "I've done a lot of wondering about what's wrong with thinking about cruising beyond Saturn, or beyond Pluto, for that matter. Simply scientific speculation. Right?"

"Wrong." Alexander hunched forward, and, narrow eyed, he fixed Garvin with an intent look. "This is between you and me, and I'm not even asking you to keep your big mouth shut. If ever you quote or misquote me, all I have to do is declare that you are a God-damn liar. Here is the answer—We do not want a lot of agitation, a lot of talk about space beyond Mars. Once the notion began booming, there would probably be too much public demand for reaching further and further into space. Every junior-grade crackpot would dramatize himself as a Space Pioneer, Space Hero, or whatever the hell you fancy.

"There would be billions down the drain—and our first problem is making progress with that Martian Ecological Development thing. If population increase makes better time than the Development, we are in trouble. *We* includes me and the rest of the Consortium. We have our limits. Is that clear?"

Garvin pulled a long face. "Too damn clear. But I've ash-canned the Saturn business. There'll be vacancies on the Mars run. My record there was good."

"And you got a big promotion. Your next step will be Works Manager, upkeep and manufacture." The hawk face crinkled. Alexander made a jabbing gesture with index and middle finger leveled pistol-wise at Garvin. "You Serfs are too stubborn to change. Once you got as far as Mars Mineral & Mining Depot, you'd refuel and take off. That would start a space stampede."

Garvin made a careless gesture. "That's a caper I never thought of. You've sold me an idea."

Alexander grimaced sourly and shook his head. "I know a lot of things that you've been thinking about."

"Such as?" Garvin challenged.

The answer he got was a setback: "Such as prehistoric astronauts from outer space, and what is stopping us? Skip that *who, me?* look, and your attempt at the expression of innocence is not convincing. A native in Turfan, a young fellow who had notions about a girl named Djénane picked up second- or third-hand talk about her stories of people from outer space. Also, that you thought the idea made sense."

"So I was promoted because spacing around was too dangerous for a newlywed? And then Djénane's bragging about having a sleeping mate who didn't sneer at Uighur Turki traditions got to Central Intelligence and I got to the Rehab Facility."

Alexander chuckled. "You figure with no detours. And there is this—a lot of your thinking we do not know, and some we never will know."

"Hence the pyramids."

"Hence the pyramids, Rod. You lead a complicated life. Even entirely in your own right, and if Flora cut loose tomorrow, you have a future. Provided you quit bucking the system. Get smart and learn how to use the system."

"Meaning, if I do what my wife tells me to, I can get anywhere but into space, provided I think the right thoughts."

"I couldn't have said it better. Forget that space nonsense, inner space or outer. You can't have the benefits of being one of the family without accepting the handicaps, the no-no-no's. We—the Consortium—do not have the fun and games life you may imagine. If a man isn't able to sweat carpet tacks, and if he isn't ulcer-proof, he'd better find job with different specs."

Abruptly, Alexander Heflin got up, thrust out his hand. "We like you. Nobody ever thought you were balmy. That was for the trained seals. And why not skip the notion of resettling in Cuzco or Khatmandu? What are you good for in those *K*-places, Kashgar, Khotan, Khartoum, and the rest of 'em?"

"Let's keep on understanding each other, and awfully glad you dropped in."

Garvin hoped that his expression of good fellowship was convincing. "Thanks, Alex. And tell 'em to double all security so I can't hijack that new cruiser, the *Garuda Bird*."

Chapter 6

Garvin found Hamlin Daly in his one-man shop, lost in a jungle of spare parts and partially disassembled electrical equipment.

"How's the Black Box coming along? Is Jim on the right track?"

"Not more than one and a half men in the whole world could understand his plans. As of right now, the half man is me. What Jim doesn't know about the workings of Central Planning Control Department you could write into a small notebook, using a four-inch paint brush."

"He worked there long enough."

Daly nodded. "That's why he got into the fruit and nut shop. His loud talk began to bother the Fat Boys. Now that they've got him where he is, they can laugh it off, saying the poor guy's got too many cards missing from his deck."

"Jim said he could include me in the resettlement deal if I wanted to get in. We'd talked in general terms about getting into an uncrowded spot, with plenty of elevation. Jim being in a restricted section, special observation, we had to go easy on talk, or the whole works would blow."

"I can brief you," Daly said. "Everyone goes to the same spot. There's supposed to be random selection from a list of applicants, but that's easy to get around. There can't be more than twenty in one draft, and no fewer than ten. No singles—they're bound to be trouble-makers. No lesbians, no homos—no point in getting them out of town, they don't increase the population."

"That's the most surprising thing I ever heard—"

"What do you mean, surprising?" Daly demanded.

"Well, it makes sense, which is something those bureaucratic bastards never make."

Daly grinned. "Jim made the rules for this one draft, just tying it into the general pattern for genuine resettlements, the strictly *kosher* kind that the Fat Boys figured out. That's where I come in, doing the programming after I figure the circuits that'll work the way Jim outlined for me. And you go to the Central Complex and hook the Black Box to the master computer unit that distributes programming into every branch of the system that would have any relation to resettlement."

Garvin frowned. "Hey, wait a minute—crank that one over again! What does it really mean?"

"I had to do some thinking, myself," Daly admitted. "But it's really simple. For instance, Education gets a briefing, and then sends out directives on pedagogy, child psychology, and diet and what-not. Public Health might send them bulletins on abortion, and first-aid, and the family medical advisor. Someone or other would contribute home gardening, house beautiful, animal husbandry and how to keep from being shot by natives you've unwittingly insulted."

"Hold it a second, and see if I get this," Garvin cut in. "How the hell can you know all the departments? Suppose you skipped important details on food arrangements. A lot of people can't go for native chow. Like Flora, she can't stand *bêche de mer*, no matter how you fix it."

"You missed the whole point, Rod! I don't have to know a thing. All I have to do is tie in with the unit that programs every department related to a basic subject. Easier to tell you what's not included. For instance, military supplies, grenades, small arms, light artillery, field sanitation—hell, no. But under subsistence, cross reference to wild game and fish, there'd be the classical sporting rifles, fishing tackle, nets—"

"And harpoons for whaling in Khatmandu?"

"You want to bet that couldn't happen?"

"Am I crazy enough to buck a frozen deck?" Garvin countered. "This business is terrific. And you can get it going with a black box that one man can carry?"

"Actually," Daly explained, "there isn't any box, and it is not black. That's a word the programming jockeys cooked up. You can stuff the four–five pounds of circuitry, silicon, and such into a mechanic's tool kit and have room for enough odds and ends, so as to impersonate a legitimate service man. You won't have any problems."

"*I* won't? Hold it, Daly! Where do *I* come in?"

"Jim is in the fruitcake bakery," Daly patiently explained, "Hoping to get out. Me, I am too busy with specialized techniques to frig around with mechanic's drudgery. That leaves you—Am I a routine working stiff? Does it take my specialized talent to walk in and go to unit number such-and-such, hook wire X to terminal Y—color coded, you know—and put back the housing cover? Then you walk out and crawl into bed with that girl, to make sure she functions properly at high elevation."

"Just walk in, *comme ça!*"

"No rule against levitation, or materializing in the right compartment of the complex. Sit *down*, Rod! I was just kidding. I mean, it's nothing complicated, like plying staff members with liquor and women. I'll get you a custom-built ID card no one can tell from the genuine article."

"One that would pass the electronic scrutinizer if Security gets fussy minded? Where do you get fakes that good?"

After a moment of gazing reflectively into further space, Daly smiled. "Fellow I know pretty well. He builds passports to order. Has other neat tricks. How come you're interested in resettlement? With you recanting the way you did, you've got the world by the tail and on a downhill pull."

"That's what my wife figured, so she squaked about dumping my fine future to fraternize with savages."

"Kind of got me wondering, too. Finally got her talked into line?"

"Neither now nor ever. And I don't mind telling you why I've set my mind on bailing out. Far as fumes and chemical and lead and arsenic dust and asbestos fiber are concerned, we've got air as pure as any in the high far mountains. It's the propaganda and thought-control crap, and all the thinking by people that buy it. The air is soaked with mental manure, psychic sewerage, emotional excrement. We're all getting crazy faster than psychohospitals can be built for us—"

Before he could elaborate, Daly cut in. "The way you put it, it adds up. If your wife won't buy the deal, find someone else."

"I've got a date with a good prospect." Garvin carefully moved a rotor and a magnetic clutch. In the table space he won, he set a bottle of genuine Bourbon. "If she doesn't like it, she can bail out soon as I find a native girl."

Daly grimaced. "I'm not used to luxury liquor. Have a real drink."

He reached into a waste basket and brought out an earthenware jug with odd-looking characters stamped into the shoulder.

"Jesus! What's this?"

"It's Ethiopic, and don't call me *Jesus*. The name's Hamlin." He slopped a dollop into each of two tumblers. Faint fumes rose from the slop-over on the table. "That smoke don't mean a thing. It's something in the lousy varnish."

"You . . . uh, drink it straight?" Garvin wondered, uneasily.

Daly demonstrated. "Good, when you get used to it."

Garvin followed suit. He choked, coughed, blinked. "Uh—huh, still got tonsils and esophagus. That wood is probably one of those lousy exotics." He thrust out his glass. "Never met a drink I couldn't learn to like."

Daly poured refills. "They ferment *dhurra*," he explained, "and instead of making their lousy beer, they distill the mash."

Garvin tossed off the slug, hitched up his chair, and resumed. "Hamlin, you may know less about computers than Jim Ward, but you're ahead of me. Ever since you began explaining things, I been mulling over an idea I was pondering on when I couldn't sleep—after that high-tension electrical ordeal, I couldn't get within a kilometer of sleep. My idea's grown into shape. During restless hours, I sketched out a letter, my farewell compliments. Instead of me sending it to the Thought Control Board, you work it into the Black Box so it'll go on the air, through all the different channels, as many as you can think of, anyway."

"I tell you, I don't have to think of all the departments," Daly repeated. "Just program things and the message will go into audiovisual, it'll be worked into abstract patterns like you saw in the wall panel behind the *Ouled Nayl* dancer, and the high-frequency sonics, like in the tape you gave me, the song and the music for the belly dancer. The whole network will get its briefing—I don't have to know a God-damn thing, and look what I can get started! Bureaucracy's wonderful, come to think of it."

"Try and sell Jim Ward that idea."

Daly shook his head. "Jim's loving this—and if he can bitch up the computer system, show it up for a horse's ass, he'll feel rewarded for all the years of being in the funny farm. Furthermore and moreover—" Daly now gestured and wore the face of eloquence. "There's Amelia! But for the stupidity of bureaucrats, he'd never have met Amelia."

"Now that you've run down for a minute," Garvin said, "pour me another one. You figure out my share of the expense of building and uh . . . integrating my message into the Black Box. I'll pay in advance. Be sure you put in, say, a thirty-day delay so I can figure my getaway from Khatmandu."

"I'll figure all that out when I get around to it," Daly assured him. "Where's your message?" He picked up the Ethiopic jug, and poured himself a snort. "If you got it written out, you don't need to tell me the blow-by-blow."

"Have I got it written out!" He dug into the inside pocket of his jacket, handed Daly an envelope. "I had a half way feeling that Cousin Alexander would give me the friendly but firm no-no about my going back to space! So I brought this poop sheet. Telling the world why the Fat Boys are against exploring outer space. It's because they want to build up Mars, and put the surplus population to work on the ecology, seven days a week, making Mars habitable."

Chapter 7

Garvin met Lani at the entrance of her gourmet restaurant. Since she had a partner for the evening, the long-legged redhead wore a sedate gray tunic, elegant of line, yet designed not to catch the questing eyes of potential customers. The gown tricked Garvin until Lani made an abrupt change of direction, heading for a nearby kiosk. She faced the low sun's horizontal beam, which spotlighted her from silver heels to silver hood.

He was dazzled, but not by the sun. What left him blinking was the red gold aureole which haloed her silver hood, and not entirely incidental, there was the sudden view of exquisite long legs which had been veiled until the instant of revelation, when the low sun reached through the ankle length skirt of clinging mist and rippling haze.

Sensing that he was not at her heels, Lani paused and looked over her shoulder. The silhouette vanished in gray mists, now impenetrable. Garvin blinked, and then, "Some shopping! I got some liquor at the groggery." He patted the parcel in the crook of his arm.

Lani pointed at the kiosk, a miniature cross between pagoda and Taj Mahal, done in Styrofoam and sprinkled with iridescent flakes.

"Let's see what the stars say."

"Stars? You mean, for us."

"Who else?"

"You have to find out *whether*, or just when?"

41

Her smile was a glowing promise. "I had my mind made up the first couple of minutes, the other day. But when I saw that funny little dome with the sun bouncing off the bric-a-brac, I got the feeling that this is important. An odd feeling, kind of a shiver down my back. Awfully important, not just fun and play." She caught his arm. "Did you have any, well, sensings like that? When I looked back you had a blinking, dazed expression—"

"That's the way I felt," he admitted. "It was sudden, like this—" He traced Lani's thigh from knee to the limit. "I couldn't believe they were real—the sun shone—"

She brushed his hand aside. "Don't, you idiot!"

"Well, they are real—"

"You didn't have to feel me up in front of nine thousand clowns!"

"Sure, I'm crude at times, and anyway, I was only reaching for ultimate reality. All right, let's see what the stars say."

Mollified by apology and his acceptance of her pet whimsy, she patted his cheek. "The ultimate reality will keep till we get home. That's really a different word for it . . ."

"You're right," Garvin conceded, "and this is the usual crowd of scummy slobs!"

The age of science had its reactionaries. The shrine next to the astrology kiosk was a survivor from the Asiatic Wars, when the GIs had brought back the custom of firing up joss sticks, just for luck. Some were white haired, stumbling and shuffling. Other veterans were middle aged. All were the congenital scoffers their status required, but they had to make their daily offerings for the luck that'd bring heavier pensions, more privileges.

At the altar, each paused to bow, and make way for the next in line.

Instead of the Four Faces of Shiva, of Kwan Yin, or Mother Kali, the astrological Kiosk housed a computer.

"Let's get a printout instead of trying to remember what the squawk-box says," Lani suggested. "There's bound to be a lot, and it's only a *pazor* extra, darling."

"You'll never let me forget that one!"

"You'd never want to forget our first meeting."

Each dialed the day, month, and year of birth, and, for an additional *pazor*, the terrestrial latitude and longitude and the hour and approximate minute of birth. The computer spewed each printout in a brace of seconds. Lani stuffed his and hers into her handbag, caught his arm. "We'll read these with our cocktails."

"Cocktails *and* astrology? What the hell are you—you told me you're a nymphomaniac."

"I'm female mystery," she retorted. "Your crudity, a few minutes ago, and now your impatience—well, it inhibits me."

Some few minutes later, emerging from the elevator at the ninety-sixth floor, Garvin followed Lani into a spacious room from the picture window of which he could see the roof of the restaurant where he'd met her: and far beyond, the tremendous bulk of the Psycho Factory, and still further, the towering heart of the nation, the Thought Control complex which he'd be invading, once Lani proved to be the girl with whom he'd share Khatmandu and then the truly isolated regions.

"Nice place you've got here," he said, automatically, as he turned from the window, and at once, felt superfoolish. "Ah—uh—what the hell—"

Not a stick of furniture in the place.

Lani laughed with delight. "I was wondering when you'd notice. Now shut your eyes, and don't you dare peek."

Garvin backed against the door and closed his eyes. The licensed girls of the PVR Corps were a law-abiding lot, yet he had an uneasy moment as he grappled with two thoughts: ". . . *just about sure there's not a pimp going to slug me . . .*" and, ". . . *if this is how she lives, we'll get along fine in Khatmandu . . .*"

"Now look!"

Lani was fingering the buttons of a consol. A lounge was emerging from the wall. It shifted to exact sitting distance from the cocktail table which had come up out of the floor. A liquor cabinet wheeled into position from a near by panel.

"I be damned! Only the upper-bracket politicos have things fitted out like this."

"I told you I'd show you a good time! And now it's my turn. That briefcase—that's not full of liquor—or is it? Don't tell me you brought pajamas and stuff?"

"Not after you told me of your stock of silk-soft paper disposables, and what a ball we'd have in your flexible bottom Roman bath tub—" He glanced about. "Where's it hid?"

"Right in front of you, honey. This is *modern* modular—push 1-6-3-7—no, over on the panel."

Between fingering the controls and seeking clues to Lani's zipperless, snapless, buttonless gown, Garvin was far from sure whether the pool-tub complex slid out of the bulkhead, or slid along it, and down from the ceiling.

"If I had known you had it this good, I would have gone AWOL the other night, let Jim die of thirst, and to hell with the recanting ceremony."

"Recanting ceremony?"

"You mean, you didn't see the newscast?"

"What newscast?"

"Up on the Pyramid, taking back all I said about driving a cruiser around Saturn and coming back with close-up pictures." He sighed, gustily. "Such is fame—"

"Rod, darling,—" She shook her head, started to take off her silver brocade hood, but didn't, and looked distressed. "I'm sorry, but I've been so busy with that restaurant, and with company nights, I can't remember when anyone wanted to look at the screen—"

"Dream Girl!" he sounded off, as if introducing her to a vast multitude. "I didn't know anyone like you existed—you really don't get your mind polluted with all that propaganda slush?"

"Mmmm . . . well, I've never been a stock model, but I've not considered myself so awfully unusual. Let's mix us a drink and you can tell me all about that, later—and about that briefcase—"

"Oh, *that*? There's a lot of stuff about a government project I'm studying. Some of it might interest you."

"What did you say you're going to have?"

"How about Fernet Branca with a brandy float?"

"Rod, you must be psychic, calling for that one, when the only bitters in the house—how about Peychaud and gin?"

"After what I've been drinking, you could give me nitric acid and I'd like it. Anyway, you built me up to expect something fancy and we weren't talking about liquor."

"Just push 9-3-3-11, and we'll have our drink later."

When Garvin turned from the control panel, he saw a boulder, a tree trunk, autumn leaves and a wooly blue blanket spread out on the synthetic turf which now carpeted the floor. There was a picnic basket. The neck of a bottle peeped from a wine cooler.

"Outdoor living, without being stared at by a bunch of male, female, and junior-grade oafs," Lani remarked, "and it's only a hundred *pazors* extra."

"How much extra if I tear off your dress?"

"I can get out of it quicker myself."

The lights dimmed automatically. Sunset in the woods.

"I'll be peeled down before you are," Lani challenged.

"Hundred says you won't—"

Garvin lost by a second.

Between the Roman pool and the gourmet snacks in the Black Forest and artificial turf as soft and resilient as a well-organized mattress, Garvin and his discovery shared hours far too crowded to allow discussion of escape to Khatmandu or the emotional-spiritual-mental pollution of their corner of North America. All that would keep until, after a ration of sleep, there'd be a languid awakening and a cozy stretch of pillow talk . . . as with Djénane Khanoum, who had devoted their quasi-lucid hours to lessons in Uighur Turki. If he talked Lani into going to Khatmandu, he'd have no cause to trade her in for a native girl.

In due course, the smorgasbord module produced skewers of mock beef *teriyaki*, imitation raw fish salad—

"Something you were going to tell me about. Remember?" Lani prompted as she offered reconstituted avocado dip. "You weren't bubbling over with joy about going back to the restaurant, and you'd been thinking about the horoscopes."

He dipped into the tangle of garments.

"You'd never find the printouts in that mixure of his-and-hers," Lani declared. "I asked if you were a lout and a clown, or just purposeful and straightforward, and if we had any future. What did you ask?"

"I asked if you were as good as you looked or whether you'd wear out after a couple of dates. After I left you, I got a lot of new facts."

"About me?"

"About us finding a new spot, out of all this mental and emotional diarrhea. You like outdoor living, how about going to some place out in the open, high mountain area?"

He gave her an outline of the doctrine he'd explained to Flora and to Hamlin Daly. She sat cross legged, spine straight-up, like one of the ivory figurines from the Indian Liberation. When Garvin had done with the run-down, Lani grimaced. "We *are* psycho, all of us. Doing things because we're supposed to. While you were talking, I relaxed, sort of hypnotized. Anyway, I got a sensing—"

A long, long pause.

"I'm listening," he finally prompted.

"For a moment, I was realizing that I'd never done anything in my life just because I wanted to, on impulse. But the psychologists and the Behavioral Science people and all the rest of the pack, they're always telling us that there's no such thing as acting on impulse—everything we do is because of some cause, or stimulus."

"It's muck like that!" he cut in. "That's just what I mean! It's time to get out—be yourself instead of a rule book pretend-to be human."

"That horoscope—oh, here it is!" She lunged for the intermingled garments and produced the ribbon of pink paper. "It says you'll lead me into a permanently new and strange way of living. We ought to be sure we're suitable for each other—"

"Just for a change, kick everything and take off!"

"Honey, I'd love it! But there'd only be foreign

women for me to be sociable with. Couldn't you and Jim get a few of my girlfriends and their steadies in on the group?"

"Easy! All we need is their card numbers, and add those and a few more names to the programming garbage."

Chapter 8

Tool kit in hand, Garvin got off the conveyor. He looked about him, eyed the complex which towered stage upon stage, and felt uncomfortably small, bucking the network which controlled the thinkings of the entire country and influenced much of the undeveloped and backward world. After a deep breath, he shook off his moment of depression. The thought machines were no brighter than the men who used them.

They, the masters of the show, had something ahead of them. Stimulated and moving with new assurance Garvin stepped into the entrance way, and flashed his ID card. The guard ignored him. A ray-actuated bell sounded. The note subsided only after he had presented identification to the scanner. Stepping to the elevator, he glanced again at his memo, pushed the button, and descended six levels.

A barely perceptible hum pervaded the place: the background music for the chatter of a printer. He noted the number and letter combinations of entrance ways and learned which was up-sequence, which down. He stepped into 123-BY-15. The area was enclosed by transparent plastic bulkheads. Thus far, he had heard not a footstep, not a voice. The emptiness vibrated from power, and from a radiation; though this was not like the menacing aura of multimillion-volt energy transmission lines, not like the force of ray generators, he became uneasy.

Garvin was in a vortex of mental force. There was something eerie in its impact and his response.

"Those things can't think," he told himself. "Bunch of wires and gadgets."

The console was right ahead of him. He referred again to his memo. Hooking up to the wrong computer would be a disaster. Got to make sure. Nothing was happening: A couple of red pilot lights glared at him, and several green ones. He started violently when all the red blinked out, and a blue went on.

For a moment, Garvin stood and faced the new combination of lights. There was nothing in his memo which referred to changes of pilot lights. A red came on again. One green went out.

"Make up your mind, you silly bastard!" he muttered.

Then a voice: "Looking for someone?"

Garvin jerked about.

A man in a white smock confronted him. Only a human. Like most working stiffs, an automaton on duty. Although it would be illegal to bury him, he wasn't truly alive. Merely moving about. And for a dismaying moment, Garvin felt akin to Elmer Carter, as the name card on the smock proclaimed him to be. Fellow dummies.

Garvin set down his tool kit. "Hygroscopic equilibration," he announced, remembering his lines." He produced a clipboard with work order. "Sign here."

"What for?" Carter demanded.

"To prove I was here to do some equilibrating."

The man frowned, waggled his head. "I'm not signing."

"You can shove your signature, then. Who does the signing for this floor?"

"I do."

"Then for hell's sweet sake, have at it! I work flat rate, and you sitting around with your thumb up costs me money."

"Can't sign till I really understand what it's for."

"That's a roundabout way of saying *never*. You still notice that humming sound, all the time here, or have you got used to it?"

"Oh, that humming? Sure I notice, all the time."

"Can you explain it to me?" Garvin demanded.

The man eyed him, resentfully. "How about *you* explaining it?" he challenged.

"You think I can't? It's hysteresis currents in the laminations of solenoids and armatures maintaining a steady vibration at auditory level."

The man's face brightened." So *that's* how come all the buzzing." He reached for the clipboard. "A technician like you had ought to be able to explain *hygro—* what?"

"Hygroscopic equilibration. What's your bag, around this plant?"

"I'm a junior programmer's aide. Name is Carter. Elmer Carter."

"Pleased to meet you. I'm Gregory Gurdjieff. It is this way. *Hygro,* combination with or presence of water or moisture. *Hygroscopy,* observing moisture. Hence, any device for measuring humidity. Equilibration, leveling off, adjusting."

Carter signed. But Garvin's sigh was premature.

"You mean, that gear you got, it's hygroscopes?"

Garvin was stuck for a lecture course, and his blood pressure was rising. He took an instrument from the kit, snapped the switch, adjusted the zero point. "See?"

Carter nodded. "Reads zero now."

Garvin stepped to the far corner of the compartment. "See the reading now?" Without waiting for an answer, he beckoned, crossed to the opposite angle, and took another reading. "Level's different."

"Uh-huh."

"Now I got to equilibrate. Around Unit BX-422-M-3.5, especially. Which one is that?"

Carter pointed. "Right over there."

"Want to watch the doings?"

"Mmmm . . . well, now that I understand everything, what's the use of sticking around? All you do is look at dials. I'll be—" He gestured indicating a cross corridor. "That way down the hall, second hallway, and to your right, in case you need a hand."

"Well, thanks, I'll call you."

Garvin went back to Unit BX-422-M-3.5. He

twisted the spring-loaded knobs that secured the main cover plate, and got to work. First move, activate the hygroscopic instrument. In addition to buzzing and whirring, it had eye-appeal: two pilot lights, crême de menthe and deep amber, steadily glowing, with a red which flickered on and off. By twisting knobs, Garvin could produce anything except martial music.

Never could predict when the next computer jockey, next Junior Programmer's Aide would show up. One nice thing about the era of specialization: a man knew all about one thing, and nothing at all about anything else. Carter was not dumb. He was a specialist.

And then Garvin began to wish that he, too, had specialized in computers. Peering into the guts of the unit he had come to gimmick left him on the verge of collapse. Pressure at his temples promised to explode his skull. Confrontation with so many chances for error left him numb, except for that pain in his head. He hated himself and he hated everyone whom he had loud-talked into depending upon him.

"I can screw this up," he said to himself, "in two million ways, raised to the *N plus one power*."

He closed his eyes. He forced himself to draw a deep breath, to hold it, and finally to exhale, slowly. He repeated this routine until the crazy pounding at his temples subsided. Breathing regularly finally became easy. Garvin licked his lips, grinned at the array of electronic junk.

"First time is rugged, even if it's nothing but performing an abortion on a computer."

He reviewed the poop sheet. The Black Box, neither black nor a box, had been defined in one of the books he'd studied: "*Any assembly, usually electronic, which can readily be taken from or put into a larger system without detailed knowledge of that larger system's internal structure . . .*"

Here was a "larger system." Garvin's knowledge was not detailed.

He faced color-coded circuits and color-coded junctions. There was not even a jungle of glowing tubes. Nothing but silicon chips or was it "solid-state" stuff?

This was a one-screwdriver job, and he had screwdrivers to spare. He set to work. Finally, he did need a magnet. That was when he fumbled a lock washer.

Then, voices broke in. Sounded like Carter, startled and stuttering, answering someone else. "B-b-but he had a card."

The retort was terse and obscene. Comment merged into the sound of footfalls. Another interruption. Garvin had just about had his fill. He dipped into the kit, hefted a plastic sausage of fine white sand, and put it back. Not the proper cooler for settling two customers in one rush. *Kung fu*? Hard to strike a balance: you either got results fatally permanent, or you might not silence the enemy for as long as the operation required. Garvin groped for and got another answer, hooked his thumbs in his belt, and knelt there; let them write the prescription, and he'd fill it.

Carter was in the lead, and pointing. The other was in charge. His smock was lettered *Frank Higby*. His lean face had a nasty expression: mean, browbeating, with a cruel streak showing through. All he wanted was to be sure the odds were all in his favor. All in all, there was something about the man's face that made Garvin eager to rebuild it.

"Who and what the hell are you?" Higby demanded. "What's this equilibration business?"

Smiling and bland, Garvin replied, "You wouldn't understand, not even if I told you."

"Restricted signs, all over. Can't you read?"

From his knees, Garvin went into a crouch, hands positioned.

Higby snarled, "Don't try any *kung fu* on me! I'll settle you—"

Garvin had no intention of resorting to Chinese martial arts. Higby, however, had snapped at the bait. Though his gesture was by no means fast, it was revealing. From his distance, he could afford to take his time. He was reaching for a hand weapon, which he was happy to give a work out. This he could do, and lawfully, since *kung fu* was deadly. Garvin got a glimpse of an energy blaster. To disarm Higby would not be impossible; risky, yes, but there was a fair chance. And that, clearly, was what Higby expected, and what he wished.

Expecting a *kung fu* defense-attack, and watching too intently, he didn't notice that Garvin was going for the tool kit; that he'd grabbed and come up with a gas tube. Gavin flicked the release as the tube cleared the kit. What left the outlet as a missile became a greenish blob, early in its brief trajectory. It expanded and enveloped Higby and the Junior Programming Aide.

An instant later came an answering sound, click-smack. There was a black spot in the tiling near Higby's foot. From it red-hot flakes of concrete erupted. The rim of the hole fumed.

Holding his breath, Garvin watched the two crumpling like Japanese lanterns. They seemed to be telescoping instead of toppling. Slate-bluish faces gaped stupidly through greenish vapor.

When the air-conditioning system had sucked the paralyzing fumes into a vent, Garvin resumed breathing. He picked up the energy blaster, nodded, grinned, then set it down again. Refinements would come later. He turned to complete his electronic project. Three screwdriver twists secured the black box.

He scooped up the components taken from the unit, stuffed them into his kit. After clipping the panel back into position, Garvin moved his gas-victims about, so that they faced another unit. He fired two power blasts. One seared a tile. The other grazed the corner of a computer unit, and burned a circle out of the wall facing. He wiped his own prints from the projector and fitted Higby's hand about the grip.

Finally, Garvin removed a panel from the unit which the two would face when they regained consciousness. After wiping the hygrometric equilibrator clean, he set it into the exposed unit, clipped its terminals to junctions, and eyed the ensemble.

"Neat," he observed, as he regarded the green and purple and red pilot lights which blinked at irregular intervals. "The investigators studying that little Black Box will have a long-term project leading to a cozy padded cell."

Picking up his tool kit, he made for the elevator.

The gear he had planted in the unit he had *not* bugged was not hygrometric, nor was it in any way related to equilibration. As far as he had been able to follow Daly's rundown, the device was designed for no purpose known either to science or folklore, except that it did have entertainment value for specialists.

Chapter 9

After leaving the tool kit at Daly's shop, and downing two slugs of Ethiopian liquor, Garvin raced to share the good news with Lani. "Breakfast be damned!" he told her. "All I need is a shot of nourishment that'll cut the taste of the rocket fuel Daly drinks. Doll, it was a ball, I mean, at Thought Control—I wish you could've seen it."

"But you've got to eat something," she wheedled. "There's boiled reconstructed potatoes with creamed finan haddie flavored—"

"You should've seen how I creamed those two bastards. I tell you it was better the way things fouled up. Daly figures it that way, the hygroscopic gimmick will keep them guessing for weeks—tie up a staff of technicians—"

"Darling, how about Eggs Benedict?"

Garvin grimaced. Lani was acting as if they were married. "The Latvian Landing Force got nothing but dehydrated Eggs Benedict three times a day for a month. Some other outfit got all the mock breast of pheasant and ersatz wild rice."

"I begin to see why you and Jim have the idea that computers are the curse of modern living, but you should eat—"

Garvin interrupted, "You never heard the tragedy that finished a company of Marines, in another theater, but same computer foul-up. No food at all for them.

Nothing, absolutely nothing but a cargo of liquor, and the global supply of PVR Girls."

"Nothing to eat, nothing at all, for thirty days. Oh, how horrible! Did they all starve, or—"

"Not a man of the lot lived long enough to starve. The girls were all nymphomaniacs."

"Oh, you stinker!" She slapped him, right-left. "Can't you ever keep your mind on serious matters?"

The videocom buzzed. Garvin grabbed an empty champagne bottle.

"It's okay, honey," Lani said, and flipped the switch. "Licensed girls never are raided. Not even wives can get away with a raid." She sighed. "You and your conditioned reflexes! You must've led the most awful life. No wonder you and Flora can't agree on anything." Then, to the mike: "What's that? . . . it is none of your business who I'm entertaining!"

She cut the switch.

The buzzer screamed, screamed, decibel upon decibel—an unendurable crescendo. This was official. Only high bureaucracy rated using that superimposed wave. Garvin went to the panel and touched the switch. Silence was unbelievable relief. The screen glowed, and the image came into focus.

"Who and what the hell do you want?" he shouted at the purposeful yet amiable face.

"I want to speak to Rod Garvin."

"You have that pleasure right this God-damned instant, make it short, you are bitching up my breakfast with a licensed lady."

"If you don't mind, Mr. Garvin, I'd like to talk to her, too. I am Jason Ackworth, Fifth Assistant Commissioner of Resettlement. I am aware that it is early, and I am sorry, but this is urgent. Please be ready, and stand by. At thirteen hours thirty, I'll escort you—"

"Commissioner, suppose you flash your ID and the papers. Then I'd thank you to explain how come you or anyone else gets to *escort* me. It's my constitutional right to proceed solo, and only after I have had six hours to get ready."

"Pardon the personal reference, Mr. Garvin," Ackworth said, "but I am required by law to escort persons undergoing psychological reconditioning. They are an exception under the Code."

"If you had time to keep up with current events, you'd know that I recanted, and I'm released from Rehabilitation."

"I'm well aware of that, Mr. Garvin, but the computer system has not sent me a directive concerning your status, so I am required by law—"

"Oh, screw the law, but have at it! You still want to talk to Lani?"

Mr. Ackworth shuffled his papers. "She's under the same order, but of course she proceeds without supervision."

Lani pounced to the instrument. "Oh, Commissioner, how *wonderful!* We'll be ready, thirteen thirty." She cut the switch. "Does that give you an appetite for breakfast? But what'll I wear?"

"Since when've you been dressing up for breakfast?"

"I meant for resettlement."

"Anything at all, pack an overnight kit, and you've got it made. Dress appropriate for foreign areas is included in the resettlement order."

"But I ought to have some new things! I know they'll have the awfullest frowzy stuff, not even native women would look at it. I am going to do some quickie shopping—I don't have to be escorted."

"Good idea," he agreed, and then, to cut short a discussion of hostess gowns appropriate for resettlement areas, he said, "You're right about chow—you punch the buttons while I open a bottle. Or do I mix us something?"

She pushed the code-numbered buttons for boiled spuds and finan haddie. The hidden monster presently produced artificial buckwheat flour cakes, synthetic sage honey, and natural pigeon eggs, a freighter load of which had been flown in from Taiwan, in lieu of quail eggs. This time, the computer had not screwed it up. One of the Bureaucracy had put quail on the Endangered Species list.

"I was afraid of that," Garvin grumbled. "Somebody ought to put these bureaucrat bastards on the Endangered Species list and see that they stay endangered."

Then, with resignation. "It could've been Eggs Benedict or soufflé of XI Dynasty Egyptian Mummy."

"Rhine wine is right for finan haddie, but you can't drink it with buckwheat cakes."

"Who the hell says I can't? And where's the finan haddie?"

Before they made noticeable dents in the breakfast they had not ordered, the videocom again intruded, this time presenting Jim Ward. Fury contorted his voice, warped his face, darkened his color.

"How'd you bitch things up—what'd you drink, smoke, sniff or shoot—"

"Hey, what's wrong? Commissioner Ackworth called an hour ago to say he'd pick me up. We've got it made. Lani's going with us. How about Amelia?"

"He didn't tell you where we're bound for, did he?"

"I couldn't care less, Kabul or the Inca ruins."

"Now hear this, this is no drill!" Ward shouted. "The whole pack of us are headed for the manned observation posts on Mars."

"*Mars*? You're out a mile, it's dragging in the dust! You're demented! They can't send us to Mars."

"They're doing it."

Lani cut in, "No wonder they locked you up—getting us into a mess like this. Mars, oh, sweet Jesus, MARS!"

"You dizzy bitch!" Ward screamed. "If he'd kept his mind on business instead of the new positions you've been demonstrating, he'd not have frigged things up. Don't you blame me, you flutter-witted tart!"

"You old bastard, I am *not* dizzy. I am *not* flutter witted."

"You two-bit whore, I'm not old!"

Garvin shouted, "Shut up, the both of you!" Then, earnestly, "Jim, are you sure it's fouled up as bad as all that?"

"It is as bad as I said. The pack of us are going to those little plastic bubbles on the prime meridian of Mars."

Garvin raised his eyes, and faced Ward again. "Jim, what I did or how I did it makes no difference. All that counts is that I'll get a lawyer, and then I'll confess. I can prove that I was at Central complex, and that I rigged a machine."

"You mean, you're going to take all the blame?"

"Dividing it can't help me. Nothing they can do to me here that's as bad as going to those manned bubbles."

Ward frowned. "Maybe it wasn't your fault. I'll confess, too."

"I tell you that wouldn't do any good. But you can do this much—get a top attorney, and see if he can get Lani and Amelia and the rest of the party off the hook. Get started before assembly time. A court order or some other legal kink."

They switched off.

Lani clung to Garvin. "Oh, what'll they do to you! If you don't end up in the mines in Mars, you'll get some other high-radiation area just as bad."

Garvin stroked her hair. "Time for a farewell feel, and if you ever have any children, name one for me, especially if it happens to be illegitimate."

Somewhat more than an hour later, the video sounded off. Ward and their attorney were waiting at the ground level. Garvin said to Lani, "Not a chance of beating this thing, but maybe I can get a delay and we might even squeeze in a week or two in a vacation spot. Relax! I've been in worse ones. Like the time I accidentally set fire to the night club in Pohang, and they claimed I did it on purpose. Good luck and cheer up!"

He gave her a slap on the rear, and pounced for the elevator.

In the lobby, Garvin found Ward and the attorney, J. Lawton Grimes, Esq. The attorney was tall, stooped, a bedraggled old fellow at least forty, and worse yet, not as bright looking as he might have been. Garvin's optimism sagged.

Grimes dipped into his briefcase. "I filled in your names the minute I heard you were in trouble. Always carry a bundle of signed writs. You never know when these judges will be hard to find. Nothing for you to do but pay me one hundred thousand *pazors* retainer, and we're in business." As an after thought, he extended his hand. "Glad to know you, Mr. Garvin."

Garvin choked. "One hundred thousand—"

Ward screeched, "God damn you, how come you stuck me *three* hundred thousand; That's discrimination."

Grimes said, quietly. "No, it isn't. You had a total of three hundred thousand, counting accrued credits and your next three years' allowances. Mr. Garvin has only one hundred thousand, on the same basis of reckoning. When he pays off, you'll both be exactly on a par. No discrimination whatsoever. And when you are both released, you'll start out with equal opportunity ahead of you."

Garvin sighed. "That makes me feel better already."

J. Lawton Grimes no longer seemed so dull witted.

They fed their cards into the machine in the lobby. When the credit transfer was effected, Mr. Grimes said, "And that includes insurance in my favor, in the even that you do not survive for three years."

Garvin's optimism surged anew. "Hold it a second!" He bounded to the videocom and signaled Lani. "Buck up, doll! We'll beat this case yet. J. Lawton Grimes is a sharp cookie!"

Then he followed Ward and Grimes to the helijet which was parked in the neutral ground between the pedestrian conveyor belt lanes.

Straight up from the takeoff pad, and with G's that nearly telescoped Garvin's spine. Then, acceleration off. A motionless pause, and the flying pill began to sink. Mr. Grimes waggled the stick, and said, reassuringly, "Changing the plane of the jets—don't care for automation—*harrh!*"

With the driver's triumphant shout, the heli was under way, and moving horizontally. Garvin blinked as he read the instruments. He'd never until now met anyone sufficiently wealthy to own a helijet, except of course, members of the Consortium, and the Hierarchy.

As they settled on the pad of the Administration Center, Grimes announced, "We are getting a special hearing."

The hearing was informal, and in the judge's chambers. His Honor did not wear either wig or robe.

Awaiting the arrival of Garvin's group was another attorney, with his client: Wilson Grahm, Esq., and Carson Radcliffe Hayden, the stern, the venerable, the white-haired "Grandfather of the Computer Era."

The attorneys bowed to each other. Counsellor Grimes asked, "Wilson, what the hell are *you* doing here? What is *your* interest in this case?"

The Judge said, "Counsellor Grimes, I will entertain an objection, if you insist. However, if you are patient, you will soon learn that Counsellor Graham's client does have an interest. A third-party interest, as you know, having all his life been the sponsor, the champion of computerism, the fostering of the computer. Neither Counsellor Graham nor Mr. Hayden will influence the ajudication of this case, please be assured of that."

"Then why are they here, Your Honor, if I may ask?"

"Although Counsellor Graham and his client do not anticipate any sharp practice, certainly not in the presence of the court, they feel that if there were cause for objections, they would prefer to make them now, rather than on appeal. It appears that the sanctity of the computer is at stake."

"No objection," Counsellor Grimes conceded. "To the presence of these gentlemen, of course."

Grimes tendered the pleas to the clerk. He addressed the Court: "Your honor, I have of course punched the issues, to facilitate adjudication. As a matter of form, I must state that my clients protest against being resettled in Martian Manned Observation Posts, and on the ground that they fraudulently fed false data into the master computer system, knowing that the data were false.

"They, James Ward and Roderick David Garvin conspired to commit this fraud. The act of feeding such data into the system was solely that of Roderick David Garvin.

"Whether a charge of conspiracy would lie is not the essence of this petition. It is stipulated that Roderick David Garvin did unlawfully, and with malice aforethought, feed fraudulent and false statements with the intention of causing the computer system to publish an order authorizing him and James Ward, and twelve other persons, none of them parties to the unlawful act, nor having any knowledge that such act was contemplated, or committed, to be transported to the Government Research Area maintained under the terms of a treaty between our Government and the Government of Nepal, the resettlement area being some ten kilometers north of the corporate limits of Khatmandu, capital of Nepal.

In as much as the computer's decision is based upon false data, with the result that instead of being transported to Khatmandu, my clients and others are ordered to be transported to the Manned Observation Posts on the prime meridian of Mars.

"Furthermore, had the data been *lawfully* entered into the system, the resulting order should be vacated since the destination prescribed by the computer is some 43,000,000 miles, to wit, approximately 68,000,000 kilometers from Khatmandu, the order is in itself an absurdity and irrespective of illegality, is null and void.

"Accordingly, I move that the resettlement order be vacated."

Counsellor Graham got to his feet. "Your Honor, I submit my client's objection to vacating the Resettlement Order. As a matter of form, I state there is basic doctrine, with many decisions and precedents to the effect that the computer cannot render a voidable decision, not even if based on false data, as alleged. I have of course punched the issues, to facilitate adjudication."

He handed his reply and the punched card to the clerk.

The clerk asked, "Is Your Honor prepared to adjudicate?"

"You may proceed at once, Mr. Gilbey."

The clerk fed the cards into the conveyor, for transmission of its information to the legal units of the central system. In less than a minute the screen beside His Honor blazed into light. There was a printout. The clerk read it:

"Resettlement Order X-77-989-007.33 is found valid. Proceed as ordered. Checked and cleared by Computer B-5A-MM-4."

Garvin leaped to his feet. "Don't risk contempt of court," Counsellor Grimes cautioned.

Carson Radcliffe Hayden, Grandfather of the Computer Era, rose laboriously to his feet. "Begging Your Honor's pardon, and strictly off the record, time and again, I told that son of a bitch that the computer cannot lie. He has constantly tried to rig the system. I sincerely hope and trust that this will be a lesson."

Ward snarled an obscenity in Urdu and several in English.

Garvin croaked, "But the facts, Your Honor, the facts!"

"Facts, as such," His Honor said, "are irrelevant and immaterial when a matter of public policy is at issue. Under the Ancient English Common Law, for instance, it was virtually if not absolutely impossible to question the paternity of any child born to a lawfully wedded wife. Although there was a doctrine of nonaccess, the period was so absurdly long that it had no effect whatsoever.

"It must not be supposed that this was to encourage adulterous wives in their illicit relationships. Neither was this intended to facilitate the passing of lands and titles to one not a lawful heir.

"As nearly as we may infer from today's viewpoint and our scrutiny of history, and of the words of the commentators, the fundamental reason for that which on the face of it appears unrealistic, if not downright silly, was related to the peace of the realm, as the archaic phrase puts it.

"In view of the practical impossibility of convincingly and justly assailing the legitimacy of a married woman's offspring, the frequency of lawsuits and feuds was significantly reduced. The stability of succession and inheritance was fostered; and as one of the most important institutions of society, the family was assured of maximum security. This was desirable as a matter of public policy.

"Today, the sanctity of the computer and its output is equally vital. Accordingly, it must be sustained as a matter of public policy."

Chapter 10

When the retrojets fired up to reduce approach velocity, Garvin moved from the observation port to make
room for Lani and Jim Ward. Amelia apparently had
concluded that her presence was not essential to proper
landing. As the ruddy disk of Mars became larger and
larger, the domes of the space port expanded from
white specks to ever-widening disks.

"Well over to the right of the space port," Garvin
told them, as he squinted between Lani and Jim, "that's
Maritania, the big town—administration buildings,
shops, communications, entertainment, and when we
get closer, you'll see the ring of small domes—they're
the suburbs for people who don't want to live in Maritania, which is crowded with space crews, mechanics,
technicians, shopkeepers, and service people of all
sorts. Pretty much like any Terran town, only smaller
and cruder.

"Then, way over to the right," he continued, "that's
the Martian Minerals complex."

"You mean, the mines?" Lani wondered.

"Just the processing plants," Garvin answered. "The
mines are scattered all over. Radioactive ore to fire up
the cruisers. Quite a lot of mica. And rare metals. Pros-
pecting's going on all the time. So far, nobody knows
much about anything beyond forty–fifty *kay-ems* from
the spaceport."

Ward picked it up: "I remember, way back, they

told us that Mars wasn't inhabited, never would be, not until development colonies were set up, after quite a few years, I began hearing about aborigines, sort of human."

"You can strike out the *sort of*. Some work in the mines, some are good mechanics, some are office workers, and a few are technicians. The aborigines—they call 'em Gooks—nobody knows much about. Instead of going underground when the Terran landings began, the Gooks came up out of the underground air-tights."

"Underground!" Lani exclaimed. "They sound weird. Are they really human?"

"They probably wonder that about us! Like the Chinese. For centuries we figured them as backward. They called us barbarians."

"Will we see any of them?"

"Look way to hell and gone, dead ahead—see the dome, kind of greenish—that's the resettlement project. Last freight haul I made, they were finishing the main building. And those specks you can barely see, the ones going in a straight line, those are the manned stations we're going to live in."

The barren expanse of Mars was blotting out the expanse of space. Lani wailed, "There's just nothing! No lakes, no oceans, no forest; just craters, dead as the Moon. If they ever skip a shipment of supplies, we'll starve!" Lani's sob-screech-wail died out. She sniffled, blinked, licked her lips. "It had me bugged for a second."

When the passenger module was air-locked to a capsule, the Terran party disembarked. Once clear of the airport, the vehicle moved on rails to the reception center, some ten kilometers distant. As they neared the tremendous plastic dome, the largest of the group, the newcomers saw the red neon tubes light up, an archway over the air lock. Presently the words became clear: *WELCOME TO MARTIAN GARDENS.*

Another air lock. Garvin stepped out, Lani and the others following him toward six-story buildings of celluglass. Walkways reached across springy turf. Tall columns towered into the misty heights of the dome. These supports were linked by a lattice-work of cross and diagonal members. Vines twined to conceal much of the stark structural skeleton. Fountains spurted a meter or more from the pools which dotted the grassy expanse.

"All it needs is some tombstones," Garvin grumbled. "Nobody living here!"

A crew member, bringing up the rear, corrected him. "It's orders. First place, everybody except the staff is working in the gardens. Second, you'd get psychic trauma if they turned out to gawk at you. Take the left branch—yes, thattaway, please."

They filed into the lobby of the Administrative Offices, and then to a small conference-lecture room with stage, videoscreen, projection screen, sound equipment, and forty–fifty chairs.

"Sit well up front," the guide directed. "The Director will welcome you right away."

They had scarcely found seats when a blocky, white-haired man wearing unceremonial green jacket and slacks stepped from the wing, hopped nimbly to floor level, and seated himself at a desk.

"I'm Sam Blanding. They call me Director. Actually there is nothing and no one to direct. Our ecological system manufactures the climate and produces most of our food, the basics, that is. Luxuries are still scarce. They're imported when there is surplus transport space, which isn't often.

"The code book outlines your duties, the regulations, the privileges, and the penalties.

He regarded the group, cocked his head; eyes twinkling, he said, "Once you learn to love Martian Gardens, the penalty will be to go back to Terra. Until you love this place, penalties will consist of permission to stay an additional six months, or year, or two."

This did not get the appreciative laugh he expected. Undaunted, Sam Blanding continued, "During the orientation period, you may see me at will. No appointment required. Prowl about the gardens—talk to your fellows in resettlement. In the social hall there is a library alcove where you can read up on Martian Development, the history of this project. I want you to feel at home.

Blanding smiled engagingly. He meant what he said.

"This *is* your home. It's wonderful, being a pioneer. As soon as the strangeness wears off, you'll share this feeling with me."

"How many outside stations?" Jim Ward asked.

"Fifteen, all on the prime meridian, except for two east and two west, on a parallel of latitude. No polar stations. The tropical latitudes are our present field."

Garvin spoke up: "Any choice of duties, stations?"

"Yes, within narrow limits. And it depends on your educational and technical background, and of course, the psychological screening."

"Thank you." And Garvin whispered to Lani, "*Merde* for our side. Amelia has the best chance, and Ward's ahead of me. Don't waste any time—scrounge around all you can, during orientation. See you as much as I can, but how much that'll be—"

He had read the book, while in transit. Blanding's remarks were entirely canned, except for the summing up, and in that, the old man's enthusiasm took charge.

". . . We began by cultivating various lichens, Martian and Terrestrial. Next step was the cultivation of legumes and edibles, and eventually, shrubs and trees . . . began by releasing carbon dioxide to make the artificial atmosphere of the domes congenial to plant life—and as the number of human residents increases, their exhaled carbon dioxide will take the place of that which was industrially produced. Correspondingly, plants, shrubs, eventually, trees, will exhale oxygen . . . Martian minerals will supply the nitrogenous component of the atmosphere of each dome."

His two-arm gesture suggested domes girdling all Mars.

"Each of you newcomers, and those coming after you, will be increasing the life-supporting potential of this planet, the second home of expanding humanity, until in the fullness of time, our successors can live in a Martian outdoors, with an atmosphere of the sort which our Terrestrial home has enjoyed."

Blanding got up, made a gesture of dismissal. He did not wait for applause. There was none.

The emigrants spent their orientation periods in getting used to the space gear required when venturing out of the domes, and into the extremely thin Martian atmosphere. Then, there was exercise, calisthenics to accustom the new arrivals to the gravity of the planet, about one-third that of Terra.

Although the chow was far short of gourmet, it could have been worse. Lani grimaced, prodded the fried thing on her plate. Garvin said, "Too bad your restaurant didn't come with us. What is this, soya imitation pork chop?"

"It's deflavored fish, with pork and brown gravy synthetics built into it, along with whatever binder they need to give texture."

Garvin nodded. "From aquarium to processing to mess hall."

Jim Ward added, "And when it's recycled in a couple weeks, they'll serve it to you again. Mock pheasant and wild rice, maybe."

Lani gagged and hurried from the table. Amelia merely gulped and laid down her fork. Jim met her bitter glance, grinned, and said, "Ecology is ecology, same as back home."

The biscuits were reconstructed fish protein and dehydrated-algae flour. Garvin declared that there'd been a gross oversight: they'd skipped lichen brandy.

Jim corrected him: "I talked to one of the headquarters staff. In one of the agricultural domes, someone planted some smuggled corn and some ditto rye. The stuff they cook off isn't much worse than what the dispensaries back home are peddling."

"You've been getting around."

"More or less," Jim admitted. "I did a bit of dealing with one of the home-bound party who'd done his two years. I gave him a warehouse receipt for things I put in storage when I got locked up. I'm just about sure to take his place here at headquarters. That way I can keep in touch with Hamlin Daly and find out about our chances of getting transferred out of here. And keep in touch with you and Lani and the rest of us."

"Who figures job assignments—personnel department or the computers?"

Ward shrugged. "Don't think it's a definite *either*-or

arrangement." He fished a card from his pocket. "Look what a lab technician gave me."

Nadya Saran—PVR License. Garvin looked up, eyed Jim, nodded. "The problem is figuring what really is her line?"

"Far as *that* is concerned, nobody is interested except Nadya and her customers. But there's another angle, and it does rate some figuring."

"Sound off."

"Female technicians are scarce. Funny thing, there aren't any ration books at the commissary. Talk about a monopoly! And now what happened? A couple or three worn-out bags get competition from Lani's half dozen friends, every one of them ultra choice."

"Life in the Martian Gardens is going to be complicated."

"That," said Jim Ward, "is where the right job assignment will mean something."

The cubicles of the transients' dormitory were so small that it seemed that they had been designed to prevent double occupancy except by acrobats immune to claustrophobia.

"No problem," Garvin told Lani. "We'll put our gear and spare things in one cell, and we'll not be too cramped in the other one. But first thing, I've got to study the maps in the library, and then we'll have something to talk about—such as preferences we might put over after the computers get done lousing things up."

"Honey, you and Jim are innocent optimists! When you two are all done with your reckonings, come back and I'll tell you a few things. And don't get into the wrong cell."

At the end of the indoctrination period, Garvin learned that Lani's forebodings had been justified. The first detachment of newcomers included every one of Lani's elegant PVR girl friends: and they were sent to the northernmost stations on the prime meridian.

"Don't tell me that that was random selection," she flared, as they watched the electrically powered ground capsule wheel away from the central dome. "Or that job qualification had a thing to do with it! Just because that old bastard of a Blanding can't remember what to do with a woman is no reason why he had to let those female battle axe technicians rig the thing this way."

Garvin shook his head. "If those friends of yours worked around headquarters, there'd be murder, rioting and all around hell in no time. Sure the six of them have enough of it to go around, plenty to take care of the whole colony, but it won't work that way, never does, when there is really something deluxe.

"Anyway, you and I have done damn well. I got a hunch Jim rigged that part of it. For a newcomer, he did a neat job, and he could not push his luck too far."

"Honey, I hope you're right." She squeezed his hand, and sighed from the hips. "Oh, God-damn science and God-damn space!"

Early next morning, Garvin, Lani, and four others boarded the vehicle which was to take them to their stations. Although the bus had its own air system, each passenger wore a space suit and kept his headgear right at hand.

The driver said, "When I come down the aisle, each of you check the oxygen valve, so I can see that you've learned how. Keep helmet ready. You'll need both, if a meteorite or a rock flung from the wheels of another vehicle knocks a hole in this shell, and we start losing atmosphere."

The bumpy trail paralleled the surface-laid plastic pipeline which followed the meridian from polar ice cap all the way to the equatorial central station. The line was insulated to prevent freezing at night.

Road and pipeline diverged from the meridian whenever it had to skirt one of the tremendous craters which scarred the othewise unbroken desert. Above the humming of the motor, Garvin heard the dry rustle of windblown sand.

At each station the vehicle's rear end was air-locked to the dome so that passenger and dunnage could be unloaded. At each stop, the driver went with the alighting passenger for a checkout of quarters.

Although those departing, whether for Terra, or to a better job in Maritania, downplayed their excitement, they didn't fool Garvin. The glint, the shift of their eyes, the taut lines of faces sharpened by incessant anxiety and vigilance betrayed them. He whispered to Lani, "They've learned to look over their shoulders without even turning their heads. Don't get that way. It's twenty *kay-ems* from my station to yours, but I'll manage to see you."

"Over this horrible desert? All alone—darling, you *can't*!"

His glance shifted. "Your station coming up. With the low *G* they have here, I can do it walking on my hands. Listen, woman—we started out playing and having fun. But going this far with you, I'm serious. At times I'm damn near loving you."

"Rod, in a spot like this, all I can say is, Bless you."

"Considering it's my fault you're here, there's lots of other things you could say!"

Chapter 11

At Station Six, Garvin got barely a look at his predecessor.

"Luck," the man said, and bolted with his bags.

The driver jabbed a button on the panel of the dome. The squawk-box sounded off, "Headquarters, Martian Gardens, Joe Gates.

"Checking Six. Smallwood. You call back. Over."

The box sounded off, "Calling Six, Smallwood. Joe Gates."

Smallwood, the driver, checked Five, Lani's station, and Seven, the next station north. "OK, you got communication north, south, and headquarters. Good looking pussy, back there." He grinned. "Twenty *kay-ems*, long walk, but you got neighbors."

"Lot of good they'd do!"

"Talk to them. Makes you feel like you belong. You relate better. You know, get more identity."

When inspection of the dome was completed, and Garvin knew where to find every control and safety device listed in the manual, Smallwood said, "Work routine's in the book. You're on your own."

Of this, Garvin found evidence aplenty. There were cylinders of compressed air in case the dome was punctured by a meteorite so large that the self-sealing shell would have to be patched by hand. Emergency food; a grim little First Aid book—*Be Your Own Surgeon*—and medical hit.

Aquarium, with fish that lived on algae. Mushroom cave, plastic, and above surface, legume gardens, with record of tests made to determine the soil's gain in nitrogen.

Rock hound gear: bag, hammer, and the rest. In the center of the dome, a miniature core driller and a stack of drill tubes.

An assayer's kit with manual, and reagents for identifying refractories, fissionables, and other minerals of technological value.

When Garvin came to the anemometer indicator, he exhaled a long, quavering sigh. He said aloud, "If these autocratic, bureaucratic, autoerotics ever quit playing with themselves long enough to realize that the wind offers a lot more electric power than the whole modern mess of solar energy systems for recharging batteries to run this place, they'd vanish in a flicker of blue flame."

He prowled his private world, and tried to account for his restlessness, his uneasiness. There was plenty to think about. The Manual which was to be digested was anything but dull. Survival depended upon it. He flipped the book aside.

There were two chairs, well contoured. Each had a generous range of adjustments. Two small alcoves, each with a bed somewhat broader than minimum solo requirements. Garvin stretched out on one, and on the other. He sat up, shaking his head.

"Room for me and one thin Martian girl. Homelike, optimistic touch. Some genius figured it'd be good for the morale."

The refrigerator had a heating element constantly at the focus of a convex lens which moved by clockwork to keep it in line with the sun. He opened the box. He found drinking water, sour dough starter, dehydrated vegetable cubes, and a couple of catfish from the pools.

Stepping to the battery fired hot plate, Garvin presently was amazed to learn that the fried fish were tasty, and that he liked the sour dough pancakes. The dried pinto beans from the garden needed nothing but cumin, oregano, some lean beef and some *jalapeña* peppers—and a Martian girl to do the cooking.

Windblown dust made sunset colorful. It was practically Terran, except for odd shades of violet and apple green. Darkness came suddenly. Garvin checked the battery charge indicator, the temperature, humidity, CO_2, oxygen—all okay.

The impact of wind-driven sand telegraphed through the structural members of the dome and came to Garvin as a rustle, a whispering, an eerie, unpleasant ghost of sound. It built up almost to easy hearing intensity, then subsided into silence. After an interval, the cycle was repeated.

The silence was the worst. He began to wonder what was behind him. *Who* was behind him . . . He understood now why station keepers picked up on the northward run appeared to be able to look over their shoulders without turning the head.

He'd never minded being stared at. What made so unpleasant his feeling that someone was regarding him intently, pointedly, critically, was the fact that no one was nearer than twenty *kay-ems*.

"Nobody," he corrected, "is supposed to be closer."

A thermostat clicked. Garvin jerked as though prodded by a hot iron. He searched every corner and curve of the dome. It was not until he had completed the search that he felt foolish about having taken a kitchen knife, just in case.

Then he had an idea. "I'll fool the son of a bitch," he said, aloud, and cut off the lights.

When his eyes became accustomed to darkness, Garvin quit the living quarters and edged through the deepest gloom of the aquarium-hydroponic farm area.

"Water gurgling. Fish making noises, plopping up."

Very logical. Now that he had identified each sound of the blend, all was well. Nevertheless, he continued his prowl.

Phobos and Deimos, those puny little moons, were combining their light. The former raced along, moving from horizon to horizon in less than five hours, making shadows shift at a rate unnatural to Terran eyes. The latter seemed to stand still. By Martian moonlight, one could picture whatever he fancied. It could be motionless or it could be moving, according to the observer's apprehensions.

Someone was at it again, staring.

"You, out there!" he shouted. "Come up to the door and I'll buy you a drink or I'll knock your head off and feed it to the fish! Name it and get it!"

No one answered. Garvin's moment of feeling extremely foolish ended abruptly. He remembered Lani. He turned, stumbled several times and nearly fell into a fish pond. Three long bounds brought him to the intercom.

"Calling Station Five. Garvin, Station Six."

Lani answered before he had done pronouncing identification.

"Oh, Rod, it's so good hearing you! This is the craziest-weirdest!—I nearly blew my top when I heard the buzzer."

"Someone staring at, eyeing you from just beyond your field of vision. No matter how quick you turn, you never see anything."

"How'd you know?"

"I've been getting the same. Figured you might be having troubles, so I called."

"Oh, I'm so glad you did! But who—what?"

"We're imagining things. It's like the hallucinations the early astronauts got when they had the moon behind them, and headed for Mars, wondering if they'd ever make it, or wondering if they'd ever get from Mars to home again. Wear something stare proof as long as the lights are on. Looking don't mean a thing. Now, if they start feeling you up, then you'd better call me."

He cut the switch before she could burst out with hysterical endearments. The entire system might be bugged. All this could be part of testing newcomers.

He fell asleep, sitting in his chair.

The buzzer awakened him. It was Lani, and more terrified than ever. He said, "I tell you, it's imagination. I bet we're all having a time of it. Listen to me—do not buzz headquarters. Do not squawk. All you'll get is something worse. It'll ease off, soon. Daylight isn't far off."

He repeated his words, and repeated the emphasis. Then he cut the connection. He hoped that she'd get the point of his studied and overdone brusqueness, and realize that it was intended as a promise to see her as soon as he could contrive to.

Before dawn, Garvin ate and put on his space suit. At sunrise he hustled the station's power-cycle into the lock, evacuated the lock to avoid oxygen waste, and emerged to meet the Martian desert.

Going afoot, he circled the dome, scanning the ground. Each circuit spiraled. When for the third time he came abreast of the parked bike, he realized the futility of his attempt. He had left no footprints. A skilled tracker undoubtedly could have picked up traces of his final circuit. Garvin fancied that he could see signs as far back as a dozen paces. With hard surface, irregular, rocky, and dust and mineral drift incessantly stirred by the wind, he could not hope to find any trace of whoever or whatever had been staring at him, and at Lani.

Hallucination? Or, organized and purposeful spying? He had one guess—the aborigines, but this was something he'd better not share with Lani. Maybe later, but not now.

Mounting his bike, Garvin made for the center rim. The brisk upgrade beat the cycle to a crawl so slow that it barely maintained equilibrium. Presently he was well beyond the pattern of prospect holes dug by his predecessors, and the little cairns they had made to observe the erosive effect of wind and sun.

He stopped at the edge of the crevasse. Beyond was a temendous crater. He guessed that the orbit-jarring impact of a small asteroid had made that bowl. Then, evaporating from the immeasurable heat, the disappearance of the celestial missile in a tower of fiery vapor had relieved the pressure, and thus, the crevasse had been formed.

He skirted the crevasse until he came to its beginning, then continued upgrade to the crater-rim. He looked south. From this elevation he could just perceive the pinpoint that was the top of Station Five, Lani's dome.

Garvin raised his arm in greeting. "Hell, I could walk it!"

The climb had pulled the battery charge down to its

final ten percent. Reversing the terminals, he nosed the bike downhill and closed the switch. Gravity furnished the power to spin the motor. Thus driven, the armature cut the residual magnetic field, and generated current, charging the battery.

No problem: push the bike to the rim, coast downgrade and build up the battery, and also, charge the spare. This would be a lot quicker than depending on the sun-heated thermocouples which supplied electricity for the dome.

To reduce the number of spare parts to be freighted to Mars, the computers worked to get the maximum interchangeability of components. The gears of the drive train which operated the core-drilling rig could be reversed and coupled to drive the bike-motor as a generator. Hand cranking beat pushing a bike uphill to the crater rim and coasting down.

The following afternoon, a service bus hove into view. Smallwood, who had taken the newcomers to their stations, had returned. Stepping into the vestibule, he hailed Garvin and explained, "This is a routine checkup. Not an inspection. That'll come later, when Inspector Morgan gets around to it."

"You said that last as though he's no treat."

"Mmmm . . . well, I'd not go so far as to call him a son of a bitch, but he could qualify with not much effort. How'd you make out?"

Garvin decided on frankness. An open-face reputation would come in handy when dissimulation became useful. "Twitchy-uneasy—I've not done much sleeping and what little I did wasn't restful."

"Standard." Samllwood's tanned face crinkled in a good humored grin. He shook his head, shrugged. "I know how you felt."

"I feel foolish saying it, but I had the notion all the time that someone was staring at me."

"Think nothing of it. Didja read up on space hallucination?"

"That didn't make it any more fun."

This blocky, good-humored bus driver looked right minded; still and all, he was a bit too casual when he continued," Didja *see* anyone or anything?"

"What am I supposed to be seeing?"

"An occasional character sees women."

Garvin chuckled. "You probably got to be here awhile for that. And then some would see boys, and others would see sheep. Or—"

"That's not as funny as you seem to think, but usually, it is women."

Garvin eyed him intently. "Listen, Gene. I used to be a freighter, and for a while I made passenger runs. Know my way around the spaceport and Maritania. Maybe it's hallucinations, and maybe it is Gooks."

Smallwood's face registered quick changing expressions, and then, "I wouldn't say it's Gooks."

Garvin grinned. "Sure you wouldn't say it's Gooks. If you did say so, you'd get your ass burned plenty. Now if I ever said that you'd told me it was Gooks, and you said I was a God-damn liar, and hallucinated to the hilt, who'd they believe?"

"I'm not saying its Gooks. I'm not saying it ain't. I'm just not saying."

Chapter 12

That night, Garvin called Lani "Any orientation problems?"

"Plenty, but none I couldn't handle."

"If there are any tough ones, give me paragraph and section, I'll study and call back. Remember what I promised you."

She gave several numbers, and then, "You're sweet, thinking of me. But I'll get used to the staring."

"I'm groping for answers, and I think I've almost got some. So I'll call you back. Maybe kind of late. May wake you up."

"Oh, who cares! Call anytime!"

She cut the switch.

Garvin was sure that she'd be expecting him. Previously, she'd clung to the intercom until he signed off. He put the charged battery into the bike and loaded the spare on the rack. That done, he headed southward, following the pipeline.

Well over an hour of hitting the bumps brought him to Lani's dome. During the final five hundred meters, he kept the headlight on, to warn her of his approach.

She was waiting at the air lock.

As the outer panel squeezed against the gaskets and the inner slid free to admit him, Lani cried, happily, "Oh, darling!" and extended her arms. Garvin yanked his helmet, evaded her, and gestured.

"Hold it! Damn near a hundred below, outside. Two

of your outstanding charms would get frost bitten from grazing this armor jacket!"

The eye pieces of the helmet were already thickly crusted with frost. Spirals of mist drifted from his space suit. He followed her into the living quarters.

"Get out of that smoking gear while I fix you some coffee. Imagine, ice building up on your boots!"

"You been outside yet?"

"Am I crazy?" Lani shuddered. "They want to know how different Terrestrial types respond—all right, I'm one they'll learn plenty about. I am not prowling around picking up pebbles and scraping lichens." She turned from the hot plate and filled his cup. "You working?"

Garvin nodded.

"Oh, Good God! Why? You shouldn't! If we all fumble and fall on our faces, they'll know it was a mistake, and we'll go home, they'll want to get rid of us."

He regarded her, earnestly, intently. Her face changed. "Rod, the way you're looking at me—what *is* on your mind?"

"I hate to tell you this, but I got you into this mess. Getting you out maybe isn't impossible, but we're not supposed to go back. We're stuck until they find a worse place."

"Has Jim told you anything?"

"He doesn't have to tell me anything. We've never been true believers. That settles us, and you—you're wrong because you and I were paired off for this trip. Makes you a wrong thinker, like me and Jim. So, it's up to you and me to pretend we are believers, that we've come to Jesus, holy jumping Pioneers. Now if you got knocked up and produced the first Terran-ancestored infant in the Martian Gardens, you might, just *might* be ordered back for a tour to sell Resettlement. Meanwhile, until you get that way, make a game of pretending you're bubbling over with Martian Reclamation Spirit. As long as we're stuck with it, getting interested is easier than sitting on our tails, hating it. I've been studying on cooking off pinto bean whiskey, and without needing a copper worm."

Lani got to her feet. "Just in case anyone's lurking

and peeping—" She snapped the master switch. "If you can find me in the dark, I'll tell you whether it's for love, for fun, or for a hundred *pazors*."

When moonlight aroused Lani, she nudged Garvin, and ever the perfect PVR girl, she murmured, however sleepily, "When do you have to be back home?" But before he could answer, she sat up, and well awake. "How'd we get out here in the garden?"

"When I said that each bed was too wide for one and not wide enough for two—"

"Oh, now I remember! We moved both mattresses out, and I said it was almost like my apartment except we didn't have special lighting or automation."

"And so you don't get your hundred *pazors*! But there's a laugh at the peeping Gooks—" He checked himself, but not in time, then carried on, "They must've been staring at where the lights went out."

"Why'd you stop short when you mentioned *Gooks*, still halfway talking in your sleep?"

"I didn't want to tell you about the Gook girl who crawled in with me, at Station Six—there was plenty room for two."

"Don't try spoofing yourself out of that slip. I am not asking you whether she was a good lay, or whether it's crosswise, I am sticking to my question—this *peeping Gooks*. Rod, did anyone at the Gardens tell you anything about Gooks?"

"Hell, no, darling! Remember, on our way from the spaceport, I was telling—or was it during the approach?—Jim cracked off about Gooks being almost human, and I sounded off? What's the point?"

"It's this way, lover! They're old stuff in your life, you've seen them working in the spaceport, and female Gook taxi dancers in the night clubs. But you were being stared at, same as I was. It's not hallucination, see what I mean? Old timer, new arrival, same feelings. And then you tried to change the subject." She twisted about, caught Garvin by the shoulders. "Tell—or next one won't be for love, it'll be a hundred *pazors*."

"Twenty would be fair. There's no sunset lighting, and the government furnishes this lawn, and you're not paying rent—"

"I don't know why I'm so fond of a son of a bitch like you. But I won't even settle for the head of John the Baptist—either you tell me, or you can start chasing female Gooks across the desert."

He told her how Gene Smallwood had reacted to his query as to snooping aborigines. He concluded, "He's halfway an Honest John type, when they try to falsify, you know it before the mouth opens. So I figured it is aborigines spying. Well, I was curious about women in Turkistan, and in China, lots of us were, but we didn't do any spying or peeping."

Lani frowned. "Wondering whether they're human— you can bet they hate our guts. How many are there, who and what are they, where'd they come from?"

"They may have come from Earth so many thousands of years before our history began."

"But that's ridiculous, Rod! We made the first Moon flight—" She counted on her fingers. "Hundred ten–fifteen years ago. And the first little sputtering prop plane wasn't sixty years earlier." She regarded him sharply. "I don't say you should've been locked up in the fruit factory, but I'm not too surprised they did."

"Now hear this! When I was freighting pipe and drilling stuff into Chinese Turkistan, I met some natives in a small town at the edge of a desert that makes Mars look like a rose garden. That God-awful Takla Makan.

"The people are kind of Turks. Not the kind we hear about so much—those are Osmanli Turks. Then there were Seljuk Turks, they ruled Iran a couple of centuries. And there were the Uighur Turks. My guess is that they're the original, the oldest of the breed.

"I learned to haggle their language pretty well. They didn't laugh—they loved to hear me speak Uighur—I could do tricks with it that they never heard of."

"Oh. Long-haired dictionary?"

He nodded. "Name was Djénane Khanoum. Lady Djeane. I used to call her Lady Jane in English."

"Was she—well, high class and expensive?"

"She was high class and whenever I was in town, her dad told her to sleep with me and she did, and in no time, we got to like each other a lot."

"So of course you dumped her, and married that high-nosed bitch that's a cousin of the holy family?"

"If I didn't really like you, I'd spank your fanny till your nose bled."

"I'm sorry, Rod, I didn't mean to insult your wife."

"That's not it at all! You're simply ignorant and running off at the mouth! Long as you stick to things you know something about, you're the smartest girl I ever met. But—"

"But what?"

"Just this. I did not dump Lady Jane. But sleeping with her did not mean she or her folks thought I was good enough to *marry* her. I might've qualified, in time."

Lani regarded him perplexedly.

"Darling, it is all very simple. They consider us to be barbarians—crude bastards, with nothing to commend our society except bombs, bombers, artillery, and the like. But they're not racists, they just think they're a lot better than we are. Well, I don't agree entirely, but I respect them. Unless a man thinks he's better than I am, I'd despise the son of a bitch, he's no good. And of course, I think I'm better than he is. Simple?"

She sighed and shook her head. "But we got off the track. This business of the Gooks having come to Mars a million years ago."

"When Lady Jane—Djénane Khanoum—and I got to know each other, and she trusted me not to ridicule her traditions, she told me a lot of confusing yarns. According to some stories, some of her people quit the Earth to go to Mars—this was while Mars still had water and a climate humans could live in. Other stories had her people coming from outer space, some stopping on Mars, some coming to Terra."

"Well . . . she must've been awfully nice. You do have good taste in women. I got a good look at that wife of yours when she appeared in newscasts. But the people Lady Jane learned those traditions from could have been mistaken."

"They could have, and that's what I thought, but I had sense enough to keep my big mouth shut."

"She must've been a good piece, or you couldn't ever have kept from sounding off."

"It paid off. We rode out, way out—no, not camel back, but in a company jeep—out into the desert, the damndest, deadliest muddle of dunes and desolation. She showed me a space cruiser. It wasn't crash landed, far as I could tell, though being pretty much buried in drifting sand, I wouldn't be sure.

"She gave me the complete tour. I took a few samples of the fissionable material that powered the cruiser. I got a long look at the power plant. In the machine shop I found a piece of metal that had been turned, and one end threaded.

"The pitch was foreign, and the threads were not English, and not metric. From power plant to such details as cutting threads, I took along some lathe shavings, and a lathe tool—Lady Jane told me to, if I wanted—Finally she gave me a wise, very affectionate look, and said, 'Now you believe me. And I trust you not to tell where you got those samples.' So I promised her, and then I spoke of next time I flew into Turkistan. Lady Jane said, 'Tonight is our last sleeping together. Before you come back, I will be marrying one to whom I was promised, a long time ago, and you won't be seeing me, not ever.'"

Lani sighed, shook her head. "I did talk out of turn, didn't I! What did the samples of the space ship prove?"

"I sawed off testing samples, and threw the rest away, so no one would look long enough and start wondering. A radioactivity test indicated that the alloy was something like a million years old. I can't say that it's non-Terrestrial, but it left the metallurgist talking to himself, and I knew I'd better dump every scrap into the river, and I did just that."

"They might not have put you in the booby hatch if you'd had those samples."

Garvin snorted contemptuously. "And I might've been doped with hypnotics till I'd told where I got the things. And I wouldn't have been hustled to the Psycho Factory, and I wouldn't have got you into this mess."

After a long silence, Lani got back to Gooks: "You suppose their spying is the start of some kind of revolt?"

Garvin shrugged. "From way back, the Turki people have been reckless and dangerous fighters, no surrender. Death never scared them the way it does most westerners. Whether a general massacre could succeed, I couldn't guess. Anyway, they may just be snooping to see if we have anything new and worth while in our ecology plans. How much we learned from them, that's another I-can't-guess. If they date back to ages while Mars had plenty of air and water, they coped with conditions gradually—we're just busting in, quickie."

She looked at her watch. "About an hour and a quarter for the ride to Station Six. We've got plenty of time . . ."

"For fun or for love?"

"Let's try each, honey, and then make up our minds."

Chapter 13

Garvin quickly learned that however he got the bike battery recharged, there were no shortcuts. Cranking the reconverted core drill was rugged work. Despite the low *G* of Mars, pushing the bike to the crater rim took a lot of leg-power. Coasting to level ground was a ride too short for recuperation.

He considered hiking. "I can see a service truck long before the driver sees me. Flop behind a rock or in a swale. Get an early start in the afternoon, get to Station Five by dark. Three hours each way—nothing to it."

Nice work, until he realized that he would run out of canned air in the six hours the round trip would take. Biking was the only way. He'd see Lani often enough to keep her convinced that their best play was to keep up a pretense of pioneering spirit.

One morning before he had more than started breakfast the printout from headquarters began clacking away. This was odd. Quite too early for instructions. He tore off the perforated strip, and read, "*Attention all stations stop. Inspector Morgan on the way looking for trouble stop. Destroy message stop. Do not repeat not discuss with anyone.*"

Garvin figured that Jim Ward had sent the warning: at this hour, no one would be in the field.

He dismantled the battery-charging arrangement and got the core driller gears reassembled. But he had not even a length of boring for a rack of exhibits when Inspector Morgan showed up.

Garvin had met that thick-necked, aggressive character during the indoctrination period at headquarters. He had not seen enough of Morgan to learn to like him. This had not left Garvin feeling culturally deprived. And as they exchanged greetings in the lock, Garvin felt that fraternization would not change matters greatly. On the other hand, there was no animosity on the surface.

Morgan had, as the job required, a check sheet: on this he entered the readings of gauges and of graphs as taking and replacing the indicator cards was part of his routine, he logged humidity, temperature, CO_2, oxygen level; odometer reading of the recon bike; he made a couple of jabs with a tread gauge and noted tire wear—on and on until at last the top layer of the duplicating log book pages were removed. There were no new core drillings, but there was a handful of specimens in the geologist's field bag.

No questions. Garvin made no statements. Finally, "Comments or suggestions?"

Garvin eyed the big man from head to foot. "No beefs."

"I didn't ask for complaints. I asked for suggestion and comment."

"Anemometer log shows twenty-five-knot wind round the clock, except for short cyclic lulls. Put a windmill outside and generate a good many more KWHs than those thermocouple things can dream up, even on the brightest day."

"Not enough power?" Morgan seemed interested. "Explain?"

"Not enough power. We've had cold nights, and the insulation is not very tight. If we had beefed up lighting, photosynthesis would be more productive, more oxygen released. Every time sun radiation falls off, oxygen output drops. Can't build up a surplus to compress for longer field trips."

Morgan picked up the field case, set it on the study table and plugged in. This was a miniaturized computer. Punching the inspection report took less time than Garvin expected. Morgan set for the radio circuit which was beamed for headquarters only. He fed the card.

The report came back as a duplex printout.

AQUARIUM AND HYDROPONICS GOOD ENVIRONMENTAL CONTROL GOOD OPERATOR COMMENT CONSTRUCTIVE CREDIT RECORDED OPERATOR WASTEFUL AND ERRATIC EXCESSIVE FIELD TOURING AND MINIMAL SPECIMENS OBTAINED QUERY WHY NO CORE DRILL SAMPLING.

Garvin read his file copy.

Morgan asked, "Comment?"

Garvin studied the squarish face, the narrowing hazel eyes: their feral-feline expression was unpleasant. "Better than comment," he said, and pounced for the desk. From a drawer he took a handful of rock samples. "Been studying these. Forgot to show them to you sooner. Sorry about that."

They regarded each other for a moment. Morgan's face twitched, but his voice remained level. "Interesting. How come?"

"Long field trips on the edge of the crevasse. Climbed down and in. Saved a thousand feet of core drilling. How you like?"

"Hold it! Give me a close look."

He plucked the specimens from Garvin's hand. "No core drilling, but you've got the damndest biggest callouses on your hands from bending on the drill crank I've ever seen. And all the kilometers you've run up. And the way those tires have worn."

It was time to grin amiably, to be whimsical. In case *that* kicked back, and sometimes it did, try *kung fu*. It left no marks.

"I could tell you about hill climbing contests with friendly aborigines, but the fact is, riding the rim of that crevasse, the full length of it, and around and along the far side, to find a spot where I could climb down, way down, wearing nonfeatherweight gear, took a lot of *kay-ems*. That rim rock is sharp. Cuts tires, you know."

Again each studied the other, and less amiably than

before. After a long silence which was nearing the breaking point, Morgan said, "You are up to something. Keep at it long enough and I'll know what it is. And what to do about it."

"Since you are the Inspector, it would be improper for me to tell you to screw yourself. You have a long and interesting career ahead of you."

Morgan left without answering.

As the Inspector drove away, Garvin realized that he had not played things the way he'd told Lani the game should be played.

After reassembling the core drill gear train to make a battery charger, he set to work, bending on the crank. By intercom he gossiped with his neighbors. "The Inspector came up from Headquarters," he told them, "gave me a neat eating out, made a neat U-turn, and headed back south again. If I have enough trouble with that son of a bitch, the rest of you get off easier."

Every evening he called Lani to tell her how the batteries were building up: and the third day following Morgan's inspection, Garvin said, "Extra bright sun, and overtime on the crank did it."

"For fun, for love, or for money?" she quipped, and as she turned from the intercom, she flipped her jacket to the nearest chair, kicked her shoes after it and sent her jeans flying to overtake them. After a contemptuous glance at the sorry stuff she'd bought at Martian Gardens commissary, she realized that discarding the first layer of awfulness had made her feel better—but she was reminded of the environmental insults which covered quite too much of her elegant femaleness.

Panties and bra joined the revolting heap.

There wasn't a three-panel mirror in the entire settlement. She snatched the chrome-plated mockery, hurled it at the bulkhead. The metal rebounded, tinkled to the deck. She retrieved and put it back on its peg.

"Mmm . . . think I'll wear *Spirit of Mars*," she mused. "Lani was thinking of the horoscope printouts she and Garvin had found so amusing. "*Desire, passion, battle . . .*"

She dipped into her luggage, the contents of which she knew by heart; the review, item by item, was nostalgic routine. ". . . damn science and double-damn space . . ." she said, bitterly.

It had become ever more natural to vocalize her thoughts, even the most trivial. Lani looked at her mirrored image. "Look like I always did, but for how much longer . . ."

She'd packed hastily for takeoff from Terra. Absentmindedly she'd included the brocaded kit containing a tiny hypo, a vial of yellowish fluid, and a vial of tablets. *Life Savers*, the professional girls called these things. If a client developed notions on flogging, on outright beating, or became just plain nasty, flip a pill into his drink, or jab him with the needle and he'd be out for hours to come.

A second kit contained a pale green play-gown, bedroom play, that is, with built-in scent. Too serene for her mood. A third came to hand. This she unsnapped, and unfurled another of the few luxuries she'd smuggled aboard. The wad of tightly packed fabric shook out, expanded, lengthened, exhaling its built-in fragrance. *Red Mist*, this party gown was called. The fourth compact—it would keep. Her mood was red, Martian, and impatient, although not as extremely so as she'd been, that first romancing at Station Five.

There'd been no sense in dressing only to undress—

Tonight, plenty of time. Too much time. An eternal couple of hours. He'd be cycling slowly to save energy until he figured a way of keeping the batteries charged, and despite Morgan's suspicions.

The clack-clack-clack of the printout startled Lani. She read the paper ribbon:

CAUTION. INSPECTOR DRIVING NORTH SURPRISE CHECKUP DESTROY PRINT OUT.

"Oh, that mother-lover," she cried. "That—that—"
There was death in her voice, and it choked her. She bounded to the intercom to call Station Six. No answer. Garvin was on the way. And he'd end up in the mines if Morgan reported him.

Red Mist and all, Lani got into space gear, grabbed a marking crayon and a pane of emergency patching plastic. Rolling her bike out of the lock, she rode northward.

There were kilometer markers, numbered, for emergency vehicles to follow up an inspector's report of a leaking pipeline. One of these posts had been clobbered by a swerving capsule. She'd noted this on one of her field trips. It was three kilometers from her dome. She headed straight for it. She hit it, head-on, and spilled. Picking herself up, Lani backed away and belted it again. The marker yielded. With rocks she propped it in the middle of the narrow track. On the emergency patching tape she crayoned, INSPECTOR. That done, Lani mounted up and biked homeward.

Once back in her dome, she shed the space suit, shook out the *Red Mist* play gown and got back into the loathesome jeans. As she sat waiting in darkness, she wondered whether she'd ever be in the mood for anything but murder.

Neck against the low back of the chair, legs stretched out, she mentally dismembered Morgan. She'd fed more than half the pieces to the dogs when reflected light alerted her. Presently, she heard the crunch of tires on the road bed.

A moment after the headlight of a ground capsule blinked out, the buzzer sounded. She dragged her feet toward the air lock. She had decided against ignoring the buzzer. That would do nothing but alert Morgan and set him off for Station Six, and catch Garvin off limits. She and Rod and the others of that exiled fellowship had no choice except going with the current. Revolt, however passive, would bring reprisal.

She snapped a switch. The flourescents at the entrance came to life. As the lock closed behind Morgan, she asked, "What's happened? An emergency?"

Once in the living quarters, she continued, "Coffee? There's not a drop of contraband in the house."

Morgan took off his helmet. "I brought the contraband." Flipping off a glove, he unsealed the space jacket and produced a five hundred milliliter flask. "From Terra. Not the stuff they're cooking off from legumes. You said something about coffee?"

As she headed for the galley, he continued, "You were wondering about emergencies?"

"Well, yes, I did." She stepped from the galley. "Tell me."

"A lot of you folks have been fidgety. Not a one of you that hasn't talked about being stared at, after dark."

"So I'm not the only one. That's as bad as it's good."

Her summing up left him wondering. "Wait a minute! Play that one again."

"I'm glad I'm not a freak, and it's rugged, hearing that there really must be someone, something prowling around a whole line of stations, some of them more than twenty kilometers apart." She grimaced, shuddered.

As Morgan set to work getting out of his space suit, he went on, "We figured not all of you'd be hallucinating. And it couldn't be tricks of the wind. Still guessing, it might be the abos."

"Lani frowned. *"Abos?"*

"Aborigines. Sorry—I forgot you've not been here long enough to speak the language. It's against the rules, calling them Gooks."

"Someone did mention them during indoctrination. Are they dangerous?"

"Never any rioting, never any ganging up on prospectors or other Terran folks going about alone. A lot of grumbling, sure, and complaining about being slaves. They never had it so good. Instead of scratching away, round the clock, to survive in their leaky halfway airtight undergrounds, those that are for us get modern systems. Higher standard of living." Morgan shook his head. "They don't make sense. I'd not trust any of 'em too far."

"Could they break into a dome? What would it get them but trouble? We outnumber them, and we have modern weapons—"

"They outnumber us, and if it ever came to weapons, it could wreck the whole project. Maybe they didn't tell you at indoctrination that this is an international project—we're picking up the check, as usual, but every-

body and his brother, including all the half-pint ba-
nana republics and cannibal kings gang up and put us
in bad with the rest of the world."

"Oh . . . this is complicated." The *beep-beep-beep*
from the kitchenette brought Lani to her feet. "Water's hot," she said, over her shoulder, and went to stir
up the coffee. She barely had the serving tray on the
table when she got back to aborigines: "What would
their prowling get them?"

"If enough of you in the manned stations get shaky
and stay locked up, indoors, for security, the whole project might bog down. It's not just you women—
everyone's twitchy. It could keep this operation from
expanding enough to count. Like they must've told you
at Martian Gardens, the next step is solar power to
break up minerals, make synthetic atmosphere. Tap
subsurface water, irrigate the desert—do what the
Gooks have been doing on a bare subsistence basis, but
do it on a bigger scale."

"You make it sound so real—I've heard the words
before but none of it sounded the way you speak it."

And this she really meant: Morgan was a son of a
bitch, but in his way, he was impressive. She still hated
science and space, but in a different way.

The Inspector untwisted the cap of the contraband
and splashed a dollop into each of the steaming cups.

"Oh, you caught me off guard! My coffee'll ruin that
liquor!"

"All wrong! Even worse liquor than this would improve commissary coffee! Try it and see."

She raised the cup, eyed him over the edge, took a
dainty sip. "Mmmm . . . this does improve the mud!
Good luck, Inspector."

"The name's Phil, and I'm not on duty."

"Thanks, Phil," Lani smiled her most winning smile.
After a moment of sizing up the rugged face and prob-
ing hazel eyes, she was thinking, *"He'd not be at all
bad, if he weren't such a bastard."* Her wonderings as
to the outcome of this bitched-up evening disturbed
Lani. She was certain that her warning would not scare
Garvin back to Station Six. Quite the contrary, and that

was what was getting her keyed up, twitchy, moment by moment.

Rod wouldn't arrive all prepared to break and enter, but whatever he might do when he saw the Inspector's capsule parked at the entrance, something critical would happen. *"Before we're through with this jam-up, Rod's going to kill the stinker, which would be bad. And if he doesn't kill him, he'll be transferred to the high-radiation area of the mines. If the right answer doesn't show up in a hurry, I'm due for a raping."*

Lani was twitchy and tense from toenails to eyebrows, all in the mood for a drooling lover, not a twenty-*pazor* trick. Although business had always been business, she'd selected the customers just to her taste, thanks to her restaurant. The idea of anyone but Rod's attempting to complete the unfinished business for which he and she hadn't had sufficient time, the other night—the idea was revolting!

Wrath and dismay when she read the intercom tape had bemuddled Lani's wits. She'd left the "safety kit," the whore's best friend, in her sleeping alcove. If only she'd brought it to the kitchen, he'd by now be doped until he wouldn't know his own name for the next three days or more.

No use putting up a fight and be all mussed up when Rod arrived. Better relax, spread her legs, cold meat, and needle Morgan. One jab of the little hypo—when Rod arrived, the inspector would never know the difference, and neither would she.

If she made for the sleeping alcove to get at her kit, he'd follow her and if she wasn't laid in bed, he'd get her on the floor.

Hot panties, professional pride, female cussedness— and, the principle of it. Her thought took shape in silent words: *"I'll make you eat shit, if it takes till judgment day. And that's a promise!"*

"Phil—" She glanced over her shoulder, shuddered, and again squinted, craned her neck, peering into outside darkness. "Climbing the walls of this dome is tough but I'll be doing it, and soon. I'm closer to the booby hatch than I can stand. Let me have the straight of it—

you know our history—mine and every one else's in the
handful of us that arrived to relieve the people who had
done their time—when can I go back home."

Lani's voice went up an octave. It was not a lovely
soprano. It was like a nail scratching glass. Morgan
winced when she reached her limit, half an octave
higher. "I can't take it," she wailed.

Morgan poured another jolt of Bourbon for each,
and laid a reassuring hand on her shoulder. "Lani, it's a
good act, but you're no nearer crazy than I am. And
even if you were, I'd not mind, not one bit."

They eyed each other, read each other. He smiled
indulgently. "Nobody's fooling anybody. We've both
been plenty of places. Someone tipped you off. You
don't look it, but you smell like an important date.
Enough time to call if off. Not enough to wash off the
perfume, which is too good to waste. It's for company."
Morgan sat back, nodded approvingly. He raised his
cup. "You're good, and I'm drinking to you."

Lani recognized genuine admiration. There was no
mockery behind his whimsy. She raised her cup.
"Thank you, Inspector."

"However your friend in Station Six manages it, he's
been seeing you evenings. Cycling, I'll bet."

Lani smiled, shrugged. "You're brilliant and talented, Inspector. And what's your next move?"

Morgan met and accepted the challenge. "Even if
you'd never been a PVR Girl, you'd still be enough
woman for any half dozen of us. There's no need to
transfer Rod Garvin to the thorium plant. No need for
you to go to the Gardens where that lab technician, Nadya Saran, wouldn't like competition. Why do you suppose you were assigned to Station Five?"

"Rod did say that that bitch had a monopoly on mattress drill—she and another battleax."

"Nadya and two other bags. Even a female snake
would get a lot of business at the Gardens. And you'd
die, accidentally, if you got a job there as a file clerk.
So—better for me, better for Rod, better for you.
Right?"

Morgan had all the answers. Morgan had it made.

"You've just about made me a proposition."

Her voice was seductive, rather than acquiescent as he'd expected it to be. Morgan grinned happily, gave her a smack on the thigh. Lani went on, "Maybe you can get Rod an extra battery and charger? You can pretend you don't know, he can pretend he doesn't know. And nobody'd be a fool with wounded vanity."

"You smell as good as you sound!"

"I'll wash off this *Red Mist*—"

"I'll wash your back."

"There are two other play gowns. Why not whiff each and take your choice? Just a minute—" Lani darted to the bed alcove, and without skipping a beat, she returned with two fat purses, *Sea Sylph* and *Jungle Passion*. Stately and formal as a Burmese dancer, she opened the first. The green gown and the scent billowed out in waves of fragrance and color.

He reached for a handful, but she evaded the almost grab.

"You can't improve on *that!*"

"I want the one that puts me in just the right mood— we've got lots of time."

He wasn't thinking of rape yet, but he was getting too anxious to have much judgment left. Lani whisked away and as she made for the shower, she called, "I've got to get *Red Mist* off me!"

Behind the curtain, she flipped out her garments, piece by piece. The hissing of the shower warned him against wasting any more time. He got shed of shirt and of shoes—"

She cut the shower. "Close your eyes, dearie. Surprise—don't peek—don't you dare—not till I tell you—"

Morgan got into the spirit of things. Peeping past the edge of the curtain, she could tell from the lines of his face that he wasn't cheating. Deftly, Lani nudged the curtain, smoothly, without a betraying sound. Stepped to the threshold, she poised herself—

Stately: elegant long legs, belly drawn in, breasts thrust out, and all of her agleam with drops—head high and proudly carried, Lani stood as though she had invented the female body, and was modeling the first one, after which all others would be production line—nice, but, production line stuff.

As so much woman on the hoof, she was a shapely and pleasing parcel, well above average: but now, pride in her femaleness gleamed through, and with it, her smouldering wrath, and the anticipation of the moment of keeping her promise to the clown who took quite too much for granted—

These made Lani magnificent.

Chapter 14

The moons of Mars fascinated and irritated Garvin. "The Gooks wouldn't put up with them if they'd ever seen a better one," he grumbled . . . wonder if two full moons at once will make Lani all-out wild . . ."

The apparent diameter of Terra's moon was three times as great as that of Martian Phobos, and twenty-one times as great as that of puny Deimos. "Better than nothing," was his summing up. "One barely moving, the other racing like crazy and eclipses till you get dizzy."

Despite the eerie illumination, the kilometer post poking up from the middle of the narrow road was conspicuous. Garvin pulled up, snapped on the headlight, and sized things up. The marker was kept upright by three rocks. He pulled the patching tape from the metal, and got a good look at the word, INSPECTOR.

The crayon scrawl looked like a large-scale specimen of Lani's lettering on her report sheets.

She must've written it. Couldn't have been here this afternoon when he went south, or he would have taken it out of the way. Or fixed it up, temporarily.

"Three *kay-ems* to Station Five. Sure she marked it." He squinted at the post. "Tire prints. Hmmm . . . she must've hit it and busted it off . . ." He didn't bother to look for tire prints in the dust or sand drift. Not being a tracker, he couldn't figure the probable time of her hitting the post, by figuring from prints visible, or, by lack of prints. The Abos could, probably.

"I've taken it slow," he summed up. "Before she'd bike three *kay-ems*, she'd call me. Hour and twenty minutes, thirty minutes ago, she would have caught me at the Dome. So, written warning—"

He flung the marker to the roadside, but kept the patching material. "Either he's been there and has gone, or he's still there." Garvin scowled. He cut the headlight. He dipped into the tool kit, found a chrome-vanadium steel wrench. It wasn't heavy, but a crisp flip of the wrist, and one man no-have-got.

"Gene Smallwood made a crack about good-looking pussy at Station Five, and Morgan knew about that before Smallwood . . ."

Gavin switched on the power, and despite his impatience, he took his time covering three kilometers. He had to think things out. He was a realist. Lani was in a nasty spot, and a Martian station was one step short of the graveyard for a girl with her wiring diagram. She might have meant for him to stay away, while she turned a trick, well, to gain important advantages.

"If that's what she wants," he told himself, "I'd be a stinker to butt in—I'm the son of a bitch that got her into this mess: She likes me, but getting away from here is a whole hell of a lot more important to her than I ever could be, or ought to be . . ."

He cut the power.

"But suppose she wants me to take a hand in this? And I screw it up, trying to do the right thing by going back to Station Six?"

Garvin resumed his ride. See what was going on at Station Five.

Moon glimmer and the material of which the dome was made kept him from seeing his destination until he came close to it. The irregularity in the curve of the dome resolved itself into the mass of a parked ground capsule. Whether from data fed into the a computer, or from relying on intuition, Inspector Morgan seemed to have arrived at conclusions concerning Garvin's unusual bike mileage and the lack of rocks from the field. And who wouldn't want to share the wealth?

Garvin would not, of course not.

He cut the power and paused. "So, that *chingado*, that *bugao*, thinks he is also a meat inspector. He's got to have a taste of the only article in the system so far not taxed or government stamped."

Garvin quit the road. He got well clear of the pipeline and made for the rocky waste. When he gained perhaps two hundred meters of offset, he paraleled the road, going southward until he was abreast of dome and parked capsule. Then he made his way domeward, afoot, and screened by the Inspector's vehicle. Near his objective he racked his bike in the lee of a boulder, and continued afoot.

Instead of the wrench, he brought with him the hammer from his field kit.

The capsule was not secured to the air lock. Garvin found the tool kit and pondered simple ways of sabotaging a capsule—for instance, shorting out the battery.

"Stranding him here would embarrass him but it would make Lani conspicuous, which wouldn't help her, not one bit," he cogitated. "If I could just *think*, for one half minute . . ."

He got out of the vehicle. He had just the right answer—

Then he tried to make sense of what was happening beyond the garden-aquarium-hydroponic area. He was sweating at a rate beyond the air conditioning of the space suit. The face plate was misting badly. All he could distinguish was motion, blurred figures. One was white, gleaming, female and amazingly agile. The other, whoever he was, made no difference.

Garvin clawed the road shoulder, snatched a ragged rock the size of a muskmelon and clouted the shell of the road capsule. The alarm sounded like a battery of fire sirens. He sidestepped, got a clear view of the pursuit and evasion. The female figure was diving for the bedroom area. The other scrambled for a floppy dark mask and a helmet.

"Woman crazy or not," Garvin was thinking, "good man, going to plug a leak . . . duty first." He hefted the rock, picked a handier one from the roadside. Not knowing much about capsules, Garvin watched the fast-

moving dark shape until it started from the hydroponic
and aquarium sector and bounded for the air lock.

Lani was still out of sight. Morgan—it had to be
Morgan—paused in the air lock. Garvin heard the
evacuation pump.

"Good spaceman," he applauded. "Won't waste air,
not even with Lani on the brain."

Garvin began to relish the situation. The mist which
clouded the face plate had thinned. He stretched out
alongside the berm and as he waited, he fondled a ragged chunk of rock.

Morgan had a square of pressure adhesive patching
he'd grabbed from the emergency kit at the inner door
of the lock. Agile despite the cumbersome suit,
Morgan circled the vehicle, feeling for a meteorite
puncture.

Garvin came up, a long-legged stretch, a second—
poised as daintily as a ballerina, he clouted Morgan
with the rock. The glove cushioned the impact against
Garvin's palm. The Inspector crumpled, and ceased
twitching, ceased clawing.

Garvin heard a thumping sound. It distracted him
from thoughts of how to dispose of the body, just in
case he'd overdone things. He looked toward the dome.
He raced to the lock. Lani, drawing a robe about her,
was gesturing.

Garvin dragged Morgan toward the lock. Lani got
the message. She fingered the controls, and the door of
the evacuated lock swung out. Garvin got his prey into
the compartment. As pressure built he took off his helmet, and high time!

"Open the door," he yelled. And when Lani gave
him a hand, dragging the Inspector clear of the lock,
her skimpy gown revealed her from knees to collarbone.

"Good and faithful spaceman," he said, grinning
sourly. "Duty to the uttermost, breaking away from the
pursuit of all that!"

"Did you kill him?"

She savored each wide-spaced word. An eerie light
glowed in her eyes. Her breathing was strange—it

wasn't from outracing pursuit. It made him think of her moments of recovering from all out lovemaking.

Garvin shook his head, and he saw her moment of regret. "Doll, we can't kill the louse. The story is, a meteorite knocked off the alarm. He came dashing out and another one dusted his helmet."

"Get out of that gear, darling, get me a drink—I need one, I was at my wit's end. If you'd been later by a minute or two—oh, get shed of that frozen hardware!"

"Jesus, woman! You look good enough to eat raw—" He eyed the Inspector. "I'll tie him and gag him—"

Lani raced for the sleeping alcove. In a flash, she came out with a small, brocaded kit. She took a tiny hypo and a vial from the container. With shaky hands, she loaded the former. "You're going to be busy till sunrise," she said, and knelt beside the Inspector.

"What the hell?"

A jab, a flick of the plunger, and Lani looked up. "He'll be out until well after sunrise, and with a puking hangover when he comes out of it. He'll live and he'll be wishing he didn't have to. Now let's have a drink of the Inspector's liquor."

Garvin glanced at the bottle. "Didn't make much progress."

"I wasn't being plied with liquor, honey. I was too busy stalling till you got here. And overplayed it, and —well, I might've got at my needle, but I'm glad you got here when you did."

Garvin glanced toward the lock. "Maybe I'd better tie that clown, just to make sure."

"If you'd ever had the treatment yourself, you'd not have any worries about him."

Lani dug into a locker and got a trouble shooter's light with a long extension cord. "While you're tending to him, I'll get cleaned up from racing all over the vegetable patch—and which play gown shall I wear?"

"Put it on later, while you're resting up," Garvin suggested, and set to work securing the Inspector.

Not many minutes later, when Garvin stepped from the shower, Lani called from her alcove, "For fun, for love, or for money?"

"That depends on what you're wearing!"

The alcove light snapped off.

"Hundred *pazors* say you can't call the color from the perfume."

"Hundred says I can!"

He stepped into the fragrant gloom, sniffed. "*Red Mist*, and I'll take it out in trade." He groped for a moment, found Lani, and then, "You little bitch!"

"You lose! I'm not wearing a red gown—or any color gown—but I'll take the hundred out in trade."

When Lani stepped into the galley, to cook an early breakfast for Garvin, she wore her sedate sea-green gown. Its fragrance. *Sea Sylph*, was neither aphrodisiac nor seductive. She and Garvin regarded each other as might a couple twice their age look back at an opulent lifetime, well expended.

"Never appreciated your gourmet restaurant," he said, almost wistfully, "until I tackled space-cuisine. Anyway, here's your story. You saw a flash and heard a siren and began scrambling. You figured it was your alarm. Morgan knew a meteorite had poked a hole in his ground capsule. He'd know what was what, a newcomer wouldn't. He got out of the air lock. There was another flash, a streak. He keeled over. You had a time of it, dragging him into your station."

Lani frowned. "You think he'll buy that one?"

Garvin grinned happily. "He'd love any story, unless he could cook up a better one. Being so far off base, he'll need a cover-up. Prowling abos explain why he was making an inspection tour—he might've seen something near the road, got out, and a pip-squeak meteorite nicked his helmet. He's only an Inspector—he's small fry, he doesn't rate a damn, except in the field, running it over people like us."

Lani sighed, shook her head, frowned. "Honey, I'm not too sure of that. Some of the things he said, I've not got around to telling you."

"Me savey plenty, darling, It was a busy night!"

"He said," she resumed, "that I was plenty for you and for him. He led up to that by saying I'd better be sweet about it all, because you could be transferred to the thorium mines, or the plant."

"What I don't see, don't bother me. After all, I am married to a woman I couldn't get rid of, if she did not want me to get rid of her. But if that pig-fucker thinks he can run it over me, he just does not understand me, not at all.

"I studied a lot of maps while I was making the shuttle run, and even if he does get me transferred, I'll be seeing you, and I'll be seeing him *before he sees me*."

Lani's eyes widened. "You're thinking of that enormous crevasse, the one between my station and yours?"

"That crevasse," he said, deliberately, "won't be filled up, not today and not tomorrow."

Lani let Garvin out the lock, and watched him cycle away from behind the enormous boulder, well off the road. He waved his good-bye, and settled down to looking for spots in the story he'd given Lani. In her business, she'd acquired resourcefulness in a measure which three conventional women, working as a committee, could never approach. In the entire history of the PVR Corps, there'd not been one Jack-the-Ripper victim. On the other hand, there had been a number of deaths, always caused by person or persons unknown, and each victim had been a man with a record of sadism, or other games which could cause a girl too much harm or pain to be worth the hundred *pazors* extra.

A bit too much of the needle, or one pill too many . . . Garvin had often wondered whether the PVR Girls were a sorority, the equivalent of one of the deadliest of all secret associations, the not *entirely* masculine Chinese White Lotus Society: a group which no man in his right mind would ever needlessly offend. Odd, that the infallible police were never able to track down a woman suspected of being responsible for a fatality.

Nonetheless, Garvin was concerned. There was no one he could blame for the bitch-up which had landed him and Lani and others in this Martian *arschloch*. He, Garvin, had promoted the idea of going to Khatmandu, or Cuzco, and no matter who screwed it up, it finally was his baby. Resourceful all his life, he'd always got away with his own hide intact. This was the first time a bundle of other hides were jeopardized.

Although his thoughts were unpleasant company,

they engrossed him so completely that he was startled when Station Six loomed up. Nor was that more than a small piece of things: a ground capsule, not a rental vehicle but without official markings, was parked at the entrance. Garvin became homesick for Terra. Here, no matter how agile, he could neither outrace on the road, nor escape afoot.

The dome light made the vehicle a big blob of yellow glow. He pinced the finger-switch of his helmet mike and speaker: "What's going on?" he challenged, and stepped clear of the bike. Under cover of his mount, he took the tappet wrench from the tool kit. Some Terran genius had computerized the contents of the kit. He'd never heard of an electrical rig that had tappets, but maybe the men awaiting his return needed theirs checked for clearance, and adjusted.

"Garvin, Station Six?"

He jerked a hand toward the road marker. "I'm the friendly native that lives here. What the hell you want?"

The vehicle was headed southward.

"Let's get indoors. Or do you have to see our papers first?"

Two men got out of the car. Garvin said, "You wouldn't be crazy enough to come out here without orders!" It was not entirely politeness that made him gesture for the two to go ahead of him when he opened the outer door of the lock.

"Straight ahead," he directed. "And take off your helmets. Pressure's okay." And when the inner door opened, "That way—"

It wasn't until they were past the aquaria and the hydroponics that one said, "We drove from the spaceport and took a branch road, an old one, and a bitch."

The taller of the pair dug out a paper. "I'm Harland. My driver, Bromley. If you want to read the fine print, you're entitled to. Otherwise, pack up toothbrush and spare pair of socks and come with us."

Garvin didn't like this a bit. He eyed the pair: the short one, Bromley, was towheaded and open faced. No doubt he could drive or he'd never made it by the old road which cut the main line about ten *kay-ems* north of Station Six. The dark, angular-faced character, the one who claimed he was Harland, also looked okay, but the night's events had left Garvin in a mood somewhat less than trustful.

"You—" He leveled his index finger as though pointing a pistol at Harland. "Seal up your jacket, all the way to the collar."

Harland looked puzzled. "Ah . . . what—"

Garvin made a quick side step which brought him against the work bench. Dropping the tappet wrench, and with the other hand closing on the geologist's hammer, which had a pointed pick as well as a burnished head, Garvin said, very quietly, "Zip that jacket all the way up. Back up to the bulkhead, over there, and you read me that paper, slowly, while I'm watching you." With his left hand, he brushed a switch. The dome blacked out. "We can play hide and seek in the dark, or you can start reading when the lights go on."

Lights on, and his visitors stood there, blinking. They backed off, and Harland read the order. It sounded official, not like an improvisation. When Harland had done with the text, Garvin gave a short moment to thought.

He recalled the map, and the abandoned road from the spaceport. It intersected the improved road from spaceport to the nearest Gook colony. He was far from sure what he'd do with the information, but he was taking nothing for granted until he boarded the Terran-bound *Space Princess*.

"Sorry to be sticky about things," he said, pleasantly. "But I have nothing to pack up that I can't get from the ship's comissary. And I'm riding in the back seat." He fingered the hammer handle. "I'll take that paper and read it once we're in the spaceport."

Chapter 15

Flora Garvin wanted to exploit her family connections as never before, but the way the election had gone made her shrink from confronting Cousin Alexander. After Rod's outrageous caper she felt like staying totally out of sight, as though her influential kinsman might forget that she existed—until, hopefully, he'd remember her kindly once the Consortium had coped with the by-products of her husband's scandalous behavior.

However unbelievable the outcome, there was no arguing with facts: the Black Box had got Garvin, half a dozen women and an assortment of men ranging from psychos all the way down to pimps and general purpose renegades transported to Mars for resettlement. Months of thought control had smoothed that over—humorists had got to work, converting it all into a high-hearted caper. Biologists took their turn, and they declared that there had not been any women in the group—the resettlers were all male, and they'd be shacking up with female Gooks, a scientific experiment to determine whether the latter were sufficiently human to produce half-breeds. When the sociologists had their turns, the story was that there had indeed been women in the resettlement party, but that they were to be dance hall hostesses to elevate the cultural level of Maritania.

The disaster which could not be talked away was the result of the election which the Consortium had planned, the usual vicious campaign, with victor predetermined months in advance. The Benefactor of the People was swamped. The wrong scoundrel had been wafted into high office. Garvin's contribution to the Black Box had destroyed every flake of political science and of psychology at the command of Thought Control. There were long, long faces. Each authority doubted the competence of his colleagues. Garvin's message had been simple, as subtle as a double-bitted axe. Yet it had buggered an expertly planned election. The computers were analyzing the message to determine why the words of a blundering ingnoramus had been so effective.

Garvin's terse address, intended as his farewell to a culture whose influence he'd escape the day he and Lani could ride yak cart or pony back out of Khatmandu and into free country, drove immediately to the point, thus:

He told the electorate that the most competent spacemen had been locked up in fruit and nut factories to discredit them. That the actual reason for downplaying trans-Saturnian cruising had been to concentrate on converting Mars to well-watered land with a breathe-able atmosphere. That thousands of the Plastic Populace, working seventy hours a week, instead of the usual five, could rejuvenate Mars.

The solution was simple. Instead of slave labor to develop airless Martian wastes, develop Terrestrial deserts, swamps, jungles making employment for jobless natives of each region. Out with hand-picked political favorites—make way for an administration dedicated to the construction of trans-Saturnian cruisers built according to plans which former governments had suppressed by propaganda pumped through the media until the public had accepted the swindle. Time now for a new approach, new names, new faces, and no exiles to do seventy hours a week developing Martian deserts.

To get Rod off the blacklist and to save him from severe penalties, Flora had to convice Cousin Alexander that his upsetting the election had not been from malice; that the disaster had been the unforeseen result of a caper gone wild. To do this, she had to understand what had been done, and how it had been done, else her plea could not be plausible. Her only resource was to consult Hamlin Daly.

Daly scarcely concealed his amusement at Flora's change of expression when she stepped into the jungle of wires, instruments, insulation peelings and shreds of packing material. She recoiled a short pace, glanced about her, bewildered and unbelieving. He recognized her before she give him her name. The media had made her a public figure.

Charm—looks which, divided between two or three plain Janes, would have made a glamor girl of each— and she dressed to catch the eye. Flora at the races, Flora sponsoring homes for indigent Sunday School teachers, Flora presenting medals to Space Scouts. Only one reason she'd missed being *Mother of the Year*.

Deviously, indirectly, the Consortium had blocked her every effort to go underground. She never suspected that the Consortium needed her to build up its own image; no one with a wife such as Flora could be a renegade—a whimsical, a daring eccentric, of course, but so progressive.

But the disastrous election—that still demanded much effort.

Daly dusted a chair. "If you had let me know you were dropping in, Mrs. Garvin, I would have cleaned this one up, and a clear alley right up to it. What's on your mind?"

"I don't quite know where to begin—"

Daly dipped into the waste basket to get the ceramic jug with Ethiopian characters on the shoulder. "I'll get a glass. You can bet it'll be clean; I'll wash it here and now."

Flora declined with thanks.

"While you're getting your thoughts assembled," he went on, as he flipped a cigarette butt out of the nearest tumbler and poured a hefty jolt of liquor, "I'll take one for me and one for you. Just pretend you drank yours. Good health, madame."

"I understand," she began, "how Rod's declaring that computers could be tampered with could . . . ah . . . embarrass a computer-oriented social order, but what puzzles me is this—after all the audio and video appearances I went through, everything was smoothed over. You remember, it wasn't until four or five weeks later that he attacked the restricted space program. How he did it—I've been so busy with a sudden flurry of civic obligations—I haven't had time to think!"

"That," Daly explained, "was to give him and his buddies time to get to Khatmandu, then out of that spot and into country where he couldn't be extradited. But something fouled up, and they all went to Mars instead—see what I mean? The man's a genius! He missed his mark by 69,000,000 kilometers and lands in an international area—and no extradition. So you can relax."

"Oh, but I *can't*! He did more than denounce the space program—he assailed the integrity of the administration. It's all so frightfully puzzling, confusing, how an impulsive caper could have such long-lasting effects—a political upset, reversing a trend and offsetting a whole campaign. Everyone had predicted just the opposite result—the experts, I mean."

"Mrs. Garvin—"

"Let's not be formal. To Rod's friends, I'm Flora."

"Flora, I'm a bit surprised to rate so high. Some people even hint that I put him up to that trick. There seem to be things about this that you don't quite understand."

"It's driving me right to the edge!"

Daly hunched forward over the table. "Let's take it from the start. Rod ran off at the mouth about the space cruiser he could design and so he's sent to the Psycho Factory where he meets Jim Ward. Jim got there account of sounding off about computer boners not being corrected because the bureaucrats wouldn't admit there were mistakes. He said he could show how anything could be fed into a computer and he could correct it. You could make a computer say anything you wanted it to, and whenever you wanted it to, and that that was what ailed the whole damn system.

"Jim and Rod figured they'd demonstrate that point, and they gave me the specs of a Black Box which would get them far away from the Magnificent and Plastic Society. I'd do the wiring, and they'd hook it up."

He tossed off a jolt of Ethiopian Terror, paused for breath.

"Now hear this, Flora! I'm getting to what made the election go against the experts. Part of the Black Box programmed the basic policies of the country. Technicians are spattering paint and mosaic according to designs that artists are cooking up, and nobody knows what or why he's doing it, or who's going to use the stuff. Everyone from the cellar to the roof is obeying a computer. High-frequency sound you can't hear is dubbed into background music. Slogan specialists invent slogans for departments which don't know how the overall scenario fits into a level one step closer to the public that gulps it all.

"I bet propaganda was needled into your fashion show openings, audio and video blobs, into your Better Nutrition drives.

"Rod and Jim told the central master computer what *policies* to follow, and the machine knows nothing—and it tells other machines that don't know a bit more—"

Daly doubled up, laughing until he gasped and choked.

"Jim and R-Rod—they forgot—what they told—the d-d-damn—machine."

"You mean, *nobody* can stop it?"

"Every computer from here to the Pacific Coast is spewing it out. Maybe Jim could figure a way. Maybe they'll have to take the network to pieces by hand, unit by unit—Flora, I just can't help laughing, it's so silly!"

She sat there, wide eyed, awed by the scope of what Rod had set in motion. Not knowing what possessed them, the citizen mass had remained hostile about the limitation of the space program and the thought of long working hours. They felt that they'd been voting a wrong set of trained seals into office, and they'd corrected their error.

Alexander and the Consortium had cause for worry. The monster they'd created, impressionable millions acting as a single colossal idiot, trained to accept any suggestion, however preposterous, could in one emotional blast destroy not only the Hierarchy but the Consortium and the entire Magnificent Culture.

"Have I made it clear?" Daly asked solicitously.

"I hope there's nothing more to tell me." Then she brightened. "Maybe I can put in a word for Rod. I know now that he couldn't possibly have realized how far he was going."

Flora headed directly for Central Administration. Recently won prominence got her express service to Cousin Alexander's office. Stately as ever, *Caesar Minus Laurels*, the power behind Democracy-Dictatorship was on his feet to welcome his fifth cousin.

"Alex—"

He caught Flora with both arms, kissed each cheek, held her at arm's length. "Every time I see you, you're more gorgeous! Why do you stay away so long?" He clapped his hands; from the refrigerator panel came the bar cart. It followed him to a conference alcove. "Flora, this is grand! Make it oftener, so I won't be so surprised. What's on your mind—I know something's troubling you."

"Oh, everything. I'm still—well—all upset about Rod!"

Alexander chuckled, gestured magnificently. "Can't you find a real problem?"

She'd expected a sympathetic hearing, but not this! Apparently he'd dismissed her problem before he'd even heard of it. His hand wavered between the four leading bottles.

"Over the rocks? With soda?"

Flora had to get herself reorganized, balanced. "Let's have an *Herbsainte Frappé*? With all my troubles, I need a holy herb!"

"You came to the right place." He filled the deep goblets with finely shaved ice. "A cube, or straight?"

"Sugar spoils it."

"Right! You're still my girl." On each goblet he set a glass saucer with a pinhole piercing the center. Into each saucer he poured the greenish liqueur. For a moment he watched until the spot beneath the dripper center turned cloudy-white. "Let's hear it. The floor's yours till every drop's dripped. Better than an egg timer sandglass?"

One black brow rose to a Gothic arch; the other leveled a bit, almost veiling a twinkling dark eye. The lurking smile encouraged Flora. Alex let other people do his worrying for him.

"And when the drops have dripped, I hush up and listen?"

"Unless you want a refill."

Flora sighed and relaxed. "I've been worried silly! I've heard rumors that you were *furious*."

"What about?"

"Why—well, I told you, Rod's awful caper."

He chuckled. "Half a dozen whores and a psycho. But Rod always was an individualist."

"That's not really what I meant—I mean, the really *gruesome* business, upsetting the election."

"Your friends must've been drinking something a lot more potent than anything I have." He gestured toward the refreshment panel. "This is a democracy. Upsets from time to time remind the public that it is actually the final arbiter. Rod did not louse anything, not really."

He put palms together, gazed into outer space, and spoke as though to himself. "It is true, we do often prescribe in detail for the common good. Yes. Ultimately, however, the people tell us what they want us to think in their behalf." He parted his hands, making an expansive gesture, and addressed Flora: "*Vox populi* and that sort of thing, you know."

"Then—" Tension eased off; she slumped comfortably, and sighed. "Then Rod isn't working in the mines?"

"Mines!" He chuckled. "Of course not! You've been out of touch?"

"I was so mortified—first wave of gossip, you know—and then I got myself involved chin deep, in civic things as a conspicuous way of hiding out. I knew you'd all hate me for bringing a congenital outlaw into the family—which is what Rod is, I think, but there's no malice in him."

"Initiative." Alexander nodded. "The pioneering spirit that made this a great country."

She regarded him shrewdly, and risked another move. "You were awfully influential before I was born, but you've been another of those pioneers—still are—"

"*Touché*!" he acknowledged. "I have a surprise for you." His glance shifted to the drippers. "Mission accomplished." He plucked the drippers from the goblets, and handed Flora her glass. "We have something to drink to—hold it, not yet—"

He turned to the intercom, fingered several buttons. When the speaker answered, "Spaceways Development," Alex said, "Send me Roderick Garvin's file. That's all. Thank you."

When the orderly entered the office, Alexander opened the folder, took out one sheet, and dismissed the messenger. Then, to Flora, "Want to read the fine print?"

"Oh, skip the fine print, just tell me!"

"We are bowing to the people's will. The election proves that they want space development. Not Martian Gardens, Martian fields, but flights through the asteroid belt, flights beyond Jupiter, beyond Saturn, and I won't even speculate as to what else it'll go beyond. So, Rod's coming back to design power plants and special shielding against the garbage ring between Mars and Jupiter. Armor and also magnetic repulsion.

"To speed things up, we'll use a cruiser completed but not yet fitted out for normal service."

"You mean, using his ideas on propulsion and all the rest?"

"Rod has the job. He's in charge. What he says, that's what it's going to be."

Lipstick tracks showed how thoroughly she'd kissed Alexander. And then, "Oh, how I'll drink to *that*."

Alexander licked his lips. "Nice flavor you're wearing. Makes me sorry we're cousins." He sighed, then brightened. "I'll start a refill, so it'll be ready when we need it."

Chapter 16

The Consortium had not been amazed when the general election went against the candidate scheduled to win the office of Supreme Hierarch. When the Consortium assembled, each face, whether round, square, ruddy, tanned, or the opposite of one of those specifications, was troubled; the eyes were haunted and somber, regardless of color.

And then the Moderator, Alexander Heflin, arrived. He waggled a hand, set down his *Pernod frappé*, and didn't even bother to call the meeting to order, much less whack the gavel. His presence sufficed.

"This is as bad as it looks, as your looks made it. I do not blame you." He turned his glance on the Consort at his left. "Ambridge, let's hear your views. The tapes will be for reference at this meeting only. Before adjournment, they will be destroyed. There will be no leaks."

These were not prophecies. They were commands.

Ambridge's beetling brows, stern mouth, and swarthy, squarish face expressed scepticism. "Can we be sure of that?"

Alexander smiled reassuringly. "The magnetic field protecting us has probably knocked out every conventional watch among you. Now that that's settled, let's hear your thoughts."

Deliberately, Ambridge chopped his words. "For those bastards to support Lacoste was a kick in the teeth. Never mind telling me that it makes no difference whether Lacoste or Norton was elected, it's the principle of the thing."

He paused. Wrath pushed concern from his rugged face. Alexander cut into the sink-in pause. "Do you object on principle, or is it from irritation because our Plastic Populace went unplastic, mocked and needled us when we're not accustomed to such doings?"

"Both," Ambridge answered candidly. "Once they know their power, they'll begin to kick us around. A lion trainer knows that if he ever lets the beast gain an advantage, he's finished."

"Lions and tigers do not have minds that can make monkeys of them. If people had minds, we'd not be here. That's just a reminder, and I admit that people can be dangerous. But the question is, how do you feel about what Ambridge has said? Raise a hand for acceptance."

He noted the unanimous agreement with Ambridge. He gestured to the man at Ambridge's left. "Dawson, give us your thought."

"I pass. You've heard it."

"Next."

A beak-nosed, sandy-haired man responded, "Before the Populace became plastic, a careless and overconfident Consortium was mobbed. Your great grandfather was one of the three survivors."

The Moderator amended, "Two and a half survivors, really. Absent without leave, but he lived a bad fourteen years. Pardon the interruption, Irvin, and carry on. Recommendation?"

"How about mobilization because of, for instance, threat from Celebes-Macassar. Carefully screened troops, in case we have to declare martial law."

"You think it'll come to that?"

"The Consortium didn't think so, and only three survived to know they'd made a mistake. I've made a recommendation."

"Anyone concurring, raise his hand."

Three joined Irvin.

"Well short of a concensus, but four is too many to ignore."

So it went along the table, Alexander Heflin baiting each into an expression. Wrath began to center on Garvin, all the more so since he was a cousin-in-law of the moderator and more than reprehensible—a traitor to his borrowed status.

Life sentence to working in the thorium mines of Mars . . .

"Which is never an awfully long sentence," one Consort interpolated, with gusto. And another, "A firing squad—that makes sure there'll be no pardons, no paroles, no probation nonsense."

Finally, Alexander rose. Stately and withdrawn, he stood until his silent presence commanded group attention. When the silence became alive and vibrant he said, "Acting as a body, the Consortium could relieve me of the responsibility of condemning my cousin's husband to death, whether sudden or gradual. If I saw value in any such action, I'd lead, not advise against it." A dark pause, and then, "I must remind you that it would be dangerous for you to make a martyr of Roderick Garvin."

There was a cross fire of dissent, acceptance, incipient wrangle. All this he ignored. Arms folded, he stood there, mortally weary, yet enduring, patient. At last he resumed, "Magnetic screening has probably knocked out the refreshment automation. Why don't some of you roll out the carts and relax for a glass? Most of you are as hoarse as I'd be, if I'd shouted as you have."

Before the shuffle and scrape of feet made it necessary for him to raise his voice, he resumed, "I've spared my larynx because I'll make a summing up before we adjourn."

This drew the Consortium together, even though the members flocked about the carts, each mixing his own potion. Alexander sat back, viewing the group as if it were too distant for him to hear the waxing babble. He had no glass at hand. His withdrawal was so complete that when he emerged from the depths of his high-back chair, the move silenced the group.

Alexander Heflin smiled whimsically. "Now that I've heard you, it's your turn to hear me."

"Sound off!"

"Let's have it!"

"Hear the Silent Consort!"

"I'll refresh you on what you already know." Weariness, coming ever more to the surface, shaped his majestic features, inviting each of the consortium into the fellowship of tiredness. "We've become so accustomed to the concept of Democracy that we're inclined to feel as if it has always existed. We are prone to forget that it's been a gradual growth, with many a reversal, many an approach to extinction.

"In the earlier years, there were a few centuries of lunacy, mob impulse, catering to the imbecilities of half-baked children who believed themselves experienced adults. Adults they were, in body, but with juvenile minds, parrot-intellects, echoes of what any glib half-wit or calculating scoundrel could tell them. There was no force to act in the place of parents or guides.

"Rash dictators, themselves maniacs of great force but petty minds, devoid of principle or good sense, almost ruined democracy.

"Custom and the manners of each reaction of despotism restricted the succeeding expansion of despotism. There lingered in the mass psyche the rudiments of what had been. The witless leaders who baited and who duped the witless populace overdid it.

"A few were kicked to death, manually dismembered. Others died more quickly. Bombs and small arms did a cleaner job, and to the disappointment of those who craved action. Mouthings of Democracy which so often won the gullible word lovers, word worshippers, left imprints which were detonators to explode the mass psyche.

"Remember that for half a dozen generations of population ever more plastic has been developed. They've become psychic sponges—they'll accept and believe the ultimate absurdities. Each individual is rational enough. But a detonation wave can touch off the entire mass. One mistake at the wrong time, and we're in for vivisection, without anaesthesia."

Silence.

Then the man who had advised mobilization, ostensibly because of foreign complications but actually to have martial law at hand, raised his voice.

"What do you suggest? Knuckling down, or an issue of candy bars?"

Alexander smiled. "Children, particularly subnormal children, always settle for candy bars. There are so many flavors."

Chuckles, and one demanded, "Carry on!"

"So, they want space explored. So, since we are restricting human progress, blocking the advance of science, we'll recall Garvin. We'll put him in charge of reconverting the *Space Princess* for a cruise far beyond Jupiter and back."

"That crackpot, gets a nine-billion-*pazor* toy!"

"That is precisely my decision."

"Alex, you must be demented."

"Could be," the Moderator conceded cheerily. "But when he gimmicked our entire thought-control system, coast to coast, and threw an election right between our eyes—and gave us a farewell goosing—sure, he did go to Mars by mistake, but we're still the losers. The public wants a hero, and we are giving them one. Anyone here want to be hero?"

There were no takers.

"That's the answer I expected, and you're quite right."

But there was another objection. "I go with you. So does Hogan . . . and Simms." He gestured. "But Garvin's poison. Give them that kind of hero and he'll end by being elected Supreme Hierarch. He'll finally be Moderator, and you'll be out, living or dead."

A moment of hoarse breathing, and then Alexander carried on: "Slater, have you said it? Or are you merely out of breath?"

Slater grinned, made a gesture of futility. "I've said it. But how would you ever stop him?"

"Fair question. A challenge, and I've already accepted it." He paused. When they gripped chair arms, and leaned forward, the Moderator said. "I suspect that you want my answer. To prevent leaks, I am keeping it to myself."

He untwisted the stopper of the 151 proof rum. "As soon as tapes are off the reels, I'll baptize them. This stuff burns like rocket fuel."

Chapter 17

Back to the old Spaceways Shops: Garvin, by now accustomed to Terran gravity, to having Flora around the house, and to having no cycling and no core drilling, was hidden by a heap of blueprints, binders of specs. Looking out the office window, he could see the gleaming beryllium hull of the *Space Princess*, rechristened *Saturnienne*. Mechanics, working around the clock were dismantling the reactors and drive, to make way for new units which would go into production when Garvin had done checking the specifications.

Meanwhile, the hull was being armored with deflector plates of manganese alloy tough enough to resist the fragments which swarmed in the asteroid belt. Thought Control broadcasts kept the air vibrant, both to keep the Plastic Populace happy and to fire up enthusiasm for the issue of ten billion *pazors* in space bonds.

They had their candy bar, and the Serfs were paying for it.

"*Rod Garvin, the intrepid spaceman, will go beyond Saturn by conserving fuel—not only with his improved drive, but also by driving through the asteroid belt instead of rising high above its orbit. Space probes will actuate direction controls to evade larger meteoric fragments and the smaller asteroids. Special armor will deflect peppering by the minute fragments which would jeopardize the older hulls.*

"*Improved reactors, an entirely new power plant*

*design, will eliminate the burnouts which have harassed
cruisers of the Martian freight and passenger lines . . .
Landing on the moons of Saturn is not contemplated,
but with the* Saturnienne's *favorable power-to-mass ratio, she will be able to resist the tremendous gravitation
of Jupiter and of Saturn. A staff of specialists is developing a communication system to transmit sound and
video across the one billion, two hundred and sixty-
eight million, eight hundred thousand kilometers between Terra and Saturn when the two planets are separated by the least possible distance between their orbits.*

"Because of her power-to-mass ratio, the Saturnienne
*can approach far closer to either Saturn or Jupiter than
any unmanned explorer vehicle has thus far been able
to approach. On your home viewing screen you will see
the rings of Saturn in detail finer than that recorded by
the most powerful of Terrestrial telescopes.*

"If the captain of the Saturnienne *ventures too near
either planet, he will lose his ship, himself, and his
crew. But you bond subscribers cannot lose. The cost of
the* Saturnienne *will be deducted from his salary, which
he can't collect until he returns."*

Garvin wavered between the thrill of having advanced from the Psycho Factory to explorer, and, feeling like a phony, getting credit which his one-time fellow inmates deserved: the men whose basic concepts he
had tried to publicize. They remained the forgotten
men.

The back-slapping good-fellowship of the Consortium was exclusively for Roderick David Garvin. The
pioneers in the madhouse would remain anonymous—
but they'd have choice names for him.

Maybe, just maybe, he could contrive to shave off a
shred of the credit which he was getting as a fifth
cousin-in-law of Alexander Heflin, and transfer it to
Admiral Josiah Ambrose Courtney. He began to see
how. He had this unpaid debt, and then, Garvin had
plans in which Hamlin Daly might be helpful. Thus far,
he'd not seen that versatile eccentric.

At the moment Rod had more to do than just check
specs against the work done by the successive shifts of
craftsmen. Garvin did not trust the contractors. He had

to be on guard against the substitution of shoddy material for the refractory alloys, heat- and meteorite-resistant alloys which the job demanded. Inspectors were on the job—no individual could possibly hope to keep an eye on such an extensive project—and most of them were straight, but Rod could count on a few being among the best inspectors that money could buy.

Everything looked good. Something was too good to be true about the entire proposition. When he found slipshod work on improper material, Garvin was troubled. When he found nothing wrong, he was even more disturbed—they were outwitting him.

"So I'm becoming a paranoiac," he grumbled. "And if I do not have delusions of persecution, I am an Honest John."

Every night, after big mixing glasses of *mastika* with a dash of something or other, or whatever happened to be Flora's discovery of the day, plus heaps of good chow, there would be a suspense build-up: trying to guess what play gown Flora would wear no longer than the time it would take to sip a *pousse café* in seven colors. And there was nothing in the scenario which required cycling twenty *kay-ems* along a rutted Martian road. This, too, this last was disturbing. It put him in mind of Lani and the others who remained marooned on Mars.

Either problem was a burden. Worse yet, Flora would begin to suspect that something was going wrong.

To explain would be a disaster as overwhelming as refusing to discuss the matter.

Garvin was within an estimated hour of despair, and Flora was even nearer the questioning phase when he realized that the simplicity of it all had blinded him to the solution. The problems interlocked. And he had nothing to do but plant convincing evidence of sabotage or the use of unsuitable material in an area which was completed, and which had been passed by the inspector.

Only one problem remained unsolved: how to explain when Flora began wondering why he was no longer preoccupied, abstracted, and groping for nonexistent answers to imaginary problems.

Garvin glanced at the digital wall clock, took a fond look at the *Saturnienne*'s hull, and bailed out. It was time to see Hamlin Daly, the master of gimmicks.

He found Daly in the center of his spider web of wires and junk. The man looked up from the clicking abacus, screwed up his face to bring his pop-eyes into focus.

"God-damn high time you showed up."

"Every time I turn around, it's a problem, and half an hour ago, I got the answer. A bit off trail, confidential, of course, and just your dish."

Daly reached for the Ethiopian jug. "Tell me more while I see if the glasses are sanitary."

"I want thin, flexible masks—latex or plastic, that's for you to figure out. But they have to look natural, skin texture and color—elastic enough to cling skin tight. To jibe with the bone structure, the muscle pattern underneath.

"And I want air travel documents, ID, papers and the rest of the goods for getting some friends out of Martian Gardens and manned stations and back home. Once they're in Maritania, they can stay under cover till take off."

Daly pondered for a moment. "See if I got it right. I can get the work done from photos, those fine-grid things that look like Three Dimension. You may not remember, but the pack of you were filmed while the case was tried. For your going-to-Mars papers.

"Okay—those same photos show the technician how you do *not*, repeat, *not* want the masks to look. At the same time, the general head and face shape will jibe, but details will be changed, until the mask is someone else but goes naturally with the general body shape."

Garvin nodded. "Right on!"

"Naturally, that'll take some study, but the man I have in mind does a nice business in false faces without plastic surgery. A service for people who . . . um . . . want privacy. Some even want two masks . . . well, to confuse snoopers trying to get divorce evidence. Or any other legal evasion."

"And there's a bit more to the package—I want a couple of confidential crew members to be fitted with

masks making each one look like me. I have a friend
who can navigate. Caspar Tweed. The other, all he has
to do is be reliable and quick witted. I may want to
convince the crew that it's difficult ever to catch me
asleep."

"Keep 'em talking to themselves, keep 'em wondering. Not a bad idea at all. This is getting really ripe
stuff."

"There's one more bit. I want a disguise mask for
myself," Garvin resumed. "Being in command, I'm
bound to be conspicuous wherever I go, and I might
want to be incognito."

"Such as, getting Lani out of the Gardens, or seeing
who crew members are fraternizing with, or who's buying them more drinks and stuff than the situation calls
for. Anyway, your confidential friends that are supposed to look like you, where are they?"

"In town and I'll send them to you, so you can fit
them with me-masks. And if I don't play it that way, I
might at the last minute have them take the places of
crew members I want to get rid of."

Daly eyed him. "You're not through with your ship
fitting. How would you know who you'd want to replace of a crew that isn't signed up yet?"

Garvin sighed. "For a man of your talent, you ask
the damndest questions! In any crew of Plastic Citizens
there'll be slobs, human garbage, troublemakers. I can
count on sabotage, or mutiny, or just plain bungling
and trouble. I am betting on trouble of some kind, and
to keep it from being too much of a guessing contest,
I'm readying up for problems and taking care of details
as they shape up."

Daly frowned, and after a moment of cogitation, he
said, "You figure you might want to get rid of as many
as three of your crew?"

"I can't imagine a crew with only two undesirables!
Fool question department is working overtime today."

"With all the automation these days, I could stand a
watch."

"What's that?"

"This must be bugging you! I said, with all the automation, I could stand a watch. I been thinking for some

little while that leaving town wouldn't be a bad idea."

"This—hmmm—you really mean it?"

"I'm being suspected of having done more than just wire up that Black Box. One of the Consortium has been sleeping with a PVR girl I know kind of well. And she told me some of the thoughts he'd been dishing out to her. She was name dropping, all about how high class her customers are."

"So she could charge you an extra hundred *pazors*."

"You get simpler by the hour! She talked so I would do her some technical favors, and take it out in trade."

"Oh, all *right!* So you want to go on the cruise and come back a space hero."

"Now that you're the white-haired boy, they got to pick someone else to crap on, and prove that justice always prevails, and on general principles, I want a change of scene. Now, about those crew members you won't like. How about your throwing a takeoff party—you furnish good liquor, and I'll hustle up a few dependable girls who'll make sure that the don't-wants miss the cruise."

Meanwhile, Garvin got minimum assistance in security by engaging operators from a dective agency he knew to be reliable. Their job rating was "handyman, general cleanup." They collected bits of welding rod, swept up spilled flux, picked up metal scraps and trimmings. Each lot of odds and ends taken away as part of the effort to maintain safe working conditions was identified as to origin: the compartment or desk it had been swept from. After passing through the hands of three dummies, the stuff at last came to a laboratory whose operators knew only that some industrial or construction job was conducting tests on material.

For another of his security crews he engaged Serfs who had long and outstanding records. One of these conscientious fellows rendered a verbal report which expressed the opinion of the entire crew: "Far as we can see, there aren't any known saboteurs or troublemakers on the job, but we can't see very far."

"Look for amateurs," Garvin suggested, patiently. "Professionals wouldn't be interested. Blowing a space job, there's no repeat business."

As before, not finding trouble was even worse than finding and correcting trouble, a point which Hamlin Daly raised—rather needlessly, as Garvin pointed out.

"You're right, of course, and it was driving me over the rim!" Rod continued, "until I saw that this security business was exactly what I needed to get Lani and Jim and Amelia and the others back home."

"Your mind is so God-damn logical and keen I miss the point. Brief me?"

"I've been planting bitched-up pieces of work, stuff I made up in private, and fitted into compartments completed and inspected. Things that could fail between here and Mars, and not blow the cruiser. If nothing lets go on the way, I'll discover the shoddy welds or low-grade parts or cheap substitutions at the Martian spaceport. And then I'll tie up the flight until there's an all-over recheck and test flights.

"That'll give me time to get our buddies out of Martian Gardens. Maybe even stow them away aboard the *Saturnienne* until there's a home-bound cruiser that'll take them away. Won't be long—there's only one more thing to take care of, well, maybe two. The first is meeting the crew I'm stuck with. Giving them an inspirational talk, the crap the psychologists have cooked up for me.

"Which is good, this time. I'll meet them, and between seeing the faces and studying the records, I'll know which three are the best to get rid of—you'll take care of that at the party I'm throwing for my gallant band of no-good sons of bitches and tramps."

"And what's the other thing?"

"Wasted breath, but I'm appealing to Caesar."

"Wait a minute, the name's Alexander."

"Wish I knew what my name's going to be, but I'll try to upgrade the crew, much as I can."

After meeting the spacemen, so-called, who were to herd the *Saturnienne* so close to her name-planet that she'd scrape the rings, Garvin requested and he got an immediate interview with Alexander. Instead of a private and man-to-man conference for which he had hoped, the entire Consortium confronted him, in the boardroom, not in the Moderator's suite of offices. The group sat in a compact crescent, with Alexander at the center of the arc, so that an eye shift would be directed to members to his right or left. And the eyes of the entire Consortium focused on the podium to which a secretary had guided Garvin.

Alexander got up from his chair, stepped up to welcome the guest-speaker, and presented him to the Consortium. "Now that you've met us," Alexander Heflin concluded, "we'll be sitting—you'll be standing. You know what you're going to say—we do not. We're the captive audience.

"My colleagues and I—our eyes have been opened by your unorthodox approach. Shock treatment, one might call it." He grimaced ruefully, glowed with good fellowship, a total acceptance of Garvin's well-earned victory. "We believe in you. Ask, and we'll answer questions. Tell us, and we'll listen."

He stepped aside, paused for a nod and a gracious gesture, then resumed his chair. The other faces ranged from noncommittal to hostile.

Garvin could not recall any previous encounter which had left him feeling so overwhelmingly outnumbered. Abruptly, bluntly, he declared, "I want my crew to consist of the spacemen you've kept locked up in the psychofacility. Unless I have veterans, experts to man the *Saturnienne*, I'd be jeopardizing the most spaceworthy cruiser ever to take off: the changes in her reactors, her outboard interceptors of minute meteorites too small to activate the magnetic shield—I'll not tick off any details—these extras alone have cost as much as a standard space cruiser.

He paused, stepped back from the podium. The faces showed no change, yet he sensed that he had made an impression. He resumed, "You have given me a crew of bin-scrapings. I've looked up their records. Each dossier shows that the higher the IQ, the longer the record as a troublemaker and a versatile no-account. Such intelligence as some of these fellows undeniably have makes for optimum obstructionism."

Alexander was too gracious, too tactful to suggest that Garvin himself had a colorful record. This left no chance for a well-prepared rebuttal. Instead, he sighed, shook his head, and wordlessly expressed regret—his expression did that, and eloquently. Then, "We are—I am awfully sorry, most deeply sorry, but our public information service extended itself to the limit in proving that you are sane and wholly right in all respects, doctrine included. Considering that their effort was required so soon after your recantation ceremony, they did a phenomenal job of building up your merits as a prospective space hero. They restored the Masses' faith in the System.

Alexander's pause was impressive, his smile, benign. He resumed, "It would not be Democratic to man the *Saturnienne* with High Brass, as the saying goes, or members of the Executive Caste, persons traditionally devoid of feeling for the Plastic Populace. Your having been recalled from ecological service demonstrates the paramount importance, the emphasis on Democracy. As you recall, during your absence, the populace protested by spectacularly defeating the candidates we had sponsored. This was the mandate, and we cannot wish to go against it, or seem to do so."

"I can't imagine what'd be more democratic than having retired captains and a retired admiral putting on hot suits and taking a hand when a reactor starts playing tricks. And there are plenty of other duties just as nasty though perhaps not as hazardous. We need good men on every watch, not bin scrapings!"

Alexander countered, "There is a minority which persistently speaks of the underworked and the overfed citizen's incompetence. We are here for more than fitting a cruiser to test the validity of the ultraradical theories you and others have advanced. This exploration cruise is to vindicate the merit of those called the overfed and underworked, the norm of our Democracy. You, the only Serf on the roster, are of necessity an exception. Although you are scarcely the norm, it would be unfair to hold that against you, and penalize you for outstanding inventiveness."

"God damn it, Sir! I won't take off with a crew of dopes and zombies!"

Alexander smiled indulgently. "Rod, you'd take off

in a Lunar Shuttle cruiser if you had no other choice. Be a good fellow and don't force us to be tough."

As one man, the Consortium nodded. Their concentrated stares, the shadow of contentment at knowing that Alexander Heflin had not wavered, assured Garvin that they had agreed on making his a suicide mission. He'd be the only kind of hero who could help rather than menace the Consortium.

Garvin wagged his head, shrugged, then grinned amiably. "Alex, and you other gentlemen of the Consortium, you are quite right. I never imagined I'd get a chance like this, and I'm lucky to be able to set out, odds and all. It'll be fun announcing mission accomplished, and thanks to every one of you."

Chapter 18

When he was eighteen years and a few months old, Rod Garvin had regarded Mars as a goal, an escape from dreary commonplace things and people: the way of adventure and of experiencing life. Now, eleven years after his setting out, Mars was an unpleasant extension of things Terrestrial, with a single remaining merit—it was his launching pad for Saturn, five times as far from Mars as Mars was from home. And here he was, in command of the *Saturnienne*; she sat on her landing struts, air-locked to Maritania's spaceport dome.

Instead of being thrilled, Garvin was dog tired from having been incessantly on guard against that which had *not* happened: with sixty-nine million kilometers behind him, somewhere ahead waited the ultimate, the critical test. But now he slumped comfortably in his chair, sighed from the hips, and eyed First Officer Caspar Tweed and Warrant Officer Hamlin Daly.

"I called you so we can brief each other on what the book calls *personnel*. We have our own words for what we've got aboard, but we'll stick to the book."

Remembering that he was in the skipper's stateroom, Daly shifted the dab of Martian fungus-snuff from right molars to left, instead of spitting the varnish-eating juice against the bulkhead as he would have done at home. Whatever concessions circumstance demanded, he remained Hamlin Daly. Papal miter or the Double Crown of Egypt would have left him unchanged. Garvin's glance shifted from the pop-eyed and immutable Daly to a more commonplace type. Although Caspar Tweed was of Garvin's build, there the likeness ended. The difference began with the wide-open china-blue eyes, guileless, blinking as they reached around or through the straw-colored cowlick which persistently invaded his coffin-shaped face. Without suggesting that Caspar Tweed was dull-witted, Garvin from the beginning of their association, in their earliest spacedays, had considered the man brighter than he looked. In this respect, Tweed was deceptive. In three continents of Terra there were unmarked graves, the resting places of brighter-looking men who had taken him at his face value.

"It's time you gave me your ideas on the crew," Garvin continued. "You've been making private notes on trifles you've not entered in the log? Good—flip them on the table. I'll show you a thing or two.

He picked up a record cassette about 5.5 by 6.5 centimeters and less than two centimeters thick, slipped it into the microretriever, glanced at his crew roster, and punched off the index number of each man.

"There's a picture and dossier for every man who's been in space the past fifty years. What I'm going to show you is the serial numbers, faces, and histories of the crew. Each index number I just punched is what a man applying for this cruise signed on the papers. If a face that's aboard doesn't jibe with the record, I'd not be surprised, but I'd be interested in knowing how come."

He twisted the control switch. Automatically, image succeeded image on the screen, each showing a face and a history. After a fifteen-second exposure, two prints were ejected, whereupon a new face and dossier appeared.

Garvin dealt the prints as he would cards. "Each of you take a hand and study the details, while I'm comparing your notes on what you thought of each man and officer. No hurry—we'll be here longer than the Fat Boys back home have reckoned.

"Questions?"

"Sir, you expecting problems?" Tweed wondered.

"You must be psychic, Mr. Tweed. This has so far been a happy ship. Double base pay for special duty. Mustn't call it a hazardous or one-way cruise. They get double time toward retirement. A list of benefits as long as an opium dream. But once we get into the asteroid belt and we're peppered with meteorites till seams begin to leak and rivets get loose, and every son of a bitch aboard, including me, begins to feel that there is an asteroid with his name on it, there'll be too much thought of *home-sweet-home*.

"Near as I remember my reading, Columbus had a tough time convincing the crew that they weren't about to sail off the edge of a flat world and drop into space. The further they sailed, the closer he got to mutiny."

"Too bad they wouldn't let Admiral Courtney join us," Tweed contributed.

"That's what I thought, but more and more, I figure that they did me a favor and didn't realize it."

"You mean," Daly asked, "you're finally beginning to think that his deck might be short a few cards? Like, imagining he's Emperor of the Galaxy?"

"Don't sell him short? Admiral Courtney is the best. Not only scientifically and technically, but he's been accustomed to command for more years than any of us have lived. But being aboard and not being the final authority, that would stick in his craw.

"So, we're lucky. But getting back to problems—you both are the only ones aboard who know that I've got some friends stuck in the Martian Gardens Ecology Project. No matter how the Black Box screwed things up, it was my talking that got Lani and her friends mixed up in it. So, before we take off for Saturn, I am going to get them aboard a home-bound cruiser."

Daly nodded. "Uh-huh, we did a lot of figuring."

"That was from far away. Now that we're within a handful of *kay-ems* of where they are, I see it isn't as easy as it looked. So, I have to stall and make shake down flights while I get squared away for the rescue raid. Any thinking you come up with, let me in on it.

"Now the orders of the day. Caspar, publish them.

"The Mayor of Maritania's holding a reception for officers and crew. Except for guard and essential services, officers and men will attend, and in proper uniform.

"When reception's over, ground leave for all except guard and necessary services. No ground patrol needed, Maritania police are sufficient for the drunk and disorderly.

"Mr. Tweed, you will wear the Skipper Mask and take my place at the reception. I'll be in town, incognito, sizing things up." He dipped into his desk, got a paper which he handed to the First Officer. "Here's my speech. Till I come back, you're in command. Daly, when you're not on duty, prowl the town and see what ideas you come up with."

"Before you leave," Daly said, "be sure you've got your Special Agent badge."

Garvin chuckled. "It could come in handy! Okay, take your posts. And when you're in town, remember you're officers. Act like officers at all times."

Tweed brushed back his cowlick, and looked perplexed. "Sir, I don't quite get that—that covers a lot of territory—"

"Simple, Caspar! Don't get stumbling-fighting-puking drunk, and stay out of whorehouses that are restricted to enlisted men. We are impersonating *gentlemen*—never forget that."

When Garvin quit the *Saturnienne* and followed the pressurized passage to the tremendous dome of the spaceport, he wore knee-length jacket, slacks, and a felt skull cap—all gray, except for black shoes with substantial soles silenced by sponge rubber. Except for his purposeful walk and self-assured carriage, he was a standard nonentity. His Special Agent badge, palmed and flashed as he neared the guard, got him into the spaceport.

Once inside the vast enclosure, he stepped to the concealment of a compound column of structural duralumin and put on his mask. Except where it changed the contour of nose, and altered the angle of cheek bones, the disguising film was extremely thin and porous.

Approaching one of the cabs waiting for passengers, he said to the Gook driver, "Maritania's a lot bigger these days." He gestured. "More domes. Six–seven years since I was here."

He spoke the "pidgin" which bridged the gap between the language of the aborigines and English, the universal language of international Maritania. Then he made an elbow-bending gesture, followed by parentheses, vertically repeated: the female silhouette. No further talk was required.

The driver grinned, wagged his head. Garvin got into the battery-powered cab, and the vehicle nosed into the eight-kilometer stretch of tube which connected the spaceport with Maritania. As the cab whirred along, making something near twenty kilometers an hour, he leaned back and got a ground view of the barren planet.

A second and a third circle of hemispherical segments now girdled the central dome which had enclosed early Maritania. A fourth ring of hemispheres was under construction. Far to his right the gleaming columns of a hoist rose from the mouth of one of the mines which supplied isotopes superior to their Terrestrial counterparts. A narrow-gauge line reached from hoist to processing plant: the rails mirrored the ruddy light of a sinking sun. A train of ore cars crept along the tracks. Presently, as he neared the domes of the city, Garvin could no longer see the big bubble of the Ecology Project, much less distinguish the manned stations along the meridian.

"Inspector Morgan," he mused, "probably bought Lani's yarn about the meteorite that conked him, and by now, Lani's concluded that he's a lot better than no customers at all . . ." He grinned and winked at an imaginary presence. "But if she likes him so well that she'll turn down a chance to go home, I'm buying drinks for the house."

And then he was in the green girdle of Maritania: trees, shrubs; vines which twined the full height of towering columns. Once through the concentric circle of residential areas, where apartment buildings reached six and eight stories without crowding the lower hemispherical segments, he approached the fringe of the business district. Shop fronts peeped from behind veiling vines. Despite his extensive travels, freighting and soldiering in Liberation campaigns, he saw now an amazing array of flower and foliage the like of which he'd never previously encountered. Maybe he'd been too distracted by girl-watching to be observing botanical subjects.

As the dense vegetation obscured the lowering sun, street lights were coming on. Ahead, neons blazed red and blue.

"Far enough, here," he told the driver, and got out. "You know good places?"

The sharp-faced Gook pointed. "Plenty, that way," and gave him half a dozen cards. "One is my card, Igor that's me, when you need a cab. One, good place for prospector-digger things. Rent truck, space hat and coat. Other good places? *Luna Tavern, Silver Palace*— give my card, they treat you right. You go that way, up straight ahead."

As Garvin strolled, never free of thoughts on liberating Lani, he nonetheless wondered more and more about the aborigines, the contradictory yarns about their origin, their mode of existence before the first Terrestrian explorers found them, the Nonexistent who could not be explained away. As a young spaceman, he'd never bothered with question or answer; he'd been too busy meeting life to have time for questions beyond the problem at hand.

He'd drunk the fermented juices and the distilled spirits which the Gooks made, he'd eaten the strange fruit and vegetables they grew in their subsurface caverns and crevasses, but he wasted no queries on how they had conserved or manufactured an atmosphere so near the Terrestrian that they could get along readily in the synthetic atmosphere of Maritania.

He had never gone with the universal notion that Gooks were somewhat less than human: they resembled Orientals in many respects, such as facial structure, head shape, and for several centuries, Asiatics, Malays, and others had been accepted as quite human, though scarcely the sort of persons with whom one would associate, except to demonstrate belief in the mandatory doctrines of Democracy.

The Gook females who worked in shops and offices and as technicians often seemed brighter than their terrestrial counterparts, and when tricked out, as some were, in Terran garments, just as attractive; and the *piquante* exotica, somewhat more so. But these the space crews ignored, and the girls seemed not to object to discrimination.

Probably there was never a whore or taxi dancer so crude as to let a customer suspect that she considered herself far more civilized than he or any other Terrestrian. And this question did not crop up until after the space boom fell apart, and Garvin turned his hand to freighting irrigation gear into Turkistan, where he met Djénane Khanoum. He learned why his people were neither loved nor respected as they craved most pathetically to be, and why instead they were exploited and played for chumps and suckers, ever the despised easy-marks.

"Most of you look down on anyone, on anything different from you. At the same time, there's your passion for meddling and trying to force your beliefs on the backward people, your social and your religious muddlings. Always the pretense of benevolence and always feeling so superior because you're wealthier. You're incapable of friendship yourselves, so, you try to buy friendship, not knowing any other way."

He had no rebuttal, nor any words for a long stretch, until the obvious occurred to him: "You've made me welcome—all right, one of the family."

She'd laughed happily at his perplexity. "You're *different*! One of the exceptions. You really like us and our customs, and you're not pretending, the way most of your people do. We see through them and their false front and their missionary-superiority!"

In retrospect, he had begun to realize how blind he had been during his space days. The more he saw of Djénane and her people, the more he felt that between them and the Gooks there was a kinship, though he knew little enough of Gook thinking.

Same old Mars . . . old stuff, just more of it. Although really too young for nostalgia, Garvin had aged beyond his years. Once more, he'd come to one of life's crossroads. The first had been when he quit home for a war and for the space life. And then, that marriage—

he'd married a social order. But this, his here-and-now, was the ultimate venture. He was about to make Mars a Terran suburb: and his memories made him ever more aware that Destiny walked with him.

He paused in one of the shops which sold, rented, and serviced electrically powered capsules and four-wheel-drive trucks. Picking up leaflets and a price schedule, he moved on. In another, he got answers and a card. His reflection in a shop window assured him that his mask would not draw a second glance.

Across the street, a hotel, with a vacancy notice in blue neon. Right at hand, space gear for rent—helmets, suits, oxygen kits—whatever prospector or mechanic need, here it was.

The salesgirl explained in Gook-English, "Pay when bring back. No bring back, no pay, work in mines, you onnerstan plenty?"

"Me savvy plenty," he told her, and figured that his fool question had established him as a newcomer.

From the beginning, Maritania and the remainder of the planet was international: the Gooks didn't count. Although North American financed, administered, and policed, Terra's first colony had become a miniaturization of all his Terrestrial soldierings and freightings. In a few blocks of strolling he had heard more languages than he could recognize, much less understand.

A song writer had predicted that there would always be an England. More than the colors, and the imposing Consulate General of the United Kingdom sustained the prediction: although the several which Garvin identified did not have umbrella in hand, neatly furled and serving as cane, and the *London Times* thrust into side pocket, these isolated, these self-contained men wearing conservatively tailored worsteds of classical design could not be other than English.

Had there been no Japanese, he would have been amazed: had the Chinese been lacking, he would have considered himself out of the galaxy. Greeks, Hindus, and Armenians—standard equipment. The Europeans—these he couldn't identify, for they were look-alikes.

More lights, brighter lights, now that he was out of

the shop and office area, and into the fun center of
Maritania. He glanced at the cards which the cab man
had given him, and looked ahead—

*Beefeaters Rendezvous, Spirits, Ale, Stout, Porter,
Selim's Shashlik Loqanda, L'Auberge Martienne, Mars-
burgers Biggest & Best, MacDougal's Magnum-
Burgers, Mandarin Chop Suey & Chow Mein.*

The electric blue and frosty silver of the winking sign
which reached far out over the sidewalk reminded Garvin that Igor had favored the *Silver Palace* and a cab
driver in Maritania rated every bit of cumshaw he got
from restaurant or hook shop to whom he steered a
customer. With enough breaks, Igor would buy the cab
and be in business for himself . . .

Garvin was about to set out for that spot when a trio
of the *Saturnienne*'s crew emerged from the *Silver Palace.* Three abreast, they hogged the pavement as they
bore toward him.

Edging into the entrance of *Rentals & Parkings,* Garvin just missed being brushed against the wall. His flare
of resentment was cooled by the realization that during
their long flight, these men had been restricted by narrow companionways, narrow passages, cramped quarters. In comparison with the *Saturnienne,* Maritania was
a city of boulevards and lordly promenades.

Before Garvin emerged from shelter, the crewmen
halted, gabbled for a moment, then crossed the street.
They stepped into the *Luna Tavern.* Disregarding Igor's
recommendation, Garvin followed. He relied on his disguise, and he had no scruples against spying or eavesdropping. Whatever he learned was going to be used for
the ship and her crew; and he had not a qualm about
putting himself first of all on the list of prospective ben-
eficiaries.

Destiny walked with Garvin—*destiny,* or *pure luck,*
these were merely words, not the reality which he
sensed—the three he had barely avoided were high on
his list of especially interesting members of the crew.

And then he recalled that few aboard the *Saturnienne* were not pointedly interesting. In any spot as
small as the capital of Mars, one didn't need coinci-
dence to lead him to encounters more than casual.

Chapter 19

Garvin took a booth adjoining the one occupied by the trio from the *Saturnienne*: Landis, Roswell, Parker, drinking but not drunk.

"How's it stack up, so far?" Landis demanded, apparently resuming talk they'd quit when the waiter took their order.

"Everyone's a bit too nice to us," Roswell grumbled.

"You'd gripe if they were hanging you with a new rope."

"They don't expect us back."

"Who says so?" Parker challenged.

"Well, no one, not in so many words," Landis continued. "It's the way they look at us, and it's the voices."

After a moment, Parker—Garvin was sure the voice was Parker's—picked it up: "Mmm . . . come to think of it, it has been different, this time."

Roswell got back in: "I don't know enough of the lingo to talk it but I caught words that fit together, and too damn well."

"Such as?"

"We'll get hammered to junk in the asteroid area."

"Manure! We're equipped for it. How would these Gook monkeys know, anyway?"

"They acted like they did."

"No Gook ever acted as if he knew anything."

"This was a she. The Mayor's secretary."

"What'd she say?"

"How dangerous it was, a million years ago, when her Gook ancestors used to fly as far as Jupiter, and figured it wasn't paying off and so they quit and tended to home business, caging the air here on Mars before it all got away."

"I told you, nothing a God-damn Gook says means anything."

"Uh, did she look like a good piece?"

"Anything's good after a long cruise."

"More I think of, the more I'm for jumping ship."

"Jesus, you can't get away with it, you'd be picked up and put to work in the mines."

"The hell I would! The union would show that the skipper was arbitrary, cruel, and unusual, and it might end up costing his ass!"

"Well, you'd miss your bonus and retirement."

"Getting socked with an asteroid is sure retirement, but you don't get no pension."

Parker, the veteran got back into the trialogue. "I still think it's not so good a pitch. She's got radar and deflector panes and shields, and anyway, the union would crap in your mess kit—the skipper's married into an important family. If he preferred charges, you might end up by just liking it . . ."

Ordering anything as expensive as Terran liquor would make him conspicuous, so Garvin shuddered in anticipation, and gulped the fungus gin the waiter had brought him. The spying was hardly worth the time and the drinking ordeal. Or so he reckoned until the voices came in stronger again.

". . . I tell you, Barrett tried jumping ship, and got his tail burned proper . . ."

This was an interesting sidelight, all the more so since jumping ship hadn't been recorded in Barrett's dossier. Hadn't kept him from getting a Warrant Officer's rating.

"Now, if the skipper got cold feet," one began, hopefully.

"That son of a bitch hasn't sense enough to change his mind," Roswell grumbled. "We must've all been doped to the eyebrows to get us signed up."

As far as Garvin could recollect, this was the first piece of independent thinking that any of the Plastic Populace had attempted in a long time. Unfortunately, it came at the wrong time and place.

". . . now, if something happened so we had to haul ass back home . . . you mean, for refitting?"

Music was making eavesdropping difficult.

". . . who'd want to stay here, even if he wouldn't get picked up? . . . Moving in with the Gooks would not be a treat . . . their God-damn popskull . . . Well, sure you can get used to drinking the stuff. Some of them Gook girls are good screwing . . . For Christ's sweet sake, they're not really human. What the hell's the matter with that one over there . . ."

About time the talk got to girl-watching, Garvin figured, and then, glancing back and toward the entrance, to cover the entire field of view, he realized that he'd missed something. *"The one over there,"* the one sitting alone at the table next to the entrance—no wonder that the talk about jumping ship had been dumped!

"Looks like she's waiting for someone . . ."

"Bet she's lonesome . . ."

"There's three of us . . . One of us ought to make it."

"Match for first turn—"

"Odd man first . . ."

Garvin was sure that the girl was not on the prowl for pickups. She wasn't looking about to catch someone's eye, anyone's eye—and she wasn't dressed right for a hooker. All in all, she was high class—even if she was a professional, she was no pickup, of this much, Garvin was sure.

She wore the usual tunic, which exaggerated her slenderness. It was pearl gray, with piping of brocade, and maroon frogs to secure it. Her finely modeled features had the repose of a mask: she sat there, withdrawn and far behind the lovely front. The eyes, however, were all alive and restless; oriental, yet with only a suggestion of slant, just sufficient to harmonize with her check bones.

Her feet, shod with gilded sandals, were slender, small, with elegant ankles. A velvet hood with spangles

and pendants outlined the shape of her head. Her blue-
black hair, twisted in a gleaming knot at the nape of her
neck, was secured by Chinese style pins, each conspicuous as a stiletto with an agate haft.

She sensed that she'd become a subject of discussion.
The dark brows moved as in recognition. But by then,
the three spacemen had matched to see who would be
the lucky man.

Parker crossed the floor to claim his prize.

An elderly Martian, wearing a skull cap, knee-length
tunic, and flopping black pants approached in time to
explain that his daughter was going home, and at once.

"Sit down, she's dancing with me!" Parker announced.

Garvin knew that the worst this girl faced would be
annoyance. If the Gook bouncers couldn't handle Parker, or simply did not wish to take sides, the patrol
would say it with nightsticks. This was none of Garvin's
business. But for his prowling incognito, this would be
routine business: put Parker under arrest and send him
back to report to the Master at Arms. What got Garvin
to his feet was that the Martian girl brought Djénane to
mind—not so much a resemblance as a likeness of flavor, or presence, and especially when she came to her
feet, confronting the lout.

She broke away from Parker's grasp. It hadn't been a
commanding grip, a strong detention. It could have
passed for a nudge toward the dance floor, had she
been willing.

Objecting, the old man got a backhanded slap that
knocked him against the adjoining table. Glassware
spilled. He took a back flip over a chair.

The affair had not yet reached the point when a
North American could reasonably interfere on behalf of
a female Gook.

This one, Asiatic seeming in the way of Djénane,
had a finer nose, almost aquiline—or, might one say,
almost straight? Now that she was on her feet, her posture revealed her quality: there was about her carriage,
straight up, regal resentment, without a touch of alarm.
This was a superior person, vainly defended by an old

man with more spirit than physique, yet proud as his daughter.

Each was a person of quality, as Garvin reckoned things. Whatever the Gook custom, in Turkistan honor would demand that Parker's life should end within seconds. The laying on of hands in an unrespectful manner was a mortal insult—a weapon, however deadly, was resisted but not resented among gentlefolk.

Landis and Roswell, alerted by the shattering of glass, were on their feet. And now Garvin was alarmed. Where he had last seen and loved such a girl, the women were proud and deadly. What appeared to be a hairpin usually was good for a fatal thrust.

If she wounded that clod, she'd be in trouble. Garvin hoped Parker would back away rather than tangle with a stiletto-wielding hellion.

True to type, she reached for a hairpin.

Garvin stretched his legs, readying not to go to bat for a lady who had been affronted but to keep her out of serious trouble. And then things did become sticky. The old man brushed the girl aside before she could draw a hair pin. He snatched the agate haft, plucked a fine sliver of twinkling steel from her hair. For a woman to avenge the mortal insult inflicted on him, that would be the ultimate dishonor.

Garvin shouted, startling the girl, her father, and Parker, checking all motion. He addressed the old man in the Uighur speech of Turkistan. "Hold it! He's mine!" He turned on Parker, and roared, "*Kupuk oglu!* Son of a whore—"

The old man knew that he had an ally, one whose intervention he could accept, honorably. Whether he got even a word of Garvin's haggled Uighur was immaterial—the speech was not English, and that established the stranger as a friend.

Parker also got it. He snarled, "You Gook bastard!"

Parker's shipmates were on their feet and stretching their legs. In moving toward Garvin, they crowded each other more than they should or need have. Other Terrans, spacemen or emigrants, were moving from their tables, though they were taking their time. They were only interested. A miniature race war had not yet broken out. Garvin did not know how much time he had, but it was little enough. He had to clean up before the spectators decided that he was a Gook getting quite too far out of line.

The crewmen followed Garvin's baiting move. In principle, though certainly not in detail, it was comparable to a bull fighter's drawing the beast off balance and into a new line of attack. The big fellow, Landis, broad and well over six feet tall, was now nearest of the trio. The group, still moving as a group, had two parts of the steam roller blocked by the most formidable one, the spearhead.

Poised, ready to pounce, Garvin avoided anything resembling a *kung fu* or *karate* posture. No sense in telegraphing his intent. As Landis struck out to clobber him, Garvin evaded the blow and with both hands, caught the fellow's forearm. He got his shoulder under the taller man's arm, sank to one knee, shifted his weight.

Landis threw himself—he'd charged and had nowhere to go but over Garvin's nearer knee—thigh nearly horizontal, like a low hurdle. His flip-flop ended in a floor-shaking thump.

What had happened to the man's arm was easy guessing for Garvin. Whether Landis would be able to make the cruise was a question which would concern Landis only when he regained consciousness and began to feel what had happened.

Bounding clear of his victim, Garvin whirled to confront the survivors. He got a glimpse of the girl: she swayed a little, and her teeth showed a little, and there was a deadliness in her eyes which made her a participant. The old man's pose was tense, however withdrawn he now was, and he still had his daughter's hairpin, an extention of his lean, boney hand.

But most of all, Garvin saw Parker, dagger in hand. Like many a seafarer or soldier in foreign service, he was one who never went abroad without being prepared for trouble. He'd learned early in life, and habit went with him.

The flash of steel which the old man had drawn from the girl's hair had drawn a natural response, and Landis, lying there, a groaning heap of twitching meat, was alarming. So Parker closed in, point first, the double-edged blade good for stab or slash.

Parker hadn't seen how Landis had stepped into trouble.

Garvin swayed, evading the thrust. He was inside Parker's guard before the man could slash. Instead of the finger-stab to the throat, with the risk of killing his man, he caught him on the point of the chin; heel of the hand did it, and so thoroughly that Garvin didn't waste a kick to make sure. Instead, he snatched the dagger, and confronted Roswell.

"Next man? Knife? No knife?" This was in English. The survivor didn't recognize the voice. Garvin was quietly deadly. Spectators backed off toward the booths they had quit.

The girl took the unused stilettto and sheathed it in her hair.

Meanwhile, someone had turned in an alarm.

A patrol came trotting in, two Gooks and two white men.

Garvin, badge palmed, gave the chief of the group one look and said, "Take 'em where they belong. Not that it's any of your business, but I cooled them by hand. This knife used to belong to that one—" He pointed. "I'm keeping it to remember him by. Now I am taking my friends home."

Whether "Special Agent," serene effrontery and self-assurance, or the display of hand-cooled meat did it, Garvin got no argument.

The girl addressed the patrol chief, and in English which, for all its alien intonation and cadence, was quite understandable. She offered an ID card, as she said, "Whores and taxi dancers are found in some of the other places, but never here. Which is why I sat here, waiting for my father. This gentleman—" She indicated the still unconscious Parker. "Made a mistake. He wouldn't listen when I tried to explain that my father, Samgan Manioglu, would be here, any moment."

The patrol chief gave Garvin a long, hard look, an afterthought, in all probability suggesting that he'd bought self-assurance a bit too readily. Garvin closed the distance between them, and said, quietly, "You're doing some guessing. You can make an ass of yourself, putting your guess on record. Or, I'll string along with you and keep this confidential. Use your judgment. Thank you."

He turned his back on the patrol and addressed the Old Man.

"*Tura,*" he began, in quasi-Uighur, "let me call a taxi. Or get a rental car, right next door. If you don't understand—"

The girl cut in, "Sir, my English is no worse than your Gook, which I'm sure you didn't learn here. Our car is parked next door, in the garage-parkings. Won't you ride with us and have refreshments at our home?

Garvin glanced over his shoulder. The patrol was waiting for an ambulance. One of the group was saying, "Shut up! Whoever he is, he didn't get around to you. Must be your lucky day. All you lost is your knife."

Garvin followed Samgan Manioglu and his daughter to the parking spot next door. There Garvin unpeeled his mask. After a moment of approving scrutiny, she said, "You look much nicer this way! But the killing-face—oh, that was beautiful!"

"That reminds me," Garvin cut in, and dipped under his jacket. He produced Parker's dagger, and presented it, haft foremost, to the old man. "I do not give this. I do not sell it. The man sends it and says that he is un-armed, and hopes that you will not kill him if you meet him again."

Samgan smiled, inclined his head. "He is young. You could have killed him—" A bit of pantomime toward the throat. "But you didn't. And I am too old to carry grudges. You gave him his life. Could I begrudge it? Or could Azadeh?"

Once they had the air lock of Maritania behind them, Azadeh asked, "Sometimes you speak Gook, sometimes English, but how comes it you speak words almost like our real talk, the not-Gook talk of my peo-ple? Like it, but hard to understand?"

Before he had done sketching his Turkistani days, Azadeh had swung from the main road leading to the mines, angling out and across a flat expanse. Presently

Azadeh observed, "So that is why you knew that when dad took my hair pin, it was for honor, and you knew that no matter what happened, even if it killed him—"

"I learned a few of the customs of those people—your cousins maybe? There would have been too much trouble, so I took a hand. That fellow is a clod. Never heard of honor."

Presently, Azadeh snapped off the headlights, snapped them on, and then off again. Ahead, as though from the ground, a warm glow began. The road dipped gently, and Garvin saw a surface curved as an inverted saucer. Once the car was a foot or two below the rocky expanse, it leveled off.

Buzzer notes, shorts and longs, apparently a signal: an air lock gate opened and Azadeh drove on, as though into Maritania's dome. Beyond was a softly lighted indefinite expanse of gardens and stunted trees, among which nestled little dwellings of sun-dried brick. Finally, she turned into a walled inclosure, a courtyard whose further extremity terminated in a low, squarish house of brick.

Garvin followed Azadeh and her father into a room which reminded him of his freighting days. Rammed-earth benches skirted two walls. At the vertex of the angle they made was a fireplace. Whether this was purely symbolic, reminiscent of days when fuel abounded, or whether the aborigines had a source of fuel was another of the many queries which would have to wait. Samgan Manioglu and his daughter left him without any desire for the details of their living.

Instead of rugs like those of Khotan or Yarkand, there were floor and bench coverings of vegetable fiber pounded to make a sort of felt. At Samgan's gesture, Garvin seated himself by the fireplace: presumably this was the place of honor. Not knowing, he made no show, as he would otherwise have, of declining the guest seat until his host insisted. He drew a deep breath, exhaled, watched Azadeh going down the hall which led to the rear of the house—he liked the way she carried herself: Fore or aft, the view was elegant, graceful.

He glanced about, nodded. "I'm at home. I belong here."

The old man smiled. "You have been here before."

Whimsically, Garvin said, "A million years ago?"

And then Azadeh came back with a copper tray on which were glazed earthenware cups the size of Chinese wine cups and of similar shape. From the flask she poured smoky tasting-gin—he could think of no better word for the drink.

"Our life is primitive," she said. "We enjoy the dome city sometimes and some of the things freighted in from your world." The old man said, "We'd invite our neighbors. But there are things you want to ask?"

"There are, yes."

"Please ask. If we say *I don't know,* that may mean that we really don't know, or that it is forbidden to say what we do know."

"That is understood," Garvin answered, and waited while Azadeh refilled his glass and her father's. "Your good health, *tura!*" He bowed, set down his glass. Then, "Several years ago, I used to come from Terra to your home, in freighters. This time we came at a different angle, not the small ship's way. So I noticed what I'd never seen before. Well away in a flat bottom bowl, it looked as if engineers had leveled the ground."

"You saw something unusual?"

Garvin nodded. "Yes. Not bright, I knew it was metal."

"The shape of the thing?"

"It looked like a space cruiser. I never heard or read of one that crashed on Mars."

"There are many stories," Samgan observed, reflectively. "No two are alike. None are all truth, none are all falsehood. One thing is sure—our people were here before this planet lost so much air, so much water. We had centuries to learn the things which your people are trying to do in a few years.

"What you saw did not crash. It was landed by people who did not want to leave." Azadeh and her father exchanged glances. The girl said, "You're more than ever interested? I knew you would be. We know all about your *Saturnienne.* So many of us work in the offices and shops."

Samgan drew a deep breath. "I'm too old and battered, but it's not late for you. Azadeh, drive our guest out for a look." He got to his feet, laboriously. "The house is yours." Bowing, he turned to the hallway.

"Good night, Dad!" Azadeh turned to Garvin. "I'll find a couple of capes. We'll need them."

Presently, Azadeh and her guest drove out of a mica-roofed crevasse to the surface, and after a kilometer or two, set out across open country, weaving in and out among boulders and jagged outcroppings. They had gone no more than ten kilometers when they came to a rim, beyond which was a sandy bowl. A thousand meters ahead, Garvin saw something like a space cruiser lying half buried by drifting sand. Jutting from the surface were latticed metal members, part of the rigging gear for lowering the shell, and to raise it to its landing struts, ready for takeoff. This was no junk center. This was business, lurking since days long before history's beginning.

Garvin shivered, as though a chill had raced down his spine.

"Cold?" she mocked, amiably malicious, fully aware.

"If I weren't a guest, I'd spank your bottom till you—till—you know what the sight of that—"

"My bottom, *tura?*"

"You little bitch, you know what I mean! That ship's waiting, it's been waiting—how many centuries, millenia?—waiting for takeoff day! I saw one like it in Turkistan. I'm seeing truth—Sure it gives me the shivers!"

"Put on your helmet, we'll go in. I have a flashlight."

He followed Azadeh to a port. It responded to her touch. The beam of her light picked out details different from yet comparable to the fittings of modern cruisers. Something odd about it all: the inclined plane from the bottom of the bowl to the port was firm, a walkway of rammed earth.

Through his mike he said, "Those are well-trained winds you have around here, doing a job like that, keeping the approach just right, just at threshold height."

She secured the port, flashed her light, found and twisted a valve. "Solar power gives us current for the colony, and our chemical workings—air and water and what-not. You must've guessed as much?"

"Had to. Gook ways and means are never discussed."

"I suspected that," she said, and as the pressure built up, took off her helmet.

When vapor tubes came to life, Garvin saw what was partly ancient and partly salvage from Martian Spaceways shops; and, some from the stores of Maritania.

The most ancient was a shrine of metal in which was the image of a woman wearing a tall miter from which depended ornaments of gold and of tinkling jewels. The odor, heavy and sweet, and timeless: incense had been burned. The most modern furnishings were sofas, chairs, a small table and a coffee service.

"Oh, yes, Rod, the thieving Gooks steal what they can, and buy what they can't steal. Oh, yes, there's a kitchen, when we have festivals, we need one."

Garvin nodded. "The cruiser that brought your people from wherever it brought them—now it's a temple." He went to the shrine, put his hands palm to palm and bowed three times. "In some of the civilized parts of my world, a stranger always bows and says *how-do-you-do* to the gods of the house."

"You learned that from the *Gooks* of your world?"

He nodded. Azadeh went to the shrine, bowed thrice, and faced Garvin. "I gave thanks to The Lady for the hoodlums, the human garbage, the trash—because of them, we met." She caught his hand. "You want to see more? Some of the ship has no air."

Once helmetted, he followed Azadeh aft. However strange it was, he felt at home, and finally took Azadeh's flashlight, to lead the way. There was a likeness of plan and layout. In the power plant he saw that Admiral Courtney had been right, whether by guess or intuition. The reactors were familiar. The ore in the bunkers however was unlike any of the thorium isotopes which came from Terra or Mars. He picked up several chunks, hefted them. They were amazingly heavy for their bulk.

"Mind if I take a sample?"

"There's enough left for five ships," she answered. He handed Azadeh the light and followed her to the quarters supplied with air. Before she touched the switch to evacuate the lock, she stood, wavering, half turning toward the shrine room.

He said, "We'll bow good night to The Lady?"

"Oh—" Clearly she'd been thinking of something else. "Of course! Yes . . ." This, absently. "I was thinking . . ."

Instead of making for the shrine, she shifted toward Garvin, looked up, eyes dark and magnificent. The kiss was open-mouthed and everlasting, or so it seemed until their lips parted—while the embrace became closer than ever, Garvin managed to say, "You're dangerous bait—quit looking so God-awful beautiful."

"Close the eyes, and don't see me how I look," she mocked, and raised her mouth.

"Gorgeous wench!" He slapped her behind, making a ripe, mellow sound. "Break away before it's for keeps. Listen to me—"

When Azadeh relaxed, there was between them a gap of at least a millimeter. After a breath, a deep breath which made her tunic swell beautifully, she said, "Do I stand listening—to nothing?"

"Hear this—this is no drill! I have a wife at home, a Number Two Lady in the Ecology Department—and some responsibilities."

Her smile was Infinite Wisdom, Universal Knowledge.

"I am not married, I have no Number Two Man, and, none of the responsibilities. Oh, yes! I remember, now. When you interrupted my thinkings, it was this— something I was going to tell you, I was reaching for words—but now the English, how to say it? . . . I will sleep with you tonight. We can stay here, we can go home. When my father said, 'The house is yours' . . ."

"It would be a lot more polite, going home!"

They forgot to bow to The Lady, but they did remember to bundle up in their capes, put on their helmets, before they raced to the car.

Chapter 20

Azadeh stretched luxuriously, twisted from the waist, and made the most of body and of a gown which had not come from any Martian commissary. It was deluxe Terran, a shockingly expensive outfit with so many panels of lace inset that Garvin couldn't decide whether she was dressed or naked. After a long moment to relish his appreciation, she drew a deep breath, exhaled, nodded contentedly.

"Now I know you like me."

"*Now*—well, when did you think I didn't? Beautiful idiot!"

"I wasn't so sure. You know, in the temple when I said, tonight I sleep with you, your eyes changed, you forgot our kissings, something troubled you."

He frowned, and then he remembered. "You're a mind reader! But you didn't understand what you read."

He tried to kiss her, but she evaded him. "No, tell me first."

"Oh, all right! I remembered that your father told us, 'the house is yours,' and left us, with his good-night. As good as telling you to sleep with me."

"And you didn't want to, but you had to be nice with me," she mocked.

"I wondered whether you were obeying orders or if *you* were inviting me for the night."

"Now you know? And suppose it was both, obedience and want to?"

"Twice as good, of course! Double dip!"

"Double dip," she echoed, and savored the words, until in her thinkings she returned, fully present and with a fresh query: "Something else worries you, what is it?"

"Do I look worried?"

"Mmmmm . . . no, but there is something maybe I have not tell you enough?" She saw now that he was shaping thoughts, groping for words. Azadeh carried on, "Some of me, you know all about, some of me you don't know any of it."

"We speak part Gook, part English, two bits' worth of Uighur Turki, and do our best when we're not talking at all."

"So, you are a scientist? an engineer? All must be precision? Say it part Gook, part book English, part Uighur, and then with sign language—and, don't I read your mind anyway?"

"Then why the hell don't you just *read* it?"

"More fun when you are talking it."

"Here we go. There's not a stretch mark on you." And it was time for sign language. He traced belly and thighs, sleek and unblemished. She twisted her hips and hoisted the elegant gown to facilitate. He cupped a breast, and with delicate touch, described a tiny circle about the nipple. "All new—not a line—Past two, three, four hours, you've acted as if you couldn't get pregnant, no matter how long you worked at it."

"Never have, not yet, but the idea is not alarming."

Garvin tried to read the dark eyes, long lashed, glowing, cryptic. "*The idea is not alarming*—and we lost no time tumbling into bed because we'll have little enough time together, my chances of coming back from a war are a lot better than coming back from Saturn."

"That is a true speaking. Too much truth for happy loving tonight. But not the first true thing."

"Tell me, before you forget it."

"So few Gooks—there have to be only a few, and we know herb medicines, never too much pregnant women—not enough room for many—and our people have lived here so long, everyone is everyone else's cousin.

She made a billowing lavish gesture from navel and downward, and cupped her breasts. "When you come back from Saturn, if I have dark nipples and stretch marks, you'll know you've put new blood in this colony. You'll be what your people call Space Hero."

She made a whimsical play on words relating to filling an empty space.

"If you invite me back often enough between now and takeoff, you may be that way before I leave. While I'm resting up from exploring—you called it the Well of the Angels—let's get back to what I was saying before you interrupted me with questions."

"Of course I interrupted you! Sometimes I think in North America nobody knows how to appreciate a woman."

"Between now and takeoff time, I could learn. Tell me now, what was wrong with Terra or wherever your people came from? Every time you tell me something, the story is different."

"You'll have time to hear all my stories, then you can make up your own."

"Time! God damn it, woman, what little time I have, I am stuck with that problem I told you about—seeing my friends at Ecology."

"No problem. You can't even get into the dome."

"How do *you* know?"

"Like I told you, I work in main headquarters, in Administration offices. Every kind of job nobody else doesn't like to do. So, I learn a mix-up of things."

"And so?"

"There was a message, an order to the important man, Sherman Wesson, chief exile he calls himself. No visitors to Ecology. Severe penalty for attempting communication. Too much I don't know yet. Your girl in Station Five, maybe her fault, maybe not, but she is complicated—involved, I mean."

"She would be. Could you get at the intercom with main dome Ecology, and give Jim Ward a message?" He saw her expression change when he pronounced "Jim." Then, "Darling, no! I'd not ask you to help

Lani. I should not. I'm trying to get a dozen people out of the mess I got them into—as I told you—"

"You do not own me. I do not own you. I have borrowed you for a little while, you have borrowed me, but no one and nothing can take away our rememberings."

"My wife's behind all this mess!"

Azadeh appraised him, looking through him. She almost smiled. "Lover, you said that. I did not. But, you are right, saying it.

"You hate to ask me to help your girl at Station Five. Lani, is it not? You think I would not help her get home? I tell you that I do not own you, but you can't believe. Because you are a slave-owning people. And whoever owns a slave is a slave himself." She shuddered. "Being the slave of a slave!

"Among my people, no one can own another, not as parent, not as spouse, not as government. When my father in a round-about way told me to sleep with you, he knew that I would not mind, that I'd want you to have the restfulness, relaxingness of a woman's body, just as you'd need food or water—you don't have to love the food or the cook." She patted The Well of the Angels. "Where else could you get new life for what you lost facing my enemies? And my father's?"

Garvin knew the truth, though he'd never heard it put in those words: and he had nothing to say, being too busy learning. But, having nothing to say, he did say something:

"You don't like my people."

"Again, that's your saying. I loved you from that killing moment at the *Luna Tavern*. Each man, you could have killed him, beautifully, with bare hands, empty hands. I saw your fingers shape for killing jab to the throat, then they changed and with the hand-heel, you struck the chin, and out!

"Extravagant with your own life and lavish with another's. Someone said that your people are afraid to live and afraid to die, and that is true of most of you. The all-of-you—" She shrugged and made a gesture of disposal for keeps. "Savages, clowns, overgrown flabby children—with exceptions, yes."

They eyed each other until her expression softened,

ever more, as she saw Garvin, and not the invading, savage oaf.

"The all of you—the mass—we are maybe a million years older, maybe only a hundred thousand, but long enough. Of course we are superior, and we know that there is no equality among people, some are more excellent than others."

Looking beyond her words as words, he knew that Azadeh had spoken what he had sensed at least half his life. She was so very right, though it took him moments to swallow the unpalatable fact. He caught her under the arms, raised her to sitting up. He chuckled, shook his head. "Darling, you should meet our Plastic Populace! Maybe I can smuggle you to North America and—"

"You think I haven't? Where I work? Where we Gooks work, in mines or any place?" Azadeh swayed, twisted, and clung to him. "You're almost like one of my own people, or I'd never have made room between my legs, no matter how badly I wanted you."

After long moments of remembering much of his short life and its peaks, he said, "I wish I knew whether you Gooks were ever Terran people, or far-off star people."

"We're sure of a little. We've forgot our first home, but we remember much of Terra. So long ago that there was a pole star not the one that now marks north. The Terran folk were scientists, tremendous minds, magnificent intellects, idiots, half-witted children, no wisdom, and playing with deadly toys, besotted by insane religions and queer superstitions.

"They bred cattle and they bred plants, and had no use at all for scrubs, except where humans were concerned, and in that, they ignored heredity, they denied the aristocrat, rejected the best, and glorified the slob, the scrub, the lowest of the race was the ideal they followed.

"Your people are not yet where *they* were, but you do your best, and you may be more successful this time."

He frowned. "Succeeding where we once failed?"

She nodded, smiled happily; she glowed from an inner light. "This time, you may destroy most of yourselves, and Terra will be clean again, happy again, the Terra-Soul will be happy again when the vermin is exterminated."

He chuckled, but there was no mirth in him. "You do hate us!"

"Not really. My people, wherever we came from, we had much science and no wisdom—we went into space when we didn't know how to live in our own home. You're doing the same. You're breeding like flies in manure and looking for new worlds to ruin. And here you are, you'll release water and oxygen and nitrogen from minerals, and make an atmosphere like we used to have, like the one we made bit by bit, indoors as air and water left Mars . . . You outnumber us beyond all hope. If we killed all of you, others would come from Terra to exterminate us. So we have to wait till Nature is weary of you and helps you destroy yourselves."

When he knew that she had done speaking her thought, he said, "That must be true, too much of it anyway. You looked like The Lady in the shrine. Now you're Azadeh again."

In a flash, she was on her feet. She whisked the honeymoon gown over her head and reached for more practical garments. "You expect trickery and treachery, so you need sleep-sharpened wits. I'll drive you back. And when you can see me, call me at the office, I'll pick you up."

A few moments of dressing, and then, "Some at Ecology dislike you, some hate you. Take care of all your friends and when you have no more obligations you'll be free and we'll be together every night, for a little while."

Chapter 21

"Where have you been all day?" Tweed demanded when Garvin stepped into the officers' mess, where he and Daly were dallying over their afterbreakfast coffee.

"Studying trans-Martian space."

"You smell like something a lot warmer and cozier," Daly observed, and plucked a long black hair from Garvin's collar. "Not short and curly, but it might be radioactive."

Garvin plucked the long hair from Daly's dainty grasp. "If you'd soldiered in the Far East you'd know that what you're quipping about isn't curly—most of it's just slightly wavy."

Tweed got into the play: "Sir, I'll find solvent and get the lipstick wiped off. You're smeared all over."

Garvin countered, "If I hadn't practically shanghaied the two of you, I'd have you in the brig for insubordination. What's been going on since the reception? How'd ground leave go?"

"Parker's been conscious the past couple hours. Landis wishes he could stay unconscious, his arm wouldn't hurt so much."

"Any other casualties?"

Tweed carried on, "The funny-looking character who got sore when they started trifling with a Gook wench got tired taking care of two, and didn't tear Roswell apart. Police patrol brought them in. Want to see the report and prefer charges?"

"Seems to me they've been taken care of well enough."

The post mortem was interrupted by an orderly from the Administration building. He handed Garvin an envelope. Garvin sighed and opened the message. It was brief, but he said nothing for a good ten seconds. Then, "I'll be a son of a *bitch!*"

Tweed asked, "Sir, something go wrong?"

"The answer is yes, but it shouldn't be." Garvin turned to the orderly. "Give me that message pad and wait for my answer."

Writing the reply took little longer than had reading the disturbing words. The orderly was scarcely on his way when Garvin said, "Admiral Josiah Ambrose Courtney is at the Palace Hotel."

"Is that bad," Daly demanded, "or just unusual?"

"Both." He eyed Tweed and Daly. "You are too tactful to ask if he's here to rank me out and take command. In case you don't recall, I told both of you that I wanted a crew of veterans aboard, and that the Fat Boys back home said no to that notion."

"I remember. Democracy on the hoof. What do you make of this?"

"A retired officer couldn't ordinarily be put in command of anything, but my wife's cousin Alexander Heflin doesn't follow the book, he writes the book. A retired officer can be a consultant according to the regulations. Until I go to town and pay my respects and read his orders, it's a guessing game.

"Daly, inspectors are coming aboard to check her out after the shake down cruise. You remember where we planted bits of slip-shod fitting, after the inspections were finished at the shop.

"You keep an eye on this recheck. If they catch the botches we can figure that they're doing a tight job of looking her over. Seeing the Admiral is going to keep me busy."

When Garvin stepped into the sitting room of Admiral Courtney's suite the tall, slightly stooped veteran was on his feet to receive his visitor. He did not look as though he'd spent the past fifteen years in the Psychic

Rehabilitation Facility. Far back as Garvin could remember, the Admiral's hair had been white, the tanned face smooth, with a youthful ruddiness which contradicted the deep lines of the forehead and the grim, down-turned grooves at the corners of the broad mouth.

They regarded each other for a moment. For the first time, Garvin was sufficiently close to that controversial veteran to note the biting gray eyes which lanced from beneath bristling brows.

"You lost no time dropping in, Captain Garvin." The lean face brightened cordially, and he extended a long, firm hand. "I dare say you've had your hands full ever since you took command. Sit down—we have a lot to talk about."

"You can tell me a good deal more than I can tell you."

"You're sure of that?"

"Admiral Courtney, I doubt that you ever heard of me until quite recently. A good many of us have heard of you and your insisting that there have been prehistoric astronauts. That our space age is old stuff, just as our science in general is.

"While I was freighting in Turskistan, I found evidence that sustains your statements. There was more persistence than good judgment in my talk. It got me some time at the Psychological Rehabilitation Facility. I haven't the least idea whether or not you heard of my public recantation, after which I was released as having been rehabilitated. My being in command of the *Saturnienne* is one of the by-products of that charade.

"I am indebted to you for the basics in my modifications of what was to have been the *Space Princess*. I don't know whether her change of name will help her circle Saturn or bring her bad luck."

After a pause, Garvin resumed, "Admiral Courtney, I don't rank asking whether you are traveling under orders, or what those orders are." He got to his feet." All I have left to say is, *welcome aboard*. All I have to do is hear what you care to tell me. It's your move, sir."

The Admiral almost smiled. "Sit down, Captain. Sit down. I am traveling under orders." He twisted about in his chair, reached for a briefcase for a paper which he handed Garvin. "Your copy. I am not here to take command of the *Saturnienne*. I am going along for the ride. Being retired, I am qualified only as observer or consultant. I am an afterthought."

The quiet bitterness of those four final words added much to Garvin's apprehension. Having an unhappy admiral aboard could range from unpleasant to disastrous.

"Sir, you have just given me something to say."

"Let me hear it."

"When I appeared before the Consortium to give them—or should I say, 'it'?—my views on the crew I needed for this project, I asked for you and other retired officers who were physically fit. I made it clear that a handful of the most competent space men in North America had been my fellow inmates at the Rehab Facility, and that I wanted the benefit of their experience.

"Since I had recanted, had gone on the air to deny every word of my retraction, and had ended by being put in command of the *Saturnienne*, some of my comrades in unorthodox thinking should have a share in the enterprise. Any comment, sir?"

"As to your logic, it is self-evident. Please carry on."

"The answer was an uncompromising *no*. They wanted a cross section of American Democracy. They did *not*, repeat, *not* want a crew of the Elite."

"An Elite from the Psycho Factory," Courtney said, and this time the admiral's bitterness told Garvin that his apprehensions had been justified. "An afterthought!"

"Their afterthought, sir. Not mine. I don't like this one damn bit more than you do. History—the facts—everything entitles you to take command.

"Come aboard. Meet the crew. If you will accept command, write me to that effect. I'll attach my resignation and forward it—My protocol is all screwed up! You forward my resignation with your offer to take my place. The Consortium will either approve your request, accept my resignation, or it'll do something else."

The Admiral's smile was thin, frosty as his eyes, but there was nothing belittling in his voice when he said,

"Your wife got you this command. I don't doubt that you mean what you say, but Alex Heflin knew what he was doing and why he was doing it. He'll change nothing whatsoever."

"Admiral, those are your words, not mine. They are all too damn right. I do not rate asking you whether you are here because you wish to be, or because you were ordered to go aboard as consultant, as observer, or whatever else may be legal. Whatever the answer, it's your business, not mine.

"I tell you again, welcome aboard. Meet the crew. Read the records. If you have any choice, you can make it before takeoff time. If I misunderstood my orders and took off a day ahead of schedule, you wouldn't lose any retirement allowances for having missed the flight. If it would make it easier for you, I could, through pure muddle-headedness, give you incorrect information.

Garvin cocked his head, grinned, winked. "Admiral Courtney, if I circle the rings of Saturn and came back, there's little the Consortium could do to me or about it."

"Rod, you make this interesting. One question, though, and it's none of my business, and let's forget rank. About that evidence of prehistoric astronauts—in Turkistan, I think—did you bring evidence back? Such as nuclear fuel? Metal from a space cruiser, some spare part."

"I did. Unfortunately, I talked too much, and with too many decibels. I had sense enough to destroy the samples after I got a strictly private anlysis. Using a custom built ID and watching out for stray fingerprints."

"Interesting. Your reasons?"

"To tell you that I knew what had happened to better men than myself would be dishonest. It would be a piece of the same if I pretended that by playing it the way I did, my rehabilitation would be under limited restriction, allowing me limited liberty. That's the way it worked out, but it was blind luck. The fact is that if I'd offered my samples as proof of my story, proof of your statements, the Fat Boys would have checked up, and caused too much trouble for the friendly natives who let me in on some of their traditions."

"Troubles, such as?"

"Meeting western culture and science. So far, history doesn't record one instance in which the natives haven't been screwed. Anyway, those samples would've got me locked up in maximum security. But they are not through with me. Not yet."

"That's just a bit . . . ah . . . opaque, Rod. Clarify?"

"Since it's purely opinion, suppose I hold out until there is something along the line to justify it." Garvin got up. "It's been good, meeting you. Sorry I have an appointment for cocktails. As I said, welcome aboard."

Garvin saluted, meticulously, and set out to get a rental car. He'd be following Azadeh to Gook Town.

Chapter 22

Samgan Manioglu welcomed Garvin most cordially yet with formality in word and gesture, begging him to accept the seat of honor—and the guest earnestly protesting that he merited no such distinction. Azadeh, standing by, yet at a respectful distance, awaiting orders to serve wine: remote, elegant, exquisite. In spite of his past experience in Turkistan, he was left groping and scarcely able to believe that this was the girl he'd been inspecting for stretch marks some eighteen or twenty hours previously.

Smoke-flavored gin and strange snacks and the lingering scent of incense and Azadeh's perfume as she filled the glasses, her posture and her gestures stylized; ear pendants tinkling as she moved. So remote. He could not quite believe his memories, and the facts of the previous night became fantasies which someone else had experienced with some other woman.

After inquiries, host and guest regarding the well-being and health of the one another, the old man begged leave to withdraw and get the rest which his feeble frame required.

Her father had scarcely cleared the entrance of the hall when Azadeh became a fluttery wench with at least two conflicting urges demanding immediate expression, each to the exclusion of the others.

"No—don't kiss me—not yet—I must not get rattling headed—first I'll tell you all about it."

"All about what?" The change from stately hostess to bubbling female left him bewildered. "Did I fumble something?"

"See what I mean? Still dizzy from our sleepings last night!" She caught him with both arms in a clinch that began at knee level and built up, mouth to mouth. When Azadeh sank to her heels, she said, "Now I remember . . . something to tell you all about."

When they'd picked their corner, where cushions padded the brick bench, she continued, "I talked to your friend Jim ward, at the Ecology Garden Dome.

Garvin frowned. "Last night, you told me no phone calls could get through. And I said it was my wife's doings."

"Oh, yes, strict orders. But, I did not phone. I went to see him, so we talked, nobody hearing. While he signed the papers, the document."

He caught her by the shoulders. "What papers? Where?"

"In the Ecology Gardens, where else?"

"The paper—I don't get it!"

"Of course not! I am so rattling brained. In the office where I work, there are quit claims, with affidavits. So I filled one in—your friend, Jim Ward, he will hold the Administration safe and harmless, and not bring a lawsuit. He has no claims whatever against anybody."

"What the hell's been going on? An accident—or was he claiming false arrest—illegal detention—"

Azadeh laughed happily. "Oh, nothing happened. But I read things in Volume Six, Title 855, *Manual of Procedure*—I was turning the pages, looking for something for the boss, and '*quit claim*' caught my eye, no, I don't know why I saw it, maybe I was thinking about when I must quit claiming you—

"So I read the paragraph and that was the idea. How to see Jim—easier than phoning. Get a quit claim with affidavit, and a seal, and I get into the Ecology Dome. That is the nice thing about the mind of bureaucrats. Nobody understands anything except maybe his own little duties. Often, not even that much. Everyone pretends to know everything, especially when talking to a Gook who is very dumb.

"I borrowed the seal of a notary who is in the hospital. Any seal is good, but better if the owner is not there. With the document and the seal I got into the place where the inmates assemble, in the garden, for a coffee break. I handed Jim the paper and I said, 'You sign here, where it says, *I have read and understood the above* . . .'

"Jim asks me what in hell is this, and I tell him, please to lower the voice, and pretend to be puzzled. Jim said he did not have to pretend, it came natural. So I said, don't talk so loud, just sign very slow, and listen while I tell you—Garvin wants to know how it is with his friends."

"Jim said, 'Except for me, he does not have friends. They all believe he used his wife's family to get him back home, and he left the rest of us here. That girl, she hates him. The Inspector makes it all the worse. He blames Garvin's wife for keeping them all locked up. Lani, that's the girl, thinks he should help us. I am waiting for my chance to program the computer and get us all out of here. I know Garvin won't run out, he'll do what he can, but be damned if I will sit here, waiting."

It took Garvin some moments to digest the details.

Azadeh caught her breath and resumed, "So Jim signed the quit claim, and I made like a notary, witnessing, and stating that Jim Ward, known to me to be such, had solemnly sworn and affirmed the foregoing."

"You got away with all that?"

Azadeh nodded, beamed all over. "Easy. I am dumb Gook, nobody thinks I know enough for tricks."

"So they all hate my guts except Jim. It does look bad for me and I can't blame them."

"When you come back from Saturn, you will be a national hero on the audio-video screen and the important people will let your friends out, and if your wife asks her cousin, then, no problem."

"Darling, I want them all out of there, now. I'm going on a long trip. It'll be months and months. And I'm going to—don't forget those masks I told you about. Like the mask I wore last night.

"The friends in the manned stations on the meridian, I can haul them away in a prospector's truck, disguise them, get them into a hotel or boarding house in Maritania, and home on the next cruiser. Unless they're caught before takeoff.

"The only tough business is getting Jim and Amelia out."

Azadeh frowned, pondered. "Too bad you did not have your friend Daly get a Gook mask . . . my father don't need one . . . maybe I can fix up a *subpoena* paper to get Jim and his girl to Maritania for an imaginary court trial for something . . . Oh, I forgot—your wife, she wants all your friends kept here, they are a bad influence, troublemakers. Maybe without them, she can make you amount to something. You see, the freeze-up, no talking by phone, maybe your Flora is using her influence."

"That doesn't add up! She's not bitchy. Sure, she is a meddler, she's got to have security all around, *take care* is her life's motto—she doesn't want me spacing around, she wants to have me shackled to a nice steady job back on Terra."

"Mmmm . . . maybe this Inspector Morgan don't like you."

Garvin chuckled sourly. "He doesn't, and I hate his guts like he hates mine. If I ever owned a private graveyard, I'd want him for my first customer." Abruptly, he snapped to his feet, and caught Azadeh's hand. "You've told me so much that I have to digest it before I can tell what is what—but your tricks with documents and seals—I begin to feel lucky about the mess I kicked up."

"What time do you have to be back to the *Saturnienne*?"

"There's lots of time for us, and I'm tired of thinking in circles. If you don't get some sleep once in a while, you can't keep on thinking up Gook ways of doing impossible things."

"That," she agreed, "is something to sleep on."

Azadeh slept restfully, while Garvin's thoughts raced in an idiotic whirl of elements of his recue plans— documents, masks, *subpoenas* for imaginary court cases, cruiser schedules, escapes synchronized to take- off times, and permutations and combinations of these and many other elements. Toward dawn, Garvin gave her a pat on the hip, stroked her hair.

She stirred sleepily, and her drowsy smile warned him that he'd better bail out instantly, or revise the day's plans.

"Don't wake up . . . I have a plan that won't let me rest. You've got a couple more hours."

She fell back asleep and away from their kissing.

Garvin lost no time in getting his rental car to the surface. Whatever plan he'd finally pursue, he had first of all to gain the confidence of those who believed he'd run out on them.

Near the spaceport, he made a U-turn: he'd overshot his mark. Backtracking nearly two kilometers, he recognized the abandoned road which he'd missed. This was the one which his escort, Harland and Bromley, had taken to reach Station Six, that night they'd been waiting for him on his return from clobbering Morgan at Lani's station.

Weaving, pitching, twisting among jagged outcroppings, he came to the junction of the pioneering trail with the road which followed the meridian on which the manned stations were aligned.

The drive had taken longer than he'd reckoned. The nearest marker told him he was about nine kilometers north of his old station. The moons were blotted out by the rising sun. He read the exterior temperature and shivered, wishing he'd stayed subsurface with Azadeh. He had the feeling of one who returns to a long ago scene of his childhood, or of a battered survivor of an ancient battle: something to remember but nothing he'd want to experience again. Something had happened to him, and insidiously, so that his awareness was an awakening so sudden as to be a shock.

Garvin realized that obligation to a comrade in mishap was all that moved him to see and to reassure Lani. Although he'd had no romantic illusions about Lani, he had seen her as much more than a deluxe play girl: her eagerness to escape with him to Khatmandu, or Cuzco, away from the Plastic Population of phoney-land had been genuine, had proved her to be a kindred prisoner, a free soul, an individual none the worse for being a whore. Now she was no longer the image of escape, of spreading wings. Nevertheless, Lani was the catalyst without which there would not have been the detonation, the critical firing up. His indebtedness to Lani remained but the currency in which he'd pay his obligation—that was beyond foreseeing.

First installment, liberation from Mars.

Perhaps that would be the quit-claim. Since no lover could own Lani, certainly Lani could not own any lover.

And all became clear to him: he recalled Azadeh's thoughts on possession and possessiveness, and these, in an utterly different context, answered everything and at the same time, answered nothing, nothing.

Azadeh, if she delivered in due course a parcel of vigorous barbarian blood into Gook Town, would be a benefactrix of Gookdom, neither being owned by nor wishing to own another.

Everything was clear as far as Lani was concerned. The only problem was to Jim Ward and his girl on the way home. Bluntly, Jim's formula for the Black Box had contained one small error whereby destination became Mars instead of Khatmandu. Jim's error, or the error of Jim's expert, Hamlin Daly. But no logic, no quibbling could liberate Garvin. The skipper is responsible for everyone's bitch-ups.

And then Garvin pulled up at Station Six, his first Martian home. He put on helmet and jacket and got out. He went to the lock. The voice of the intercom would have aroused, or should have, whoever was in charge. The hydroponic section didn't look right. He hammered, bell punched. No response. The place was unmanned, or perhaps, unwomanned . . . some son of a bitch taking too long saying good-bye to Lani . . . he jammed the face plate against the plastic. The Martian muscovite-mica panes that the Gooks used in roofing their subterranes were as clear as the plastic and a lot less prone to scratches.

Garvin got back into the rental car. Twenty *kay-ems* to Station Five. Wondering what to say to Lani and how to say it bothered him. She'd know without being told that obligation had brought him back, and that this wasn't the first step toward Khatmandu. If he didn't tell her, she'd be offended.

No frost on the visor. The sun had burned out the night chill.

He pulled up at Station Five, to pound on the door, and then to lean on the buzzer button.

Lani's expression was not what Garvin had expected. It took him a moment to realize that she mistook him for an inspector, or the inspector, showing up far earlier than he should. And of course everyone looked alike in space gear. The lock opened to admit him. She remained apprehensive until he shed his helmet. In amazement, she backed off a step. He caught the twinkle of chrome and saw the hypo she'd used to make sure that Morgan remained out, totally out, for a long time.

"Rod—how'd you do it—I—what's been going on—oh, get shed of that jacket and tell me—" She ran fingers through her tawny-red hair, licked her lips. "Sneaking up this way—I'll hate the sight of me while I'm putting on my complexion."

She raced to the rear. He followed slowly.

When Lani returned, wearing make up, a commissary robe and gilt slippers, she shook her head, sighed. "Give me time to get used this." She backed to a chair, and gestured to its companion. "Rod, I've been hating you so long, wishing you were dead. That morning, after *he* left, I called and called and called you. No answer. You just vanished. There were all kinds of rumors. First, that you were shacking up with the Gooks, and it'd be against Administration policy to make a search. Not unless you'd committed a serious crime. And then the story that your influential wife got you out, provided you forgot your riffraff friends. Yesterday, I got word from Jim. Just saying that you'd not dumped us."

"Jim seems to be the only one who hasn't put me on the black list." He grimaced sourly. "Uh-huh, I have been busy—shacking up with a Gook while honeying up to my wife whose influence got me out of this ecology mess. And she's so happy she got me a job of remodeling a space cruiser to go past Saturn."

"What cruiser? What's this?"

"You mean, someone skipped the only news I have had a thing to do with? The one piece of all out fact, no mention? I just landed her, we're not through yet checking her out after the shakedown cruise from home. The *Saturnienne*, you know."

"All we get is closed-circuit stuff."

"Ummm . . . custom built, I bet! Now listen to some more. I am going to get you out of here on the next home-bound cruiser, and anyone else who is in a manned station. Jim and Amelia are a tough problem, but I have a thought."

"Rod, don't fool me—I couldn't stand—"

She choked up, bent over, elbows on her knees, face buried in her palms; her shoulders twitched as she sobbed.

"Do you suppose I'd drive out from the spaceport to play games? Sit up, Doll, I have to get going—I'm a wage slave in command of a crew."

She sat up, blinking, choking.

Garvin continued, "Think, and give me the straight of it. *First* I was shacking up with a Gook, and *then* my wife got me back home. Was it in that order?"

"Yes."

"Sure? I got a reason for asking."

She nodded.

He said, "That son of a bitch Morgan has been feeding everyone, but especially you, a scrap of fact and a scoop of manure. Put me on your shit list, and you wouldn't throw rocks at him." Garvin eyed her for a moment, and then, "I've never seen you kill anyone, but now I know how you'd look if you did." Garvin looked at his watch. "Got to bail out. Keep up appearances. I'll have to get you out by night. One strike is out, in this ball game."

"Your Gook lady, is she nice?"

"Yes, and she knows all about you. Jim told you?"

"In a cagey, left-handed way. She sounds good."

He kissed her too gently. The pat on the rear didn't sound rich as it used to. Before the lock pump built up pressure, he said, "I have to play it all by ear. Trust Jim, but be damn careful what you say to *anyone*."

Chapter 23

Before Garvin could complete his time-and-motion study for Lani's liberation he had to digest the flight schedules of homeward-bound freighters. This was complicated by bulletins on the passenger space available. Furthermore, *personnel* traveling under orders had priority; after them, persons traveling for own convenience; there after, in theory, it was a free scramble. However, the nonpublished, universally denied, but well-known fact had always to be integrated into all other variables: that favored travelers got precedence according to the Consortium's pleasure. Planning was a shortcut to madness. Consulting the *I Ching* or the Tarot was recommended.

Finally, Azadeh gave him unofficial information from headquarters which contradicted all published statements.

When not coordinating those variables, Garvin was concerned because of the Guest Admiral, whose rank did indeed bring privilege. At first he preferred to enjoy Greater Maritania; later, he wanted a tour of the mines and processing plants. He cut this short, deciding that he should move to his stateroom aboard the *Saturnienne* to get acquainted with the ship whose performance he was to observe and to whose skipper he would be a consultant.

"If he was a female admiral," Daly grumbled, largely because the orders of the day could be counted on to be countermanded by the previous day's orders for which he and others had prepared. "I'd figure he was pregnant. The old bastard canceled inspecting the Martian Gardens—canceled the mine tour—screamed like an eagle when he got turned down on a tour of Gook Town. When he comes aboard, you'll have mutiny before takeoff."

"His or the crew's?" Garvin asked.

"Both," Daly snapped back.

Garvin shook his head and sighed. "As if I didn't have enough private problems, the Lani deal. Here's something you can work on—remember in those historical novels you used to read whenever you were sober long enough to keep both eyes focused on the same page? How officers of sea-going ships used to be piped over the side?"

"Sure I do. I forget about ensigns and lieutenants, but there was a grade that began with two side boys, and each grade higher, two more side boys. I don't remember if they got guns, like for generals."

"Lucky we don't have saluting guns, so forget it," Garvin advised.

"We've got no side boys, and there's not a boatswain's pipe on the whole damn planet!"

"Don't tell me you can't or there isn't,". Garvin flared. "You see the mayor's secretary, the Gook lady who was talking to one of the crewmen who got clobbered the other night. She might have some answers."

"What would Gooks know about bosun's pipes?"

"For the most resourceful man aboard, you are a letdown. How many centuries has it been since anyone's heard a bosun's pipe? Cut down a flute or something, and have twelve Gooks in uniforms practice the twitter-twittering—"

"How do you know the sound?" Daly challenged.

"I read about the twitter-twittering—"

"I meant, about Gook flutes and pipes cutting them down?"

Garvin burlesqued picking an imaginary long, long hair from Daly's collar, held it to his nose, sniffed daintily. "That is none of your God-damn business."

"Aye, aye, sir!" He saluted with hammed-up snap.

"*Merde, alors!*" Garvin growled, and returned the salute.

And his thought was, "*If I'm right, it'll buck up the old man's* morale, which he deserves. If he rates more than twelve side boys, I am on the black list for life. If I turn out sixteen, just to make sure and if a dozen is the highest in the book, he'll figure I am ribbing him, and that'll be dung in the fan."

Then he turned his thoughts back to Lani.

This was cut short by the arrival of dispatches from the message center: largely, general orders for all commanders, from Lunar Garbage Shuttle to Martian Freighter; regardless of relevance, the Saturn-bound explorer was included. He waded through the bureaucratic morass because in that daily flood of verbal diarrhea there might be something which he should read, and be guided accordingly. There were also two radiograms.

He opened the first. It was from Flora, aboard the *Space Queen* en route for Maritania. Heroically, she was striving for telegraphic terseness:

DARLING I'LL BE SEEING YOU SOON AFTER YOU GET THIS STOP IT WAS MY URGE TO SURPRISE YOU STOP—

Garvin stopped. "Mission accomplished, darling girl. Sweet Jesus, is this real?" He squinted at the date line, at the three-coordinate spatial position of the cruiser; he accepted the disastrous incredible, and read on

I LOATHE AND DESPISE SPACE BUT WANTED TO WISH YOU BON VOYAGE STOP A SURPRISE PARTY STOP SO MUCH FOR US TO TALK ABOUT OUR FUTURE STOP YOU COULD NEVER GUESS WHAT I DESIGNED FOR MY TAKEOFF DRESS STOP NOW I HAVE TO CHANGE IT FOR OFFICIAL CEREMONY STOP ALEXANDER RADIOED ABOUT DARLINGEST CEREMONY MARITANIA WITH AUDIOVIDEO FOR TERRAN PUBLIC LOVE FLORA.

Garvin didn't know whether to be deeply touched, dismayed, or furious. It was simpler to be all three simultaneously. Flora was exasperating in her worship of the Magnificent Society and its doctrines. She was a silly bitch and she was also colorful, fascinating. An all-out, sweet girl.

"I could kick her million-*pazor* fanny till her nose bled, and then kiss it and patch it up with Redi-Plastik bandage-stickers. She's a curse, a plague, a shackle, a stumbling block but what can you do to write off a wench who hates space and flies sixty-nine million *kay-ems* for a *bon voyage* party?"

The only answer: turn out damage control. Get Lani off the scene and under cover. That would be easy. Telling Azadeh that their pre-takeoff honeymoon had been shot down in flames: that would be grim.

Impatiently, he waited until Azadeh would have had time to drive home, clean up and put on her romance makeup: her kind of yoga for relaxing from and forgetting the Maritanian day . . .

When Azadeh heard him park his car in her walled front yard, she went to stand in the doorway. She wore Terran dress, a long, sea-green tunic, Tang Dynasty, and tall head gear, with kingfisher breast feathers and jeweled pendants: but it was her stately carriage and expression which made Garvin pause instead of grabbing an armful.

"With no honeymoon romancing," she said, "this hair-do is for looking at, not letting down." Reading his perplexity, she added, "I read copies of those radiograms before you did."

"Hell you did!"

She nodded. "I have friends in Communication Center."

"They know about you and me?"

"All Gooks know, and so do many non-Gooks."

This left him groping.

Azadeh continued, "Some like to mock the North Americans—famous space captain, romancing with a Gook. But much they do not know. The Ecology Station people, new ones, always feel that something stares at them at night. In the morning, the station keeper comes out to look for footprints. Yes, Gooks studying barbarians." She smiled. "Man of Station Six, cycling to see lady in Station Five. Now, come in. I wanted to tell you about your Flora's surprise visit when Dad can't see your face changing. I'm awfully sorry about this, but as you tell me, we can't win them all."

The Old Man was in the guest room, stepping from the ceremonial hearth. "Azadeh gave me the news—please spare yourself the explainings—it is so awkward, and so needless here."

Having become somewhat more than a guest, Garvin avoided the seat of honor at the hearth, and Samgan Manioglu did not observe the ceremony of objecting.

Crosslegged, stately as The Lady in the temple, Azadeh sat facing the hearth, and well back, so that she could easily address her father and her lover.

Samgan resumed, "With your wife so soon to arrive, your first action is taking your Number Two Lady from Station Five?"

"Yes. My no longer Number Two Lady can hide, in disguise, in Maritania till the *Space Queen* goes home, or other cruiser takes off sooner."

"Late today there was a notice of one leaving sooner," Azadeh told him.

"So there'll be no awkwardness. The Saturn Ceremonies will keep my wife busy until I take off. Maybe I can persuade Flora to get her cousin to get my other friends a permit to leave Martian Gardens stations. Keeping Lani out of sight should make it easy.

"I've caused Lani a lot of trouble, getting her into this mess. Once she's back home, that'll be the last I'll hear of her."

Azadeh and her father eyed each other; and the old man spoke for both: "We think with you."

Azadeh added, "You think the mask-film will protect her when Maritania is crazy with audiovideo teams, all the media going wild with human interest stuff, personality stories?"

Garvin pulled a long face. "You have a point there. Each complication breeds a new one."

Azadeh's glance shifted to her father. He nodded.

Garvin had scarcely time to wonder how far the two had gone in digesting the afternoon's complications when Azadeh said, "Gook Town is never searched unless there is a serious crime. We can find Lani a room with neighbors, well away from here."

However far this was from the Terran social pattern—it would never have occurred to Garvin to ask for a hideout for Lani, however clear it was that she had become an explaymate—the offer did not surprise him: now that the invitation had been extended, it seemed absurd to fancy that it could have been otherwise.

The Old Man got to his feet, bowed, and courteously gave Garvin permission to depart. Azadeh went with him to his car.

"Lover, you looked surprised! We mean it. Bring her as soon as you can. No Gook will talk in Maritania or the spaceport. No one has talked about the time you—how do you say it—conked the Inspector." She patted her tall headgear. "Drawing two pins will bring hair to my hips—and we'll have a miniromance until Flora leads you to face the camera and the sound to amuse the Magnificent Democracy."

Chapter 24

Now that the road was more familiar, Garvin made better time on his way to the meridian. Heading south, he surmised that his old home, Station Six, remained untenanted, and wondered whether Inspector Morgan had to fake reports for an imaginary station keeper. The thought of encountering Morgan had become amusing.

"Cold caulk the son of a bitch," he mused, "and then Lani gives him the needle, and around noon, nothing to do but cook up a story. After she's been on the intercom, saying good-bye to her neighbors." He did not in fact contemplate any such games, but the whimsy enlivened the drive.

From full headlight range, Garvin saw the silhouette of an ecology car. He cut his lights. Whether for fun or money, Lani's party shouldn't be interrupted at an awkward moment. He swung from the road and by moonlight picked his way toward a rocky outcropping larger than his vehicle, and parked behind it. The dome was lighted, but he was not near enough to size up the action. This was good, very good indeed. All he wanted was one good whack at Inspector Morgan, not for tumbling Lani into bed, but for being Inspector Morgan.

Garvin was so eager in picking his way among knee-high boulders that he overworked the air conditioning of his helmet. The face plate was misting. Finally he was leaning against the dome, well away from the lock but able to scan much of the interior. As his breathing eased up, the glass disk cleared a little. There was motion. Two figures stumbled into view. One was dark, bulky, awkward: a man without helmet but wearing a spacesuit. The other, slender, a woman in a gray robe which swirled wide. If she wore anything under that garment, it was too flimsy to count.

Lani saying no and meaning it.

The other must be Morgan. She gave him a thrust which apparently caught him when he was off balance, or he may have tripped over something lying near the low table in the all-purpose room. There was a jacket and slacks and helmet on the table.

Instead of taking a full sprawl, Morgan somehow recovered, staggered, lurched toward her. Although Garvin could see more clearly, his vision was far from good. The gesture however, was eloquent. Whatever Lani's words—and Garvin was sure that they were infuriating—they were irrelevant. Her thrust had almost floored Morgan and her blessing completed the job. Morgan lashed out, open handed, to slap her into the middle of the ensuing week. She ducked, stumbled to her knees, checked herself by grabbing the table.

Missing his mark threw him off balance, and before he could recover, she was on her feet. Metal twinkled: it looked like the standard field hammer, the geologist's implement, with pick for prying a specimen knocked loose by the head.

The man collapsed.

The ballet was over.

Garvin pounded the air lock, yelled, finally pawed the button.

The gray length jerked, froze, stood, staring, gaping—moving like a mechanical toy, step by step toward the lock. She still gripped the spiked hammer. For an instance he had the urge to run before she could get to the lock. Her face frightened him.

He stood fast, and gestured meaninglessly. Of course she couldn't recognize him while he wore his headgear. She might guess. And then it seemed that she did remember.

Lani dropped the hammer, and closed the switch. Separated by a space of almost vacuum, they stood, staring, each at the other. He could feel the pulsation of the pump and its cessation told him that pressure had built up.

"Pretty if she killed him . . . maybe it's only a graze . . . what's the next move . . ."

A whirl of answers trampled each other to a pulp.

She opened the inner door. Garvin yanked off his helmet.

Lani's staring senseless eyes made him recoil. Her color shocked him. Her pallor exaggerated the red of her upper lip. The lower had not been rouged. Her teeth were like a row of tombstones by moonlight.

Recognition made her eyes human again.

"Come in and look."

As he followed, he got out of his jacket, and saw the frost whitening it. On the floor he saw one of her field boots, and another, well away from it: the one over which Morgan had stumbled.

Garvin knelt beside Morgan. He heard none of that hoarse breathing of one knocked out and recovering— or, dying. The man lay face down. Neither hand twitched. Almost as an afterthought, he felt for some trace of pulse. He got up, shook his head.

"Hell, I've seen enough of 'em, I don't have to check by the book. Doll, you creamed, you totaled him."

"I knew that when I smacked him." Her frozen face began to twitch. She choked, screamed, caught Garvin with both arms. She ran her tongue impossibly far into his mouth. She drooled and moaned. "Darling, darling—get out of those icy things—"

"Jesus, woman—"

Lani's knees sagged. She toppled off balance. Caught off balance as he tried to get free of the rest of his space gear, he sank with her to the floor—

Moaning, pelvis twisting, clinging, she finally could cry words: ". . . love me . . . oh, Love me to death . . ."

There was no denying her, and he didn't want to deny her.

When each had depleted the other, they were wallowing against Morgan's body. Lani exhaled a long, quavering sigh of ultimate emptiness, utter exhaustion.

"Oh . . . I needed that . . . first time I've ever had enough. That slob might've known I wasn't in the mood, even if he didn't know you came back to prove what a lying bastard he'd been . . . thinking I could be had like a bowl of instant noodles." And now beauty lighted her face. Garvin had never seen ecstasy such as Lani radiated. The woman was transfigured. She raised herself on an elbow, hitched a little to get away from the corpse. Wonder lighted her face anew. "Thanks, Inspector," she said, affectionately, gratefully. ". . . never had it that good before."

Garvin, on his feet, was thinking, "*All she needs is a halo, and she could pose for a madonna . . . who's going to find her another slob to clobber?*"

She extended her hand, and he gave her a lift. Though the glory and the splendor were gone, her beauty remained radiant, contented. "Honey, I hope you can die this happy, some day. I could, right now. What're we going to do with *this*? What can we do about the whole mess tonight?"

Garvin closed his eyes, shook his head. "Even if I beat you up, knocked out some teeth and dragged you all over the place, you'd be wasting breath, claiming you were raped."

"Well, that's one of the handicaps of being a hooker!"

"Hooker, my ass! Just before I took off for Mars, there was a California case where a girl who wasn't a hooker pulled a knife and gave a guy a slash. The judge said that rape was not bodily harm and she was lucky the man didn't sue her for assault with a deadly weapon. And Mars goes by North American law.

"Get into your space gear and give me a hand. I got a thought."

When Lani returned, dressed for Martian outdoors, Garvin was still studying the area maps. "Once we get this cold meat loaded into his car, I'll give you a run-down."

"Honey, I just had a thought. Ever since you left Station Six, that slob threatened to have me transferred to

Gook Town if I didn't come across, and dumped there.
Or, sent to work in the mines. So, I could claim it was
burglary."

"Burglary? Hell's fire, doll, I don't get it?"

"Oh, I know some law. On the books no matter how
you ignore them, rape is a felony. Well, burglary—"

"I still don't get it. How burglary?"

"Burglary," she explained patiently, "is breaking into
a dwelling or a place of business, at night, with intent to
commit a felony. And that son of a bitch was breaking
into my place of business."

Garvin regarded her with awe. "Darling, you
shouldn't ever have been a hooker or a gourmet cook.
You'd be a perfect Chief Justice of the Supreme Court
of North America."

Between them they got the corpse into the Inspector's vehicle. Back in the dome, he said, "Clean up.
Pick up. Go over every inch of metal or plastic and mop
up my fingerprints. It's okay for his to be around. Inspectors are supposed to look around."

"And feel around—"

"Wipe that map, I pawed it. Clean up the blood on
the floor. I was wearing gloves when I pounded the
outer door, but wipe the inside door of the air lock, I
had my gloves off."

"You think of everything! I'll take a shower all over,
with detergents—"

"Calm down for a careful checkup. No time for
hurry."

They made a deliberately paced circuit, reconstruct-
ing each move from the beginning of the Morgan hassle
to the moment at hand.

When Lani stepped from the shower, she said, "See
any finger prints anywhere?" Then she dressed, and followed him to the Inspector's car.

Garvin said, "I'll drive this one. You drive my car,
follow me closely. Take it easy when we leave the
road."

Though there was time aplenty, he had to fight the
urge to hurry, to panic. Lani's unnatural calmness
might blow up in hysteria—she was a nonstock model,

but he could not count on her not falling apart after having had her final spasm, her ultimate jollies, while sandwiched between a lover and a dead enemy. The only certainty that Garvin had was that he'd never want to shack up with that fascinating and talented redhead. She might again be in a mood which demanded a corpse and a lover—then what? Or, who? He wasn't finding fault with Lani. Garvin still recalled that he had neither kicked nor screamed enough to count.

Garvin drove north until the odometer indicated that he should quit the road. After doing so, he walked back to Lani and said, "Follow me, slowly, to the dip that's just ahead. Once you're in the swale, pull up alongside and get in. I'll go back and see whether our car can be seen from the road. If not, we'll carry on."

Once reassured on that detail, he returned and they drove on. Finally the staff car nosed up and over the rim of the swale. Garvin then bore in a nearly northerly direction until at last they came to the rim of a crevasse, one he had studied during many a kilometer of biking. He halted, chocked the wheels with rocks and beckoned for Lani to follow him.

"I found this while I was studying ways to bike to your front door," he explained. He paused to have a good look at the steep drop into distant blackness. "Good place."

Back again at his car, he said, "You follow with a hefty rock to chock the wheels if I stop. The armature began to hum as the vehicle's speed was whipped down by the grade. Finally, he halted near the rim, got out. "As I feed her the juice, you bend your shoulder to the rear end—"

Reaching in, he fed the power, shouldered the door frame.

"Heave!" Turning on full power, he leaped aside. The car went over the side. Seconds elapsed before he heard the thump-whop-crunch, followed by a second, and after a long interval, by a final impact.

Once back at the car, Garvin said, "I forgot to have you put on the disguise mask, the one Daly got for you. But you won't need it yet. Wearing space rig, no one could tell whether you're male or female. We're going to the *Saturnienne*. There's a confidential spot that the crew doesn't know about."

Once they got off the meridian road and on the pioneer track, he told Lani about his talk with Azadeh, and of Flora's impending arrival.

"If they hunt Morgan and by some fluke see the wreck, there's no telling what they might do. Or if you and Morgan and the car stay missing, they might think you two are shacking up in Gook Town and start a search. So you can't move in with Azadeh's neighbors."

After a long silence, Lani asked, "Suppose they search the *Saturnienne*?"

"That's a risk you're stuck with. But if it comes to that, I can flood the approach passage with carbon dioxide—fire extinguisher gas—they'd blink out like a match in a typhoon, and when they're resuscitated, they'd hurry home, happy to call it a day."

"You think of everything!"

"Hell I do! We didn't pack your clothes."

"As if I ever want to see that awful stuff again! And I did grab my little brocaded purses and tucked them into my blouse before I put on the space jacket."

"Your perfume and party dresses?"

"When I'm back home, I'll have to start all over."

"Give me your measurements and I'll have Azadeh pick you some things to wear on the homeward flight. Now relax—we're boarding my ship, and in space gear. No one'll think you're not a crew member."

Chapter 25

Now that Lani was stowed away aboard the *Saturnienne*—conversion of a freight and passenger ship to space explorer had left compartments and staterooms blocked off and idle—Garvin had only to keep Admiral Courtney happy, await Flora's arrival for *bon voyage* ceremonies, and devote the remainder of his hours to Avadeh.

As honeymoons went, this would not, not even at the best, be a long one. Garvin and Azadeh realized this could not be the romantic wallowing of a standard honeymoon, of persons in ordinary circumstances. Normally, it would be an emotion-binge, a farewell to reality, an interlude of unreality, and then the plunge into becoming acquainted with each other and with a shocking, dismaying, grimly revealing mode of life.

Garvin put it into words only because Azadeh wondered why he had made a point of speaking the Gook language whenever the situation permitted circumlocution, fumblings, and the laughs generated by a natural linguist's venturing into a new language.

The scholarly type studied, got everything sorted out, attained a perfection which few natives could equal or approach. The instinctive variety boarded a plane, took from his pocket *Gujarati Phrase Book, Conversational Tagalog,* or *Basic Pakhtu,* learned the words for *how much, how many, one-two-three-four-five* (whether it was bottles, women, meals, or any minor benefits, you

187

never needed more than five), and wheedled the native stewardess, if any, into auditing his pronounciation. Setting his feet on ground at flight's end, he took charge, in unfaultless Gujarati or whatever and made his way. There were always natives to correct his grosser errors and to be fascinated by the strange and entertaining things which a novice could do, tricks no native had ever dreamed of.

Accordingly, Azadeh wondered, and Garvin told her, "The way to get acquainted with a woman is to speak her language. It's going to be a long cruise. The more I can speak Gook, mixed with Uighur and three or four others, but mainly Gook, the more of you I'll have with me while we're spacing."

"But how about me?" she countered.

"*Madame*—Azadeh *Khanoum*—every day at work, you speak English. You speak so well it is not funny to hear you, it's just nice. Anyway, you'll not be dodging asteroids or wondering when the mutiny is going to start. And one more thing—"

"You never give me a chance to argue."

"Of course not! I'd always lose! Now, the one more thing is this—the halfway spot, when we're circling Saturn, we'll be transmitting images and talk to Mars, for relaying to Terra."

"Why not directly to Terra?"

"Censorship, darling. A bit of dressing up, editing, with Thought Control and propaganda dubbed in. The Plastic Populace would be bored by facts—there'd be rioting. Worse yet, they'd all go to sleep and vote wrong when they awoke. And for that reviewing here, I'm awfully glad."

"Glad?"

"Of course! And glad because Flora's coming back for the halfway ceremonies. That way, you and I can see and hear each other, just before I start back. On the outbound way, just radio routine reports, until we're near Saturn."

She sat bolt upright, eyes wide. This she had not anticipated.

"But of course!" he continued. "The drama, the human interest—Flora and I exchanging words and looks across space, and with the rings of Saturn in the background. If Saturn isn't tilted the right way, we can change our course and get the right view.

"Now, here's where you can come in. With your record as an employee, civil service rules will give you a chance to take examinations and transfer to communications.

"Tell 'em you're pregnant and you want a leave of absence, someone will take your place, no trouble then getting a new spot when you go back to work. Be a technician and finagle your way into the transmitting station, after hours or during a tour of night duty. I'll sell them the idea that they should have more reports than they've got scheduled now."

And while Garvin's idea was seeping through the bureaucracy's strata, Azadeh busied herself with preparing for her change of civil service.

He had not told Azadeh why he hadn't brought Lani to Gook Town the night he had set out to liberate her from Station Five. It was as though the subject had not been mentioned during the discussion of Flora's coming to Mars for the takeoff ceremonies. And when Azadeh and her father had for some days refrained from posing any question, or dropping even a hint, Garvin finally said, "If I don't say where I went or what I did that night I left so early, it'll be better for us, if there is ever any official question."

The old man smiled, wagged his head. "That is why we have not asked—we did not want you to tell us. Whatever story gets into Maritania's gossip, you will know that my daughter and I could not have repeated what you didn't say."

And some days after that terse exchange, Garvin remarked, "When something which you are sure would be news is never mentioned, that in itself is sensational news."

Father and daughter exchanged side glances; as usual, Azadeh well away from the hearth, so that she could catch the eye of either without shifting her head. Samgan gestured, a twist of the wrist, a nod, a flip of the palm.

Azadeh said, "We think with you. It would be not-amiable to keep away from you what so many know."

"Yes, *Khanoum*, it would not be gracious, and not necessary. There has always been talk about Gook spies who watch the domes along the meridian."

"*Tura*—Great Lord—" Azadeh was at her most stately-remote-elegant manner. "Some have said that the Terrestrian Devils have put Jim Ward in Station Six, and a female person, Amelia, in Station Five."

Garvin solemnly considered this, and finally observed, "Strange experience has come to at least one person once stationed at Six." Possibly my friend Jim Ward asked for a transfer, hoping that strange things might happen to him."

Azadeh remarked, "If I hear such news in the offices of Maritania, I'll suspect it of being bait."

"If you hear that my friend, Inspector Morgan, has been relieved of duty, I won't know whether the words are bait, or not-bait."

"Gook spies say there is a new inspector. No one in Maritania mentions inspectors."

Garvin did not ask whether prowling Gooks had looked into the depths of any crevasses between Station Five and Station Six. He said, "Changing the subject abruptly, are there Gook settlements well away from Gook Town?"

"Quite a few, quite small, not easy to find," Azadeh said.

All in all, Garvin inferred that the silence at Headquarters indicated that the Administration didn't know what had happened to Lani and Morgan, and was pretending that nothing had happened to anyone. Regardless of masks and custom-built travel permits, or legally paid transportation, attempting to put Lani aboard a home-bound cruiser would be risky, perhaps a critically disastrous error. For her to risk moving to a hotel in Maritania would be worse. More and more, it seemed that she'd have to set out for Saturn. And if some subtle mind had figured that moving Jim and Amelia to Stations Five and Six would bait a rescue party, Garvin decided not to bite.

Not reporting the disappearance of Lani and Morgan was the giveaway. It would have been great propaganda, telling the Electorate that Mars was a planet of romance and elopment.

When the Old Man laboriously got to his feet, bowed, bade them good night, and did not give Garvin permission to depart, Garvin knew that he had been briefed on all but one detail: to wit, whether Morgan and his vehicle had been discovered.

Vultures did not soar in the thin air of Mars. The answer could well have been "No."

Rather than speculate on the thus far unrevealed thinkings of Administration headquarters, the quasi honeymooners found a subject far more relevant:

"If I dodge all the uncharted little asteroids and the rest of the cosmic rubbish, we can look at our future, close at hand. It'll begin the day after landing in Maritania. After all that fine publicity for Marvelous Mars, the Terran Suburb, we'll tune up, refit, fill in and smooth out the dents, and yo-ho for setting her down for a final vote-getting fiesta in North America."

"Our future," Azadeh pointed out, "doesn't really begin until things and happenings show us that we have a future."

"And that, we do have—if I make the round trip. Whether pioneering on Mars, or going to Turkistan, so you can see for yourself whether the people there are your cousins."

"You're already married into what you call the holy family—but a concubine is no problem, as long as everyone pretends she is not a concubine. I wouldn't mind at all, and once you're great and famous, a space hero, everyone would be happy to do all the pretending that your strange customs require."

He saw that instead of being oppressed or depressed by what Azadeh called her propsects, she considered the situation the most amusingly ridiculous thing she'd ever heard of.

"Sure it's funny—so God-damn, silly-funny I've laughed myself punchy most of my life. But the Consortium—Cousin Alexander, the head of the family that runs the show—have it figured that I won't come back. The only good hero, the only permanently valuable hero is the one who dies dramatically, with tragedy, glamour.

"That election I screwed up, purely by accident, is haunting Cousin Alexander and his family. I am a mocker until I become a Space Hero."

"But, you have so many things for dodging cosmic debris."

"They fitted me out with a crew wired for sabotage or mutiny or both."

Azadeh frowned perplexedly. "Rod, sometimes you have what is it you call it, the paranoiac persecution ideas. Sabotage in space! That is—really now, no kind of crew—in space, everyone dies with the ship when something happens."

"Beautiful Lady, Azadeh Khanoum, Dream Girl, you are an ignorant Gook. You do not understand the brain-washed Plastic Citizen of the Magnificent Society. He believes anything. He'll follow any suggestions. You don't even have to hypnotize the impressionable slobs—they're psychic sponges!"

"Ah, for that reason, you said, *hell's fire, no!*, when I said I'd stow away, and keep you too busy to sleep with Lani."

"Lani's got to hide out until the Inspector's mysterious disappearance no longer interests anyone." He caressed the area which began around her navel and extended to what he'd whimsically called The Well of the Angels and, sometimes, The Bottomless Pit. "Just in case you have something to remember me by, let's not risk it on a cruise like this one. Outwitting Cousin Alexander and his clique takes lots more figuring and persistence than getting you knocked up."

Chapter 26

At last Garvin had all the ceremonial behind him. Sound and image racing across space had dramatized Flora in her gown of glittering sequins, each Saturn shaped. Seven Gook women in brocaded tunics carried the silver-threaded train. Of these, there were three on a side and a seventh at the end. Flora, though scarcely over medium height, towered majestically because of her headgear which was styled to suggest an ascending space cruiser surmounted by Saturn. The takeoff blast stream was metallically threaded gauze shaped as neck and shoulder drape which trailed past her hips and blended with the train of the gown.

There had been field music to herald her stately progress to the dais, after which Martian percussion instruments and wailing pipes preceeded Garvin, who wore full dress uniform of space-black, with gilt. After him, Admiral Courtney had followed, ahead of the flight officers and crew.

Awaiting them on the dais was the Supreme Hierarch, representing North America. He was grateful to Garvin for the Black Box fiasco which had swept him into office. Two of the Consortium, inconspicuous fellows, had appeared as names and window dressing.

Then spaceport officialdom, clerks, secretaries, the staffs of Administration, and Azadeh, Ceremonial Secretary, intently noting each Great Man's every word, as though each word were not being taped, edited, synched with video before setting out for Terra.

Thus far, all had been as planned. Then, during the moment of each celebrant's taking his post, according to the briefings of the Master of Ceremony, Azadeh had had her chance. Poised as though to write, Azadeh said, "You will not be seeing me tonight. Your wife has all your time, and there is no help for this thing."

Garvin in his orbit, Azadeh in hers: after speeches came ruffles and flourishes, and departure for cocktails. Only important persons had received tickets for this and for three minutes of screen time.

Smooth—elegant—the Supreme Hierarch himself, the two members of the Consortium, and four members of Security escorted Garvin and Flora from the cocktail lounge to their suite in the Spaceport Hotel. The seven girls of the spectrum had not followed the mistress. "Flora's maid couldn't make the trip," Mr. Consortium Number One said, smiling amiably. Mr. Consortium Number Two had carried on, "Captain Garvin, you'll have to help with the spaceship tiara, and the train."

Hierarch and Consortium waved good night.

The media recorded Captain Garvin picking up and holding Flora's train as she blew kisses to the guests. After an elegant pose, a final hand wave, she crossed the threshold. The door of the suite closed behind them.

"Someone goofed," Garvin said, bitterly. "I should've carried you. Trailing train, trailing skirt, and with the sun low and reaching through the window, the media could have given Terra a view all the way to your navel."

She flung the tiara aside, ripped the gown neckline to waist, and stepped out of the billowing wreckage.

"Rod—I didn't rig this tableau, this—oh, I wanted to see you, be here to wish you luck. I talked it up, persuaded Alex—but I didn't—" She choked, caught him with both arms, "I didn't cook this up—this charade!" She backed away, blinked, wailed, "I didn't!" Then fiercely, "Everyone knew about Lani, and then your, your native girl. You drive every night to Gook Town. Of course the story got to Terra, and this show was to prove that there wasn't anything to such gossip."

"That a space hero couldn't possibly play games with anyone who wasn't the government-certified North American blend! That there wasn't any female Gook—never could be. If there had, you'd have stayed far away from Maritania!" Beginning to understand, Garvin sighed, shook his head. "So, let's get it straight. As long as the Plastic Public bought the demonstration, the facts make no difference, and here you are—there was and there is. She and I said our good-byes in the Throne Room."

"*There*, in the crowd?"

He nodded. "She pretended to be taking notes on my last-minute statement, for tomorrow, just before take-off. A big name columnist or commentator gets the by-line or screen or both. Of course nobody noticed her. She just said, 'Good luck, and see you when you get back.' "

"But they can't keep you *here*."

"They don't have to *keep* me here. You didn't make it a political commercial, you didn't even suspect that you'd be on a million screens, flipping lavender panties with little rose-bud embroideries and saying, 'Rinse them in *Sudz-Oh* before you fly to Saturn'—you're here, and you hate space like snakes."

More and more, Garvin recognized Flora as a covictim, a sacrifice to the happiness of the Plastic Populace, another pageant illustrating the wonders of Democracy. And since she was here, he could no longer resent the solicitude which had made her pull him out of space-faring. He hoped that she had not noticed that the four security men remained in the hall: the Consortium, he suspected, was making sure that no camera men would have a chance to get a picture of Space Hero heading for Gookville.

"I'm glad you made it," Garvin continued, and he meant it. "I've been a slug and a headache. Just being myself, no harm intended. Too busy doing things to have time for intentions."

"Slug . . . headache . . ." Flora echoed his words, looked up, kicked aside the muddle of metal fabric and gauze. "I've been your evil genius. We liked some of the same things—it was not hating enough of the same things! That was the trouble. I've done a lot of thinking about us."

"You've had company. Carry on, doll."

"One thing—Rod, I hope you'll believe me—that month or so before we married, I really did think I was pregnant, and I was so scared and worried that I'd never take a chance again—"

"We would have married anyway—the samples were too damn out of this world good—and I hope you believe me. Nothing was ever wrong with you except that everlasting *take care* attitude—no, you never used the words, so there wasn't a blunt-instrument murder, but every time I heard someone speak them, it reminded of why I got taken off the Mars run and fitted out with the biggest ground job Cousin Alexander could dream up. And when you balked about getting out of the country and heading for Khatmandu or Cuzco, that's where Lani came in and from there on, there's little or nothing you don't know—anyway, no gripe, darling, this is take-off eve, and don't tell me that's a Freudian slip."

"Lani . . ." Flora mused. "I looked up her dossier—is she actually so marvelous at gourmet cooking?"

The question left Garvin groping. Flora laughed, amiably mocking. "Of course I'm not interested in her bedroom manners! If any cards in her deck were missing, you wouldn't have wanted to take her to bed, much less to Khatmandu." She rearranged herself, neither stretched out on the sofa, nor quite sitting up. A friendly, cushion-supported posture, an amiable smile, whimsical. "What I've really been wondering about . . ."

Voice trailed off.

"This is our *hail, Caesar*, we who are about to head for Saturn salute thee! Nothing's a foul tonight. Neither can be griped by what the other says. God damn it, madame, if we'd got down to talking out loud and to the point at the very beginning—"

She smiled ruefully. "Lover, we'd have blown it up from the start. With sense enough to look at the facts—"

"We'd have designed the five-acre mattress and lived

happily ever after. You had something on your mind, didn't you? Wondering?"

"About your . . . ah, local girl."

"You and your female snooping curiosity! Well, I guess it's professional interest."

"If it weren't takeoff eve, I'd call you a bastard and slap your face!" Her eyes narrowed, her lips thinned, and then she laughed happily. "Takeoff eve is fun, sad fun, but fun—just for tonight only, I think you're right—*professional.*"

He wagged his head. "Sure— you have a long-term legally binding contract, one customer, no matter how dull the son of a bitch. Lani has or used to have half a dozen interesting part-time customers, and she doesn't own a one of them, so she has to be sweet. Hence the pyramids!"

"You are a stinker!"

"Want to argue?"

She made a mocking grimace. "About your being a stinker, or about—oh, shut up! You can't sneak out of the question that way, getting me wrangling about the *professional* angle. Never mind what she's got, I am just curious."

"With everything you've got, how can you be curious about one Gook girl? Okay, doll—she's one of a mysterious people. Whether her folks came from outer space, or whether they are prehistoric refugees from one of Terra's troubled cycles, I leave that to science to figure out. My guess is that they were spacing while our people were having first thoughts on how to quit being Neanderthal."

"I'm glad you said *Neanderthal* instead of simian. So, they are really civilized?"

His eyes changed color and his face tightened.

"Rod, I didn't mean it that way. All I've ever heard is the Terran stories. Let's talk about something else. Give us a *bon voyage* glass—"

"She's a lady. No leprosy, no VD, and *it* isn't crosswise." And as he made for the bar, he looked back, grinned. "Been jailed a number of times, but never with a luscious package of woman in my cell."

Garvin came back from the bar with champagne, Armagnac, Peychaud bitters, and glassware crowding the tray. "For leave takings, nothing else does it." Glasses clicked, and over the rims, spouses condensed their tempestuous years. There was about it something of duellists, each regarding the other over the guard of his *épée*. And then the affection which rarely accompanies sword or pistol meetings blossomed. Garvin said, "Next to our premarital honeymooning, this is the peak."

A taste, and Flora set down her glass.

"When you come back, you'll be famous—the pioneer—would you have to keep on spacing, always further? To Alpha Centauri, only four light-years away?"

"Before we go into that, and there's a lot to go into. Funny, takeoff eve, we can lay it on the line. When you get back home, needle Alexander into sending for Lani, Jim Ward, Amelia, and the rest of the folks I got to Mars by mistake. I owe them that, and I have a long trip ahead of me. It's tough out where they are, in Martian Gardens and the Manned Stations on the Meridian."

She reached for her glass. "Rod, I'll radio Alexander soon as you're in flight. That's a promise."

"Let's drink to it."

And they drank.

And then, "I asked a question, and you changed the subject."

"Not mentioning names, but I'm as bad as some women."

"A woman can be a bastard, but no woman ever was a *son* of a bitch."

"Radio that to Women's Lib, and I'll tell you about spacing. The night I was prowling Maritania—that was half an hour before I met Azadeh, the Gook Lady—a thought came to me. If I make the looping of Saturn and come back, I've had it. I've made Mars a suburb of Terra. And you can shove Neptune and Pluto and Alpha Centauri. Let some other chump make that flight."

Flora's eyes widened, and her brows rose.

"You can believe me like you never have before. Now hear this, this is no drill. To make the next breakthrough, beyond Saturn, beyond Neptune, beyond Pluto, out of the solar system—the poor chump who does that will be wallowing chin-deep in the Magnificent Muck of a secure, take-care society. I can, I could take it, but be damned if I am going to. I'm retiring to far-off high places that never heard of North America. I am not going to keep on being bigger and better—I am not going to bust my ass to amount to something. Being me is a full-time career, and I'm pursuing it. You love the Magnificent Society and all its trimmings. I know what it means to you."

Flora did her bit of blinking and gulping and trying to digest the substance and the implications. "But she is in love with you."

Too polite to say, *"You are in love with Azadeh."* Garvin ignored that fine distinction, and replied, "Azadeh and I spoke a good deal about you. And she said, *'We'll take your wife along, and I'll be your concubine, your Number Two Lady, or whatever else you might call me.'* Even if I'd wanted to break away from you and have my final night in Gook Town, she'd shake her head and close the door. She doesn't own me. You don't own me. I don't own either of you. Azadeh isn't wired up, North American style, so this is your turn, your night, our night—she knows that whoever owns another is a slave owner, and the least free of all people is the slave-owner. If I'd wanted to turn my back on a woman who'd come all the way from Terra, Azadeh would know that I wasn't the sort of person she'd want to sleep with. How you lik-ee? But don't answer, not yet. It'd be wrong to hold out on you, and I don't think I am."

"I don't know what you've skipped!" Flora said, and she was amiable beyond every rule in the book.

"Here we go. Alexander and the Consortium have it figured out for me not to come back. There's an odd and peculiar alloy in the shell of the *Saturnienne*. It wasn't originally planned for sabotage and it is one of the best alloys for spacing, but you can blow the whole cruiser up in a puff of flame if you know how to use the reactor rods in ways they were not designed to be used."

Flora recoiled, licked her lips. She leaned toward him, caught him by the shoulders. "You wouldn't say that unless you believed it. You're a thorough bastard and too arrogant to be a liar. But how could *saboteurs* be so crazy as to blow themselves up?"

"It's the system, darling, century and a half of gullibility. They'll do anything they're suggested to do, never suspecting that it wasn't just a gag for a slow-down, or whatever the pretext! That's why I'm bailing out, when I return—begin to understand?"

Her change of color showed through her makeup. "Tell me—this could be our last time together—you've been a stubborn stinker and I've been a giddy bitch, your evil genius—" Flora smiled, she glowed, she blinked tears away. "I never saw till today, and even then I didn't suspect that they'd go as far as they did—in making a political commercial of our wanting to be together. It's a wonder there's not a *look-ee talk-ee* of us in bed."

"The Consortium had to send me out—no malice about it, nothing personal—the best way of making sure I'd be the only kind of really good hero—a dead one.

"The crew is hand picked, made up of game players, loafers, overfed and underworked slobs, citizen-dreamers, hopped up by words and slogans. They'd respond to the village idiot! . . . So, the high, unpeopled spaces—understand now?"

Flora nodded. Her eyes were wide and dark. Radiance reached from behind her face, glowed through eyes and skin. She'd gone far beyond any orgasmic peak. "I know, now . . . finally . . ." Her voice was strange and new, neither happy nor sad, but transcending both extremes. "We're high, nothing matters now . . . we'll always be at cross-purposes, always clashing . . . you're you, and I'm I—so we'll go and see and not be sorry."

"I'll fool them, the whole crew of them—"

"Whether you do, or don't—" Flora wriggled out of her slip and flipped it aside, flung bra after the slip. "No pills, no shots since you left, and I couldn't care less—"

Chapter 27

In the morning Flora and Garvin waited at the barrier which kept the crowd well away from the entrance tube which led to the passenger port of the *Saturnienne*. He was not surprised when Samgan Manioglu came edging along the barrier and toward the media teams which were covering the event.

"*Tura*," he said,, "Let your eyes follow me. I go to where she stands. You have binoculars, and she has the pair you gave her. My cap, my coat, pick me out where I'll stand, and you'll see her."

"Father, all is understood between her and me. The messages I'll send." He extended his hand, in which he had palmed a tightly folded slip of paper. "This is for you and Azadeh if I come back or if I do not come back. Thanks, peace, blessing."

Stately in his white tunic with Arabesque designs in medallions, on chest and back, the old man resumed skirting the barrier. Presently, he stood for a moment, then leaned well over the cable before drawing up erectly.

"Azadeh's father?" Flora asked. "And imagine, you took time to learn her language! Nice, if you and I had tried to learn each other's language."

"We did that last night, darling. It's only a question of getting a chance to speak it some time."

Again, communications teams got the Dignitaries, their words, their faces; and then, Garvin, with Flora

201

looking like a bride. What the camera got was not an act: there was peace between them, and their blinkings were unfeigned. Their kiss was genuine, which spoiled its camera value. Then he went to board the *Saturnienne*, with Admiral Courtney and two watches of the crew following.

Then came an unplanned bit: Garvin, gesturing, "Admiral Courtney, I led off yesterday. Your turn today. I've been following your idea from the start—Board ahead of me."

The lean, long-faced officer shook his head. "Thank you, Captain Garvin, but this is your show."

Once on the bridge, Garvin raised his binoculars, slowly scanning the faces of those who pressed against the barrier. Flora remained where he'd left her with the communications crews. She'd have stayed even if they hadn't asked her to stay where she was, so that they could zoom in when she waved as the *Saturnienne* rose on her tower of flame.

High magnification brought her image as close as though she and Garvin were standing eye to eye. She was alone now. Unaccustomed to high-powered glasses, she didn't realize that he could almost count her eyelashes—and he knew that their reconciliation had been complete. It had gone further, further by far, than forgiving him for that scandalous caper with Lani; further even than her acceptance of Azadeh as his Number Two Lady. The past night's recklessness had left its signature. *Take care* had been blotted out, blasted away. Now there was exaltation—not lover's exaltation, but that of self-liberation, self-discovery. More than that long ago honeymoon glow. Even with earth instead of Cloud Number Seven beneath her feet, she'd never forget the Cloud, and Garvin thought, "It didn't have a number, and it wasn't purple or pink or any other color—it was a don't give a good-God-damn cloud, here I go and I don't care what happens."

He'd never imagined that she could become so nearly like Azadeh, below the makeup, below the skin, below the magnolia blossom, the old ivory tinge of Asiatic skin which at age sixty has a texture finer than any North American teenager's.

Under the skin, Flora was good enough to keep.

Garvin shifted the glasses. The "indoor" bridge couldn't be filmed. He didn't have to wave back at Flora. He picked up Samgan Manioglu's conspicuous tunic and cap, and then, Azadeh beside him, her binoculars leveled. Garvin stepped close as he could get to the shatterproof triplex glass which inclosed the bridge.

Azadeh lowered the binoculars. She'd seen him. He lowered his optics to give her a clear look again, then raised them. Her lips shaped words he had to guess because they'd had too little time to practice lip reading. She gestured. He lowered his glasses and was willing to bet she'd get the words he shaped.

Behind him, a door clicked and Hamlin Daly said, "Tweed reports all clear."

"Fire up!" Garvin commanded.

When he felt the first lift, he raised his arm to Azadeh and turned away. He paused, found Flora, who couldn't see him, but he saluted the memory of their first honeymoon and of reconciliation.

Low g and thin atmosphere—Mars had a feeble hold on the *Saturnienne*. Her ascent was faster even than the final shakedown flights around Mars had led him to expect. Presently, he could see the curvature of the horizon. The domes of Mars become translucent pearls against ruddy soil which reminded him of the Arizona desert in the Kingman–Oatman area. The widespread pearls along the meridian became ever smaller specks, and ever nearer to each other.

He counted, "One . . . two . . . three . . . four . . . Lani . . . six . . ." He remembered that he and Azadeh had forgotten to wonder whether Morgan's disappearance and Lani's would ever be investigated.

Garvin reached for the intercom. "Casper when she's firing smoothly and settled down, send off-duty men to general assembly for briefing. I'm taking a walk-around."

He punched intercom buttons to signal Lani's uncharted stateroom. When he got the answering buzz, he said, "Ignore general assembly. I'll see you while the off-duty watches are waiting for me to brief them. Is your stateroom bugged?"

"Hamlin says it's okay. He checked it out."

"Keep it so."

Casper Tweed came to the bridge to take over.

When general assembly sounded and green lights blinked, alternating with orange, Garvin leveled his glasses at the ruddy globe of Mars. He traced the road which intersected the one from Maritania's emormous domes to the cleft which had housed him and Azadeh during their subsurface honeymooning. He shook his head as though to clear it.

"Be damned if I'm not getting homesick."

Not for Terra but for Mars. Whether he went with two women or with one, he'd make for a Terran High Place farthest from the areas which had the highest standards of living with *Supervision* for all.

The elevator dropped to the passage leading to Lani's stateroom. His code signal got instant response. She was fully dressed and without professional makeup.

"Any problems?"

"Not so far. But—" She glanced about, uneasily. "Was there any, ah, flare up about, uh, the Inspector's disappearance?"

"No one mentioned it to me."

"Not even your aboriginal lady?"

"She had a lot of things to attend to toward the last."

"I bet she did!"

"Low minded little bitch! There was ceremony aplenty, and what little sleep I got, it was with Flora."

Lani sighed, shrugged. "I guess there are times when even a wife is a change of pace."

"Who knows you're aboard, except Ham and Caspar?"

"Nobody, far as I know of, so far. By the way, now that we've taken off, who am I supposed to sleep with—well, I guess I should've said, who am I supposed *not* to?"

"What're you getting so anxious about? That's a new quirk!"

"Well, in the old seafaring days, a stowaway getting caught had to work his way to the nearest shore—" She shuddered. "It must've been *awful*, climbing around in the rigging, or shoveling coal. I don't know what Women's Lib sounds off about so much, female stowaways always had it better. Better pay for equal work."

"When I get through coping with immediate problems, I'll be devoting lots of thought to that one. Meanwhile, keep life simple and for Christ's sweet sake, stay out of sight and smell. I know you shower oftener than any virtuous woman ever dreams of, but you always smell like an invitation to rape." He glanced about the stark bulkheads, the open closet, the compact bath compartment. He sniffed. "*Red Mist*, I bet."

"Give you lecherous notions?"

"Not until you conk another inspector or other would-be rapist."

"Ooooh . . . Wasn't I just *awful* that night!"

"Changing the subject abruptly—" He jerked a thumb at the row of books. "When did you get intellectual?"

"Oh, that fifty-centimeter shelf of classics? Pass me the Bible, or Shakespeare or Homer."

He reached, then exclaimed, "They're all falsies! What's the wiring and stuff behind them?"

"My spy system. Ham figured it out and installed it. He did the wiring before I sneaked aboard that night. He'd figured on bugging the foos'le and elsewhere, just in case."

"And people have called *me* a paranoiac! We ought to have a psychiatrist aboard. Too late, so tell me, is it productive so far?"

"You expect faster action than a girl in a one-*pazor* house! Well, it's yes and no . . . a hooker develops a suspicious nature, account of the bastards she meets—"

"Thank *you*, you red-headed bitch!"

"Now, don't be touchy, honey! You've *always* been nice. As I was saying, turning down so many kinky customers takes intuition, sensitivity, and if you don't have intuition, there's Jack the Ripper or worse. Anyway, there is something cooking. No, I can't recognize the voices, and I missed things. I missed a lot, some of them mushmouthed. There was something about how nasty it would be going through the asteroid belt. And the thing to do is to turn around and go back before we get into the flying gravel pit. And when somebody said maybe the Admiral would talk you into backtracking before you got too far, someone told him that he was fruit, the Admiral had spent half his life wishing he had a chance to make this cruise."

"So far, it adds up, and I wasn't morbidly suspicious! And I owe you an apology."

"What for?"

"Well you're not really red-headed at all, it's tawny golden."

He was ready to dodge, but she missed that one, and he wondered until a question broke the long pause. "Rod, what do you know about admirals? Are they anything like generals and other high brass?"

"You ask the damndest questions! Now, if I wanted a rundown on high-ranking officers, I'd ask the most beautiful, elegant, and intelligent playgirl I know. Whatever you're cooking up, be discreet about it, and don't go wild."

"If you think I'm interested in being the *Saturnienne*'s whore, you're demented. Thanks, I'll be discreet."

Garvin made it to the elevator and thence to the assembly room. The moment he entered, he was sure that Lani had been right in her estimate of the talk she'd audited. That there would be silence when the skipper entered was natural enough, and so was the scuffle and scramble as Norton, the Second Officer, and the men got to their feet. Their faces had to rearrange themselves. There was nothing which Garvin could pin down definitely, yet he had the feeling that he'd broken in on something he was not supposed to hear. It was significant that neither Casper nor Ham was in the compartment, nor the Admiral.

Garvin, open faced and beaming, glanced at Mr. Norton.

They didn't know him well enough to suspect that his good-humored front was pure trickery.

"All present and accounted for, sir."

"Sit down." He dipped into the pocket of his jacket and brought out several small objects which he fumbled

without giving anyone a look; there was however a hint
of metallic twinkle, and their eyes shifted. He had them
baited, and he resumed, "While you crew members
were lolling around the fun spots, I was prowling, quite
a piece beyond the mines." He displayed a piece of ma-
chined metal, and two small chunks of dark substance.
"Pass these around. I want each of you to get a look,
then size up what you see. Officers last. Men speak up,
beginning with lowest rating. I want your opinions, your
guesses, before I tell you what I am guessing. Repeat, I
am guessing with you. I don't *know*."

The first crewman dutifully fingered, squinted, and
passed the specimens to the nearest shipmate. That one
became a bored diplicate of the first. The third muttered, eyed the piece of metal more closely, looked up,
made as if to speak, but changed his mind.

"Sims, what's so interesting?" Garvin demanded.

"Sir, I used to be a machinist's mate. Ah, um——"

"Carry on. If you're afraid of a laugh, relax. I'm
talking last and if anyone thinks what I say is funny, no
sweat at all."

"This looks like a piece of a porthole cover clamp.
The tool marks—I don't get it——" He twisted the narrow piece of metal, cocked his head. "Now I got it
again. Sir, you take it, if you hold it just right, you
see——"

"I noticed that, but you tell me."

"It shows color bands—refraction, diffraction. I
can't think of the words——"

"You're doing all right. And we do not finish metal
so needlessly smooth these days."

"Someone had a lot of time to kill."

"You're modern, Sims! And you've not given your
shipmates much left to say. That finish was made by
tools a lot faster working then anything I've ever seen."

They closed in, edging about him, to form a crescent.

"Pass those bits of ore to Hendricks. I'll get back to
the tool marks."

Hendricks didn't look overly bright, a languid stand-
up-and-fall-down. The specimen however touched him
off. He closed his fly-trap mouth, fingered the ore,
sniffed it, thrust it toward Garvin. "Sir, it's hot."

Garvin took a square of lead foil from his pocket. "That's the way I figured it." He passed the radiation-proof foil to Hendricks. "That bit of exposure won't hurt you. I had the stuff tested. You're a mineralogist?"

"Well—uh—I used to be."

Their eyes met, leveled, until Hendricks lowered his glance. Garvin saw no point in remarking on the counterfeiting rap the man had sweated out because of his metallurgical talent.

"Let's hear the mineralogy."

"Sir, that's what bugged me. Never saw ore like this, but I'd bet it's thorium."

"At will, inspect the specimens," Garvin resumed. He had them hooked. "Forget what I said about rank. Gabble as much as you please. When you're talked out, I'll tell you something."

He sat down, reached for the previous day's *Maritania Times* and caught up on the news. The media cameramen had been dawdling, as had the feature story writers. Nothing about Roderick and Flora, and how thrilling it was to start all over again.

He flipped the *Times* aside when the second officer said, "Sir, if you are ready to speak, I'll call the men to order."

"Please do so," and in the succeeding moment, Garvin was on his feet facing the crew. He had the specimens on the arm of his chair. Picking up the metal, he began, "The machining of this piece is older than any written history we've heard of. The ore you've been discussing never came from Terra or from Mars. It's a new isotope. That much the lab at Maritania decided.

"This bit of metal came from a spaceship that was set down while Mars had an atmosphere. It's an alloy different from any we know. The threads are not English, and they are not metric. None of the lab technicians could classify the machine work—it doesn't fit into any system of our machine age, which began about four hundred years ago.

"That cruiser I found out beyond the explored area of Mars had ore that you don't find in any Terrestrial mines, and none in the mines of Mars. We don't know where these samples came from, but the bits that are fused into this polished metal are the same kind of ore as the chunks you've been looking at.

"The stuff is flying around in space. Could be in the asteroid belt. And—purely as a wild gamble—this is the chance of a lifetime, find out where the prehistoric astronauts got the stuff. If we find it, we'll make it big. A bonus, and all that that you've signed up for—plus, special legislation for extra payoffs.

Chapter 28

The going proved to be worse than Garvin or the Admiral had anticipated. The *Santurnienne*'s shell vibrated from the peppering of fragments long before she came within the fringe of the charted zone. However, the repulsion field prevented damage from chunks too massive for the shell to resist, yet too small to register on the radar screen.

Presently, the directional jets got their first workout.

"We don't have to follow the course that the orders prescribe," Admiral Courtney suggested, after a succession of rugged watches shared with Garvin. "Why not go over the belt?"

"Why not?" Garvin agreed, though he did not ask whether his consultant's hint was based upon explorations and experiments not entered in the logs of cruisers he had commanded.

Whatever the origin of the thought, it was no help. The asteroid orbits proved to be more steeply inclined to the ecliptic than the charts had indicated. The belt appeared to be as deep as it was broad, perhaps even more so.

Tweed took the next watch.

When Garvin went with Daly to relieve Tweed, they gave him his chance to tell at length what he had tersely logged.

"We're going through a dust bowl. Look at the haze!"

The stars were veiled. Garvin said, "Couldn't be much worse diving through Saturn's ring."

Is the dust radioactive?" Admiral Courtney asked casually.

"Yes, sir, it was the last two tests."

"What do you think of it? The haze, I mean."

Tweed pointed to the indicator graph. "Losing speed. Too much drag. Temperature's going up—up—ten—twelve degrees."

Back in his cabin, Garvin kept an eye on the infrared spying system. The invisible light system had been wired in after the final inspection at Maritania Spaceport while the crew was enjoying ground leave. Although nothing came from Lani's audio system, infrared rays activated the video screen, which enabled Garvin to see what was happening in the dark.

Presently he spotted a group in a compartment off a passageway near the power-room. The audio hookup brought in only an unintelligible muttering. Garvin signaled Daly.

"Come on over, Ham. I'll show you a thing or two."

Daly lost no time in getting to the skipper's quarters.

"That infravisual you installed is doing the job. Take a look."

After a moment, Daly said, "They're waiting for something to happen."

"Those bastards don't have long to wait! Neither do we. No telling what those knotheads might cook up, trying to get me to turn around and head for home."

"That temperature rise bugged them. I didn't like it either, and neither did Casper Tweed, though he said little."

"They're so dumb they don't know how dumb they are. They're likely to cook up some trick that would blow us up by mistake and themselves included."

Garvin's eyes narrowed. "Ham, watch the IR visor while I try something you did not wire up. And the pipe-fitter didn't know the color coding—it wasn't in the book." He stepped to the disaster control panel and actuated solenids which operated bulkheads that sealed off various compartments, isolating them from the others.

"That broke it up!" Daly exclaimed. "Man, man!"

"Keep watching."

Eye on a pressure dial, Garvin cracked a valve. There was a faint hissing and whining. "Hold it!" Daly warned. "They're blacking out. All but one . . . now he's out!"

Garvin opened a purge valve and at the same time fed oxygen into the gassed compartment.

The intercom buzzed. Norton, the Chief Warrant Officer, was babbling and incoherent.

Garvin shouted, "Do something, mister! I'll be out directly."

He cleared the damage control panel switches.

"You hustle," Daly said, "and I'll listen."

The four spacemen were beginning to revive when Garvin stormed into the now-lighted compartment. He was on Norton's heels. The Pharmacist's Mate trailed along with his emergency kit.

The half-conscious men were trying to sit up. They muttered and mumbled. "It's got to work soon . . . We're done for if we don't go back . . . Christ, we've gone too far . . . They've got to clog up soon."

The first to regain his wits sufficiently to realize that they had an outside audience let out a yell. "He's a God-damn liar—I didn't have a thing to do with it—I just happened to come in—"

"Dargan said it wouldn't be long—"

"I didn't either—I didn't say—"

Before the end of a wild minute, everyone had denied having said anything. Garvin cut in, "Don't take so long telling me that none of you was ever in here and weren't doing anything. Now that nobody was here, what the hell brought you to this compartment?"

Everyone thought that he'd heard an odd sound.

There was the drumming of interference beats, the normal muttering of the exhaust. Garvin however caught a faint undertone. The sound was not normal. A manhole cover, not tightly secured, was vibrating. Instead of taking up on the handwheel, he slacked off and lifted the cover. Fumes billowed out. A ruddy glow broke the darkness.

Garvin said to Daly, "Let's have a look." After an

exchange of querying looks, he added, "Sure, we'll need hot suits, and bring a tool kit. The *emergency* kit, you understand."

"*Emergency*," Daly echoed. "Aye, aye, sir."

"And an open-end adjustable wrench while you're at it." He stepped to the intercom. "Mr. Tweed! I am sending Mr. Norton to relieve you. This is an emergency. Repeat, *emergency*. You do not need a hot suit. Do *not*, repeat *not*, need a hot suit."

Garvin closed but did not secure the manhole cover. It opened into the bulkhead, not into the deck. He said, "Nothing but paint fumes. Relax."

But nobody did relax, except the skipper.

Daly presently returned. He wore a hot suit, with helmet flipped back. In one hand he had an adjustable open-end wrench. In the other he carried a mechanic's tool kit, about one meter long. It seemed not as heavy as it looked: a light gesture set it on deck, right at Garvin's ankle.

Garvin addressed a crewman. "Sims, grab that wrench and take down that manhole cover. Dargan, give him a hand."

When it was unhinged, they set the heavy slab on the deck.

Garvin opened the big tool chest and took from it an asbestos suit, a helmet and a shoulder pack of oxygen.

Daly dipped into the chest and came up with an old-fashioned device which the centuries had never outmoded: a sawed-off shotgun.

Garvin wagged his head, and announced to all present, "Don't shut the manhole after me when I step in. Stand well clear."

And then Casper Tweed stepped into the compartment. He remained at the entrance. "Captain, where's the emergency?"

"I won't know until I go in and take a look. So far, there isn't any."

"Aye, aye, sir, and there ain't going to be none."

He swayed, turned slowly on his heel, covering the crewmen.

Garvin stepped into the passageway. Holes had been drilled through the insulation, and into the exhaust tube jacketting. The tube itself had a dangerous glow. Sparks darted up from it. The alloy was on the point of failing. It was on the durability of the metal that the entire cruise depended.

Garvin knelt and picked some of the hexagonal red crystals from the deck. He stepped to the intercom and called the engineer on watch: "Webber, starboard tube number four failed. Cut off and replace." Then, to the men in the corner: "Sims, Dargan—put the manhole plate back."

Garvin got out of the hot suit, and put it back in the tool kit. He addressed the First Officer: "Mr. Tweed, there never was an emergency. Resume your post and relieve Mr. Norton."

When the manhole plate was secured, he commanded, "All hands, dismissed."

All hands were happy to leave.

Garvin said to Warrant Officer Daly, "Ham, this is bound to become montonous, but I might as well give these sons of bitches the works while they are in a pliable mood. Put away that sawed-off shotgun, and when general assembly is sounded, show up with three saucers in your pocket."

"If you're thinking of what I think you're thinking, all hands ought to show up with spare pants."

When he was back in his own quarters, Garvin unlocked and dipped into a compartment from which he took another archaic weapon which in many a situation was better than modern electronic arms which were more destructive than need be: a collector's piece, for the collector who still had sense enough to combine beauty with utility, instead of, for instance, replica IXL jacknives.

It was a short-barrelled 11.2 millimeter magnum. He removed the cartridges, hefted each, and replaced them.

Then he called Lani. "I'll have general assembly sounded. There is no emergency, so ignore it. If you have company, it is okay for him to ignore it."

She called him a dirty name and cut the connection. But he was sure that Lani was smiling when she spoke.

When all hands were assembled, excepting those on watch, Garvin came to the point without preamble:

"The unexplained failure of power tubes would make it foolhardy to carry on. We'd have to turn back. And you are here because the starboard number four tube was close to failing."

He gave them time to digest what he had fed them. Then he gave all hands—or almost all—acute indigestion.

"The tube did not fail, and there is an explanation. Sabotage is a handy word whenever you don't know the answer. I do know the answer and for the benefit of anyone on deck who does not know why that tube began getting in trouble, I'll explain.

"Someone who probably did not know any better, drilled holes in the insulation and poured in cinnabar crystals. That's as bad as putting lead on platinum. Someone of this crew, though maybe not of these two watches, was trying to get the ship to put about.

"I do not know who did it, and I do not want to know. Ham, did you bring the saucers?" and then, "Go into your dance."

Daly flipped the saucers, one-two-three. None hit the ceiling, and none hit the deck. Garvin's three shots blasted the trio, in midflight.

"If I'd known who did it, he'd a got those three slugs. Dismissed!" He added, "Mr. Norton, stand fast, just a moment. You probably know why I had the manhole cover taken off before I walked into that passageway? And you may guess why I called for sawed-off shotguns instead of using my handgun?"

As to the first, Mr. Norton knew. As to the second, he did not.

"It is simple. The shotguns spoke for themselves. The handgun would not have been convincing until I demonstrated, and there were no saucers handy."

Norton's color was still sickly. "I've read the manual cover to cover but I never heard that cinnabar is harmful."

"I know you didn't. Because this alloy was made up from a formula that didn't exist when the manual was printed. Unless you crave to finish your days aboard a space derelict drifting with the asteroids, put a stop to whatever is cooking.

"And, one more thing, Mr. Norton!"

"Yes, sir?"

"Find out what the complaints are. Those fellows who were bumping their gums about the funny noise had a lot more on their minds than they wanted to spill. When you find out, tell me, but mention no names. That's all."

An hour later, Norton reported, "Self-luminous asteroids got them worrying. They're about ready to blow their gaskets. They think you are lost and too stubborn to admit it."

Garvin sighed. "Those meat-heads might know there's nothing wrong with an asteroid's being self-luminous, no more than there's much out of line if one is dark and doesn't reflect light. They've heard too much muck from someone who read what astronomers have written. All they know is what they think they saw, while pratt-sitting in an observatory. We're here and looking at things and we are among what we're seeing.

"Our radar beam could make some of those spitballs glow."

Chapter 29

Now that Jupiter and the asteroid belt were well astern, Garvin called an officers' conference. The *Saturnienne*'s shell had taken a beating. She was losing air. Although reserves could handle routine loss, the present leakage was more than routine.

"The log," he began, "shows that each has known for some while that we've been losing more air than we should. I have not called for your opinions on what to do. That's something we know already.

"The only question is, *when do we get to work?* I don't want a debate. I want each one of you to write his own opinion and hand it to me when I call the next conference.

"I do not want any one of you to discuss your opinion or in anyway try to influence any other officer. I want no one to be influenced by another's rank, experience, or other qualification."

He paused, eyed them. Sensing that the Admiral was on the verge of addressing him, Garvin quickly resumed to avoid even the appearance of discourtesy.

"*I* am included in *no one*. I want not a word from any of you until each has handed me his opinion and I have the opinions of officers now on duty. The question is, *when do we get to work?* You need not, but you are welcome to include whatever reasoning you wish to offer. That's all. Thank you."

As the conference broke up, the Admiral stepped toward Garvin; Garvin did not like the veteran's expression, least of all the firm resolution in the wintry eyes, the weathered face.

"Captain Garvin, we were dismissed, but—"

"Admiral Courtney, my apologies: but the conference has been disbanded."

"This is personal."

Garvin met the man's eyes, narrowed, and with a gleam like lance heads by moonlight. He noted the twitch at the corners of the usually unwavering, the inflexible mouth.

"I am sorry, Admiral Courtney. I cannot allow even the appearance of making an exception to my instructions. I'll be happy to hear what you have to say— immediately after I have *all* the opinions in my possession."

Garvin did not make the tentative gesture which was a hint to a subordinate that the man in charge had terminated the interview and was ready to return the salute of him who was about to leave. Garvin snapped a meticulous, ultracrisp salute, and that did it. One detail fouled it up: there was only one exit, he did not care to go ahead of the Admiral.

Without knowing why he felt as he did, Garvin shied from the Admiral's personal problems. The entire business had the flavor of trouble. With the Admiral's thirty years of seniority over the captain of the *Saturnienne*, there should not be any personal problem concerning which Garvin could counsel the dean of spacemen.

Garvin went to the observation-transmission compartment. There he looked through the eyepiece of the sighting telescope. As the cruiser neared Saturn, she'd be diving, heading for the planet's polar region to get the full expanse of the concentric rings. This would not be a repeat of what "Explorers" and "Surveyors" and all the other unmanned pots had sent back to Terran space centers. This would give a *portrait* of the magnificent planet from the optimum camera angle.

Garvin made notes, adding to his shooting script for plotting the course. He had to study the ephemeris of the thirteen moons of Saturn to see if, with the proper camera angle, he could get them all in one tightly framed scene.

Although the prospect of getting the perfect portrait of Saturn got his mind off air-loss, the Admiral's problem persisted in nagging. Garvin cursed, jabbed an intercom button. He said, "If you're alone and not wearing *Red Mist*, I'll be seeing you immediately."

That Lani did not retort with one of her stock quips was ominous. What she said was, "I've been wanting to have a word with you but gossips say you're in a stinking mood."

"On the way, and they're right!"

When Garvin stepped into the stateroom, he eyed Lani and grumbled, "Dressed, for a God-damn wonder. What're *you* looking so constipated about?"

"Oh, I'm all up in the air and worried . . . you remember . . . in a kind of halfway hinting, I let you know the Admiral was interested in me."

"You were hinting with a double-bitted axe! What's the beef? He doesn't like you, or you don't like him?"

"I just don't know what to do—he wants to marry me."

Garvin exhaled, a quavering sigh. "Is that all? I thought you were going to tell me you're knocked up. Anyway, you're over the age of consent, and if you don't like the deal, run out on him and sue the old bastard for desertion—it's easy, in California. Get alimony checks as long as a box car. What've I got to do with all this, I'm not your parent or guardian!"

"Oh, you never understand *anything!* Nobody else aboard could marry us except you—you're the captain."

"Nuh-uh! Not even a hundred years past never. He knows there must've been something between you and me, or you wouldn't be aboard."

"I told him it was entirely platonic. He could see how devoted you were to Flora, not even sleeping with your Gook lady the last night in Maritania."

"He'd still be suspicious and jealous."

"Oh, but he loves me."

"That's just what I am getting at. Now, if you were

the ship's whore, there'd be no problem. But once you're his wife, there'd be a sticky situation . . . mutiny . . . assassination—"

"Well, this situation is pretty much your fault."

"*My* fault?" Garvin shouted. "You didn't know where to dump the Inspector's carcass. You didn't have any place to go except aboard the *Saturnienne*—"

"Oh, Rod, you *never* understand me!"

"You talk as if we were married!"

Lani carried on, "When you came to Station Five, and I saw how happy you were with your Azadeh, and then when I saw the broadcast of the ceremonies and I saw how happy you and Flora were, I just got a burning urge to settle down and retire. The Admiral's awfully nice, and I'm tired of being a hooker, and the time to quit is while I've got my shape and my looks. Well, now, you see! It is your fault, looking so happy with a wife and a concubine."

"He'll keep till this cruise is over. It'll have to."

"But maybe he won't," she wailed. "Josiah has a heart condition, and he wants to make sure I'll at least be his lawful widow."

"I told you twice, God-damn it, no!"

"But *why* not?"

"While I was at the funny farm, I was reading some old true-fact crime stories. One about a beautiful model. About the time she was fourteen, big enough and eager, she was in bed with every painter, sculptor, architect, and most of the successful writers in town. And finally she met a wealthy patron of the arts and she married him. Well, he was crazier than he acted, so he killed one of the forty–fifty men who'd laid her—the one he figured was the one who ruined the girl he loved.

"Nuh-uh! Take care of the crew, after you've taken care of the officers, and all is well. But I'll not have this a honeymoon ship—I've got troubles enough."

"Can't you be reasonable? I'm really fed up with the pussy-rental business, and here's my chance to retire."

"Does he know you're going to ask me?"

"Lord, no! He's so sensitive."

"And that is what I'm afraid of."

Lani's voice changed. "Honey, I know you can't help

being a little jealous. You know that I'd never *not* want you?"

Garvin sighed regretfully. "It's a funny business all around. If I had a girl, she'd have to be all mine. And there'd have to be one for the crew. Really, one for the officers, and one for crew. Meanwhile, whichever way I decide the question of you and him will be as wrong one way as the other way would've been."

Lani sighed. Her smile was wry, but there was a fond light in her eyes. "You're a son of a bitch," she murmured. "You always were, but sometimes I almost love you."

Lani kissed the bunched tips of her fingers, and tapped them lightly on his right cheek, and on his left.

"We'll make out, somehow," she added, as he turned toward the door: and he knew that she referred to herself and the Admiral.

Chapter 30

The total kilometers cruised had become meaningless, and Saturn was looming before Admiral Courtney entered Garvin's cabin. "Captain, this is not in the line of duty. Have you time to spare?"

Garvin shook his head, wearily, and smiled. "Sit down, sir. I've been wondering whether there is anything which is not in the line of duty. Speak your mind."

"Lani spoke to you. Now it's my turn."

"Now it *is* your turn, sir."

"Do you mind telling me why you refuse to marry us?"

"Admiral, half your life or more you've known that the only time the captain explains anything is when he instructs a subordinate. Any other time, explanation is defending a judgment he's made, and once he does that, he's no longer exercising command."

"You gave Lani some reasons."

"Admiral, if there is an art of command where women are concerned, why not explain—consider me a subordinate . . . mmmm. No comment? I was afraid of that. No doubt you have plenty of reasons why I should marry you and Lani. Reasons, and any facts you can offer."

"There are no facts to prove that Lani had anything to do with Inspector Morgan's disappearance. Why she boarded the *Saturnienne* instead of a home-bound ship,

222

or why she didn't stay at Station Five—quite irrelevant.

"I know Lani's history. You needn't have any qualms. I know what I'm doing. If she contrived to disembark at any North American spaceport without being picked up, she'd have to stay undercover indefinitely. Or, get into one of the unfederated states and make a new life for herself."

Garvin nodded. "Correctly stated, sir."

"Whatever public relations calls me," the Admiral continued, "passenger, consultant, observer, state's witness, I'll be a space pioneer. As the wife of such, Lani would avoid the investigation she'd otherwise face. If ever Inspector Morgan's body or his car were discovered, it would be the worst possible publicity for Thought Control and public opinion shapers to harass the first Space Heroine in the history of interplanetary exploration."

"Provisionally conceded, sir."

The admiral paused, drew a deep breath. "I am running out of time. If my heart doesn't settle me quickly, something else will tend to me, slowly. A space pioneer's pension would pass to my widow."

"You've given me something to digest. I am responsible for her being shanghaied to Mars. A fact you were too smart to mention. I am not promising a thing—get that straight. It serves me damn well right—I should have known better than to listen to your reasons and your facts."

The Admiral got to his feet. "Thank you for hearing me, sir."

The exchange of salutes was a cordial informality.

From North America to Saturn's front yard to extricate Lani from the mess into which his blundering had got her. And with Flora getting Jim Ward and Amelia and the others liberated, Garvin realized fully and for the first time how he had been oppressed and depressed by the obligation which had taken him so long to fulfill. Between wit and luck, he'd fooled the asteroids, and had staved off mutiny. But most of all, he was glad that he was under no further obligation to Lani.

Nevertheless, misgiving gnawed at him.

As the *Saturnienne* began to circle the planet, Mars reported that reception of pictures and of sound was excellent, and that Flora and Terran dignitaries would be waiting for the critical shot, the rings of Saturn as seen from polar heights.

Aboard the *Saturnienne*, morale was far better. Short memories had toned down the rigors of passing through the asteroid belt. Uppermost in the composite mind of the crew were the bonus and retirement on double pay, with status which conferred prestige and privilege.

Poised on gimbals, the observation compartment had the positional flexibility of a three-dimensional universal joint, and its deck, on which all but the duty crew were standing, was parallel to the axis of Saturn. Thus, the observers stood with their backs to the optical system, looking down on Saturn's pole, on Saturn's concentric rings, and on the moons which paraded across the celestial blackness.

The luminous rings, glowing swarms of particles, separated by zones of darkness, were alive, pulsating as they whirled.

Garvin spoke across space, knowing well that all those who listened at Maritania station could scarcely be other than confused as he described the geometry of the downward-lookingness of himself and the others in viewing the spectacle. But that spectacle was its own testimony. And then individuals, so carefully and persistently rehearsed that they had the appearance of spontaneity, turned to face the optics which would transmit their features, close up.

As some walked offstage, to relieve men on watch, others filed in, until each had had his long look, his moment to greet the colonists and visitors in Maritania, and ultimately, all Terran watchers. Meanwhile, Saturn's image contracted, the perimeter of the outer ring gradually drawing away from the frame of the screen.

"We're still rising," Garvin said. "But which way is up? On Mars, on Terra, one has to be very dumb not to know which way is up. In space, and for us at the moment, *up* is moving away from the nearest pole of Saturn and, with respect to other markers, sidewise, or forward, or backward. But really, there's only one way—

"And that way is Marsward, homeward. You've met *almost* all who are aboard; *almost* all have been recognized as space pioneers, to be remembered, after some other cruiser goes out beyond Neptune, beyond Pluto . . ."

For a moment, Garvin faced Flora across half a billion kilometers of darkness at whose center was a far-off sun. He gestured, blew a kiss, and sounded off, "Nothing to do now but find my way back."

His glance shifted to Azadeh. They'd have their words, their final moment, later. And then Garvin resumed his address:

"And now comes another first—Lani d'Artois, of *Folies Lyonnaise*, the First Lady of Space Stowaways."

Lani swirled her sea-green gown and stepped to her marker. The do-it-yourself hair-do, with a red-bronze curl trailing from the base of the tall coiffure and along her throat to flirt with the neck yoke of the fragile green gown was different, and no doubt of that: but it didn't look homemade.

And then Garvin presented "The most distinguished man aboard, Admiral Josiah Ambrose Courtney, my consultant on this cruise, the advisor who helped me all the way to Saturn. Admiral Courtney detected the stowaway. After a summary courtmartial, the defendant, Lani d'Artois, was sentenced to marry the Old Master of Space Men. As captain in command of the *Saturnienne*, I am marrying Lani d'Artois and Josiah Ambrose Courtney. Anyone objecting to this marriage will hold his peace, or be hustled to the brig by the master at arms."

Garvin asked the questions. He heard the responses. He declared the couple to be man and wife. Then, "First Officer Tweed, Second Officer Norton—when they sign as witnesses, I'll show you the certificate. The third witness, Saturn, will not sign."

When the Admiral and his bride quit the compartment, all but Garvin followed. Alone, he waited, watching the blank screen, until, after he knew not how many minutes, Azadeh again faced him, and this time, as thought within arm's reach.

Garvin said, "*Khanoum,* I start saying some of what

I've been thinking. I'll tell you this—I was so fidgety about that wedding that I forgot to announce that when we get to the asteroid belt's edge there will be another broadcast. The pages of the ship's log from now—get a printout—if the images are clear, that's the best record you could have. If the ship is hit by an asteroid, the whole story won't be lost."

Garvin pulled the switch and learned anew how lonely a space skipper could be.

"Lani had the right idea," he muttered, almost aloud. "There's a time for retiring, and mine's been here and passed!"

Chapter 31

Now that Garvin had Saturn behind him, he settled down to evaluating the statements which the *Saturnienne*'s officers had submitted. To have made repairs during the outbound trip could have upset the morale of the crew. Had mutiny ensued, even though it had been suppressed, the mission would have been aborted. Meanwhile, he withheld judgment until the nearness of the danger zone would give the Overfed and Underworked ample motive for doing their best.

Garvin sounded officers' call and gave his judgment: "We're so near the asteroids we can smell the little bastards." He waggled the sheaf of written recommendations. "Mentioning no names, I'll give you the high spots of a couple or three opinions. '. . . *we're not losing enough air to call it an emergency . . . another go at the floating junkyard might make it so . . .*' Here's another. '. . . *can avoid serious collision as readily as we did out-bound . . . general stress causing all-over seam leaks, harder to correct than a few serious breaks.*' Here's a nice one. '. . . *with this package of slobs and clowns, nothing but a pelting of meteorites would get Damage Control to take its thumb out and get to work.*' I told you I'd decide when to take action. The facts have told you and they've told me the same thing.

"We will change our course to go with the orbit of the asteroid swarm. Less danger of collisions than if we go across the orbit. Once we are in a vacant pocket, holding orbital speed, we'll get to work. Mr. Tweed, include that in *Orders of the Day*.

Garvin again waggled the sheaf of recommendations. "Thank you, and that's all for the day."

Edging into the fringe of the asteroid belt, the *Saturnienne* adjusted her speed until, in effect, she became one of the swarm. Damage Control set to work, a compartment at a time, inspecting the shell, looking for dents, warped areas, and punctures sealed only by metal fused by meteorite impact.

The morale was good.

The *Saturnienne* had little more than found her flying berth in one of the greater empty spaces in the swarm when a new fact intruded. However gradual, however insidious, it finally demanded Garvin's attention and that of his officers. There was a gradual change in the slope of the fine line which, hour after hour, day after day, was traced on the indicator card of the gravitational meter.

Minor planetary masses—call them major debris!—made short, sharp jerks in the continuous graph. What now interested, excited, and at times worried each officer was the buildup, the sharpening of the gradient, the slope becoming ever steeper.

"*Still rising*" was what each officer going off duty reported to the one taking over the watch.

Speculation built up regarding the size of the asteroid they were going to meet; and its *g* was becoming relevant. Although by no means a problem, whatever that body was, it had to be taken into account. The mass was out of keeping with established views on asteroids.

The third time long-faced Caspar Tweed had come off duty since the graph had first aroused general curiosity, he brushed back his cowlick and spoke his mind: "Unless the sensors are out of order, whatever it is, it's a lot bigger than—" He jabbed his index and middle finger as though to impale the ephemeris. "Ceres, Pallas, Vesta—not a damn one of them has any business in this neck of the woods."

Garvin grimaced. "Difference between telescope

squinting and getting out into things. This is worth flashing to Maritania."

"Sir, is that an opinion or is it an order?"

"Both. Pass the order to Communication. Too early for the coordinates. Simply give what's been observed. Instruments indicating approach to dense body, mass half again that of Ceres, but dimensions speculative. Stand by for visual reception until further notice—hold it, Caspar!"

Tweed turned. "Sir?"

"Report as soon as you get acknowledgment from Maritania."

Next watch, radar picked it up. Garvin stood by Daly and Tweed, and the Warrant Officer, Mr. Barrett. Each was more interested in what was just ahead than he was in going off duty.

Observational data, fed into the computer, gave successive approximations of the mass and velocity of the sphere.

When visual observation picked up a globe which neither Terrestrial nor Martian telescopes had distinguished occulting a brighter body, Garvin signaled Maritania. Then, as the optical system picked up a grayish, greenish sphere, he changed the ship's course, and addressed the mike:

"The color is more and more greenish—a considerable body of water. We're dropping for better observation and a sweep to sample the surface. If conditions favor, we land. Temperature rising . . . dense atmosphere . . . quality not yet determined . . ."

Later, when Tweed was at the controls, Garvin focused his binoculars and after a moment said, "Considerable wooded area near a lake . . . there appears to be cultivated soil. Admiral Courtney, tell us what you see."

The Admiral steadied his voice. This required effort. He was hard put to maintain the poise which training and tradition demanded. "I—ah—I can't quite believe it, but there's nothing else I can make of it, we'll have to wait and confirm—"

"Tell 'em, Admiral! Signs of animate life?"

"More than that—intelligent activity, Rod. You have a look."

"Human activity . . . tilling soil . . . in nearby field, millet—a guess, doesn't look like wheat. In the distance . . . masonry—small town, walled. We're circling for a landing spot—" Then, to the intercom, "Make atmospheric tests and report."

Garvin got the first analysis soon after she was sitting on her landing struts, on hard footing. The pharmacist wasn't sure of himself. He sounded as if he expected an order to recheck. And he got it.

Garvin beckoned to Tweed. Then, to the intercom: "Ames, let's have that again. Never mind the oxygen, nitrogen, CO_2, helium."

Ames called back presently and repeated what he had first given.

Garvin said, "You might have got a sample tainted with exhaust fumes. Try again."

Thoron—thorium emanation—had such a short life that its persistence in such quantity indicated the presence of an unusually large body of thorium ore. This, however, proved to be only a minor anomaly. The planet was warm; the air dense and moist. Beyond the open space in which the *Saturnienne* had landed was vegetation of a lavender-grayish tinge, with a greenish undertone. The chlorophyl ecological cycle appeared to prevail.

Flights of water fowl rose from the distant lake. The sun, small and red, rose through swirling mists.

Barrett and several of the crew debarked to get samples of air, water, soil, to make thermometric and barometric observations, and to take samples of vegetation. Following standing orders, they remained within two hundred meters.

Later, the rest of the crew left the *Saturnienne* without wearing space gear. Meanwhile, Garvin had debarked to examine the first of the samples which Barrett had brought back until, looking up, he saw human forms approaching along the lake shore.

"Sound recall!" he commanded. "We don't want incidents. And those men—" He gestured toward a group gathered around a growth neither quite like the plantain stalk it appeared to be, nor yet like any tree he had ever previously seen. "Whatever they're picking, there will be no eating until it's been tested."

For awhile the human forms he had seen along the lake were hidden by a patch of scrubby forest. Presently, they came into view again. The first of the group was in procession, crossing the clearing. Musicians led. They played wind instruments which sounded like flutes or oboes: others had small drums, cymbals of glittering metal, probably brass; rattles clack-clacked and some which made a swishing sound. The scale was pentatonic: an eerie, alien harmony, reminding Garvin of Martian music. At times the flavor was akin to Chinese.

After the musicians came men carrying banners. Others had censers from which billowed fragrant fumes, half inviting, yet an odor to which a stranger would have to become accustomed. As far as Garvin could see, none of the procession carried arms of any sort. And there were women in the column, a fair indication that the natives were coming to welcome rather than to warn.

"Look like Gooks," a man behind Garvin observed. "Same kind of faces."

There was more than the facial structure, the high cheek bones, and noses shorter than the usual Occidental's, and with nostrils flaring somewhat more, more than the general roundness of the heads of these people—the details which Garvin noted merely sustained his own impression and that of the man behind him: these did indeed look like Gooks. The stature, predominately of medium height—the carriage, the posture—Garvin's memory flashed from Azadeh's subsurface people and back to Turkistan.

The embroidered skull caps, the knee-length, multi-colored tunics, the head gear of the women: all this was familiar from old times. The column was counter-marching, and Garvin began to understand words, an occasional phrase. And when the music subsided, he caught somewhat more, though he missed more than he got.

From his left, Hamlin Daly came up and breathed

a fog-horn whisper to Garvin's ear: "Skipper, is this as friendly as it looks?"

"Shut up! I'm trying to understand 'em!"

The procession was now halted in a square, nine abreast and nine deep. When the chanting ceased, Garvin stepped forward three paces, then halted. Now it was their move.

Behind the nine-by-nine square, Garvin glimpsed a group of women. Each had a tray. And there was a tallish man at the flank of the musicians, elderly, important looking, and carrying himself in accord. Still looking straight ahead, Garvin spoke from the corner of his mouth: "Ham, get a tray, any kind, and be sure it's clean. Stand by, about one pace to the left and three to the rear. Come up closer when I waggle my hand."

The Important Man advanced. He was about the Admiral's age. His full beard was neatly trimmed. Clearing the front of the square, he made a precise column-right, and halted in front of the middle man of the first rank.

Nine women followed slowly along the flank of the nine-square.

A musician sounded off, a long, quavering note. Then, one beat a chunk of exceedingly hard wood: *tock-tock-tock*. At the third whack, the Important Man stepped off. Acting on hunch, Garvin took three short paces and halted. His Chinese experience had helped. The Important Man had also taken three steps. It would have taken photo timing to decide who had halted first, who had bowed first.

Tock!

Three more short steps, and each halted to bow to the other.

Garvin had an uneasy moment. *"Nine women, each with a tray of stuff—sweet Jesus, where's Ham!"*

Tock!

Distance had been miscalculated. The final three steps were mincing shuffles, but the ninety-degree bows were perfect. Then Garvin faced the weathered, moderately wrinkled envoy. His age showed mostly in his dark eyes, which had seen everything, long ago, and the thin, squarish face was in accord.

"The Lord of the World, the Gur Khan, Alub Arslan, sends me to welcome the Exalted Ones to this world."

Djénane . . . Azadeh . . . two long-haired dictionaries, but for whom Roderick David Garvin would have been standing of an asteroidal afternoon, wondering what to say; thanks to each, he had an answer.

"No lord of any world sends me. I come in my own right, with my followers. It is good to be here. We are tired from travel."

"The Gur Khan sends gifts of welcome."

Daly arrived with a second to spare, He had a tray, and he took his post as the book prescribed. Nine women went past, in single file. As each paused, Garvin picked from her tray one of the nine pieces she offered. When the final woman stepped past, Garvin said to the Important Man, "You depart with my permission. Please tell the Gur Khan that I need time to prepare for paying our respects. There will be guides to show me the way to the Exalted Presence?"

"Guides have already been posted, waiting until it is convenient for you to pay respects to the Lord of the World, the Gur Khan, Alub Arslan."

Chapter 32

Rejoining officers and crew, Garvin displayed the gifts. There was a peach, a tangerine, and a plum; then, the leg of a fowl, a chop, and a filet of fish, each broiled. Finally, an hexagonal crystal of lavender-red, a slug of yellow metal, and a similar slug of white metal.

"Taking only one piece from each tray is standard Chinese, so I guessed my way. The setup is probably symbolic—one lot stands for vegetable, another, animal, and then the mineral kingdom. Bird—fish—meat, there's air, water, earth. And maybe nothing means anything, they sent what they had handy.

"Minute ago, I heard someone asking whether these people had been expecting us—they'd acted as if spaceships were standard business. That's routine—I mean, strangers from sky or water being expected by the natives, whether you're reading history or watching lookee squawk-ee programs.

"Nearly five hundred and fifty years ago, when our people had barely got used to the idea that the world was round, the Aztecs were stupid enough to think that the Spaniards were gods coming back, as had been prophesied. That was their fatal mistake. Then there were spots where the White Brothers were not mistaken for gods. The natives killed and ate them. What I am getting at is, we are in a spot where it doesn't pay to take too much for granted.

"Until further orders, you will not go more than two

hundred meters from the ship except by permission of the officer on duty. Officers, meet at once. Crew, dismissed!"

As Garvin made for the passenger port, the Admiral walked with him. "Now that we're straight up on our struts, would it be okay for my wife to come out of seclusion and get a breath of outer air?"

Garvin stopped and faced his Consultant. "With one watch working on seam leaks, and the others stretching their legs, outdoors, while I'm conferring with my officers—it would be bad business. Now, or any other time until—Sir, it's too risky!"

"If you mean that in the sense I must presume that you mean it, let me assure you that I am quite capable—"

"Quite capable of protecting Mrs. Courtney. But I prefer not to have one or two men shot before they believed that you or I meant business."

"What you're suggesting is too absurd to discuss!"

"Admiral Courtney, I am sorry, awfully sorry, to say it, but for the past fifteen years or so you have been out of touch with the social order of our country.

"The psychologists who made you one of the pioneer patients at the funny farm had been doing a lot of other effective work, and along with the sociologists, they sold Thought Control a bill of goods—the importance of self-expression, of having an identity, of being an individual, with special emphasis on social justice for the young and rehabilitating criminals instead of gunning them down for resisting arrest or gassing them after a fair trial.

"Most of our crew is of that generation. Only a month before the *Saturnienne* took off from Terra, I heard of a woman who resisted rape. This was in one of the western areas. The supreme court of that state held that since rape did not constitute great bodily harm, it was unlawful for her to shove an ice pick through the son of a bitch. She got nowhere pleading self-defense, but there's a fair chance of quick parole—she would have got second degree, but she copped a plea, manslaughter."

This left the Admiral capable of nothing more coherent than sputtering sounds. Garvin continued, "Ganging up on an Admiral's wife would be more kicks than laying a dozen female Gooks. Keep her out of sight until I've paid my respects to the Gur Khan and arranged for you and Mrs. Courtney to be his guests.

"Don't look so puzzled, sir. These backward people are pretty hard to understand. For instance, the reservation Amerindians of the great southwest take a rapist, stake him out over an ant hill and let the breeze drift sand enough to bury the bones. There is not much rape among those backward people. You'll be safe with these Gooks.

"Sir, we're delaying the meeting. Why not have a word with Mrs. Courtney and join us later. After you—"

The Admiral went aboard.

Garvin followed Warrant Officer Barrett into the conference compartment.

Ames, the pharmacist, and Hendricks, the metallurgist-counterfeiter, stood apart, waiting to report their findings.

"Gentlemen, be seated. Ames, Hendricks—let's have the report."

Ames said, "Sir, you wanted information at once. The cook and I shared the peach, the tangerine, and the plum. The filet of fish, the duck leg, and the mutton chop, all well seasoned."

"You ate every bit, none for testing?"

"Aye, aye, sir. If we don't develop actue indigestion, cramps, or cholera morbus, you can figure the chow was all right. That's quicker than laboratory testing."

Garvin raised a hand. "You have heard a true spaceman. Your laugh was out of order, Hendricks. How about metal and mineral analyses?"

Hendricks held up the yellow slug. "This is gold, not refined, but specific gravity quite high. The other slug is native silver. Fineness not yet determined. The mineral is quartz. Looks like we've struck it rich."

"Keep it so. Dismissed." And once he faced only officers, Garvin resumed, "As visitors, it is up to us to dig up presents for the Gur Khan. From what little I've seen of the people, it's just as well that we didn't bring calico, beads, plug tobacco, and knives.

"Best thing we can do is *ad lib*. I'll throw my personal watch into the pool and draw a space issue. Those who prefer to keep your personal stuff, draw an issue equivalent and put it in the pool. I'll assume all the expense.

"There are two or three instant-color cameras aboard. I'll buy one for the package, if the owner is willing to sell. Buy up all, if all are offered.

"Marmalade, chocolate bars from the commissary. Coffee and tea, always a good bet. From here on, use your imagination. The natives sent quite a reception detail. We can't begin to match it, so I'll play it just the opposite.

"I'll go alone. Daly will be my porter, carrying gifts. All hands will be aboard. Secure freight and passenger ports, and post a lookout. I think we're among friendly people, and if I am wrong, forget the rescue crap, bail out. Admiral Courtney will be in command. That is all until further orders."

Chapter 33

Following the trail trampled into the grass by the welcoming party, Garvin and Daly were some distance from the fringe of the clearing when they saw two palanquins parked in the shade of a tree. The upholstered couches sat on stubby little legs. The uprights were secured by a frame which supported a tentlike canopy of red cloth, gold brocaded, and with gilt pendants tinkling in the cool breeze.

When he came within greeting distance, Garvin halted. "Will you show us the way to the Gur Khan's palace?"

A spokesman answered, "You are tired from long travel." He gestured to the padded couches. "Let us carry you."

Porters shouldered the carrying poles. Musicians sounded off as the procession jogged along. At regular intervals, relief porters took the carrying poles, never skipping a beat; those they relieved fell in at the tail of the column, awaiting their next turn.

When the column reached open country, to skirt the reed-fringed lake which Garvin had first observed during his landing approach, he saw that the rural population was as busy as the musicians and the bearers. Nonetheless, they quit scything millet in a field not far from the lake. Pheasants swooped from distant brush. A herdsman kept only one eye on sheep grazing among the rocky outcroppings of a weed-cluttered area. A farmer hailed the procession.

As the column jogged inland, Garvin coughed from inhaling sulphur fumes from fumaroles, and the steam rising out of vents in the spongy-pumice surface. Then, leaving the volcanic stretch, Garvin looked further inland and saw several kilometers ahead, a walled enclosure along which were crenellated observation towers. Presently, the procession wound through small settlements, and past gardens, vendors' stalls, vegetable patches.

Near a bazaar not far from the city gate was a building of neatly squared white stone, surmounted by a low dome almost like an inverted saucer. Whatever it was, it sat on a terrace four or five steps high. And before he could make his guess regarding that isolated building, so small yet so solid, the musicians piped and drummed and whanged away as never before, ever louder as they neared the entrance of a masonry structure which seemed to occupy most of the walled enclosure.

Lancers and swordsmen got off their rumps and lined up at each jamb of the entrance. A dignitary in red and gold stood in the doorway. He slowly descended, one step at a time, until the porters parked the two palanquins; then he went to the leading one, extended a hand, welcoming Garvin.

Porters took Daly's bundle and assisted him from his palanquin.

The stately man in red said to Garvin, "I am Chakir Bek, Master of Ceremony." He chuckled, stroked his white beard. "My work is easy. There will be no kowtowing—when I announce you, and your friend, you will advance nine paces. The Gur Khan will come to meet you. He will walk three paces. You may bow once.

"Yesterday was most formal. Today, I can't earn my food and drink! I'll guide you."

"What happened to *The Lord of the World?*"

Chakir Bek chuckled. "That goes back so far, no one remembers. It came from a larger world. This one is ridiculously small, but it's the only one we have left.

"You may address the Gur Khan as *sir*, or, *Your Highness*, until he suggests informality. His name is

Alub Arslan. Now explain to your friend who doesn't speak our language."

Garvin said, "Ham, Chakir Bek will brief me, and I'll pass it along."

The trio turned and stood looking into a reception room with upholstered benches along the wall, and as in Azadeh's home, the seating centered on the hearth.

Garvin identified the Gur Khan somewhat because of his posture and carriage, and largely because he was the focal point of the dozen or more men, all dressed like him, who stood near the hearth.

Alub Arslan was only a handful of years older than Garvin. His beard was black, neatly trimmed to a point, somewhat like a van Dyke. Instead of the short and wide Asiatic nose typical of the natives Garvin had observed, Alub Arslan's was full length, narrow, slightly beaked—like the rest of him, lordly.

The gong blasted, shaking the masonry.

As if he had until that moment been unaware, the Gur Khan turned from his staff men, regarded his visitors as though surprised. Good staging, yet the smile of welcome was genuine, not rehearsed.

A nudge at the elbow and Garvin, followed by Daly, took the nine prescribed steps. Alub Arslan's three brought him within a millimeter of exact bowing and handshaking range. That was it: the greeting which followed was spontaneous. With a pat on the elbow, Garvin was nudged toward the seat of honor, and Daly with him.

Assistant Masters of Ceremony followed with a silver tray, one sufficiently large for the serving of sheep or pig, entire. On this they had the gifts from the *Saturnienne*.

There was no throne, no dais. The Gur Khan sat with his guests.

Speech was laborious because of the many questions regarding Garvin's origin, since astronomy and chronology and most other nondomestic phrases had been omitted by Azadeh. He said, "Before we landed, I will send a message to the red planet. When they answer, Azadeh Khanoum will speak to you in your own language, her own language.

"Maybe your ancestors used to live on her world, or on mine?"

Alub Arslan gestured, and one of the staff took a tray from a wall niche. On it were slices of dried melon, of smoked meat, a stack of millet or barley cakes, and a flask of at least two-liter capacity.

"You are tired and thirsty." The Gur Khan poured a pale yellowish liquor into small cups, after which the staff man set the tray on a taboret. "You've come a long way. Our ancestors came to this little world to work in the mines, digging for stuff used in the space birds of our old home. The miners brought their families. We brought seeds and plants, ducks and pheasant, sheep, pigs, silk worms, mulberries."

A pause, and Garvin asked, "Then, no more ships?"

"Yes, no more ships."

"Your people forgot you?"

"There was a large war. The people on the final ship said that the enemies had nearly destroyed one another. Only a few, here and there, found new homes on mountains, or small islands, or in desert oases."

"How long have your people star-traveled?"

"A hundred of our years."

Alub Arslan stroked his pointed beard, frowned, trying to translate his uncertain chronology into a reckoning even more baffling.

"What did you do before you—your people—went to the Red star?"

Garvin shrugged. "For many thousands of years, no record, and there weren't many people. Many more thousands before we learned to fly."

The Gur Khan exhaled a long, long sigh. "They didn't lie to us when they said it was a large war. In those days there were many people, too many."

"Again, there are too many."

Alub Arslan's dark eyes gleamed from beneath his heavy black brows, and he smiled, grimly and yet whimsically. "A world is a living thing. People are like the fleas on a dog. When there are too many fleas, the dog tries to get rid of them, but he can't. A world knows how to kill vermin, and when that's done, it is comfortable again." He leaned back, wagged his head contentedly. "We respect our little world. So far, it doesn't want to exterminate us. It doesn't drive us crazy, so all our wars are friendly."

When Alub Arslan gestured, one of the staff refilled the cups with high-proof spirits. Another brought and handed Daly a basket of dried melon slices. The Gur Khan got up from the bench.

"Porters will take you back to your ship. Some of your men will be working. Those not working, let them come to town, and eat with us. Porters will bring fresh food to the ship. A few of them will stay, to bring me word when the talking-thing speaks Azadeh Khanoum's words."

Chapter 34

Crew members not on duty lived in "Little Turkistan," as Garvin had tagged the Gur Khan's town of brick and of lava blocks. They had lodging within the walls, and they ate with Alub Arslan's retainers. There was no scarcity of unattached women. Palanquins took the crew from town to the *Saturnienne*.

Before setting out with Lani and the Admiral, who were to live in the Great Khan's palace, Garvin sent a message to Maritania, requesting that Azadeh stand by as interpreter, since she was probably the only person in Maritania who could convert asteroidal speech to Americanese which Communications could turn into feature stories, synthetic interviews with the Gur Khan and other natives. Thought Control and the Space Authority got exactly what they needed—that Garvin had survived thus far was no longer the misfortune which it would have been had he not blundered into his asteroidal discovery.

In the Gur Khan's reception hall, Lani proved her merit by presenting to Alub Arslan's wives a gift package which exhaled an overpowering composite scent that could have been called *Women Only*: it was a blend of *Red Mist*, of *Sea Sylph*, and of *Jungle Passion*, exhaled by her three play-time gowns. And there were other goodies which Azadeh had got for her from the stores of Maritania. The swordsmen and lancers posted at the entrance of the hall sniffed the fragrance and understood enough of Garvin's translation of Lani's presentation words to make each retainer wish he, too, were a great khan with a collection of luxuriously scented wives. They sniffed the fragrance, rolled their eyes, exchanged glances, and made gestures which might have been considered suggestive or even obscene.

Garvin addressed the Admiral: "Sir, His Highness asks you to give Mrs. Courtney permission to meet his wives and to offer them these gifts. He permits us, you and me, to have a tour of the surrounding country between now and dinner with his staff officers." He added, "Sir, that invitation is a command, and the only excuse for declining is *sudden* death. With three or four or more wives auditing everything that goes on in the palace, the prince wouldn't risk giving Lani as much as a fanny patting."

The Admiral accepted the invitation and with Garvin followed a grim-looking henchman to the porters waiting outside the entrance. There was a third palanquin for the guide, a white-bearded fellow attended by two archers armed with prototypes of the deadly reverse-curved cavalry bow with which Central Asiatic horsemen in historic times had massacred the best European troops.

The palanquins moved with Garvin's in the center, so that he could translate the remarks of Toghrul Bek, the guide.

In an area of red earth, there was a primitive smelter which men were feeding with iron ore and charcoal. Sheepskin bellows furnished the draft.

"For weapons," Toghrul Bek said, "we put charcoal into the melted metal. Sometimes a special sword is made with iron that falls from heaven."

"Weapons?" the Admiral commented. "Who'd you be fighting?"

"There are many other settlements in our world. At each mining place there is a town ruled by a *khan*. If we weren't armed some neighbor might make trouble."

"What about?"

After a moment of perplexity, Toghrul Bek answered, "People can't all the time do nothing but work. My great grandfather used to tell how our people fought in the Big World, a hundred thousand of your years ago. Our people had horses, fine ones—the ships couldn't bring horses to this little world, so we have no races."

"Ah . . . they used to quarrel about races?"

"No, just about owning breeding stock." He frowned a moment. "Not always about horses, no. When a town had too many beautiful women, there was a war until time to harvest the crops. Then all quit fighting, everyone gave everyone else goodwill presents—yes, of course, beautiful women and fine horses to make the peace binding."

Sighing, he continued the tour in silence for some while, until they came to a gulley where native silver was being washed from alluvial deposits. The miners showed the visitors wire-threads, and longish flakes of metal. However, it was the *borrasco* which interested the Admiral: a heap of grayish granules with metallic luster. Toghrul Bek explained, "That? The dump-pile? The stuff is no good. Can't melt it. No fire is hot enough."

The Admiral pocketed a sample and so did Garvin.

Further on, they paused for a look at a spaceship, the last one to come from Terra to the asteroid, until the arrival of the *Saturnienne*. Acrid fumes from steaming mud-pots and fumaroles had reduced the shell to cracked corrosion clinging to what little remained of the metal. Reaching through a hole gaping in the side, Garvin picked up a handful of the thorium ore, the stuff which prehistoric astronauts freighted to Mars and to Terra.

"*Queen of Heaven*," the guide said, and they moved on.

It was not until the porters had almost completed their circuit, and were not far from the gardens and dwelling girdle of the walled town that the old man again said, "Queen of Heaven."

He pointed to an isolated building of perfectly finished white masonry. It was cubical, and sat on a terrace. Garvin recognized it from his first approach to the citadel.

Toghrul Bek asked, "You wish to see? Pay respects to

The Lady? She brings you luck, your far traveling brought you here."

Garvin nodded. "Yes. Say thank you to The Lady."

He was saddened, wistful, nostalgic, as though it had been many years since he had seen Azadeh: and he was at the same time happy and renewed when he faced the image of a woman, grave and beautiful, sitting beneath a canopy of hammered silver . . . honeymoon in Gook Town . . .

She sat cross legged. Two candles burned, each in a tulip-shaped bowl. He sniffed the fragrance of the air. Toghrul Bek pointed.

"Incense is in the copper dish."

Garvin beckoned. "Admiral, put a pinch of incense on the coals."

His Consultant shrugged, shook his head. "I'd not know what to say, don't know Gook customs the way you do."

"*Thank you for safe landing*—say it in any language, or just think it. We still need luck."

But Garvin knew by now that his attempt at deferring to a much older man had been an error. Courtney, he sensed, had a touch of the almost universal North American contempt for the religions of all other people, especially if those were inferior folk. He was thinking, "*He's not so crude but at heart he's like the Round Eye slobs who smeared dung on the temple images in Khatmandu, and pissed on the floor . . . makes 'em feel sanctified . . .*"

Garvin said in the native language, "For the Admiral, and afterward, for myself, I pay respects, and give thanks to the Goddess of Far Traveling."

He picked a pinch of incense from the dish, sprinkled it over coals almost buried in ash, and bowed three times.

Perhaps Garvin's voice or his face betrayed him; perhaps the Admiral had mocked the Goddess, so that his own intent had made him sensitive.

"Mind telling me what you said to the graven image?"

"I said, 'For the Venerable Man and for myself, I

give thanks for the good luck of our far traveling.' I don't have a scrap of religion, eastern or western, but I've never been too proud to say thank you to whatever brings my luck."

After dinner with the Gur Khan and his henchman, the Admiral elected to return to the *Saturnienne* for a talk with Garvin, after which the Admiral would return to the palace—and Lani. The bearers would wait for him. Once aboard, Garvin followed him to what once had been Lani's hideout.

The day crew was knocking off, and the evening shift was taking over the repair work. The admiral closed the door.

Garvin smiled, and not as amiably as he might have. "Quite right, sir. No point in having anyone hear about the heap of platinum we found."

"You guessed?"

"Guessed? The natives smelt iron. And the only thing they couldn't melt in their little blast furnaces is the platinum metals. You were slick and cagey, getting the samples, but you did slip there in the temple."

"What do you mean?"

"Paying respects to the Queen of Heaven would have been smart."

"Can't say that I care to cater to native superstition."

"That is self-evident, sir, but Toghrul Bek has put you on his shi—uh, black list."

"Garvin, that's ridiculous! These fellows are only miners reconverted to farmers."

"If you think Toghrul Bek was assigned to us at random, you are mistaken. The old man couldn't understand what you were saying but most Asiatics are a lot more sensitive than we are and come close to being mind readers, and your mind doesn't read right to him.

"Anyway, you had platinum metals in mind, I imagine?"

"Right. Have the pharmacist make some rough tests."

Garvin picked the scrap up. "You mean, see if the arc welder will melt the stuff. If it's malleable when cold, and specific gravity around twenty-one or two, we'd be smart to load up with the crude stuff, ground it in Maritania, and ship it home by private carrier, with nobody any the wiser."

"You're right, Rod. We've both done time in the re-hab facility. An unofficial indemnity would be in order."

Garvin shook his head. "I was just fishing for your views. But a hod of platinum isn't worth the risk. Getting the stuff assayed, and then selling it—no, I have no conscientious scruples! Our government has spent the past century and a half buggering the public, kissing them, giving them gum drops and other pogey bait, keeping the clods happy!"

"You do look to the long term! The thing to do is start an asteroid trading and development company, buy the platinum openly, legally."

Garvin shook his head. "I don't like the idea."

"You're all for the Gooks. Our trade goods would raise their standard of living."

"You don't give a damn for anyone's standard of living except your own."

"God damn it, sir!" The Admiral's voice rang triumphantly. "You slipped that time. I'm looking out for the interests of my widow to be. And you have no such interest—not with being married to an Alexander Heflin cousin. She'd be happy with her status as a space hero's wife or widow."

"I want none of it," Garvin declared, stubbornly.

"You went to great lengths helping Lani."

"That was in a dangerous emergency. As your widow, she'll have your pension, and she'll get look-ee squawk-ee royalties for endorsing soap and breakfast cereals. I'll not trade with the Gooks."

"If we don't, someone else will."

"Then go and deal with the Gur Khan."

Courtney gave him a bitter look. "If I'd spent as many hours with a Gook playmate as you have, I would not need an interpreter."

"Sleep with the right women, next time. Porters are waiting to carry you back to the palace. And tell Mrs. Courtney that I am not cooperative."

Chapter 35

Garvin and the Gur Khan left the palace by a service doorway. The prince wore a quilted sheepskin cap, and the boots of a farmer. In the crook of his arm he had a basket of melons, apricots, barley cakes, and broiled mutton chops. Palanquins carried him and Garvin to the fringe of the clearing in whose middle the *Saturnienne* mirrored sky glow.

Garvin led the way to the ship. He carried an earthenware jug of millet spirits. He said to the man in charge of the work details, "Higgins, the Gur Khan asked us to bring you a snack. All hands knock off for a break."

Alub Arslan followed him to Communication. "Spencer, the work detail is having chow and a drink. Get in on it while there's some left."

When Spencer quit the compartment, Garvin and the Gur Khan stepped in. Garvin closed the transmitter switch. Presently, the squawk-ee sounded off, "Maritania hears *Saturnienne*. Eagan speaking."

"*Saturnienne* hears Maritania. Garvin speaking. Let Azadeh take over."

The screen glow took shape and presented Azadeh. She said in English, "*Saturnienne,* you see Maritania?"

"Seeing Maritania."

"Seeing *Saturnienne*."

Garvin resumed, "Have our reports been relayed to

Terra?" When she nodded, he went on, "Are they planning a festival?"

"If you're thinking of Flora, she's been notified. But I don't know whether they'll send for her. How is the repair work going?"

"Everything normal, but much to be done. Now turn on the charm—His Highness, Alub Arslan wants to talk to you."

Garvin stepped from the marker and nudged the prince into focus. He audited the dialog: answers interrupted by listener turned querent. There were gropings, vocal failures, emotional rises in pitch until words reached a ceiling and cracked. Azadeh was wide eyed, blinking; tears trickled down her cheeks. At times, one or the other repeated, slowly—millennia of absence from their original home had changed their speechways. To each the other was a survivor of a war in which history itself had been destroyed.

Finally the Gur Khan stepped back, and aside.

Garvin and Azadeh, facing each other, participant and uncomprehending auditor, equally burned out, so that neither could grope for meaninglessnesses, and then, "Keep in touch. See you soon. Good night."

Garvin cut transmission. They sat down to wait for Spencer to return from his snack-break. Alub Arslan blinked, licked his lips, passed the back of his hand across his eyes. "We . . ." Bunched fingertips thumped his chest. ". . . are not alone. Your Azadeh's people, my people . . . different stories, same people. She says you have seen all three worlds. She said, 'I am happier being his Number-Two Wife than being anyone else's Number-One Woman.'"

"She spoke of my people?"

"There was much I could not understand. Sometimes, words were strange. Sometimes, the thought was too foreign." Alub Arslan laid a hand on Garvin's shoulder, a moment of strong grip, then a patting touch. "You call me Gur Khan, and Highness even when others are not with us. Rod, I was Alub Arslan before I became a prince."

"Thank you, Valiant Lion."

"When the work allows it, I'll have a banquet for all the crew at once."

Several days later, the Gur Khan's household staff was keeping the courtyard adjoining the palace in a happy uproar. Whole sheep and pigs were spitted for broiling. The smell of fat dripping into beds of coal blended with the bouquet of herbs simmering in copper kettles suspended over fires. Elsewhere, barley cakes were baking on hot rocks.

Though there had never been horse or camel on the asteroid, the courtyard was patterned after that of the caravan-serai. The cubicles along the walls were ankle deep in fresh straw. However drunk a guest, he would not have to stagger homeward.

Women gathered at each of the three entrances of the court. Some were all made up, scented and painted. Others paused for a look before hurrying home for a bath, a festive dress, and a final look at a mirror.

Near the end entrance of the court was the dais where the Gur Khan would sit with his henchmen.

As the sun touched the horizon, cymbals, drums, and trumpets hailed the arrival of the *Saturnienne*'s entire crew. Deputy Masters of Ceremony guided them to the mats arranged on the flagstones.

Garvin, in full-dress uniform, leaned against the jamb of an entrance. His coat bulged from the 11.2 mm magnum he'd stuffed in his waist band. It did a sweet job of pistol whipping: A light, crisp flick of the wrist brought a man down. He didn't relish the prospect. Mixing Plastic Populace with Gooks, liquor, and women promised trouble: but to have declined the Gur Khan's invitation would have made for awkwardnesses.

As the palace staff set to work sticking torches into wall brackets, Garvin saw long-faced, stoop-shouldered Caspar Tweed slouching his way through the confusion and toward him.

"Sir, what're you looking so constipated about?"

"Our shipmates looking so God-damned superior and noble about fraternizing with backward people—actually going to sit on the paving, and not even get their lard-asses kissed to make 'em smile and enjoy the fiesta."

"Room for a lot more than our crew."

"Lot of the leading *honchos* and their bodyguards want to meet the foreign devils." Garvin brightened. "There's Ham—"

He wasted few words briefing Daly and Tweed. "Keep an eye on this explosive mixture. We've got a handful of clods who have never been further away from home among people than I've had to dig into my pocket for a phony *pazor*. No brutality, you understand. First sign of someone getting out of line, cold caulk him. We are badly outnumbered, and I am not for fighting a rear-guard action to the ship for a fast getaway—we wouldn't make it. Conk him first, question him later."

A fanfare, lots of brass, and the roll of saddle drums: the Gur Khan, the Admiral and Lani, and local dignitaries turned from the courtyard entrance to ascend the stairs to the dais. Garvin said to his aides, "I've got to sit on the poop deck with the prince—wish I could swap places with you."

Having presented three aphrodisiac bedroom dresses to the Gur Khan's wives, Lani's *savoir faire* peaked when she turned out in a sea-green silk, ankle-length tunic and gilt slippers. Pheasant plumes trailed from her embroidered hood.

Garvin asked one of the retinue, "His Highness, the Gur Khan is alone tonight. How come?"

"*Tura,* the Prince of Space Flyers has only one of his wives with him. It would be rude for His Highness to appear with four wives. Ostentatious, you understand."

Although Terran life was the nightmare of a subnormal child, it presented no such problems in *politesse*: and this reminder heightened Garvin's sense of impending disaster.

"Why not show up with just one wife?"

"My Lord, for him to leave three at home would cause ill will. Each wife is the daughter of a neighboring *khan*. Furthermore, there would be . . . ah . . . domestic wrangles."

Garvin followed a Master of Ceremony to his place on the dais. He had barely seated himself between the Gur Khan and the Admiral when another Master of

Ceremony brought a woman to the mat slightly to the rear and to the left of Garvin's.

"My Lord, if this hostess does not please you, I offer you the choice of six or seven others."

Before he fairly got a look at his dinner companion, Garvin said, "Not even if you offered me all seven! *Khanoum*, please be seated."

From tiny brocaded slippers to splendid dark eyes, there was only elegance, pale-blue silk reflecting the torch light from thigh and breast. Although the paint job rather stylized her features, it could not mask the woman's amiability, goodwill.

She sank fluidly to the mat, legs crossed and barely a toe-twinkle to indicate that she had feet. After noting Garvin's moment of admiring her elegance of motion, she bent forward until forehead touched the mat for an instant. Straight up again, she announced, "I'm Aljai. The Gur Khan sent me to please you until you leave."

"Aljai *Khanoum*, I'm here to tell the Flying Lord and the Red Haired Lady what the Gur Khan is saying. My men, down there, I have to watch them. So, my Official Hostess, I'll have too little time to see and hear you."

"The banquet won't last long. I live near the palace. We'll go there unless you'd rather we went to your ship."

"Your home, near the palace?"

Aljai gave him an amiable, mocking smile. "You thought we'd crawl into one of those courtyard kennels?"

For a while his duty as interpreter kept Garvin busy. And then Aljai had her turn. When an enormous tray was carried up and set in front of them heaped with mutton and pork, she never missed a chance to plop into his mouth a morsel of meat wrapped in a piece of barley cake.

A hostess was preparing morsels for the Gur Khan. Lani was getting gravy on her tunic, and on her hand, up to the knuckles but the Admiral fared well—as to eating, that is. Whenever he tried to get the talk around to mineral resources, the Gur Khan blocked him with questions about the way from Mars to Saturn.

Finally the Gur Khan napkinned his fingers and got to his feet. A tremendous gong clanged. The prince tapped Garvin's shoulder. Garvin called to the astronauts in the courtyard, "On your feet! Till the prince is out of the yard! Then carry on till you pass out or stumble to your quarters. No duty tomorrow. Carry on at will!"

For a moment he stood, wondering why Warrant Officer Barrett was quitting the party and heading for one of the side entrances. Perhaps some girl hadn't showed up . . . Then, with Aljai he followed the Gur Khan from the dais.

Before Garvin and his hostess cleared the gateway, Caspar Tweed detained him.

"The prince cut the hard liquor. All okay so far."

"Any woman problems?"

"So far, just friendly swapping, sort of negotiated. What I came to say was—uh—your command post—is it far from here?"

Garvin asked Aljai a question, got an answer. Then, "She says, come along and she'll show you the front door."

Aljai's cube-shaped home was within hailing distance of the courtyard. Tweed said, "Good night, skipper," and then, with a farmboy bow, he bade Aljai good night in her language.

The maid who had admitted them had scarcely quit the reception room when Garvin said, "*Khanoum,* I would have sworn my First Officer said good night in Turki."

"Surprised?" She gestured to the wall bench near the hearth, and seated herself. "Some of your crew hack away with a few words. Martian experience, only not as good a teacher as you had."

By the glow of a small forest of tapers, Aljai was not the glamorous creature she'd been by torchlight. The eyes remained splendid. Her makeup, however, keyed to outdoor illumination, left him wondering how she really looked. Aljai was neither *"so homely she's cute"* nor was she the predominantly plain type. Halfway, he guessed, between his own age and Flora's.

"Still like me?"

"Was I staring so long?"

"Oh, no! You're wondering who and what I am."

"If you were one of the party girls in the court, it would make no more difference to me than to her."

"And you want to know how I look without my makeup."

Garvin's answer would have been yes had outside events not exploded into sound many decibels higher than the happy rumbling from the courtyard. Garvin bounded to his feet.

"They've screwed it—darling, I've got to—"

Aljai caught his arm. "I don't speak your language—"

"Leave the door open!"

He was in the narrow street and still trying to pick the best direction when Tweed came running toward him. "A couple of mother lovers made passes at girls that weren't hostesses, some of the natives sneaked into the party. All under control, but the shouting got too loud and that stirs up trouble."

"Thanks, and good night. Caspar."

Three bounds brought Garvin over the threshold. He slammed the door behind him and slid the bolt.

Aljai emerged from the dimness of the hallway. When she smiled teasingly, cryptically, he realized that she wasn't as plain looking as he'd fancied. She turned, and he followed her from wavering dusk and into three-ply darkness before he caught her hand.

"Only in darkness do I take off my makeup," she said and turned to Garvin, snuggling up to him as a woman moved by inner fires and not as the hostess assigned for the duration of the *Saturnienne*'s stay.

Each fumbled with the other's alien garments until they realized trying to undress each other was delaying the long overdue.

When the sun reached into Aljai's bedroom, she was awake. Whatever of her makeup had not worn off, she'd washed off. She sat, bare and unadorned.

Garvin awakened, more because of her regarding him than from sunlight's reaching through a small window opening.

In darkness, Aljai's beauty of body could be read by

Girl Watcher's Braille. He saw that touch had not fooled him.

"Still like me?"

"After our busy night, how could I quit?"

"You've slept with beautiful women all your life."

"What do you know about my life?"

"I know from seeing you looking at me without makeup."

"Where'd you learn all those makeup tricks?" He explained in Braille. And then, "You were beautiful all over. I skipped nothing, nowhere."

Aljai clapped her hands. The maid, not significantly better looking than the mistress, lost no time appearing.

"We'll eat in the reception room. I'll dress myself and tend to my makeup." Then, again alone, she said, "Sleeping with an unbeautiful hostess didn't make you a bit unhappy. But something troubles you."

"Yes, or it'd be noon before you'd have time for breakfast. Or put on makeup. It's this way. Our people will want to come here and trade. Ore to fire up the ships. Gold, silver, too."

Aljai nodded. "Whenever the Admiral said something about a trading ship, it annoyed you. And Gur Khan has been hearing too much of trade. Those dresses and perfume and things for his wives, the time tellers and the picture-taking boxes, the sweet-eatings, and the little book with pictures of women wearing dresses from the store of Mars."

"Wait a minute! The *Admiral* saying things—he can't speak your language."

"One of the half-officers learned some words from a girl in Maritania city, so he talks for the Admiral."

"*Half*-officer?"

"Yes. Lord Barrett. Not common man, not officer. You don't like it? Maybe we can think of something . . . get him drunk with spirits and hashish by one of the steam-springs in Timur Yalik's country. The fumes kill without shedding blood, so, no feud."

And then Aljai became glowingly lovely. She said, "You told me the nicest things in the dark, all about what we'd do before I put on my daylight makeup."

Chapter 36

Garvin lost an hour sitting while the Gur Khan heard and adjudicated a civil dispute. Very little crime, and few lived to be second offenders. Finally he got his chance to say, "Your Highness, have you some place where I could lock up my Half-Officer Barrett, so he'd not be going to tell your neighbor, Timur Yalik Khan, how fine it'd be if trading ships landed in his territory?"

"My jail is empty. Room to lock up your whole crew."

"Your Highness is lavish. First, I'll warn him."

The clerk called the next case.

Garvin found Tweed and Daly at the nearby homes of their hostesses. They went with him to Aljai's reception room. After setting out the long-necked earthenware jug of millet spirits, she left the trio to confer.

"How's the crew?"

"Couldn't prod 'em to life with hot irons. Those we had to clobber are resting nicely. They'll recover."

Tweed added, "It was all in fun, for the natives. The soreheads—those bastards of ours are used to looking down on Gooks."

Daly resumed, "I remember a dance hall near Manila, for white men only. The girls were Filipino, Chinese, Thai, Japanese. No native men were allowed in the place during girl hours.

"And there was a spot on the California coast, dance hall or hook shop, probably both, with white girls for the foreign farm labor. No white men allowed. Nothing wrong with the girls in either place. God-damn men make all the ruckus. Our men, I mean."

"That adds up," Garvin admitted. "Caspar, your first chore is to find Barrett. He is not, repeat, not to go to the next-door prince's territory to sell trading ships. Nobody else is, either."

Daly eyed him shrewdly. "You must've been close to someone who's close to headquarters."

"Nothing to it. Anyone who can talk twenty words of Gook gets an Official Hostess who knows the Gur Khan's wives, and the ladies' maids who sleep with the court honchos. I heard that Half-Officer Barrett has become a sort of half-ass interpreter for the Admiral. The Gur Khan balks at trading posts.

"Soon as you've briefed Barrett, the three of us are going to the ship and grab every weapon aboard. The natives are too many for us to antagonize. We are expendable, and quickly."

They'd barely got to their feet when Aljai edged in.

"Oh, I want to go along and see your ship."

"Where'd you learn English?"

"I knew you'd not be going anywhere else."

"*Khanoum,* you are a mind reader! Ham, you hustle up four palanquins while Caspar's giving Barrett the message."

When the train of porters halted at the towering cylinder of a special alloy CX-41, Aljai looked up and up and up, from exhaust stacks to nose. "This is like the stories my great grandfather heard from his great grandfather. And when Ham and Casper are through with their work, tell them to get more marmalade and coffee and chocolate bars."

Garvin fired up Communications. He reported repair progress, gave a censored account of the banquet, and said that one of the Khan's ladies wanted to talk to the Martian–English interpreter, Azadeh Khanoum."

The weapons search was completed before Azadeh's voice and face came to the asteroid. There was the same fumbling-groping until the speakers became accustomed to each other's inflections and idioms, and then the tempo became impossible for Garvin.

When he finally got his turn, he said to Azadeh, "I never know what's happening on Mars. Asteroid days and night are out of step with yours."

"It's night here, but ever since you landed on the asteroid, I've been staying at the little hotel near Communications."

"Alone in the shop?"

"The night man left. He calls this dull stuff."

"Hold it a minute, then." When he returned he had the ship's log, he said, "Set for printing. Keep the prints for your own people—nobody else to see them." He opened the book, projected each page from Saturn until the day after landing on the asteroid. "I'm cutting those pages out and burning them. It'll be almost impossible to find this dark asteroid."

Azadeh gave him the Martian time, and he gave her the time-from-sun's-rising, on the asteroid.

As before, neither knew what next to say. They repeated the dullest banalities. Garvin broke the frustrating exchange by saying, "Pillow talk isn't for space, darling, and no other kind is important. This God-damned look-ee squawk-ee won't be any good till it's a smell-ee-feel-ee-taste-ee . . ."

"In the dark, you couldn't tell your nice hostess from me."

He pulled the switch, drew his knife, and sliced out the pages. Outside, he burned them and trampled the char into the ground.

Caspar Tweed said, "You and Aljai ride in one basket. We've got the whole arsenal except for two missing burner guns."

Daly nodded. "While you and Aljai were talking to Mars, we rechecked. All we could find is in the litter."

Garvin's face was nearly as long as Tweed's. "Whether it's for fun, Fourth of July stuff, or for king-making, some bastards have been up to trouble. Divide the stuff into three lots—one for Aljai's house, and one for each of your hostesses."

Several days later, when Tweed told Garvin that

there had been a work-slowdown and that the crew had turned surly, he was not amazed.

"It's probably because the Gur Khan's gone to see his neighbor, Timur Yalik, to downgrade the trading-post notion. The crew had been seeing each man's getting a handful of platinum for a pack of chewing gum or cigarettes."

They hadn't made much progress with their discussion of the trading-post idea or with lowering the level of Aljai's long-necked earthenware decanter of millet spirits when Garvin raised a peremptory hand.

"You hear something?"

Daly cocked his head. "Bit louder than the haggling in the farmers' market."

Tweed's hostess barged in from the street. "Something's wrong, but what the hell's she saying?"

The girl turned on Garvin, who said, "Say it slower, darling." Aljai came racing in from the hall. She got the visitor's story in one piece: "Some drunks making a riot in the market place—some of your crew."

Garvin got to his feet. "Is it serious?"

"Not yet, nobody killed, just throwing pots and firewood and rocks. No swords, no axes—not yet. Maybe stop it soon, you have enough men left for the ship."

Garvin said to Aljai, "Tell her to go home and bolt the door. Caspar, grab a blaster and head for the market. Ham, you do the same." He caught Aljai by the hand. "I can't find my way in these cockeyed alleys! Lead on!"

Half a kilometer of racing after Aljai brought him to the fringe of the shouting confusion that had swamped the market booths. Though no one was sure of anything, the surge of the crowd indicated that the trouble was well beyond the plaza.

Dusk was closing in. The flare of torches was reflected from the white masonry of the temple.

"The Lady!" Aljai cried. "See the men in the doorway? Yours!"

Though Garvin heard too much and saw not enough, he tasted disaster. Those were astronauts in the temple entrance. They found partial protection on both sides because of the thickness of the masonry jambs.

"Let go of my gun hand!" When he jerked free, Aljai pirouetted to his left, grabbed his free hand, worming and edging herself into the pack. The gap she made with her wiry slender body gave Garvin an advantage—and he ploughed through, flipping natives right and left.

They had cut the distance in half when Garvin got a glimpse of tall, lean Tweed edging through the crowd. Well to Tweed's rear, Daly battered his way along, gaining three yards and losing one.

During a lull in the uproar, Garvin shouted in Aljai's ear, "What's it all about?"

She outscreeched the resumed bellow and mutter.

"They robbed The Lady! Took gold bars."

They lurched forward another few yards. It became a cross between a back-home bargain day rush and a football game.

Being half a dozen steps above pavement level, the astronauts had one slender advantage, and they were pushing it to the limit, throwing vases, statuettes, censers, and other things snatched from the altar. The natives retaliated with vegetables, rocks, pots, and utensils, bones from the grilled-meat stand.

With Aljai he gained another ten yards.

"Why didn't your folks rush them?" he gasped.

"The Khan's away, nobody wants to kill his guests, not yet."

Several newly arrived astronauts were flanking the mob, which was not aware of their approach. Two had energy blasters. There'd be massacre until the mob trampled and kicked the astronauts to pulp.

And now Garvin drove through, Aljai trailing after, as he set a course to intercept the newcomers. He shouted, "Drop those guns!"

The beleaguered men in the temple doorway were encouraged.

"Cut 'em down, we're pooped!" they shouted. "Let 'em have it!"

Tweed's long legs had brought him up from the right and to Garvin's side. Garvin shouted, "Over to the left—the two missing blasters—fire yours at the wall, shock 'em to their tails!"

Tweed leveled off. The dull burping sound—a bluish

flash—masonry disintegrated. Incandescent chips gey-
sered like Roman candles. The shock knocked the spectators reeling. Amazement silenced the first wave of natives.

Garvin shouted, "You two, drop those blasters!"

"Screw you, jack!" one snarled and leveled his
weapon.

Garvin's 11.2 millimeter roared once, twice. A man
doubled up. Before he could crumple, the second
lurched against him, dead on his feet. His final twitch
jerked a shot. The blast melted lava pavement. Cloth
and flesh smoked as the gunner dropped across the
molten pool.

All this so fascinated the mob that no one thought of
charging the astronauts in the temple entrance.

Tweed cradled his gun in the crook of his arm. "One
move and I'll wipe out the pack of you," he said, grinning amiably.

Garvin said to Aljai, "Speak to the crowd."

She got up on the thrid step and she spoke. The
crowd was still blinking. A good show, but perplexing.
Garvin prompted her, when she paused. "Tell them that
if they let these fellows walk to jail, we'll herd them to
it." And after she had translated that message, Garvin
turned to the astronauts. "If your God-damn fool buddies had hosed the crowd with their blasters, not a man
of you would be alive now. You would have been steam
rollered."

Then, "Tweed, Daly—march them to the pokey. If
anyone makes a false move, cut him down and then
find out why he moved."

Snatching a torch from the pavement, Garvin nudged
Aljai into the temple. The floor was littered with bars
of gold and silver, little ingots apparently taken from
wall recesses. The story would keep.

What he saw told enough.

The raid had apparently started as a fun caper, fun
of the kind that made the people of Khatmandu forbid
visitors from the enlightened west to enter any of the
city's temples. Christians and Moslems had a passion
for desecrating heathen shrines.

Graffiti on the walls, in charcoal from the grilled-meat stands. Grotesque cartooning, altering the figures of the murals; the additions to the female figures were anatomically absurd and as gross as the amendments that centered below The Lady's navel.

Garvin's survey of the shrine was interrupted by the arrival of Admiral Courtney and Half-Officer Barrett. The latter had apparently served well as mentor and interpreter during their crossing the market areas.

Garvin said to Aljai, "Stand by the two dead men. Tell the people not to touch the gun-things. They're dangerous."

Then he turned and the Admiral confronted him.

"Captain, what's the meaning of all this? Barrett tells me that you killed two of our men."

"Ask your source of information for the rest of the facts. Take a look about the temple, sir. Once the Gur Khan sees it, I'll set the crew to work cleaning up."

"That should be done at once! This is bad, yes. A deplorable, a drunken prank!"

Garvin frowned, blinked, then said, "Like a campus protest, you mean?"

The Admiral brightened, hopefully. "In spite of having been sequestered for fifteen years, I have a better understanding than you seem to have."

"Understanding of youth, I take it?"

"Of course."

"I am as young as any son of a bitch aboard, and you've seen my answer to outrage. Your trading-post propaganda did much to touch off this riot. If you require protection to go to your quarters, I'll be your escort. I am armed and so is Aljai."

"We came without protection," the Admiral replied coldly, "We need no assassin to guide us back."

Chapter 37

Once the rioters were locked up, Garvin sat with Tweed and Daly in Aljai's reception room. "This is my last cruise," he told them. "Burning those log book pages was hogwash. Traders would find a way back here while scientists sat around with their thumbs up, trying to get the Government to fund the study of the long-term potential of asteroids.

"The only way to protect the natives against the Magnificent Democracy's life-style is to blow the *Saturnienne* so not a one of us can get back with the story of an asteroid whose backward people need modern living.

"If she's reported lost in space, no more messages, the Fat Boys can relax for another century, until another Garvin gooses them with a red-hot farrier's rasp. That fracas at the temple summed up the Thought-Controlled Plastic Populace."

Garvin eyed them, challengingly, as he paused for breath.

"Give us the rest, Skipper," Daly suggested. "If you build up suspense long enough we might plan mutiny."

"You and Casper got into this because of me. Here is where I can't exercise command, not where you're concerned. Except for you, the brain-washed crew would've blown up the ship, by mistakes arranged by the Consortium."

Daly's pop eyes studied Garvin. "So it's up to me and Caspar?"

"What's up to us?" Caspar Tweed wondered.

"Wipe that innocent look off your face! Ages ago I told you that the CX-41 alloy of the *Saturnienne* is peculiar. If you drilled enough holes and stuffed them with fissionable material, like the thorium-isotope reactor rods we've got aboard, or the isotope we picked up from the corroded spaceship the prehistoric astronauts parked here, you'd get something ranging from an explosion to an atomic blast. Any questions?"

"Yes. Why don't you get to the point?"

"Either of you got any important ties, back home?"

"If we had," Daly resumed, "we wouldn't have untied them for a deal with you."

"Caspar?"

"Ham's just said it for me. Skipper, you've got the biggest stake. Publish the orders, or forget it."

Garvin said, "It's all in the bag, except for one point. If Azadeh said, *Hurry home*, would I chicken out?"

"Call her, and we'll all know."

After a long silence, Garvin said, "Aljai and the Gur Khan will go with me tonight to talk to Azadeh."

Late that night, Garvin sat on the flat roof of Aljai's house. Although within a couple of meters of him, she was a million kilometers distant, and Garvin was alone. His eyes were on Mars, where Flora had flipped slip and bra into a corner, shed all the social indoctrination of her short life, so that for the first time, he and she were truly close. He sat now facing the prospect of taking leave of her and of electromechanical gracious living—turning the *Saturnienne* into a cloud of incandescent vapor which would separate him from the wife discovered after their years of reciprocal nonunderstanding.

Flora had meant every word that night. He knew now, and perhaps each had known then, subconsciously, that if he, his wife, and his concubine resettled in Khatmandu, Flora and Azadeh would be sworn sisters in no time . . . but Flora would never be happy away from the security of the Magnificent Society, from Gracious Living, and from Thought Control, so Flora would bid him farewell, take affectionate leave of Azadeh, and rejoin the Holy Family and the Consortium.

Starting with bare body, she'd peeled down, for the first time, to bare self. She'd been real, so that each knew how the other had been short changed from the beginning.

"If we'd tried it, all we would have done would be ruin the best night we'd ever had. She was so awfully real . . . "

Having cleared away confusing superficialities, he faced reality: the bare-self-genuine Flora was a flash of ultimate experience, a permanent possession. That from which he was about to break away was the everyday Flora: whimsical, talented, colorful, passionate. The God-damndest worrier in North America whose *take-care* had screwed up a career which he was now dumping because—like Lani—it was time to retire. Flora had hampered him as he had been her stumbling block. Spray her with *Shalimar* and she'd still smell of Holy Family.

Aljai finally said, "Porters are in the street. The Gur Khan is waiting."

After his short visit with his neighbor, Timur Yalik, Alub Arslan had taken a good look at the desecrated temple. The crew had been carried each day, under guard, to resume cold caulking the leaks of the *Saturnienne*. Having become accustomed to not having been torn apart by outraged citizens, they relaxed sufficiently to complain about the chow and to wonder when they could get back at the skipper for the brutality whereby they had survived.

Garvin, following Aljai to the palanquins, wasn't sure whether walking or levitation got him there. Having settled the matter of severance from Flora, he faced the horror of telling Azadeh what he had resolved to do.

At the *Saturnienne*, the Gur Khan and Aljai followed him to the Communications compartment. When the look-eee squawk-ee fired up, Azadeh answered. He said, "Alub Arslan has a story to tell you. Better cut in the tape recorder and video too. After he and Aljai speak, I'll take over."

The Gur Khan's voice and features made it appear that he was describing a curious and amusing incident.

Aljai's remarks were by no means as fluent. Toward the end, her face was troubled, yet for all her deliberation, his auditing got him nothing. More and more he realized that only with care, getting used to his diction, his slow understanding, with patience and kindness had these asteroidal folk made communication possible. And their psychic sensitivity must have contributed much.

Aljai stepped clear, and finally he faced Azadeh.

"Now you know how it has been."

"Now I know."

"I have to blow up the ship. Or, I'll come back and we'll be together a while."

He'd blurted the facts out, harshly, as if all this had been her fault. Her smile was weary, sad. "You'll do your duty, and how you hated to say it to me."

He licked his lips, and swallowed, and steadied his voice so that it wouldn't break when he lowered it to a fitting tone. "In the old days, when there was war, all but boys and crippled men and old ones went. Each knew that many would not come back, but none hid his fear behind what he called his conscience. You've made me one of your people."

"You're one of those not coming back from a war."

"Azadeh darling, I landed her on that asteroid. So I have no choice."

His voice had settled, becoming smooth, and deep, not harsh. Azadeh was radiant, glowing as in a lover's embrace, glowing and radiant as that night when they learned to name *it* the Well of the Angels. Tears trickled down her cheeks, and those lurking in her eyes were gems of beauty. "So happy I'd not been sleeping with a thing that was neither a man nor a woman! I always knew, but now I'm sure and so happy-sad—Now hear me. There's no war on Terra—not now, not yet—But your people have so ruined Terra that they have nothing left to destroy but each other. When the time comes, the Gooks will take off in the ship with The Lady. We've known from long ago how to go to the asteroid and to other places and to Terra. Next time, survivors of your people will know what my people learned, long ago."

Digging in his pocket, Garvin found a sheet of paper. "Make a printout of me and of this writing."

When she reported a good recording, he resumed, "That's my message for Flora. Send it to her with your own message."

"This is sadness and not-sadness," she said. "There is thinking—how bad, how much worse if we'd never had our sleepings together. When war or other death separates, one is gone. With us, neither is gone for as long as memory brings me to you, and memory calls you back to Gook Town."

Azadeh's radiance reached a new peak, a new promise.

Garvin pulled the switch.

Chapter 38

The Gur Khan received Admiral Courtney and Warrant Officer Barrett in a private room of the palace. After hearing the facts and fancies each set forth, he said, "Captain Garvin is not punishing your men by keeping them under guard. Once people see that The Lady isn't sending cut-worms to ruin their vegetables, they'll not be so ready to tear the crew apart."

Barrett boiled that down to basics. "Sir, he says that the natives need time to forget the mob scene." And after another friendly remark by Alub Arslan, Barrett reported, "He says that as soon as the ship is ready, he'll release the crew by night.

"Captain Garvin's been making night trips, briefing Maritania about trouble and problems, making a good case against the crew. He's gone out with a couple of natives in curtained palanquins, to talk to his girl in Maritania, so she can slant the story against the crew."

"Interesting," the Admiral conceded, "but what's that got to do with persuading him to take off?"

Presently the interpreter offered this: "Porters are getting so accustomed to night joggings to the *Saturnienne* that it's got to the no-comment stage. No one would notice an extra palanquin train, the one that carried the whole crew."

The Gur Khan interpolated a brief remark. Barrett gave it thus: "Sir, His Highness just said that some night real soon, when Captain Garvin and his cronies and their hostesses are having a private bon voyage party, he—His Highness, I mean—will send the rest of the crew to the ship, to wait for Garvin. I am sure he wasn't contemplating a long wait, sir. But there's one detail he touched on, and then moved on."

"Please ask him to elaborate."

The Gur Khan was pleased to elaborate, and Mr. Barrett rendered the substance of it, thus:

"Send Mrs. Courtney aboard solo, well ahead of time—in the afternoon, of course. For sight-seeing, for any purpose whatever, and here's the reason—if she left the palace by night, every one of your wives, ladies' maids, servants, every female creature in the entire place would be wondering whether she had a date with someone and everyone'd have to share the luscious dirt with every other gossip—it'd be in Timur Yalik's baili-wick within a couple hours: It might get to Garvin, and he'd go stubborn; he'd resent any suggestion of speeding up his plans."

"Reasonable," the Space Pioneer readily admitted. "And it certainly would be better if she were in a palan-quin train, just in case there were a leak, and some sore-head natives demonstrated or rioted."

Barrett added a concluding and reassuring bit: "She made a hit with the banquet folks, wearing native dress. They'd never *harm* her, but the afternoon tour is best."

"Mr. Barrett, please tell His Highness that I appre-ciate his thoughtfulness in so many details. And that I'd appreciate even more if he has any suggestions as to how I could talk that ass of a skipper into a better atti-tude. Garvin thinks like a native, you know, which is what makes him baffling and unreasonable."

During the next several days, the three saboteurs were busy with power drills. The crew remained locked up in town. Where they had groused about the work shifts, they now bitched about the monotony of not working. Meanwhile, CX-41 drill shavings and pulver-ized thorium isotope—the local product, which was much more active than that of Mars—were being rammed into the holes.

"When can we get an educated guess on when these hot spots get hot enough to blow?"

"I'd wondered, long before we took off from home," Garvin answered. "Pure curiosity. And I made some lab tests. More curiosity. Instrument readings are the real test. A fissionable package is funny. If it builds up in geometric progression, you can't at once tell what the ratio is. If it's logarithmic, it's even trickier. I mean, errors in plotting build up faster.

"Let's take a break! Christ, no! I am not phoning Azadeh again. I might chicken out. Let the prisoners and the Admiral bitch their little heads off. They're not going anywhere."

"Skipper, if there's any trouble, do you use that 11.2 millimeter or *kung fu?*

"Depends on my mood."

Garvin couldn't even guess how long it'd be before he'd be calling some asteroidal girl the things he used to call Azadeh. Aljai was strictly official, upper bracket, reserved for important guests, and during that one-thousandth part of a second during which the *Saturnienne* became metallic vapor, Garvin's VIP status would vanish.

Every other day, Garvin heard the Admiral's gripes. They were based on Alub Arslan's variations of temperament. "Garvin, I'd thank you if you pinned that Turk down to facts. I begin to suspect that every time he switches to a different wife he figures a new answer as to the mood of the population."

Garvin or one of his allies logged the build up of radioactivity. The curve was rising along the y-axis, but it was not yet sufficiently steep to justify extrapolation.

He warned Alub Arslan that this was a dangerous thing; that his people should stay eight-ten kilometers from the homemade A-bomb. But how explain it to the natives without causing more trouble than he could handle?

The Gur Khan chuckled amiably. "All I have to do is tell them to stay away, The Lady does not want us around foreign stuff, and no one will risk getting his head lopped off. Swords are here for more than the wars we do not have. Simple Thought Control that does not foul up. I'll make sure the population is not exterminated."

The curve of the deliberate reactor was becoming steeper.

Tweed and Daly each spent more and more time with his own Official Hostess whose status would terminate with the *Saturnienne*.

The curves which Garvin was extrapolating were not related to Miss Asteroid when Aljai told him that the Admiral, the Half-Officer, and another astronaut would like to ask his advice. Graph sheet and pencil in hand, he followed her into the reception room.

His visitors were in full dress uniform, with all decorations. Barrett and Pharmacist's Mate Ames wore side arms. Over his T-shirt, Garvin wore a comfortably frowzy Turki jacket. He was unshaved, and he was as tired as he looked. For the first time, Aljai had chalked up an error. She should have briefed him.

"Good evening, gentlemen. Be seated." He nudged the long-necked decanter forward. "Aljai, some cups for my guests."

"Immediately," she answered, but edged back and dallied in the room, which was out of character.

There was something about the trio that he didn't like. That Aljai didn't get glasses immediately was a scream of warning.

"Thank you, Captain Garvin. This is not a social visit. I must decline."

Garvin wished that Aljai was out of the room. He needed space.

The resolute faces of the trio gave him all but the details. On the other hand, their glance-shift told him that whatever their plan, each relied on the Admiral; and that they hoped he knew what he was doing.

From the corner of his eye, Garvin caught a blur of color, the red of Aljai's jacket. She was near the wall niche which overlooked the table on which the long-necked decanter sat. She was pouring millet spirits into cups from the niche.

"The gentlemen do not care for a drink, but thank you," he said, speaking slowly, to be sure that Warrant Officer Barrett would understand. And then, "If not social, sir, it is official?"

"Yes, of course. Official."

Garvin's glance shifted from Courtney's bitter-blue eyes to his henchmen. He noted their hands, their side arms, their stances. Either they were quick draw masters, or they were God-damn fools—or they would have been, if only Garvin had his 11.2 millimeter within reach. He shifted his weight, and felt the table edge touch his hip.

He could not hear Aljai, but he could smell her familiar perfume. It blended with sweat, and not love-making sweat. She knew that death hovered. She knew what she was doing. He wished that he knew.

"Official, sir?" Garvin echoed, affably.

"Yes. Captain Roderick David Garvin, I relieve you of command of the *Saturnienne* and place you under arrest."

"By whose authority, sir?"

The voice was bland, quite easy, indicative of interest, of course.

"I am acting under Title Four Two, A, on the relief of an officer guilty of misfeasance, malfeasance."

"Sir, you omitted *non*feasance."

The Aljai scent was almost gone, and so, he sensed, was she.

For an instant, the Admiral's face twitched as if he'd been irritated by levity. And then he relaxed, and looked contented. The task was going along nicely.

"Sir," Garvin pointed out, and put more of his weight on the edge of the table, a casual, an easy posture. "This business is far-fetched. Before I surrender, I'd thank you to clarify. I'll hear you out, of course. And you too, Mr. Barrett, and you, Ames. Before I call this mutiny, I'd rather like to hear your story."

"The unjustified killing of two of the ship's crew, and—"

Garvin had begun to smile, and he smelled Aljai again. From his right eye's edge he watched the armed pair. He shifted his half seat on the table, and improved the pattern, since his easy move had made one man slightly mask the other's action.

"Cut the talk and arrest me!" he shouted.

The slash-in-the-face challenge startled the trio. Garvin scooped the wine cups, splashed high-proof spirits into the eyes of all three with the horizontal sweep. Blinded, they were cold meat. He snatched the table by its edges, charged, bashing them with the flat of it, right in their faces.

But he did not follow through, with commando boot-and-knee.

The thunder of an 11.2 millimeter shook the room. Plaster fell. Though this was her first experience with firearms, she could not have missed the ceiling, from which her two shots chewed chunks of plaster, and plenty of dust. When he snatched the gun from her hand, she grabbed the pistols the mutineers had tried to draw. A boot to the chin of each made her work trouble-free.

"Get water to throw in their faces."

Water from the kitchen flushed plaster and liquor from the mutineers' eyes. Once Garvin had all the firearms within his own reach and no one else's, he said to Aljai, "Fill up the cups, and give them a drink. They need it."

Then, from behind his 11.2, "It's been wondered whether I'd use gun play or *kung fu*. It isn't everyone who lives long enough to learn that Garvin always has a new trick for an old situation. Sit down, relax, get reacquainted with your commanding officer.

"The Gur Khan and I are friends. If you think you are taking me to Maritania or anywhere else, you are nuts and fruit. Not a one of you will ever leave this asteroid."

They sat on the rug-covered bench. The Admiral had recovered sufficiently to ask, "Am I to understand that you propose to assassinate us to avoid the charges I'd prefer?"

"Sir, ever since I was a punk kid, I admired your pioneer spacing. I'd never assassinate you." His glance shifted. "Nor you two slimy sons of bitches who don't rank kissing the Admiral's ass. I am going to tell you pig fuckers a thing or two. Since the lady cannot understand English, I speak plainly.

"You are a disgrace even to a country as low as North America has sunk, and the crew is so low that you two look like heros. So, I mined the *Saturnienne* with fissionable material, and stuffed reactor rods into the mix, for good luck. You are grounded for life, do you understand? A chance to live with good people for a change."

"You did what?"

Garvin waggled the graph paper. "When you came in, I was checking the rate of buildup before she's hot enough to go up in a puff of hot-assed atoms bent for hell."

The Admiral cried out, jumped to his feet. Barrett was pale enough to wilt, Ames was shocked stupid.

"Lani's aboard!" the Admiral screamed."

He lurched for the door.

Barrett bawled, "The whole frigging crew—"

"What's that?" Garvin shouted. "Lani—"

"She's aboard—"

Garvin's first bound would have put him ahead of the Admiral, but that was his last move for a little while. Aljai, snatching the long-necked flask, stretched her legs and smacked him on the head. The glancing blow was just enough to drive him to his knees, muttering and helpless, fighting ultimate disaster and losing.

Chapter 39

Aljai knelt beside Garvin and got him to his feet. Before he could recall that someone had dealt him a glancing blow, she said, "She's all right, she's all right. The red head—"

Still punchy, he let her half drag him along. When he smelled Lani's perfume he was more muddled than ever. Lurching, stumbling, he crumpled, pulling Aljai off balance and to her knees beside him.

He was half asprawl across a Lani-smelling woman. When his eyes focused, he saw that at least two of his senses had not tricked him. Lani lay on the bed, stretched out, breathing peculiarly, but breathing. The shock tore him apart. He slumped, face against her shoulder, and sliding between her breasts as he sobbed, "Jesus, Jesus, they told me—"

Aljai stroked his splitting head.

And then yelling and pounding at the door brought Aljai to her feet and set her groping for the 11.2 millimeter. Aljai bounded past him, snatched the weapon from the table, and thrust it into his hand. With one of the arresting party's guns at the ready, she yanked the door open.

Daly and Tweed stumbled in. Each was armed.

"What the hell? Neighbor said there was shooting—"

Garvin was beginning to assemble details. "Mutiny— we quelled it. Aljai fired a couple into the ceiling and I got command—and when one of them said Lani already was aboard ship—"

Daly's face bleached. "Good God, aboard ship—"

"False alarm. She's in the back room, hopped up but okay. Aljai conked me by mistake, or I'd have been after the three of them and by now a kilometer ahead. Stretch your legs and see if you can get those fellows away from the ship, keep 'em from taking off."

He lurched for the door. In the alley his comrades passed him. The town was waking up. Driving himself fiercely, he managed to keep Daly's white sweater in sight. Presently, he caught up with the pair.

"Spacing," Tweed panted, "plays hell with your wind."

Behind them natives had turned out in a pack.

Jogging instead of racing, the trio yelled themselves hoarse. Darkness was thinning. Daly peeled out of his white sweater and waved it. Ahead, and barely perceptible, Garvin distinguished blobs of blackness moving in the gloom. They were going towards the *Saturnienne*. They must be two of the arresting party.

The one in the rear stumbled. As he scrambled to regain his feet, gold braid gleamed in the graying dawn. He shouted. That must be Warrant Officer Barrett. He and the other had a long way to go to reach the towering shell of the *Saturnienne*, whose upper portion now reflected the first rays reaching over the horizon.

Garvin yelled until his voice failed, as if he could speed the two toward their goal.

Then came thunder, and from her jets, a gush of flame that swept the flat ground. Only then did the two uniformed men and those behind them realize how far they had fallen short in their attempt to warn the mutineers.

The Saturnienne began to rise. She sat on a slowly lengthening column of flame: a pillar that became ever taller, giving the illusion of something pushing out of the earth and shoving the *Saturnienne* ever higher. She gained speed. Presently her exhaust no longer touched ground. It fanned out, became a comet-tail.

Full sunrise made the faraway metal of the *Saturnienne* gleam, a red-gold molten glow. The exhaust became ever more dim against brightening sky. And then came a flash that darkened the morning: blue-white, blinding, a great blot, expanding, coming to rest, a miniature nebula newly born in space.

The halted crowd parted, to make way for men who were carrying one whose black uniform gleamed with gold braid, and epaulettes. The Admiral, Garvin knew then, had missed the boat. The veteran's talk of a heart condition had not been windy words.

Garvin was glad that the old fellow had not overtaken the the crew who had made the flight. Garvin was sorry that Courtney had not learned that Lani was not aboard. Barrett and Ames were in the crowd, having also missed the boat.

"Trying to save their shipmates, they wasted no time with the Admiral. They're not the stinkers I thought they were . . ."

Alub Arslan, Valiant Lion and Gur Khan, emerged from the crowd. He halted. He pointed at the incandescent cloud. A lordly figure, proud beaked nose, jutting beard so elegantly sculptured. The townsmen were silent: as his presence commanded.

He spoke slowly: "The Lady! She burned them. All but the three she was pleased to spare."

Teams of porters grounded their palanquins in the cleared space. Alub Arslan gave Garvin a hand. "Rod, they'll take you to your home, and they'll take your friends, and the Old Man."

Garvin toppled to the cushions, and wavered on the fringe of blackout as the bearers jogged townward. If Aljai only had perfume to make her smell like Azadeh. It'd help a lot, in the dark . . . the law's never going to get Lani for conking that inspector . . .

Finally, the porters halted at Aljai's door.

Two men sat on the threshold. They had bags and gear which Garvin recognized: it was his own. One of the pair got to his feet.

"The Gur Khan commands us to greet you and to rub our beards in the dust. Aljai Khanoum takes leave of you. We now take you to your own house, the one that the Valiant Lion gives you."

Garvin's new home was diagonally across from the

palace. He got a glimpse of The Lady's temple. When the footmen halted at the door, the older said, "We forgot to tell you that you will not see the White-Haired Lord again. Running to the ship was more than he could stand. People found him and they knew that The Lady did not hate him too much."

"Thank you." Garvin put his palms together, turned toward the temple and bowed. "Thank you, Goddess of the Far Traveling."

"The door is not locked. The house and all that is in it is the Gur Khan's gift. We beg leave to depart."

"Depart with my blessing."

Except for one detail, the reception room was furnished as would be that of anyone of Garvin's acquired status. Narrow rugs covered the wall benches. There was a hearth, and wall niches, flasks, jugs, cups for wine, cups for spirits, and glasses for each.

The woman who got up from the hearth corner was the only one of her kind on the asteroid: Lani.

"The Gur Khan sent me here. I hadn't any choice. A little while ago, they told me I was a widow. He was right, about his heart. And someone told me two other things."

"You look as tired as I feel."

"Do I show it that much?"

"Not in the way you think I meant. When I saw you, you were sleeping and didn't look weary."

"That was *ganja*. Someone gave me a stirrup cup at the palace and so I missed the boat. Everybody in town except my husband and I and the crew knew she was fitted with a short fuse. Was it so?"

"It was. If I hadn't been conked by mistake in the mutiny scramble at Aljai's house, I could have dragged him to the ground and told him I'd run on and give the word."

"If you hadn't been conked! Instead, you went crazy as he did, you stampeded. Josiah—I always called him Joe—was old fashioned, but he was one of the two men in my life who treated a hooker like a lady."

"Minutes ago, you said there were two other things someone told me. Let's sort them out."

"I did, but there's one of them I didn't get at. I'll

show you around your new home, title free and clear, compliments of the Gur Khan. Rod, I didn't rig this package deal, my going with the mansion. Being married awhile has done things to my wiring diagram, but you and I did know each other pretty well. The Gur Khan made it plain that *everything* in the house is yours, and in this territory, that also means everyone. I'm not throwing myself at you. You and I are here for life, but you don't *have* to be sweet and keep me."

"That'll take care of itself. You're a brand new widow—oh, hell, find me a drink and show me around so I'll know where to go in case I start folding or blacking out, I'm tired!"

Taking his arm, Lani headed for the utility areas of the house. He got a glimpse of the kitchen, which reminded him that Lani was a gourmet cook, and then a bath, and a second bedroom as far as could be from the one he'd noted at the start of the tour.

Garvin sniffed. "*Red Mist.* I thought you gave those play gowns to the Gur Khan's wives."

"I did but they'd been packed with other things so long that I don't know when I'll quit smelling like Martian moods."

She went back to the kitchen to get glasses and a jug.

Her mixing was interrupted by a fanfare of trumpets and the roll of saddle drums. A gong whanged thrice. This convinced Garvin that someone had been planning his day.

"That's official!" Lani exclaimed. "I'll vanish instantly!"

Opening the door, Garvin found two palanquins sitting in the street. Men at arms stood in two ranks. Eight swordsmen faced another octet with drawn blades. A bearer stood by with a three-tiered parasol to shelter the Gur Khan as he stepped from his palanquin.

Again, a roll of drums.

The Valiant Lion beckoned. A second bearer stalked to the rear palanquin. He carried a parasol of only a single tier, though it did have a fringe of little golden pendants. The woman who emerged was veiled.

Three paces behind, she followed the Gur Khan into the house. He said, as he cleared the threshold, "You are one of us, Rod. You may not realize that I know how much you've sacrificed for my people."

"Extravagant Lion, you exaggerate. After what I dumped on your people, I had no choice."

"The red-haired lady who welcomed you to your new home is a widow. She'd be lonely among strange people." He gestured to the veiled woman. "This one is not a widow. Without her, the house would be a half-gift. If you don't get along with her, there are others you might like."

Garvin sighed. "I can't live up to all this. And I don't know protocol. In some countries, one opens a gift package at once and makes a big to-do about how magnificent. In other countries, one speaks thanks and unwraps the gift in private."

"Follow the most honorable ancient custom, Rod." The Gur Khan backed off a pace. "When you've unwrapped your present, and you don't feel too disturbed by the loss of ship . . . and other losses . . . see me. Skip the audience hall and see me at home."

Garvin stood in the doorway as drums rolled, and the Valiant Lion stepped into his palanquin.

Closing the door, Garvin turned to the gift girl. She lowered her veil: Aljai, with full makeup.

"I had to bounce that jug from your head, or you'd have outrun the Old Man to save that red-headed darling and probably have died of heart failure yourself."

"I've begun to suspect that Alub Arslan figured every detail and made sure he'd be rid of every foreigner who'd not improve the Asteroidal Breed."

She made as if to speak, but thought better of it. Then she said, "If you don't want me for keeps, I'll tell you some things about protocol."

"Time someone did."

"When I met you at the banquet, you were a stranger, and I was incognito, temporary company for a guest. Now that you're one of us, I came under my parasol. I am not royalty, but neither am I a peasant.

"If you think I'm sending you back for exchange or refund, forget it! Tell me more about protocol."

"Well, the Gur Khan gave you a house and so forth. You have to send him a present. You're not a prince, so the present doesn't have to be as important as what he gave you, but it ought to be *good*. A gun or a watch . . . mmm . . . well, if you had a good horse, a fine one . . . yes! But that long-legged red head, there's the perfect present! His wives love her, and so would he! You see, he didn't really kill her husband, but he'd planned to have him in the package, so it wouldn't be polite for him to take the widow, just because her late husband was a nuisance.

"But he could give her to you. She doesn't rate a golden parasol, but she's nice."

Protocol, and especially when it got to giving away a woman, left Garvin groping. In her ignorance of Terrestrial social ways, Aljai misunderstood his blank expression.

"Maybe you are too dumb to guess, but if I'd not drugged the red head with *ganja*, she'd be part of a glowing cloud, and you'd be sad."

Garvin guided Aljai to the bedroom that was not Lani-scented.

"She doesn't understand a word of your language, so I'll explain protocol to her. A porter will be bringing your things over?"

"He'll be here around sundown."

"Alub Arslan knew I'd not send you away."

He stepped into the Lani-scented room to clarify the customs and protocol of Alub-Land.

She had quick understanding. She said, "You'd be in a tough spot if you didn't have me for a return present. Anything less would make you look strictly chicken!"

"This whole business is so awkward it's sticky! The way you and I started out, and then stowing you away aboard the *Saturnienne*, and then marrying you and the Admiral, and now giving you away—"

"Listen, honey, you're a gentleman of the old school, and even if I haven't met many of them, I think I know how you feel. You're not really dumping on me! Don't look so dark about things, you've always been grand. A hooker hardly ever does well, marrying or shacking up with a customer. When I told you it was time I retired and settled down, I meant it. Joe was a sweet old guy, and I do wish he'd known I wasn't aboard that

A-Bomb. All the way from Saturn, legal honeymooning was grand, and he was awfully happy.

"Another thing, Rod. You're fun and I've always been fond of you, all the way. But I'd never want to *live* with a woman-crazed bastard like you. The Khan is short one wife. You've got Flora, Azadeh, and now dream-girl gift. And when I move in with Alub Arslan I'll be a princess, and I bet I'll rate a one-deck parasol."

When Lani and her gear had been moved to her new home in the palace, and Aljai's goods stowed with Garvin's few possessions the sun was low, and as far as he and she were concerned, they had done with trumpets and drums for that day. A siesta, charcoal-broiled cubes of mutton, and barley cakes had repaired the damage of a long night and a too-eventful day.

So Garvin faced Aljai who, whatever else she might be, was no longer his official hostess. They had now to start over in becoming acquainted, and it wouldn't be as easy as the first time. Aljai finally broke the comfortable silence.

"You'll have sadness a long time and rememberings all your life. For me, also a new life. My father sent me to Alub Arslan, and to send me back home when we knew that we'd never get along together, that would have been rude. You are so different, giving me to you is like giving me to another prince—so, if you really like me, all this is good for everyone."

"If I call you Azadeh by mistake," he began, groping.

She laughed. "From the first night together, you called me Azadeh when we awakened and found each other in half sleep, so I knew you liked me. Now I'll tell you things about yourself—

"Your Azadeh knew that what you were going to do would take all your strength, so she didn't tell you that The Well of the Angels is empty—she gave birth to your son. When your people have done destroying each other, you may see him and her."

Garvin sighed, regarded Aljai. "Better even than food, you're a healing of sadness. So, I'll wait until you come back with no makeup." He brightened. "That'll be our beginning . . ."

ABOUT THE AUTHOR

E. HOFFMANN PRICE (1898–present) soldiered in the Philippines and France during World War I. At war's end he was appointed to the United States Military Academy, where he entered intercollegiate pistol and fencing competition. He was graduated in 1923 and commissioned in the Coast Artillery Corps. His first fiction sale was March 1924, to *Droll Stories*. By 1932, he was writing full time—fantasy, adventure, westerns, detective. When the pulps folded, he earned grog, gasoline, and groceries by holding two jobs and by filming weddings and practicing astrology in his spare time. Thanks to his incessant motoring, he met and made enduring friendships with Farnsworth Wright, Hugh Rankin, Otis Adelbert Kline, Lovecraft, Howard, W. K. Mashburn, Clark Ashton Smith, Edmond Hamilton, Seabury Quinn, Jack Williamson, Robert Spencer Carr, Leigh Brackett, C. L. Moore, and a comparable number in the nonfantasy fields.

During the past sixteen years, Price has been known in San Francisco's Chinatown as Tao Fa, the *dharma* name conferred by Venerable Yen Pei of Singapore, and he is mentioned in prayers every new moon and full moon in two Taoist-Buddhist temples. As a gourmet, he cooks shark fin soup, sautées *bêche-de-mer* with black mushrooms, and steams "tea-smoked" duck. He declares that in addition to silk, gunpowder, and the magnetic compass, beautiful women were invented in China. Doubters are invited to meet him at dawn, on horse or afoot, with sword or pistol.